The AMERICAN HERITAGE HISTORY *of* FLIGHT

The
AMERICAN HERITAGE
History of
FLIGHT

By the Editors of AMERICAN HERITAGE

The Magazine of History

Editor in Charge ALVIN M. JOSEPHY, JR.

Narrative by ARTHUR GORDON

With two chapters by MARVIN W. McFARLAND

Introduction by CARL SPAATZ, gen. usaf (ret.) IRA C. EAKER, lt. gen. usaf (ret.)

Published by AMERICAN HERITAGE PUBLISHING CO., INC.

Book Trade Distribution by SIMON & SCHUSTER, INC.

AMERICAN HERITAGE
The Magazine of History

PUBLISHER
James Parton

EDITORIAL DIRECTOR
Joseph J. Thorndike, Jr.

SENIOR EDITOR
Bruce Catton

EDITOR
Oliver Jensen

EDITOR, BOOK DIVISION
Richard M. Ketchum

Staff for this Book

EDITOR
ALVIN M. JOSEPHY, JR.

ASSISTANT EDITORS
Joseph L. Gardner, Stephen W. Sears

EDITORIAL ASSISTANTS
Jane M. Consolino, Kenneth W. Leish

COPY EDITOR
Karen Termohlen
Assistants: Frances Cousins, Sylvia J. Fried

EUROPEAN BUREAU
Gertrudis Feliu, Chief; Claire de Forbin,
Maureen Green, Timothy Green

CONSULTANTS
Charles H. Gibbs-Smith
Historical Committee,
Royal Aeronautical Society
Marvin W. McFarland
Guggenheim Chair of Aeronautics,
Library of Congress

ART DIRECTOR
Irwin Glusker

DESIGNER
David A. Van Inwegen

ORIGINAL AIRCRAFT DRAWINGS
John T. McCoy, Jr.

 Printed in the United States of America. Library of Congress Catalog Card Number: 62-17517.

Cover: Fred Ragsdale, F.P.G. Title Page: Lindbergh landing at Croyden, England, May 29, 1927. Brown Brothers.

BIBLIOTHÈQUE NATIONALE

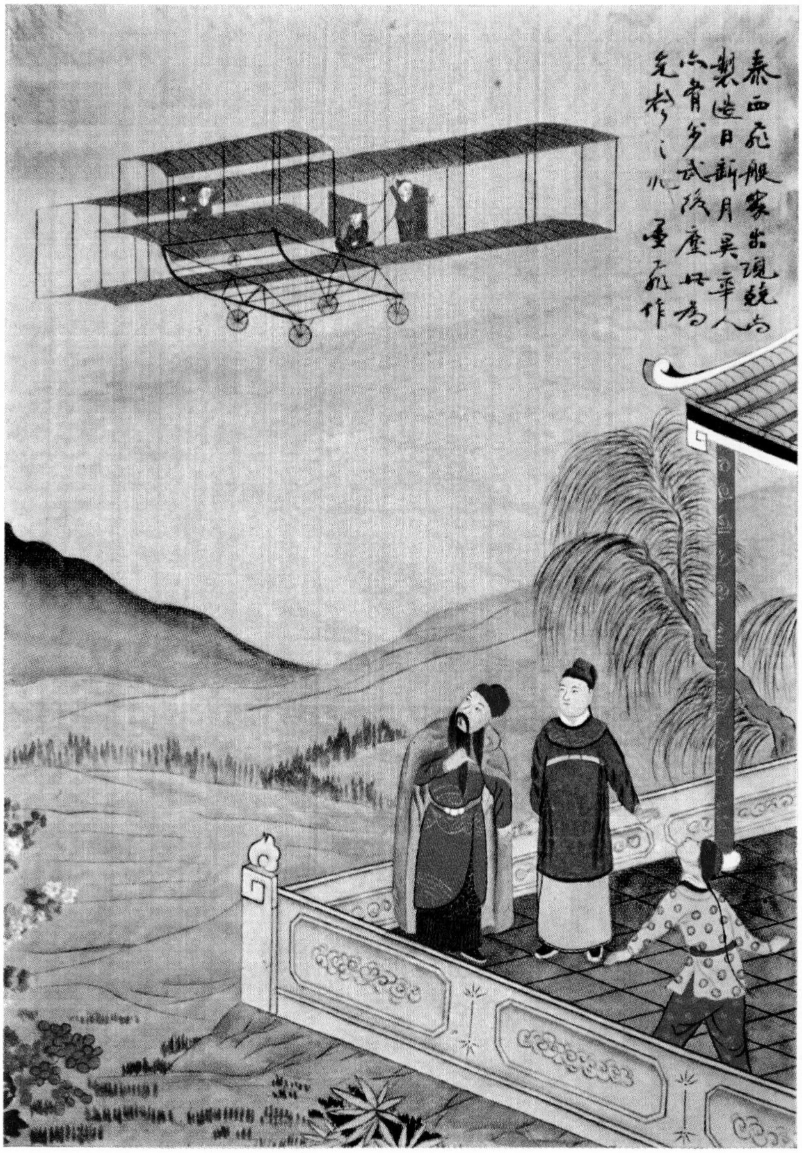

A Chinese silk painting depicts the marvel of the first plane flight in Asia.

Table of Contents

Introduction

CARL SPAATZ
General, USAF (Retired)

IRA C. EAKER
Lieutenant General, USAF (Retired)

History, like a mirror, can only look back. But, as Saroyan has reminded us, those unacquainted with history can be expected to repeat the mistakes of the past. It seems entirely appropriate to pause for a time and look back on the long way we have come in the discovery and development of flight in the earth's atmosphere before we rush farther toward the conquest of space. In that enterprise this book will be a valuable reference and guide.

This book reminds us that not all the contrails in the air world were made by fliers. Whittle's jet engine and Goddard's rocket engine were more significant than any flight except the first one. For example, too, Churchill and Eisenhower were both pilots, but they will be remembered for leadership in politics and war. However, their interest and experience in flight may well have shaped some of their great command decisions. It is clear also that the dimensions of aerospace exploration are changing. Heretofore the airways were generally horizontal, parallel to the earth's surface. As we probe for Mars, the moon and the stars, flight paths move toward the vertical.

Human experience often moves like the pendulum from one extreme to the other. The history of flight may be an example of this oscillation. The prime lesson we learn in a review of the history of flight might well be titled, "Too little and too late." At the time of the first heavier-than-air flight at Kitty Hawk in 1903, few realized the miracle the Wright brothers had wrought. There was scant interest and little encouragement for the conquest of the air. The older modes of travel by horse, boat, cart, rail, and motor car did not move over to make room for the new invader, the airplane. Military leaders failed to recognize the possibilities of the flying machine in warfare. As a consequence we entered two world wars unprepared and ill-equipped to achieve decisive results with air weapons. Too few of our people caught the vision of what aviation could do for transportation, commerce, industry, and national security. Too few funds were provided for research in aircraft and engine design and test. Now we seem determined to neglect the airplane for the missile and spaceship. For the first time in many years the Air Force is now buying no new types of fighters or bombers. The National Aeronautics and Space Administration is devoting more than three billion dollars for space vessels and boosters, and but sixty millions for all aeronautic investigation. Our race to the moon may leave our earth unguarded.

The timely publication of this history of flight may create a new interest in the airplane as a commercial vehicle and as an incomparable weapon. It is certain that no thoughtful citizen can read of the adventures of the early fliers and see the pictures of the frail craft they flew without renewed pride in their accomplishments. This book names most of the air pioneers and dwells briefly on their exploits and adventures. It recounts the air battles of the aces in the First World War, it covers that bleak quarter-century and the struggles of the gypsy fliers, the early airmail pilots, the first commercial air crews, and that little band of military aviators who proved and developed aviation in commerce and warfare. Two of its chapters recount the great air battles of the Second World War from the Battle of Britain to Hiroshima. There is a survey of the air world in the years since the last great war when the technological explosion has literally hurled men and machines beyond the earth and its atmosphere. It recounts the record of flight from the Wrights skimming the sands at 30 miles per hour to Astronaut Glenn circumnavigating the earth at 17,500 miles per hour. It touches most of the significant milestones along that span of fifty years from the first transcontinental flight by Rodgers in nearly two months to that of Titov around the earth seventeen times in a single day. It covers the power-plant story, a critical element in flight, from the 12 horsepower of the first plane to the engines with twenty million pounds of thrust now being developed for the moon mission.

Not all readers of this book will agree that it has touched all the steps of the stairway from Kitty Hawk to earth orbit. Each of us who has spent his life in air interest and sky adventure has his pet list of the fliers and flights most deserving of a place in the record. But to have included all the gallant names and remarkable feats would have required ten volumes, not ten chapters. Most of the noteworthy achievements and headline events in the history of flight find reference here.

There are many unique and commendable features in this book. It contains more than four hundred prints, drawings, and photographs of most of the outstanding air men and air vessels from the mythological ages to our time. The gliders of Cayley and Lilienthal, the first balloon, the first plane, the planes which set the records for distance, endurance, altitude, speed— all and many more are here. If a picture equals a thousand words, this is indeed a library of flight. The captions to these prints, drawings, and pictures have been done with care and a regard for historical accuracy.

Perhaps the most remarkable innovation of the volume is its inclusion of excerpts from more than seventy-five interviews with American and European air pioneers discussing historical episodes and events of importance and interest. These interviews were made only in recent months especially for this book by the Columbia University Oral History Research Office under a grant from American Heritage. It is worth recognizing that so many men and women who made aviation history are still alive. But they will not always be with us, and their thoughts and words grouped in the special sections, "In Their Words," are historic contributions in themselves and one of the volume's most memorable aspects.

One result of a book such as this may be the stimulus it must give to the youth of our country toward an added interest in aerospace. Many of our young people who read here of the air pioneers and see the wonders they have accomplished may be moved to prepare for air and space careers. It may be instrumental in removing one great handicap aerospace effort now suffers, an inadequate supply of good people. We do not produce annually as many trained engineers, technicians, and scientists as the Russians. We cannot hope to maintain our present leadership and the pre-eminence we have enjoyed in the air world during the past sixty years unless more young men and women join the effort.

American Heritage deserves thanks from our countrymen for this valuable contribution to the history of one of the most dramatic episodes in human experience, aerospace flight.

U.S. F-105B Thunderchief fighter-bomber

Wings, symbolizing the possession of supernatural power, grace the griffins from the fifth-century B.C. *Persian capital of Susa.*

WONDER OF WINGS

For half a million years at least, man lived at the bottom of an ocean of air without using it—except to breathe. He knew that the invisible envelope around him had substance, that it could move, that it could be rough or gentle, cold or warm. He saw it drive the clouds, ruffle the waters, stir the grasses, and uproot the trees. Groping dimly for cause and effect, he must have reasoned—since he could expel air from his own lungs—that the wind was the breath of some gigantic god, invisible, unpredictable, potentially hostile like everything else in his frightening world.

All about him at the same time were clues to the secret of flight. When he watched smoke drift upward, when he hurled his boomerang or loosed a feathered arrow, when the squid leaped away from him in tropic seas, man was witnessing the phenomena that he would one day utilize in his own mastery of the air: the lift of lighter-than-air substances; air pressure against wing surfaces; jet propulsion. Man saw these things, but he did not comprehend them.

Nor did man comprehend the grace with which birds performed their aerial acrobatics. He could only observe their flights with incredulity and admiration and, observing, come to speculate about the origin of their wondrous gift. Birds were a constant source of inspiration to man, who dreamed of imitating them —as well as a constant irritant, because the imitation seemed so unattainable.

The force of this stimulus was perhaps never better expressed than by a forty-one-year-old American addressing a society of French aviation enthusiasts in 1908. "I sometimes think that the desire to fly after the fashion of birds is an ideal handed down to us by our ancestors who, in their gruelling travels across trackless lands in prehistoric times, looked enviously on the birds soaring freely through space, at full speed, above all obstacles, on the infinite highway of the air." The tribute he was receiving that night for the success he and his brother had achieved five years earlier, said Wilbur Wright, was really a tribute to "an idea that has always impassioned mankind."

But as the millenia passed for ancient man, and the sky still arched above him, enormous and challenging, his imagination began to fill it with a host of strange creatures and objects: demons and dragons, angels and devils, flying carpets and flying chariots, winged horses and winged sandals, aerial boats and seven-league boots. Some of these fantasies were foolish indeed. But they expressed man's wonder at— and in a way shouted his defiance of—the incomprehensible mysteries that surrounded him.

Wherever man walked he invented gods and devils who walked with him, but there was something more urgent and fascinating about the denizens of the sky. The idea of soaring, of rising up, of surmounting or escaping from earthly cares or problems had such an irresistible appeal that wings and their significance became inextricably entwined with man's aspirations and hopes and dreams.

Almost as soon as forms of expression appear—carvings, sculpture, painting, the written word—the theme of wings is there. From the winged bulls guarding the halls of ancient Persia to the winged horse Pegasus of Greek mythology, the thought is clear and unmistakable: to fly is to conquer, to dominate, to be a god.

Into this savage company man himself came slowly and hesitantly. The early history of human attempts to fly is legend. A few faint reverberating echoes of disasters may just possibly have been based on fact, but the traditions of successful flight certainly are not. No one seems to have learned anything from the failures; there was nothing to be learned from the improbable successes.

The earliest recorded story of man in flight is Chinese. Some four thousand years ago, according to the ancient *Annals of the Bamboo Books,* the Emperor Shun escaped from captivity as a boy by "donning the work-clothes of a bird." On another occasion the versatile Shun became a flying dragon. When his father (who did not seem to care for him) ordered Shun to the top of a tall granary and then set it on fire, the youth escaped by seizing two wide-brimmed reed hats and floating safely to the ground. Such hats sometimes were—and still are—three feet wide. If Shun was a very small emperor, he may well have been the first successful parachutist.

The Chinese possess many other aerial legends. Lei Kung, the god of thunder and lightning, had the wings of a bat. In the eighteenth century before Christ, one Ki-kung-shi supposedly invented a flying chariot; the old drawings show him sailing through the heavens with a satisfied smirk and no visible means of support. Some 1,600 years later an eager experimenter named Liu An concocted an elixir that gave him the power of levitation. As he rose on high, he dropped his flask into a barnyard, whereupon the animals that sampled the spilled contents took off too.

The folklore of virtually every early civilization had its flying heroes or demigods. Kai Kawus, an ancient king of Persia, was said to have had a flying throne drawn by four hungry eagles that flapped frantically in an effort to reach slabs of meat impaled on spears just beyond their beaks. (Other legends credit Alexander the Great with a similar device, a cage drawn by winged griffins.) In northern Europe it was Wayland the Smith and his shirt made of feathers. In Africa it was a great warrior, Kibaga, who flew invisibly over his enemies and dropped rocks on them until they finally brought him down by shooting their arrows blindly into the air.

The best-known of all the flying legends is the story of Daedalus and Icarus, who fashioned wings of feathers and wax with which to escape from the labyrinth of Cretan King Minos; the flight ended in disaster for Icarus when he flew too close to the sun. The plunge of Icarus has fascinated generation after generation. Pure myth, perhaps, yet sometimes legend is a shimmering cloak for truth. Daedalus, the "cunning artificer," knew of the sail that reaches for the restless wind, captures it, and converts it into power. The updrafts where a steep cliff rises from the sea can be very strong, and Crete has such cliffs. Moreover, the principal components of a glider—light wood and cloth—were just as available in the Age of Bronze as they are now.

Could Daedalus, watching the soaring gulls, actually have attempted a glider large enough and strong enough to carry a man? H. G. Wells thought so. (Or perhaps it was Wells-the-novelist rather than Wells-the-historian speaking.) Suppose Daedalus *did* construct some such device; suppose his son *was* killed in some gallant and foolish experiment. The embroidery of the poets and the epic-singers is understandable. Beyond the miracle of flight is conflict, drama, the wicked king posting guards by land and sea. Ovid has Daedalus saying dramatically, "We'll go through air; for sure the air is free." And then the moral, with pride going before a fall.

Not all the inventions were simply legends. The windmill, an ancestor of the propeller, was known and used in ancient Rome. The Chinese introduced the kite long before the Christian era and were using it for military signaling at least as early as the third century B.C. Tradition has it that by the Middle Ages they had developed monster kites capable of lifting men, and it seems possible. The Chinese also invented gunpowder about 900 A.D. and hit upon the idea of the rocket about 1100.

The identity of the first man-made object to fly under its own power is shrouded in mist and silence. Several centuries before Christ, according to Chinese records, a contemporary of Confucius named Kung-shu Tse built a wooden and bamboo magpie that "flew for three days." It was, quite simply, a kite.

The mysterious wooden pigeon of Archytas, which astounded observers in southern Italy in about 400 B.C., however, cannot so easily be dismissed as a kite. According to Aulus Gellius, a gossipy Roman who tells the story in his *Attic Nights,* a collection of anecdotes written in the second century A.D., the dove or pigeon was caused to fly by means of "hidden and enclosed air," which in turn was activated by "some lamp or other fire within it." Puzzling over these and other descriptions, some modern historians believe that Archytas had his bird suspended by wires from a revolving arm which was turned by some sort of steam-reaction device. In any case, he seems to have had something more than a kite or a hand-propelled toy.

Actually, the first toy that flew was almost certainly invented by the Chinese. By inserting feathers in a lightweight spindle and rapidly rotating it, they achieved momentary flight using the helicopter principle. But it is impossible to assign a date to these spinning tops. They are doubtless far older than Kung-shu Tse's magpie or Archytas's dove.

Both legend and history have a good deal to say about the early "tower-jumpers," daring or demented souls who launched themselves from high places equipped with magical spells, homemade wings, or a hopeful combination of both. One of the earliest was Bladud, the legendary tenth king of Britain, who supposedly reigned in the ninth century B.C. According to medieval chroniclers, Bladud went to Athens, there studied "Necromanticke Arts," came back to Britain, and was killed while attempting to fly over the ancient site of London with a pair of artificial wings. He was also the father of King Lear; perhaps madness ran in the family.

Ancient Rome had its tower-jumpers too, one being the sorcerer Simon Magus who allegedly flew around until Saint Peter shot him down by well-directed prayers. One jump that seems to have been quite accurately reported took place in Constantinople in the eleventh century. There a Saracen mounted to the top of a tower overlooking the hippodrome. He wore a long white garment stiffened with willow poles and leaned experimentally into the wind while an impatient crowd urged him on from below. At length he did attempt to glide, but "the weight of his body having more power to drag him down than the wings had to sustain him, he broke his bones and his evil plight was such that he did not long survive."

Far from discouraging imitators, these disasters seemed to encourage them. A contemporary of the Saracen, an English monk-astrologer-mechanic known as Oliver of Malmesbury, fashioned some wings and flew "more than a furlong" before breaking his legs. After the flight, he announced crossly that the only reason he fell was that he had forgotten to fit a tail to his "hinder parts."

Some five hundred years later an Italian adventurer named John Damian, having talked King James IV of Scotland into giving him the job of court physician, apparently decided that whatever Bladud had done, he could do better. In 1507, according to John Lesley, Bishop of Ross, "he causet mak ane pair of wingis of fedderis, quhilkis beand fessinet apoun him, he flew of the Castell wall of Striveling, but shortlie he fell to the ground and brak his thee bane." Damian, who seems to have retained his sense of humor despite the broken thigh bone, blamed his fall on the fact that he had used chicken feathers which, he said, had more affinity for the barnyard than for the sky.

The first man credited with anything like a scientific approach to flying was Roger Bacon, the famous Franciscan monk whose lifetime spanned most of the thirteenth century. Actually, such credit is overgenerous. Bacon's contributions to heavier-than-air flight are limited to a few vague remarks about "instruments to flie withall, so that one sitting in the middle of the Instrument, and turning about an Engine, by which the wings being artificially composed may beate the ayre after the manner of a flying bird." He knew of a

man who invented such a thing, he said, although he himself had never seen it.

There is no evidence, however, that Bacon grasped the notion that the air was a substance which could be made to support a properly designed aeronautical machine just as water buoys up a ship, although this concept of the atmosphere as a kind of sea with a well-defined upper surface was not completely unknown. Albertus Magnus, another thirteenth-century scholastic, toyed with the idea. So did Albert of Saxony, and others.

For one hundred and fifty years after Bacon, there is little evidence of experimentation or speculation. Then, the intellectual and artistic sunburst of the Renaissance cast new light into many dark corners; and the age saw the first great scientific pioneer in the field of aeronautics. Unfortunately, he had no direct influence on the subsequent development of aviation.

Leonardo da Vinci—artist, musician, architect, mathematician, the "universal man" of the Renaissance—left his fabulous collection of manuscripts and drawings to a friend who never bothered to make them public. It was not until the late nineteenth century that Leonardo's astounding material received serious notice. By that time the march of science had overtaken most of his ideas.

But the man was a towering genius. In one almost casual notation, about the year 1500, he suggested a design for the parachute, specifying "a tent made of linen of which the apertures have all been stopped up." Nearby he sketched a pyramid-shaped parachute, giving the measurements that would enable a man to "throw himself down from any great height without sustaining any injury."

He designed a model helicopter with a helix, or spiral screw, driven by a spring mechanism and seems to have flown it. But he was well aware that no adequate propulsive unit was available to launch a full-scale machine. There is a tradition that he experimented with hot-air balloons—more likely they were small kites. But he certainly knew that heated air rises, and it is possible that he was the first man to put this principle to work by designing the smokejack, a propeller worked by the hot air in a chimney which turns a roasting spit.

He was fascinated by birds—too fascinated, perhaps, for he devoted a tremendous amount of time and effort to the study of ornithopters, or flapping-wing devices designed to fly through the air. It is curious: a man of Leonardo's intellect must have known that the muscle-to-weight ratio in man differs so sharply from the birds as to make a human-powered ornithopter a virtual impossibility. (It is only in the last few years, in the full light of modern knowledge of mechanics and aerodynamics, that some engineers are willing to hazard that an ornithopter might, just conceivably, work for a minute or two.) Nevertheless, Leonardo's notebooks show dozens of drawings of ornithopters with the operator in various positions. Had he applied a tenth of this attention to a fixed-wing glider, he might well have anticipated Otto Lilienthal, the nineteenth-century "father of gliding," by a full four hundred years.

Oddly enough, there is some evidence that a contemporary of Leonardo's did fit himself with flapping wings and attempt to fly. He was Giovanni Danti, a mathematician of Perugia, who was credited with several faltering glides over Lake Trasimeno about 1490. According to an account written nearly two centuries later, an iron brace in Danti's left wing gave way as he was trying to glide from a tower in Perugia. He fell and was badly injured.

Leonardo's stature seems all the greater when compared to some of the solemn nonsense that followed him. One theory of flight, for example, involved eggshells and dew. Since dew was thought to be "drawn up by the sun," and since eggshells are undeniably light, a dew-filled eggshell, it was stated, might very well fly—and enough of them might very well carry something, or somebody. The French author Cyrano de Bergerac used this notion of a dew-suspended airship in some lighthearted science fiction in the mid-seventeenth century. Other imaginative writers (including the great Jonathan Swift in *Gulliver's Travels*) toyed with the idea of using giant magnets or lodestones to defeat the pull of gravity.

Fantastic though their tales were, the early yarn spinners deserve some credit for keeping alive interest in flying. In 1638, for example, a fantasy by Francis Godwin, Bishop of Hereford, was published with the somewhat long-winded title of *The Man in the Moone, or a Discourse of a Voyage thither by Domingo Gonsales the Speedy Messenger*. This "speedy messenger" was an enterprising Spaniard who trained twenty-five geese to pull him to the moon on a sort of flying trapeze. The tale was of no significance in the history of flight, but it did fire the imagination of another bishop, John Wilkins of Chester, who did some serious thinking on the subject of flight, "than which there is not any imaginable invention, that could prove of greater benefit to the world or glory to the author."

Writing in 1648, Wilkins classified previous attempts to fly under four headings, by spirits or angels, by the help of "fowls," by wings fastened to the body, and by a flying chariot which he regarded as "altogether as probable, and much more useful than any of the rest." Wilkins made no attempt to build such a device, as he clearly understood how difficult the basic problems were, wondering "whether an engine of such capacity and weight, may be supported by so thin and light a body as the air," and "whether the strength of the persons within it, may be sufficient for the motion of it." In any case, he said firmly, "if [a] Fowl . . . can so very easily move it self up and down in the Air, without so much as stirring the Wings of it, certainly then it is not improbable, but that when all the due Proportions in such an Engine are found out, and when Men by long Practice have arrived to any Skill and Experience, they will be able in this (as well as in many other Things) to come very near unto the imitation of Nature."

There is some evidence that a friend of Wilkins's, the English physicist Robert Hooke, constructed small ornithopters and a helicopter "which, by the help of springs and wings, rais'd and sustain'd itself in the air." This happened—if it happened—about the time Cromwell became Lord Protector, and nothing more was heard of it.

Through the whole history of man's quest for flight runs one persistent and mysterious thread, the phenomenon of levitation, or human flight with no mechanical contrivances whatever. Various mystics and saints allegedly have had this power, the most famous being the "flying monk," Saint Joseph of Cupertino. It is difficult to say where mythology ends and the supernatural begins, but Saint Joseph's case was well-documented by the sworn statements of those who witnessed his amazing feats.

It is perfectly true that something in the modern mind balks at the notion of Saint Joseph taking gracefully to the air "with his customary cry of 'Oh!'" But it is difficult to read the biographies of this unassuming little Franciscan friar without becoming half-convinced—momentarily, at least—that he actually *did* fly. And not only in the obscure village of Cupertino, but in Assisi, in Naples, even in Rome before the astonished eyes of Pope Urban VIII. Here is a description of one of Joseph's seventy recorded "flights" that were sworn to under oath by eyewitnesses after his death. The writer is Father Rossi, Minister-General of the Franciscan Order:

"While the Lord High Admiral of Castile, Ambassador of Spain at the Vatican, was passing through Assisi in the year 1645, the custodian of the convent commanded Joseph to descend from the room into the church, where the Admiral and his lady were waiting for him, desirous of seeing him and speaking to him. To whom Joseph replied, 'I will obey, but I do not know whether I shall be able to speak to her.' And, as a matter of fact, hardly had he entered the church and raised his eyes to a statue . . . situated above the altar, when he threw himself into a flight in order to embrace its feet at a distance of twelve paces, passing over the heads of all the congregation; then, after remaining there some time, he flew back over them with his customary shrill cry, and immediately returned to his cell. The Admiral was amazed, his wife fainted away; and all the onlookers became piously terrified."

Toward the end of his life Joseph became so famous that his superiors had to confine him in the convent of Osimo, so that his life should "not be disturbed by the concourse of the vulgar." After his death the Church studied his case and weighed the evidence for ninety years before proceeding with his canonization.

Leaving supernatural intervention aside, a more scientific attempt to achieve flight was made by a contemporary of Saint Joseph's, Francesco de Lana. In 1670 this Italian Jesuit proposed a vacuum-balloon ship to be lifted by four paper-thin copper globes, each twenty feet in diameter, from which the air was to have been evacuated. De Lana, who came close to determining the actual weight of air at sea level, was the first to grasp the concept of controlling a balloon by carrying ballast to govern the rate of ascent, and readmitting air into the spheres in order to descend— but he underestimated the atmospheric pressure, which would have instantly crushed his spheres.

The pious de Lana doubted, however, that God would ever allow such a machine to fly, "since it would cause much disturbance among the civil and political governments of mankind." His prophecies of aerial warfare were devastatingly accurate. An aerial ship, he said, could swoop down on conventional naval vessels and cut their rigging, "Or even without descending so low, iron weights could be hurled down to wreck the ships and kill their crews; or the ships could be set on fire by fireballs and bombs. Not only ships, but houses, fortresses and cities could thus be destroyed, with the certainty that the airship would come to no harm, as the missiles could be thrown from a great height."

It was exactly this prospect that moved a British Prime Minister, Stanley Baldwin, to remark in 1935, two and a half centuries later: "I wish for many reasons flying had never been invented . . . somehow we have got to Christianize it."

Ten years after de Lana's proposals held out some hope of lighter-than-air flight, another Italian scientist threw some very cold water on the tower-jumpers or would-be birdmen who still believed that muscle-operated wings could sustain human beings in the air. In his 1680 treatise *De Motu Animalium*, G. A. Borelli demonstrated forcibly that man's pectoral muscles, even combined with leg muscles, were too weak to enable him to imitate the birds. "It is impos-

sible," he wrote, "that men should be able to fly craftily by their own strength," and he added rather sourly that he had "no faith in any invention designed to lift man from the earth."

Borelli may have had in mind the claims of a French locksmith named Besnier, who two years earlier, in 1678, insisted that he *had* achieved flight through muscle power. Besnier's apparatus was said to consist of two light rods which he balanced on his shoulders, holding one end with his hands, the other end being attached with cords to his ankles. Each rod was equipped with cloth panels that were hinged so as to close on the upstroke and open on the downbeat. According to Besnier, he jumped from higher and higher places, until he finally flew over a barn. But few of his contemporaries believed him, and Borelli certainly did not. In fact, when the German philosopher Leibnitz and other distinguished men of the day endorsed Borelli's conclusions, the whole idea of heavier-than-air flight was virtually abandoned for the next hundred years.

And yet this was the decade in which Isaac Newton, having stated his Third Law of Motion (to every action there is opposed an equal reaction), prophesied with remarkable foresight, "This is the principle which will enable mankind in later centuries to undertake flight to the stars."

After de Lana and Borelli, the dream of lighter-than-air flight was not only kept alive but seems actually to have been realized, in a small but impressive way, by a Brazilian-born Jesuit, Father Laurenço de Gusmão. In 1709, Gusmão requested the King of Portugal to grant him a patent for a flying machine, and the request was granted. Early engravings of Gusmão's *Passarola,* or "great bird," show a weird-looking contrivance with a bird's beak and tail, a billowing sail, and totally inadequate wings. But the pictures were the work of a misinformed artist. Gusmão's model—by no means as grotesque as it had been depicted and actually displaying a rather advanced design for its day—may indeed have been successfully flown as a glider. If he did build a full-size, man-carrying ornithopter, it certainly never flew.

But a few years ago the British historian Charles H. Gibbs-Smith rescued Gusmão from centuries of ridicule by presenting evidence that he made and flew a miniature hot-air balloon seventy-three years before the famous experiment of the Montgolfier brothers. He flew it, according to separate accounts from two eyewitnesses, on August 8, 1709, in the presence of the Portuguese king and nearly set His Majesty's furnishings on fire in the process.

Gusmão's device, according to a manuscript dated about 1724, "consisted of a small bark in the form of a trough which was covered with a cloth of canvas. With various spirits, quintessences, and other ingredients he put a light beneath it, and let the said bark fly in the Salla das Embaixadas before His Majesty and many other persons. It rose to a small height against the wall and then came to earth and caught fire when the materials became jumbled together. In descending and falling downwards, it set fire to some hangings and everything against which it knocked. His Majesty was good enough not to take it ill."

There is some indication that the Inquisition was not very pleased with this demonstration, the idea of flight still being widely associated with witchcraft or sorcery. In any case, no one in Portugal was inclined to follow up Father Laurenço's experiments.

It is extraordinary that the hot-air balloon was not invented long before Gusmão—for thousands of years man had watched smoke rise from a fire; and for centuries he had possessed, in silk, a material capable of capturing and holding that smoke.

But as the decades of the eighteenth century rolled by, progress in aeronautics seemed virtually at a standstill. In fact, contemporary comment often shows a marked degree of disillusion with the whole subject. Writing in 1713, the English satirist Joseph Addison said that as far as he was concerned, he would discourage "any person from flying in my time," primarily because of the baleful influence it would have on love affairs. "You should have a couple of lovers make a midnight assignation upon the top of the Monument, and see the cupola of St. Paul's covered with both sexes like the outside of a pigeon-house. . . . or a gallant giving chase to his mistress, like a hawk after a lark."

Fiction writers continued to endow man with wings, but there was little serious scientific speculation. The Swedish mystic Emanuel Swedenborg offered some ideas for an ornithopter with wings "to be worked up and down with a spiral spring." But he never got past the idea stage. Neither did Joseph Galien, a Dominican friar, whose vivid imagination conceived of an enormous cube-shaped aerial transport. Buoyed up by "rarefied air," he said, the airship would be capable of transporting whole armies of men to Africa, or anywhere else. But he recommended that its construction be left to "experienced engineers," virtually the only sensible suggestion he made.

About 1742 one of the last of the hardy breed of tower-jumpers appeared in the form of a misguided French nobleman, the Marquis de Bacqueville, who attracted a large crowd of Parisians by announcing that he was going to fly across the Seine. With some sort of wings attached to him, he leaped from the roof of his riverside mansion, came plummeting down onto a washerwoman's barge in the river, and broke his leg. The shades of Danti, Damian, and the rest must have smiled.

It was the French, in the latter half of the eighteenth century, who showed the most sustained interest in the will-o'-the-wisp idea of flight. Even as the storm clouds gathered around the ill-fated Louis XVI, his subjects continued to experiment with *voitures volantes;* but their ornithopters left the hopeful inventors rather firmly planted on the ground.

Meanwhile, across the Channel, the English chemist Henry Cavendish had succeeded in determining the weight of hydrogen, then called "inflammable air." Describing its properties in a paper read before the Royal Society in 1766, he announced that "inflammable air" was considerably lighter than ordinary air.

The aeronautical significance of this seems to have escaped Cavendish entirely, or perhaps he simply was not interested. But Joseph Black, a chemistry professor at Glasgow University, realized at once that a very light container filled with hydrogen would be lighter than air, and would therefore rise. Believing that a demonstration would amuse his students, he made arrangements to obtain the lightest bladder that he could think of—the allantois (part of the umbilical cord) of a calf. But by the time one was made ready, he was teaching another part of his course and never got around to carrying out his plan.

Hearing of this intended experiment, Tiberius Cavallo, an Italian scientist who had settled in England, decided to follow through with it. But none of the containers that he tried seemed light enough. In the end, "tired with the expenses and loss of time," he gave up—having come as close to the invention of the balloon as was possible without actually achieving it. Ironically, the dawn of the air age was only a year away.

The isolation of hydrogen made the development of lighter-than-air craft possible. But strangely, the final leap of imagination came from two men who had no experience at all with hydrogen. It was a far older phenomenon that finally carried man into the hitherto unchallenged air.

The clues had long been there, plain for all to see. Even the Bible contained them. "Man," wrote the gloomy but eloquent author of the Book of Job, "is born unto trouble, as the sparks fly upward." But thirty more centuries had to pass before the message of the upflying sparks took root in men's minds.

It came in the form of a question so simple that no one had thought to ask it before. If sparks did indeed fly upward, then why could not the power that raised them be used to lift other things?

In the year 1782, to an inquisitive pair of brothers, the question came. And with it came the answer.

The Wings
of the Ancients

As long as man has dreamed, he has probably dreamed of flying. But for long ages the object of his yearning seemed so completely unattainable that he could only gaze into the skies and ascribe some special sort of divinity to winged creatures. In his awe he gave wings to many of his first gods, ranking bulls, lions, and jackals with eagles and hawks.

In time, his animal deities were transformed into gods in human form. Many of them were still endowed with the characteristics and powers of the birds and animals from which they had evolved, and the pantheons of the ancients were filled with strange and imaginative figures: eagle-headed women, winged dogs, and birds with human heads.

To the Egyptians, Assyrians, and other peoples of the ancient world, flight was mysterious and awesome. It was proper that their gods should have power in the realm that man himself could not reach.

In the detail above, from the stone sarcophagus of Rameses III (twelfth century B.C.), the Egyptian goddess Isis appears in a characteristic pose, with wings outstretched to protect the dead. The fame of this universal mother figure, who was also the star of the sea and patroness of travelers, lasted into the Greco-Roman period and spread as far as central Europe.

At right, a clay impression of a stone cylinder seal from Assyria shows a winged hero confronting an attacking lion. The cylinder, dating possibly from the ninth century B.C., was rolled across soft clay that covered the cloth wrappings of a person's private possessions, sealing the contents with his mark of ownership. In this impression, the bold hero holds a slain bull.

Ahura Mazda, the Persian god of gods, is represented as a winged disk at the top of this bas-relief of colored tiles from the palace of Darius I at Susa (circa 490 B.C.). Below the disk, guarding the faceless divinity, are two bearded sphinxes, the familiar winged lions with human heads that occur in the myth and art of the ancient world from Egypt to Greece.

Gods and Heroes in the Pagan Sky

By the time the Greek poet Hesiod compiled the first genealogical history of the gods about the eighth century B.C., the belief that they possessed the power of flight was well established. It was taken for granted that the immortals could span time and distance at will; and only when the plot of a particular story required winged steeds or aerial chariots, were such dramatic devices added.

To explain the course of the sun the Greeks gave their sun god Helios a golden chariot, drawn by fire-breathing horses. Other gods in the crowded Greek pantheon possessed simpler aids to flight: Hermes (who later reappeared as the Roman god Mercury) sped his messages with the help of winged sandals; Eros (the Roman Cupid), capriciously aiming his arrows of love, was a winged child; the handsome youth Ganymede ascended Mount Olympus astride an eagle. And the hero Perseus, after slaying the serpent-tressed Medusa, made his retreat on the winged horse Pegasus which had obligingly sprung from Medusa's bleeding neck.

The power of flight which the Greek and Roman storytellers bestowed on the immortals was a happy literary device also, for it permitted the gods' many interventions in the affairs of man—especially at crucial moments in a battle—and usually brought the amorous adventures of the deities to a swift and successful conclusion.

Outstretched wings of triumph dominate the magnificent Greek statue "Winged Victory" at left. Carved by an unknown sculptor, probably early in the second century B.C., it commemorated a naval victory.

On the Greek amphora above, Odysseus, bound to the mast of his ship, resists the seductive calls of the Sirens, the woman-headed birds that lured sailors to destruction. At right, Aphrodite riding a swan is pictured on an exquisite drinking cup executed about 460 B.C. Even such dark creatures of the underworld as Hypnos (Sleep) and his brother Thanatos (Death) had wings. The detail from a Greek mixing bowl below shows the pair carrying the body of Sarpedon to his father Zeus.

Daedalus
and Icarus

*The climactic moment in the ancients'
most famous narrative of flying is por-
trayed in this oil sketch done about 1636
by the Flemish painter, Peter Paul Rubens.
Daedalus, the father (left), a mythical
Athenian architect credited with the invention of the ax and saw, watches help-
lessly as the sun's rays melt the wax on
Icarus's wings, and his son falls to the sea.*

21

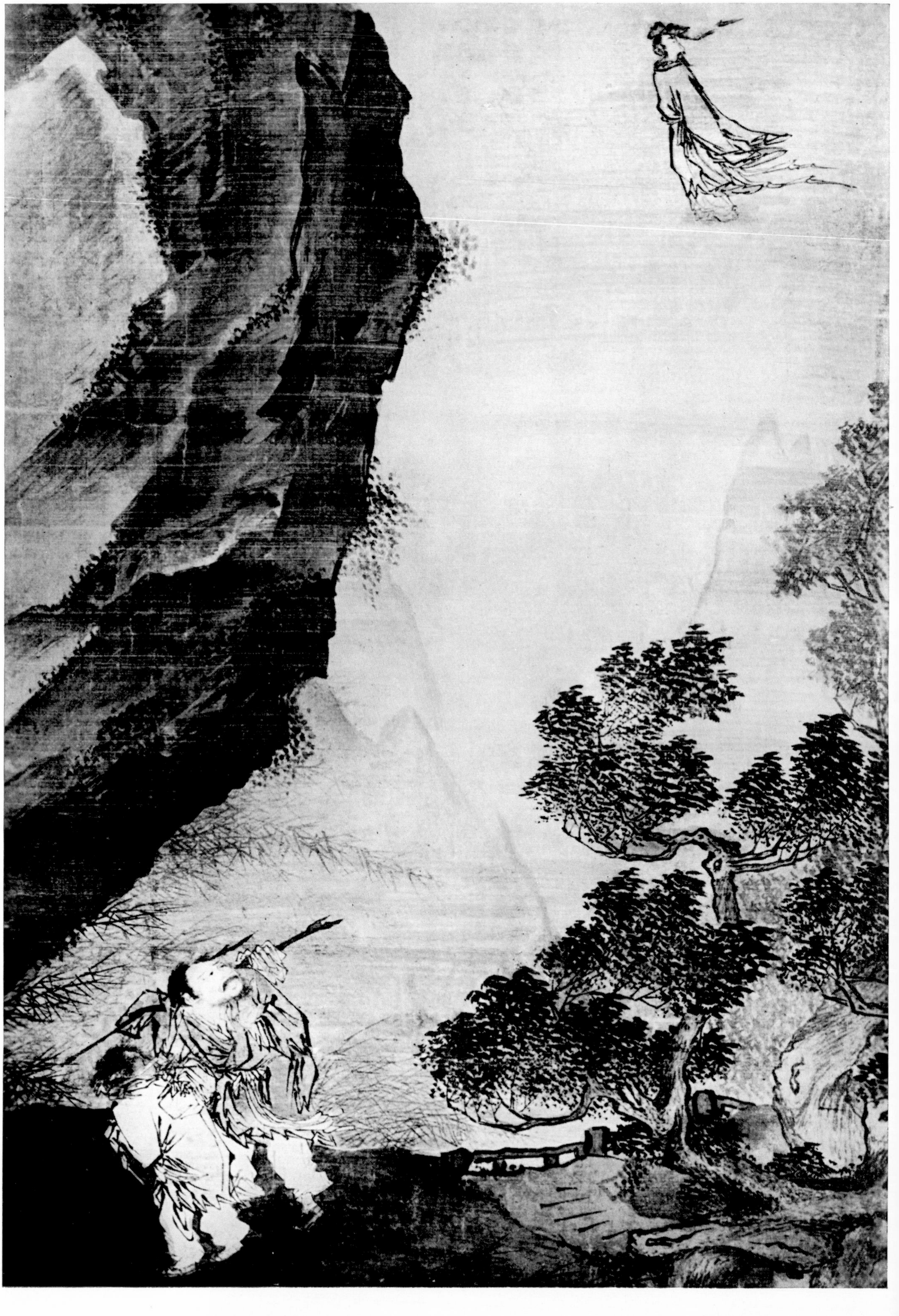

The Image of Heaven

Through the ages and around the world, wings appeared and re-appeared as supernatural attributes in the different religions of man.

The legends of the Near East, India, and the Orient—like those of Greece and Rome—contain numerous references to winged creatures, aerial chariots, and flying gods. When Christianity replaced paganism in the West, wings—far from being abandoned — were incorporated with renewed emphasis in much of the art and literature of the young religion.

Jewish law had prohibited the making of graven images; but when Christianity assimilated the Old Testament, it also borrowed from Greco-Roman art to depict angels as human figures with wings. At first, they were decorously clothed in flowing robes—a departure from the anatomical frankness of classic art. Eventually, however, even Eros-Cupid, the messenger god of love, reappeared in Christian form as a plump, innocent, and unclothed cherub, complete with the wings that were an indispensable part of man's image of divinity.

ABOVE: *Wings are not mentioned in the Old Testament account of the angel who wrestled with Jacob. But the thirteenth-century artist who created this mosaic would never have dreamed of omitting those standard marks of the supernatural.*

LEFT: *The soaring Taoist saint in this Chinese drawing (Ming period, 1368-1644) needed no wings for his effortless movements through the heavens: Taoists believed that they could achieve flight simply by starving themselves into weightlessness.*

RIGHT: *Persian peris, like the one in this sixteenth-century miniature, were endowed with such graceful wings that their legendary descent from fallen angels, which committed them to lives of unending penance, might almost have been overlooked.*

23

Flying Carpets and Chariots

The folklore and legends of people everywhere provide an unbroken record of man's envy of birds and his desire to get up in the air himself. Often, he achieved success (in his mind) with the help of elaborate and ingenious aerial contrivances.

Chinese tales credit the Emperor Shun (*circa* 2200 B.C.) with the world's first flying chariot. Shun's successors, unfortunately, proved incapable of copying his vehicle, and later fliers had to rely on winged dragons. By the third century B.C., the Chinese had kites, an invention that might have turned their minds to practical methods of achieving manned flight. But a kite was too modest a device to satisfy the needs of storytellers, and twelve hundred years later travelers in the *Arabian Nights* relied on flying carpets for aerial trips.

ABOVE: *According to an eleventh-century Persian tale, the hero Barzou tamed the flying dragon Simourg and then mounted it for a satisfying aerial jaunt. In this eighteenth-century A.D. manuscript illustration, a smug winged houri sits at left.*

LEFT: *The slightly apprehensive figure in this eighteenth-century Persian miniature is the legendary flying king, Kai Kawus (circa 1500 B.C.). Wing-flapping eagles, stretching for pieces of meat impaled just beyond their reach, had been trained to carry his royal throne through the air.*

OPPOSITE: *An Indian painting, also from the eighteenth century A.D., shows demigods in bathtub-shaped flying machines (top) scattering flower petals on dancers who sway to the music of flute and gong. Four winged figures peep from behind the clouds to complete the nocturnal fantasy.*

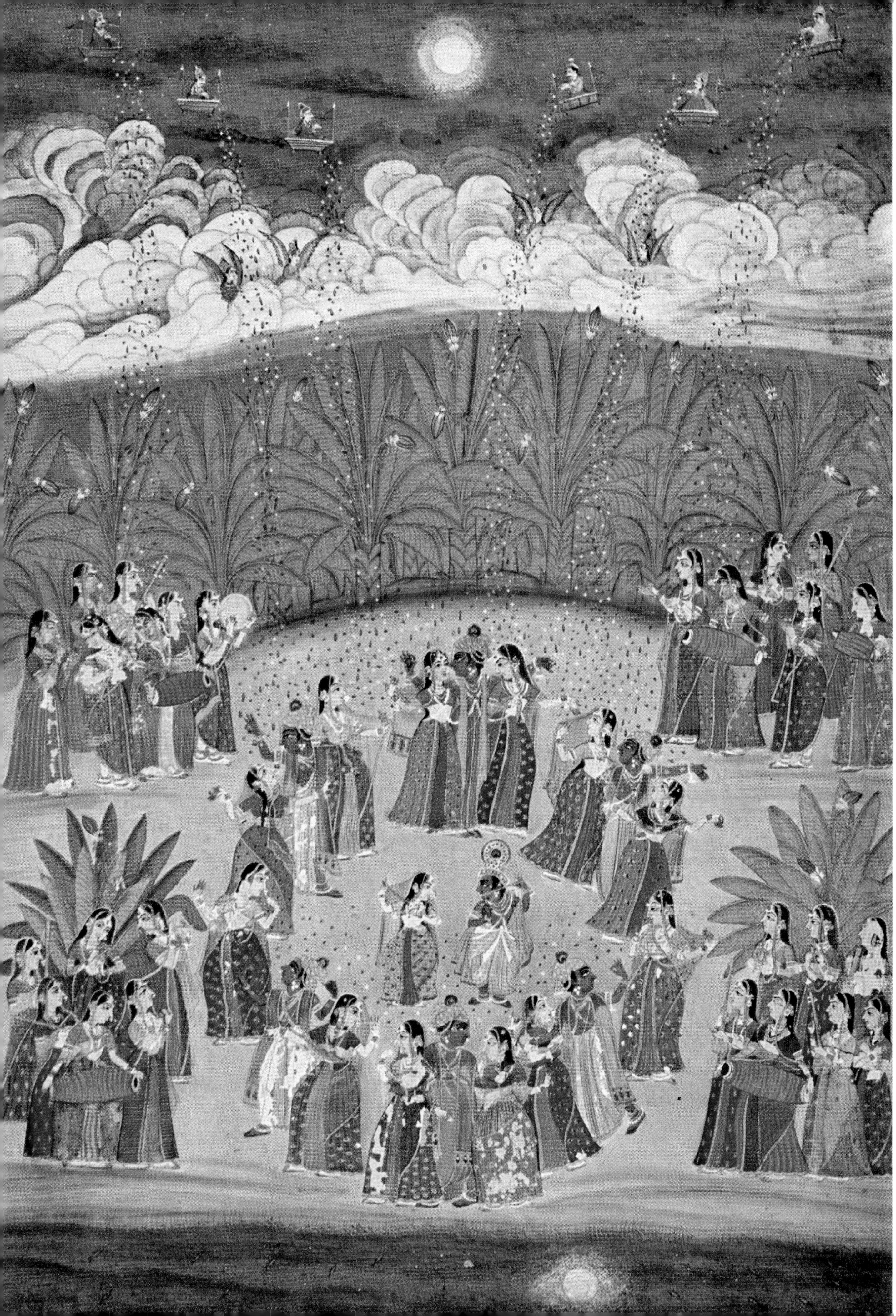

HENRY E. HUNTINGTON LIBRARY

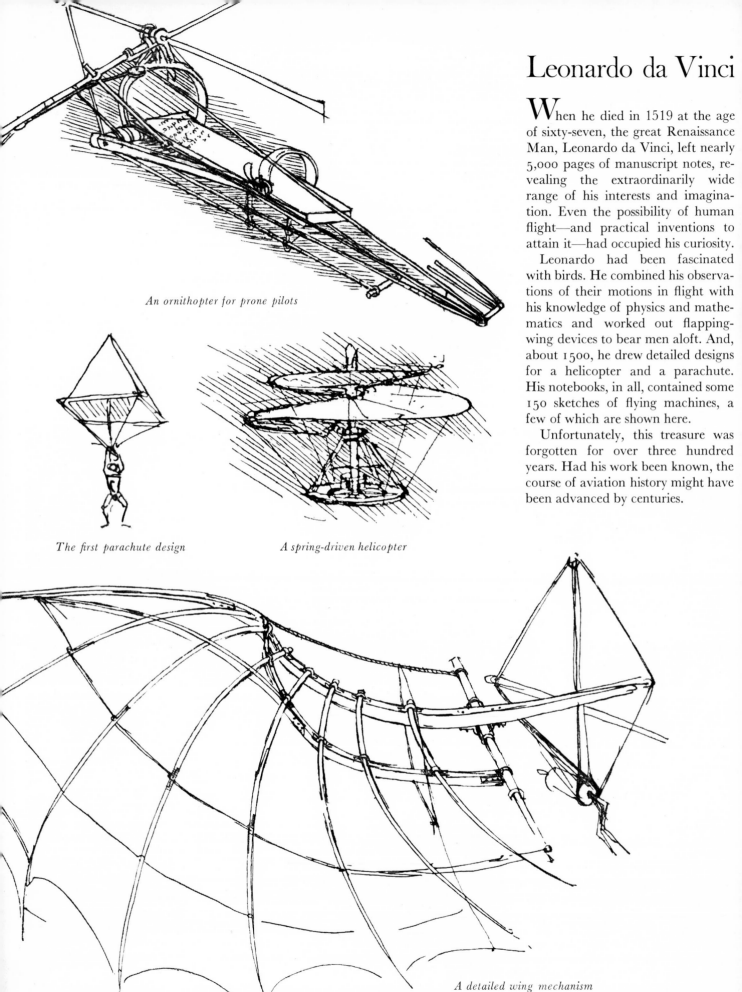

Leonardo da Vinci

When he died in 1519 at the age of sixty-seven, the great Renaissance Man, Leonardo da Vinci, left nearly 5,000 pages of manuscript notes, revealing the extraordinarily wide range of his interests and imagination. Even the possibility of human flight—and practical inventions to attain it—had occupied his curiosity.

Leonardo had been fascinated with birds. He combined his observations of their motions in flight with his knowledge of physics and mathematics and worked out flapping-wing devices to bear men aloft. And, about 1500, he drew detailed designs for a helicopter and a parachute. His notebooks, in all, contained some 150 sketches of flying machines, a few of which are shown here.

Unfortunately, this treasure was forgotten for over three hundred years. Had his work been known, the course of aviation history might have been advanced by centuries.

An ornithopter for prone pilots

The first parachute design

A spring-driven helicopter

A detailed wing mechanism

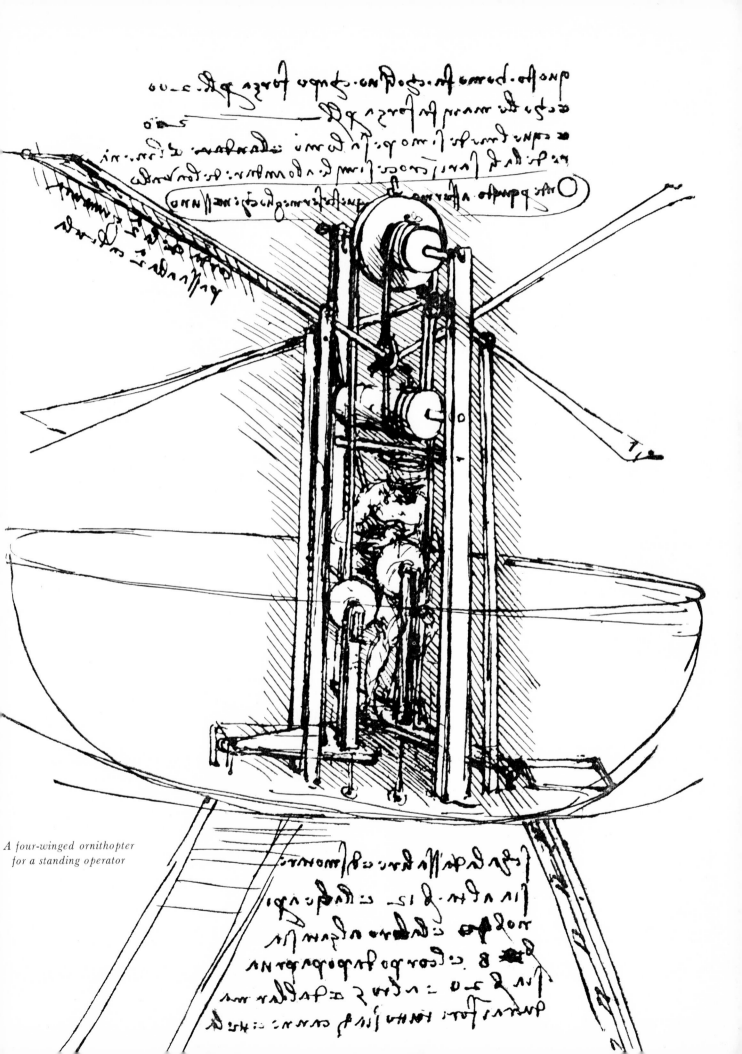

A four-winged ornithopter
for a standing operator

Dreamers and Visionaries

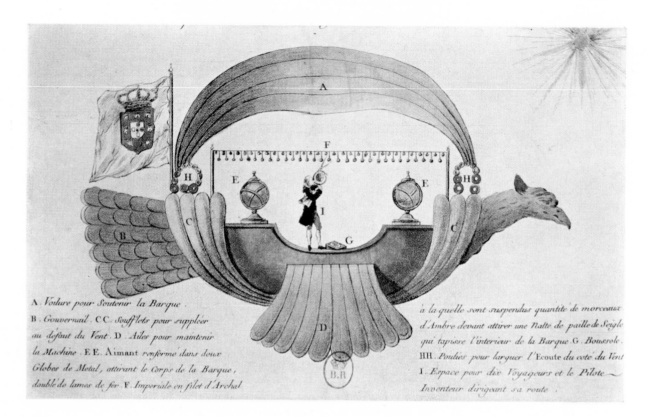

A. *Voilure pour Soutenir la Barque.*
B. *Gouvernail.* CC. *Soufflets pour suppléer au défaut du Vent.* D. *Ailes pour maintenir la Machine.* EE. *Aimant renfermé dans deux Globes de Metal, attirant le Corps de la Barque, double de lames de fer.* F. *Imperiale en filet d'Archal*

à la quelle sont suspendus quantité de morceaux d'Ambre devant attirer une Natte de paille de Seigle qui tapisse l'interieur de la Barque. G. *Boussole.* HH. *Poulies pour larguer l'Escoute du coté du Vent.* I. *Espace pour dix Voyageurs et le Pilote — Inventeur dirigeant sa route.*

For a century and a half after Leonardo's death, there were few practical contributions to aeronautical progress. Then, beginning in 1670, several visionaries appeared, proposing ideas that showed, at least, the searching work of serious minds.

The aerial boat designed by the Italian Jesuit Francesco de Lana in 1670 contained at least the germ of truth: the lifting power of a vessel lighter than air. But his scheme of draining air from hollow copper globes was wildly impractical. In 1709 another Jesuit, Laurenço de Gusmão, was granted a Portuguese patent for a man-carrying ornithopter that combined the use of flapping wings and a sail. Later that year Gusmão seems to have bolstered his aeronautical reputation by experimenting with small hot-air balloons.

Though scientifically unsound, the work of these men helped to stir a new interest in flight.

The fanciful representation of Gusmão's Passarola *("great bird") above interpreted his 1709 flying machine literally—with drooping wings, feathered tail, and beaked head. The lifting power was mysteriously ascribed to two magnetic globes (E), actually meant to be navigation devices. The Portuguese inventor is pictured on the deck.*

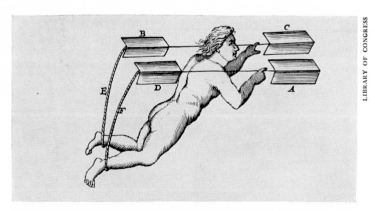

In 1678 the French locksmith Besnier claimed to have flown (with more modesty, perhaps), using the ingenious device pictured above. Motions of his arms and legs manipulated the rods and hinged panels.

The two passengers riding in de Lana's airship (opposite) are blithely unaware that atmospheric pressure would instantly have crushed the hollow, airless globes used in their imaginary journey through the skies.

Aerial Fantasies

The engraving at left shows Cyrano de Bergerac in a dew-fill bowl being drawn upward by the sun toward moondwelle Godwin's Man in the Moone (above) flew by harnessing gee

The theme of air travel fascinated many seventeenth- and eighteenth-century European writers, who wove exciting plots about heroes who flew not only across the earth, but to the moon and sun as well.

One of the early science-fiction fantasies, *The Man in the Moone,* was written by Francis Godwin, Bishop of Hereford, and published posthumously in 1638. Godwin's hero, Domingo Gonsales, harnessed twenty-five geese to his flying apparatus, devising a system of pulleys and weights that distributed the load equally and thus enabled him to reach the moon.

Gonsales commented that it is "farre more honour to have been the first flying man, than to bee another Neptune that first adventured to sayle upon the Sea"—an early appreciation of the fame that awaited the first man to fly.

Cyrano de Bergerac, the French author, was another who wrote tales of solar and lunar flights. His stories, which appeared from 1657 to 1662, told of aerial journeys accomplished with the help of dew-filled flasks and small rockets.

The vogue for fictional ascensions reached a peak in the eighteenth

Jonathan Swift's Gulliver (left) sights an island in the sky. The handsome winged woman above is a Gawry, the exotic heroine who was rescued and married by Robert Paltock's Peter Wilkins.

century, when more than fifty different works on the subject appeared in England and France. Imaginative as well as entertaining, the romances often contained references to equipment that one day would become practical realities. Crude parachutes, rocket ships, and electrical flying machines were described, and most of the vehicles employed in these adventures were heavier than air.

Jonathan Swift's *Gulliver's Travels*, published in 1727, foreshadowed today's satellites in its description of a flying island. The people of this "vast opaque body," powered by a giant magnet, intimidated nations by hovering above them, excluding the sun and rain, by flinging great stones down, or even "letting the island drop directly upon their heads."

Glums and Gawrys, strange winged creatures inhabiting an island near the South Pole, peopled *The Life and Adventures of Peter Wilkins*, written in 1751 by Robert Paltock. As a reward for helping them defeat their enemies, the hero of Paltock's book married and lived happily ever after with one of the winged ladies, of whom the English critic Leigh Hunt later wrote, "A sweeter creature is not to be found."

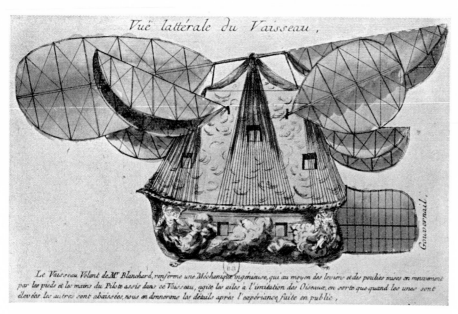

Le Vaisseau Volant de M.ʳ Blanchard, renferme une Méchanique ingénieuse, qui au moyen des leviers et des poulies mises en mouvement par les pieds et les mains du Pilote assis dans ce Vaisseau, agite les ailes à l'imitation des Oiseaux, en sorte que quand les unes sont élevées les autres sont abaissées, nous en donnerons les détails après l'expérience faite en public ;

In the engraving above, Blanchard's Vaisseau Volant *of 1781 appears as an elegant bark, decorated in the best rococo style and furnished with a ship's rudder and six hinged, beating paddles meant to supply direction and movement. A white drapery, painted to resemble the clouds through which it would pass, concealed the vessel's mechanical details.*

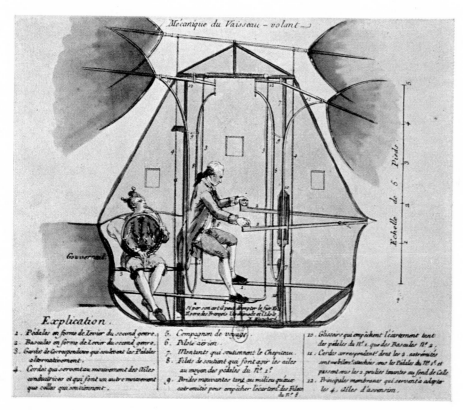

A cutaway view exposes Blanchard's ridiculously inadequate source of power: a lone pilot whose leg and arm movements were supposed to operate the paddles while a passenger with a curved trumpet provided appropriately soothing music. Later, as a famous balloonist, Blanchard retained aerial paddles which he stubbornly maintained provided dirigibility.

On the Eve of Flight

The late eighteenth century saw a quickening of interest in aeronautics. Some experimenters were misguided and others unlucky. But work in all branches of science provided a foundation for historic breakthroughs that were soon to come.

In 1772 a French priest, Canon Desforges, built a wicker car with wings and a parasol to protect him against unexpected descents. Manual operation of the wings proved too great a labor for the inventor, who failed to make good his claim of a 75-mile-per-hour speed in the air.

In the next decade C. F. Meerwein, a German architect, made a nearly correct calculation of the wing surface necessary to support a man; but he, too, clung to an impractical flapping-wing device and got nowhere. The same year, 1781, Jean-Pierre Blanchard designed the equally unrealistic flying machine which received wide publicity through the illustrations on these pages.

While such schemes were capturing the interest of the public, better-trained and more practical scientists were quietly at work on studies that would lead eventually to successful flight. By 1766 the English chemist Henry Cavendish had determined that hydrogen weighs less than oxygen. Joseph Black, a Scottish professor, concluded soon afterward that hydrogen-filled vessels would rise through the heavier air.

Twenty years passed before man acted successfully on this conclusion to create the balloon.

The optimistic artist who pictured Blanchard's machine in imaginary flight (opposite) added, for good measure, a kite and a soaring figure, foreshadowing the man-shaped balloons popular at a later date.

The writings and voices of the pioneers of flight—some of them romantic, some prophetic, and some significant contributions to an advancing science—provide an intimate dimension to the long history of man's attempt to conquer the air. In these special sections is recorded a personal chronicle, era by era, of many of mankind's aerial visions, hopes, labors, and triumphs.

In Their Words . . .

AERIAL DREAMS

Flying Carts

Some of man's earliest legends of flight have been traced to China in the eighth century B.C. *The following tale is from* Myths and Legends of China *by E. T. Chalmer Werner.*

Situated to the north of the Plain of Great Joy, the Land of the Flying Cart joins the Country of the One-armed People on the south-west and that of the Three-bodied People on the south-east. The inhabitants have but one arm, and an additional eye of large size in the centre of the forehead, making three eyes in all. Their carts, though wheeled, do not run along the ground, but chase each other in mid-air as gracefully as a flock of swallows. The vehicles have a kind of winged framework at each end, and the one-armed occupants, each grasping a flag, talk and laugh one to another in great glee during what might be called their aerial recreation were it not for the fact that it seems to be their sole occupation.

A Hindu Chariot

Several centuries before Christ, India's most celebrated Sanskrit poet, Rishi Valmiki, based an epic poem, the Ramayana, *on the legend of Shri Rama, an incarnation of the Hindu god Vishnu. This wondrous description of a flying chariot is taken from Hari Prasad Shastri's translation.*

. . . the vast aerial chariot Pushpaka, gleaming like pearl, planed above the highest buildings . . . Fashioned of plated gold, embellished with lovely images . . . an incomparable artistic achievement, travelling in space like a guiding light in the orbit of the sun, it was immeasurably resplendent. No detail of that car had been executed unskilfully, no ornament but appeared to be a jewel of great price nor was there anything surpassed by the chariots of the Gods, every part being excellently wrought. . . . it repaired wheresoever its master directed it by the power of his thought. Irresistible and swift as the wind, a source of happiness to those magnanimous beings given to pious deeds, who had reached the peak of prosperity and glory, capable of ranging the firmament, containing many apartments and furnished with innumerable works of art, captivating to the mind, stainless as the autumnal moon, resembling a mountain with splendid peaks, borne by thousands of demons whose cheeks were graced with earrings, voracious eaters, of large unwinking eyes, who travelled through space with exceeding velocity day and night, that aerial chariot, Pushpaka, splendid to look upon, covered with flowers [was] fairer than spring itself . .

The Fall of Icarus

The most famous myth of flight was related by the Roman poet Ovid in The Metamorphoses, *completed in 8* A.D. *This English translation was made by Samuel Croxall in the eighteenth century.*

In tedious exile
  now too long detain'd,
Daedalus languish'd
  for his native land;
The sea foreclosed his flight,
  yet thus he said:
"Though earth and water
  in subjection laid,
O cruel Minos, thy dominion be,

We'll go through air;
  for sure the air is free."
Then to new arts
  his cunning thought applies,
And to improve
  the work of nature tries.
A row of quills
  in gradual order placed,
Rise by degrees
  in length from first to last . . .
Along the middle
  runs a twine of flax,
The bottom stems
  are join'd by pliant wax:
Thus, well compact,
  a hollow bending brings
The fine composure into real wings.
His boy, young Icarus,
  that near him stood,
Unthinking of his fate,
  with smiles pursued
The floating feathers . . .
Or with the wax impertinently
    play'd,
And, with his childish tricks,
  the great design delay'd.
The final master-stroke
  at last imposed,
And now the neat machine
  completely closed;
Fitting his pinions on,
  a flight he tries,
And hung, self-balanced,
  in the beaten skies.
Then thus instructs his child:
  "My boy, take care

Icarus, a sketch after an ancient statue

To wing your course
  along the middle air:
If low, the surges
  wet your flagging plumes;
If high, the sun
  the melting wax consumes. . . .
But follow me: let me
  before you lay
Rules for the flight,
  and mark the pathless way."
Then, teaching,
  with a fond concern, his son,
He took the untried wings
  and fix'd them on . . .
When now the boy,
  whose childish thoughts aspire
To loftier aims,
  and make him ramble higher,
Grown wild and wanton,
  more imbolden'd, flies
Far from his guide,
  and soars among the skies.
The softening wax,
  that felt a nearer sun,
Dissolved apace,
  and soon began to run;
The youth in vain
  his melting pinions shakes,
His feathers gone,
  no longer air he takes;
O! father, father!
  as he strove to cry,
Down to the sea
  he tumbled from on high,
And found his fate;
  yet still subsists by fame
Among those waters
  that retain his name.

"I Made Myself Wings"

*Lucian, a Greek satirist of the second
century* A.D., *ridiculed the ancient
myths in dialogues like the* Icaro-
menippus. *This passage is from the
William Tooke translation.*

MENIPPUS. Marvel not, my com-
rade, if I appear talking to you on
superterrestrial and aerial topics . . .
I have travelled in the stars. . . .

FRIEND. . . . But tell me how
you contrived to climb so high, and
whence you procured such a monstrous ladder? . . .

MENIPPUS. . . . In my ascent I had
no need of a ladder nor an admiring
eagle . . . I made myself wings.

FRIEND. You were not afraid of
encountering the fate of [Icarus] . . .

MENIPPUS. No fear of that. I
used no wax . . .

FRIEND. How did you manage it
then? . . .

MENIPPUS. . . . There seemed
but one method: . . . to procure
wings of some kind or other, and
by their assistance to ascend in my
own person to heaven. . . . That
even feathers and wings would grow
out of my back, I thought pure impossibility: if however I should find
out the art of grafting eagle-wings
or vulture-wings . . . I had no doubt
that I should succeed in the attempt.
Whereupon I caught those two
birds, and dexterously cutting off the
right wing of the eagle and the left
wing of the vulture, I next fastened
them with proper thongs about my
shoulders, and fixed to the extremi-
ties of the long-feathers a sort of
handle, by which I designed to regulate the wings. This done, I made a
trial of what I could do, by leaping
upwards, and . . . endeavouring by
constantly striving upwards to bring
all the muscles into exertion for aid-
ing the flight. Perceiving now that
the project succeeded, I grew bolder
after every experiment . . . And, as
my courage increased with my dex-
terity, and I now might pass for a
perfect master in the art of flying, I
determined no longer to confine myself to essays, only fit for the cawing
brood, but ascended Olympus . . .
and being now come quite close to
the moon, I felt myself, by long exertion, particularly in the left wing
of the vulture, somewhat faint. I
therefore landed on it; and sitting
down to rest awhile, I amused myself with contemplating the subjacent
earth from that elevated station . . .
and now I am sorry, that when I
was preparing for my journey I did
not pluck out both my eyes, and
insert a pair of eagle-eyes.

A Churchyard Miracle

This tale in Otia Imperialia *by Gervase of Tilbury, a thirteenth-century Englishman, is from G. G. Coulton's* Social Life in Britain.

On a certain holyday in Great Britain, after High Mass, the folk were thronging forth from the parish church, on a morning so misty that it made a sort of twilight amid the gross and watery vapours. Here, on a stone tomb within the precincts of the churchyard, they found an anchor fixed, with its cable stretched tight and hanging down from the air. . . . they saw the rope move as though men had been labouring to weigh the anchor. . . . Soon, when they found their labour to be in vain, they sent down one of their fellows, who . . . appeared hanging to the rope and descending with alternate interchange of hands. When, however, he had torn the anchor from the tomb, he was caught by those that stood around, in whose arms he gave up the ghost, stifled by the breath of our gross air as a ship-wrecked mariner is stifled in the sea. Moreover his fellows above, judging him to be wrecked, after an hour's delay, cut the cable, left their anchor, and sailed away. In memory of which event the iron bands of the doors of that church were forged, by a cunning counsel, from that anchor; which bands are still there for all men to see.

Leonardo on Flight

Among the many subjects that pre-occupied Leonardo da Vinci during the forty years preceding his death in 1519 was the study of the flight of birds. The excerpts below are from the Edward MacCurdy translation of Leonardo's notebooks.

Write of swimming under water and you will have the flight of the bird through the air. . . .

You will perhaps say that the sinews and muscles of a bird are

A self-portrait of Leonardo in old age

incomparably more powerful than those of man . . .

But the reply to this is that such great strength gives it a reserve of power beyond what it ordinarily uses to support itself on its wings, since it is necessary for it whenever it may so desire to double or triple its rate of speed in order to escape from its pursuer or to follow its prey . . . and in addition to this to carry through the air in its talons a weight corresponding to its own weight. . . .

Man is also possessed of a greater amount of strength in his legs than is required by his weight. . . .

Observe how the beating of its wings against the air suffices to bear up the weight of the eagle in the highly rarefied air which borders on the fiery element! Observe also how the air moving over the sea, beaten back by the bellying sails, causes the heavily laden ship to glide onwards!

So that by adducing and expounding the reasons of these things you may be able to realise that man when he has great wings attached to him, by exerting his strength against the resistance of the air and conquering it, is enabled to subdue it and to raise himself upon it.

Space Travel—1686

The French philosopher Bernard de Fontenelle trained his elegant wit on the subject of flying. In A Plurality of Worlds, *written in 1686 and translated by his contemporary John Glanvill, he pursued his premise in a dialogue between himself and a skeptical countess.*

. . . shall any one say there shall never be a Communication between the Moon and the Earth. Did the Americans [Indians] believe there would ever be any between them and Europe, till it came to pass? 'Tis true, you must pass this great Space of Air and Heaven which is between the Earth and the Moon; but did not those vast Seas seem at first as impassable to the Americans?

You rave, I think, said she, did you not own the Americans were so ignorant, that they had not the least conception of crossing the Sea; but we who know a great deal more than they, can imagine and fancy the going through the Air, tho' we are assur'd it is not to be done.

There is somewhat more than Fancy, I reply'd, when it hath been already practis'd, for several have found the secret of fastning Wings which bear them up in the Air, to move them as they please, and to fly over Rivers, and from Steeple to Steeple; I cannot say indeed they have yet made an Eagles Flight, or that it doth not cost now and then a Leg or an Arm to one of these new Birds; but this may serve to represent the first Planks that were launch'd on the Water, and which were the very beginning of Navigation; there were no Vessels then thought of to sail around the World, and yet you see what great Ships are grown by little and little from those first Planks.

The Art of Flying is but newly invented, it will improve by degrees, and in time grow perfect; then we may fly as far as the Moon. We do not yet pretend to have discover'd all things, or that what we have discover'd can receive no addition; and therefore, pray let us agree, there are yet many things to be done in the Ages to come.

Were you to live a thousand Ages, said the Countess, I can never believe you will fly, but you must endanger your Neck.

I will not . . . contradict a fair Lady, but tho' we cannot learn the Art here, I hope you will allow they may fly better in the Moon; 'tis no great matter whether we go to them, or they come to us, we shall then be the Americans, who knew nothing of Navigation, and yet there were good Ships at t' other end of the World.

"Sir . . . Man Will Float"

In his 1759 romance, Rasselas, Prince of Abissinia, *Samuel Johnson had his hero discuss the possibility of flight with a skilled "mechanist."*

Sir . . . you have but seen but a small part of what the mechanick sciences can perform. I have been long of opinion . . . [that] man might use the swifter migration of wings; that the fields of air are open to knowledge, and that only ignorance and idleness need crawl upon the ground.

I am afraid, said [Rasselas] to the artist, that your imagination prevails over your skill. . . . Every animal has his element assigned him . . . So, replied the mechanist, fishes have the water, in which yet beasts can swim by nature, and men by art. He that can swim needs not despair to fly: to swim is to fly in a grosser fluid, and to fly is to swim in a subtler. . . .

But . . . swimming, said the prince, is very laborious. . . . I am afraid the act of flying will be yet more violent . . .

The labour of rising from the ground, said the artist, will be great . . . but, as we mount higher, the earth's attraction, and the body's gravity, will be gradually diminished, till we shall arrive at a region where the man will float in the air without any tendency to fall . . .

In a year the wings were finished, and, on a morning appointed, the maker appeared furnished for flight on a little promontory: he waved his pinions a while to gather air, then leaped from his stand, and in an instant dropped into the lake. His wings, which were of no use in the air, sustained him in the water, and the prince drew him to land, half dead with terrour and vexation.

Inflammable Air

On June 20, 1782, Tiberius Cavallo, an Italian scientist living in England, described to the British Royal Society experiments with paper bags inflated with hydrogen in which he came close to inventing the balloon.

Admitting, according to the common notion, [the] impermeability of paper to common air, and presuming that it was impervious to other permanently elastic fluids also, I determined to make use of paper for an experiment; which, though repeatedly attempted with other substances, had never succeeded. The experiment was to construct a vessel, or sort of bag, which, when inflated

An engraved likeness of Tiberius Cavallo

with inflammable air [hydrogen], might be lighter than an equal bulk of common air, and consequently might ascend, like smoke, into the atmosphere; it being well known, that inflammable air is specifically lighter than common air. . . .

Accordingly, having procured some fine China paper, its weight was ascertained, and, after making the necessary calculations, a vessel or bag of a cylindrical shape, terminated by two short cones, was made of such dimensions, as, when inflated with inflammable air, it must have been lighter than an equal bulk of common air, by at least twenty-five grains; consequently, it must have ascended, like smoke, into the atmosphere.

After trying this paper vessel by inflating it with common air, the usual mixture of iron filings, and diluted vitriolic acid, for the production of inflammable air, was put into a large bottle; and, by means of a glass tube adapted to the neck of the bottle, and likewise to the aperture of the paper bag, which was suspended over the bottle, and out of which the common air had been expelled by compression, the inflammable air, as soon as it was produced, was made to enter the vessel; but I was surprised to observe, that, notwithstanding the production of inflammable air was very copious, the paper vessel was not inflated in the least, and the smell of the inflammable air in the room was very strong. Suspecting that a hole in the paper might give exit to the inflammable air, the whole apparatus was attentively examined, the effervescing mixture was renewed, and every precaution, I could think of, was taken; but, after all, nothing else could be concluded, but that the inflammable air passed through the pores of paper, just like water through a sieve.

Cavallo failed, but the first practical balloon was only a year away.

CHAPTER 2

St. Louis crowds, drawn by the spectacle and sport of ballooning, await the start of the 1907 Gordon Bennett International Race.

BALLOONING

In all the folklore of flying, only one fairy tale seems to foreshadow the principle that first lifted man from the earth. According to ancient Arabian legend, a jinni, or spirit-demon, was able to fly "by swallowing air." Granting that a jinni, being a somewhat infernal creature, was probably also hot, here is a faint indication that some long-forgotten watcher of the desert sands knew that heated air rises and that it might conceivably lift something as insubstantial as a jinni.

It is doubtful that Joseph or Etienne Montgolfier, French papermakers of Annonay, near Lyon, ever heard the legend—or paid much attention to it if they did. They were well-educated eighteenth-century gentlemen who did not let their paper mill interfere too much with scholarly pursuits. Science in particular intrigued them. As children they had heard of Benjamin Franklin's famous electrical experiment with a kite. Later they read a translation of Joseph Priestley's treatise on the properties of air. The elder Montgolfier, in fact, constructed a parasol-type parachute in 1779, and tested it successfully with a sheep.

And it was this same Joseph, gazing pensively into his fireplace a couple of years later, who suddenly asked himself why he could not capture the "gas" or whatever it was that was lifting the smoke and sparks, and use it to elevate something more interesting. If clouds could float in the sky, he reasoned, why not capture a cloud and enclose it in a bag?

Cloud capturing was not very feasible, but anyone could build a fire and trap the smoke. Joseph first tried it with an oblong bag made of fine silk. When he burned paper beneath an opening in the bottom, the bag swelled into an awkward sphere and sailed to the ceiling of the room, much to the "great surprise" of his landlady, who had supplied the silk.

This indoor experiment took place at Avignon in November, 1782. To his brother Etienne at Annonay he wrote excitedly, "Prepare promptly a supply of taffeta and ropes, and you will see one of the most astonishing things in the world!" At Annonay the brothers repeated this experiment out of doors. This time the bag rose about seventy feet before losing its buoyancy and descending gently.

Still unwilling to announce their discovery, the Montgolfiers made two larger "aerostatic machines," as they called their balloons, tested them, and found the lift strong enough to break the cords that held them down. The second aerostat rose to a height of more than a thousand feet and came down almost a mile away. By now the inventors were using a fire made of chopped wool and straw that produced great quantities of noxious smoke and left them more convinced than ever that their "flying globes" were being lifted by some hitherto unknown gas. The notion that heated and therefore rarefied air alone could exert such an upward pressure did not occur to them.

By the early summer of 1783 the brothers were ready for a public demonstration. Their aerostat, a paper-lined linen bag, had a circumference of more than one hundred feet. On June 4, in the presence of "a respectable assembly, and a great multitude of people" they lit a fire in the market place of Annonay and began to inflate their strange contrivance. Soon, to the astonishment of the onlookers, it required eight strong men to hold it down. When Joseph finally gave the release signal, it shot into the air, soared to an altitude of 6,000 feet, according to careful measurements made with "philosophical instruments," and finally landed more than a mile away.

When news of this triumph reached the Academy of Sciences in Paris, it caused great excitement. The members promptly invited the Montgolfiers to come to the capital and demonstrate their aerostat. They also authorized a young French physicist, J. A. C. Charles, to carry out further research.

A coolheaded scientist, Charles realized from the start that the lifting agent of the Montgolfier machine —whatever it was—was not nearly so effective as Professor Henry Cavendish's "inflammable air." He decided, therefore, to use hydrogen for his experiment. Paper and linen, he knew, would be too porous to retain the gas. But he had heard of a pair of brothers named Robert (the brother team appears with curious regularity in the history of aeronautics) who had devised a method of coating silk fabric with rubber. From them Charles ordered a small "flying globe" some thirteen feet in diameter.

On August 23, 1783, the balloon was judged ready for a trial. Charles had endless difficulty in generating enough hydrogen to keep the balloon filled, but on the night of the twenty-sixth the balloon was partially inflated and ready for transport to the Champ-de-Mars, where it was to ascend. By this time popular excitement was so great that the balloon's sponsors decided to move it before daybreak, hoping to avoid the crowds. But the Parisians turned out anyway, and the occasion became a spectacular torchlight parade. Why the open flames did not explode the 22,000 cubic feet of hydrogen in the leaky envelope is a mystery, but they did not.

All the next day a crowd of more than 50,000 eager people waited while Charles struggled to inflate the silken bag. Finally, at five in the afternoon, in a "copious shower of rain," the balloon was released and rose into the low-hanging clouds. Craning his neck among the spectators was Benjamin Franklin, envoy from the infant United States. "Interesting," some skeptic remarked to him as the balloon vanished, "but what use is it?" "What use is a newborn baby?" growled the old genius. He hastened to inform scientific colleagues in London, Vienna, and Philadelphia of the new invention, stressing to them its military potential.

In the meantime Etienne Montgolfier had come to Paris and was completing a handsomely decorated aerostat some seventy-four feet high. Etienne demonstrated his new creation so successfully before members of the Academy that a royal summons arrived to repeat the performance before Louis XVI and Marie Antoinette at Versailles on September 19, 1783.

Etienne built a new balloon in four days (the other one had been damaged by rain). To determine if the upper air could sustain life, the brothers decided to attach to the balloon a cage containing a sheep, a rooster, and a duck. Up rose the first aerial menagerie,

soared for eight minutes, then drifted to a landing a mile and a half away. The King was delighted, awarded both brothers the Order of Saint Michel, and ordered a gold medal to be struck bearing their profiles and the proud accolade: "Pour avoir rendu l'air navigable." Soon hot-air balloons were to be called montgolfières, to distinguish them from the hydrogen-filled charlières.

When the cage of animals came down intact, the first man to reach it was Jean-François Pilâtre de Rozier, a young physician from Metz. Within a few weeks his curiosity and enthusiasm were to make him the first balloon pilot in history—and within two years the first aerial fatality.

Full of confidence, the Montgolfiers now set to work to construct a third giant balloon so that it could carry aloft not only a fire but a two-man crew to stoke it. In view of the risks involved, the King was inclined to order a pair of condemned criminals to make the first ascent, their lives being their reward if they came down in one piece. But others felt that the honor of being the first men to fly should not thus be wasted, and in the end this view prevailed. Since the most articulate and persistent volunteer was the eager Pilâtre, he was chosen.

In October, Pilâtre made several tethered ascents, twice taking passengers with him. Going up in a captive balloon sounds tame enough today, but it required the courage of any first step into the unknown. And indeed the flimsy linen-and-paper balloon, with an open fire blazing beneath it and no means of directional control, was much less predictable than a modern space rocket. Then, as now, the rewards were the soaring sense of adventure and achievement and the heady acclaim of the crowd.

The first free flight took place on November 21, 1783, when Pilâtre and the Marquis d'Arlandes, an infantry major, stationed themselves on opposite sides of a wicker gallery attached to the straining montgolfière and "at fifty-four minutes past one o'clock passed safely over some high trees and ascended calmly and majestically into the atmosphere," waving their hats triumphantly to the gaping crowds below.

The journey, lasting some twenty-five minutes, took them more than five miles across Paris. At one point sparks from the grate scorched holes in the balloon and threatened to set the cordage on fire. The gallant Marquis (who later was cashiered for cowardice in the French Revolution) met this emergency with a wet sponge. When the balloon finally settled gently to the ground, the dream of the ages was a reality at last. And the glory belonged to France.

Ten days later the methodical and scientific Professor Charles made the first flight in a hydrogen balloon. Having raised enough funds by private subscription, he had designed a big charlière that incorporated most of the essential features of modern balloons. With one of the Robert brothers as a passenger in a car well equipped with food, extra clothing, scientific instruments, and even bags of sand for ballast, he took off from the Tuileries Gardens on the afternoon of December 1.

The voyage was a resounding success; Charles himself described it as "delightful." In the first two hours the wind carried them to Nesle, some twenty-seven miles from Paris. There Robert got out, and Charles decided to make another ascent without him. With only one passenger, the balloon leaped from the shadows and rose to 9,000 feet, giving Charles the unique experience of seeing the sun set twice in one day. Somewhat troubled by the cold and a sharp pressure-pain in his ear, he came back down, making an expert landing.

The excitement created throughout the civilized world by these early flights was extraordinary. Balloons and ballooning became a craze: montgolfières and charlières appeared in science fiction and in cartoons, on plates, vases, and snuffboxes. Amid all the acclaim a few gloomy voices were heard. "I hope," wrote Horace Walpole darkly, "these new mechanic meteors will prove only playthings for the learned and the idle, and not be converted into new engines of destruction to the human race, as is so often the case of refinements or discoveries in science."

The Montgolfiers evidently had no such qualms. On January 19, 1784, the largest hot-air balloon yet made went up at Lyon with seven persons aboard, including the first airman, Pilâtre de Rozier, and Joseph Montgolfier. It was the inventor's first and only flight.

In September the craze came to London when a handsome Italian, Vincent Lunardi, took time off from his duties as secretary to the Neapolitan ambassador to popularize ballooning in England. His balloon balked at lifting another intended passenger, George Biggin, so Lunardi left him behind. He did, however, carry a dog, a cat, a pigeon, a bottle of wine, and some food which he could not eat because it fell into his sand ballast.

He also took a pair of aerial oars but soon dropped one of them. According to Lunardi, a young lady who saw the oar fall thought it was the balloonist himself, and was so upset that she suffered "a seizure" and died. However, balancing this tragedy, he also claimed to have saved a life. At another point along his route, he said, a jury deliberating the fate of a criminal heard of his approach, reached an instantaneous verdict of not guilty, and rushed outside to see the spectacle.

After a brief descent at North Mimms where Lunardi put out the cat ("the poor animal had been sensibly affected by the cold"), he flew on to Standon, in Hertfordshire, where he landed to find himself a hero—to everyone but the glum Horace Walpole. "One Lunardi," Walpole wrote, "is the first *airgonaut* that has mounted into the clouds in this country. So far from respecting him as a Jason, I was very angry with him: he had full right to venture his own neck, but none to risk the poor cat."

Lunardi's balloon was a charlière; he considered montgolfières with their open fires too hazardous. And his second aerostat became almost as famous as his first. The next summer it carried aloft the first Englishwoman to fly. Mrs. L. A. Sage was a statuesque beauty weighing close to two hundred pounds. With Lunardi's friend George Biggin as companion (the balloon, under the circumstances, balked at carrying three), she took off from London, on June 29. The flight was uneventful except for one small scientific disaster when Mrs. Sage knelt on the barometer. After a satisfying lunch of chicken, ham, and wine, she and Biggin landed safely in a field near Harrow, to the huge delight of the Harrovian schoolboys and the fury of the farmer who owned the land and objected violently to the sight of the massive Mrs. Sage tramping all over his beans.

Lack of directional control was to plague balloonists for more than a century. From the beginning they tried to achieve some degree of control with aerial oars, paddles, and revolving fans that were the crude forerunners of propellers. But these hand-operated devices were useless in the face of the pressure exerted by the wind on the balloon itself.

Two other problems became vividly apparent in that first breathless year of ballooning. Once hydrogen was valved off to check an ascent, there was no way to get the lost buoyancy back except by jettisoning valuable ballast. Furthermore, if expanded hydrogen were released at high altitudes, the balloon tended to lose its shape as it came back down. Pondering this, a French lieutenant in the corps of engineers proposed the inclusion within the main envelope of a smaller sac which could be filled with ordinary air by means of a pump. This *ballonet* could be used to some extent in varying the weight of the whole balloon. It could also help the airship retain its shape after any loss of gas.

This young lieutenant, Jean-Baptiste Marie Meusnier, was one of the first great geniuses of aeronautics. He realized that to be "dirigible," or steerable, a balloon should have an elongated shape, with a bow and a stern like a ship. In 1785, with astonishing prescience, he designed an airship that was almost a century ahead of its time. The gas envelope, football-shaped, was to be 260 feet long. Slung below it was to be a car powered by three propellers and steered by a rudder in the form of a sail. The propellers were to be worked by man power. Meusnier even sketched a hangar to house his brain child at its home base, and a portable canvas shelter to protect it in the field. Nine years later, having risen to the rank of general, he was killed at the Battle of Mayence.

One of the most dramatic events of that dramatic year of 1785 was the first aerial crossing of the English Channel. The pilot was a courageous if somewhat waspish little Frenchman named Jean-Pierre François Blanchard. His passenger was an American-born doctor, John Jeffries, who—disapproving of the recent and successful rebellion against King George III—had made his home in England.

Blanchard's interest in aeronautics went back a long way. According to his own story, he was experimenting with parachutes as early as 1777. In 1781 he designed and built a "flying chariot" with four beating wings which, like the other man-powered ornithopters, never flew. With the success of the first charlière he turned eagerly to lighter-than-air craft, and soon made successful ascents in both France and England.

This brought him to the attention of Dr. Jeffries, surely one of the most ardent amateurs in the history of flying. So determined was Jeffries to go on the voyage across the Channel that he organized the flight, provided all the money, and even agreed to "get out of the car" at any point if lightening the ship became necessary—no small pledge for any sort of flight.

Blanchard, apparently reluctant to share with his patron the honor of being first to cross the Channel in a balloon, did all he could to discourage the eager doctor. At one point he secretly weighted himself with lead in an attempt to demonstrate the balloon's limited lifting capacity. This resulted in a quarrel that was settled only by the personal intervention of the Governor of Dover Castle. Finally, on January 7, 1785, with a favorable wind, the balloon took off with both men.

Blanchard had with him some aerial oars and a hand-cranked *moulinet*, or propeller. In addition the balloon carried thirty pounds of sand ballast, two anchors, two cork jackets in case of a forced landing at sea, a bottle of brandy, provisions, and a large parcel of pamphlets to scatter over France.

At first all went well; the balloon sailed serenely over ships in the Channel which saluted by dipping their colors. But at about 2,000 feet it became necessary to release some of the expanding hydrogen. In the process the balloon lost too much gas, and went into a terrifying series of ups and downs. The ballast went overboard first, then the pamphlets, then everything movable except the life jackets. The two men managed to unscrew the *moulinet* and throw that out. Next went the two anchors; then the aeronauts began to cast away their outer garments, Blanchard even discarding his "trowsers."

At last, near the French coast, their lightened balloon went into a slow up-run. Shivering in the frigid January wind, they found themselves plunging down again—this time into a forest. They tossed out the now useless life jackets, and Dr. Jeffries reported candidly that in desperation they resorted to one last "curious" expedient to lighten the ship. When the car bounced through the treetops, they managed to pull it along to an open space where they opened the valve and sank gratefully to the ground some twelve miles inland from Calais.

On both sides of the Channel they were acclaimed as heroes, which indeed they were. Blanchard made many more flights in Europe, and one notable ascent in Philadelphia on January 9, 1793, under the watchful eye of President Washington. It was the first aerial voyage in the United States, though thirteen-year-old Edward Warren of Baltimore had risen into the air in a captive balloon nine years earlier.

For more than two years after the Montgolfier brothers had first demonstrated their *globe volant* in 1783 no one, miraculously, was killed. But this remarkable safety record could not go on forever. The end came when a misguided attempt was made to combine the merits of the hot-air montgolfière and the hydrogen charlière in a single airship. This deadly hybrid was designed by the first man ever to achieve flight—Pilâtre de Rozier.

Impressed by—and perhaps a little jealous of—the praise showered upon Blanchard and Jeffries, Pilâtre decided to attempt an east-to-west Channel crossing. To avoid the loss of hydrogen that had almost brought Blanchard to disaster, he would use both hydrogen and hot air. Underneath the spherical charlière would be a cylindrical montgolfière with the usual open fire. The pilot would be able to vary the total lift simply by controlling the fire. Such was the theory behind Pilâtre's balloon.

Some historians have claimed that Pilâtre was ignorant of the hazards involved, but this hardly seems credible. The explosive properties of hydrogen were well known. Besides, that clear-minded scientist, Professor Charles himself, told Pilâtre that in effect he was trying to mix fire and gunpowder. What is more likely is that Pilâtre, having obtained a grant from the French government to build the balloon, got himself so far out on a limb that he could not go back.

He was anything but optimistic about the voyage. He told friends that he was "certain of meeting with death," and vowed that if he did reach England he would give up ballooning for the rest of his life.

His qualms, apparently, were not shared by two of his countrymen who competed furiously for the honor of going with him. One was Pierre Romain, manufacturer of the balloon. The other was the impetuous young Marquis de Maisonfort, who offered two hundred gold louis for a place in the balloon. Pilâtre objected so strenuously that in the end the Marquis grudgingly withdrew. It was well for him that he did.

Early on the morning of June 15, 1785, with what seemed to be a favorable wind, the balloon took off from Boulogne with Pilâtre and Romain aboard. In half an hour it had risen to 3,000 feet, but was making little progress toward England. Watchers on the ground saw the occupants doing something to the fire basket that swung below the montgolfière. Instantly a blue flame appeared, a muffled explosion was heard, and the car came hurtling down, trailing smoke and shreds of silk. It struck the rocks near the coast at Wimereux. Pilâtre was dead when the would-be rescuers reached him; Romain was breathing, but died in a few minutes. The air had claimed the first of many victims.

The tragedy marked the beginning of the end of the hot-air balloon. Montgolfières continued to fly (particularly to carry aloft stunting parachutists), but confidence in them was badly shaken. Four years later, when the French Revolution burst in all its fury, even the charlières went into partial eclipse. Between 1783 and 1790 seventy-six lighter-than-air ascents were recorded in France. In the next decade the number of civilian flights dropped to six.

The significance of these new toys had not escaped the military, however. In 1793 the French Government authorized an air arm, and the next year the Revolutionary armies began using captive hydrogen balloons for reconnaissance. But in 1802 Napoleon disbanded the balloon corps.

By the beginning of the nineteenth century a certain amount of disillusionment with balloons had set in. The "cloud enclosed in a bag" had liberated man from his bondage to earth, but it had proved an intractable creature, a plaything of the winds. For the next hundred years the history of lighter-than-air flight is the story of man's struggle to make his cloud-in-a-bag go where he wanted it to go. This proved to be so difficult that as the decades passed some of the best scientific minds in both England and France turned back to the ancient dream of wings as the most promising means of flight. But the balloonists, both in Europe and America, kept doggedly on.

One of the greatest was the Englishman Charles Green, who made his first flight in 1821, using coal gas instead of hydrogen because it was more readily available and considerably cheaper. Green was the first to make practical use of the guide rope, a long rope designed to act as automatic ballast. Trailing below the balloonist's car, it regulated lift in proportion to the amount of its weight dragging along the ground. At night it could warn the balloonist of rising terrain. It could also, on occasion, cause considerable havoc on the ground, from bowling over unsuspecting lovers to demolishing haystacks.

The most famous of Green's flights took place in 1836 when with two companions he took off at noon from Vauxhall Gardens in London, flew all night over France and Belgium, and landed the next day near Weilburg in the German Duchy of Nassau, a record distance of 480 miles.

One of Green's two passengers on this voyage was Monck Mason, a flutist of note who later became one of the first air historians. His description of night ballooning thrilled his contemporaries: "An unfathomable abyss of darkness visible seemed to encompass us on every side; and as we looked forward into its black obscurity . . . we could scarcely avoid the impression that we were cleaving our way through an interminable mass of black marble. . . "

Mason was more than just a passenger or a reporter; he was also a designer. A few years later he constructed a model dirigible forty-four feet long with a propeller driven by clockwork. It was exhibited in the Strand and traveled short distances at a speed of about 6 miles per hour.

Charles Green's counterpart in America was John Wise, whose long career in the air covered more than forty years. His greatest contribution was the invention of the ripping panel, which allowed balloonists to deflate their gasbags instantly on landing and thus not be dragged all over the countryside on windy days.

Wise also saw clearly the immense potential of aerial warfare. In 1846, with the United States at war with Mexico, he proposed that a captive balloon on a long cable be positioned over the Mexican fortress at Vera Cruz, where it could drop bombs and torpedoes on the garrison while soaring out of range of any counterfire. The War Department looked askance at his proposal, but it was not so far-fetched as it seemed. Three years later, in 1849, the Austrians had the dubious honor of carrying out the first air assault in history. Besieging Venice, they sent small hot-air balloons over the city, each carrying a thirty-pound bomb with a time fuse. Damage was slight, but Father de Lana's grim prophecy of over two centuries before had come true.

By the middle of the nineteenth century, however, balloonists were still vainly struggling for directional control of their capricious craft. As some anonymous rhymer had put it, back in 1786:

To Montgolfier the Invention's due
Unfinished as it lies,
But his will be the glory who
Direction's art supplies.

Again the glory, such as it was, fell to France. In 1852, nine years after Monck Mason's little clockwork model dirigible had sailed sedately around the Royal Adelaide Gallery in London, the famous French engineer Henri Giffard slung a small, 3-horsepower steam engine under an elongated balloon. He hooked his crude little engine to a huge three-bladed propeller. Then, tugging down his flowered waistcoat and settling his top hat firmly on his head, he chugged off through the air at 5 miles per hour and did not come down until he had covered seventeen miles. Although the man-carrying, dirigible airship was thus realized, nothing much came of it, principally because steam engines were too heavy to be practical.

Observation balloons came back into use during the American Civil War and again, nearly a decade later, during the 1870-71 siege of Paris in the Franco-Prussian War. But, still, lighter-than-air travel languished for lack of a powerful, lightweight engine. In 1872 another Frenchman, Henri Dupuy de Lôme, built a well-designed dirigible, but he had to rely on human muscle power to spin the propeller. In the same year a German, Paul Haenlein, flew a dirigible powered—just barely—by an internal combustion engine that ran on coal gas.

Next the designers turned to electric motors, and in 1884 two Frenchmen, Charles Renard and A. C. Krebs, flew their dirigible around a five-mile course. But electric motors, like steam engines, were too heavy for successful adaptation to aeronautics.

It was not until 1885—more than a century after the invention of the balloon—that the solution appeared on the horizon. In that year a German, Karl Benz, built the first practical gasoline-powered automobile. Even so, thirteen more years elapsed before anyone arranged a successful marriage between the gasoline engine and lighter-than-air craft.

The man who did it was Alberto Santos-Dumont, a rich Brazilian living in Paris. He was one of the city's first automobile enthusiasts, and, in 1898, he decided to see if the sputtering engine of one of his tricycle motorcars could be made to drive a balloon. His persistent attempts to build a practical dirigible were plagued with bad luck: one airship collapsed upon landing; a second rammed into trees and was damaged; a third was destroyed by vandals; the wind from another's propeller gave the inventor pneumonia. Before he was through, however, this fearless little man with the high stiff collars and odd Panama hats designed and flew twelve small airships.

In Germany, a former cavalry general, Count Ferdinand von Zeppelin, was planning the first of his great dirigibles, to be over four hundred feet long; by comparison, Santos-Dumont's creations were little more than flying bicycles.

The airship came of age as a practical vehicle with the successful flights of the 190-foot-long, semi-rigid *Lebaudy,* named for her sponsors, Paul and Pierre Lebaudy, and designed by Henri Julliot. The first ascension was made at Moisson, near Mantes, on November 13, 1902. The following May the *Lebaudy* traveled twenty-three miles. In June it easily covered sixty-one miles in two hours and forty-six minutes; and in November it completed a thirty-eight-and-one-half-mile flight from Moisson to Paris. These voyages, made at respectable speeds of up to 26 and 28 miles per hour, were the first long-distance flights by a powered airship.

Parisians admired the achievements of the *Lebaudy,* but Santos-Dumont remained their pet. One pleasant June morning in 1903 he sailed across Paris in dirigible number nine, his "little runabout," he called it. "I might have guide roped under the Arc de Triomphe," he wrote solemnly afterward, "had I thought myself worthy." Down the Champs Elysées he flew to his own handsome house where servants drew the little runabout to earth and held it steady while their master went into the house for coffee and *croissants.* After breakfast he sailed off again.

That same summer, in Dayton, Ohio, two methodical and persistent brothers were hard at work. Before the year was out another dream, the ancient one of flying with wings, was also to come true.

Joseph Montgolfier

Etienne Montgolfier

The Triumph at Annonay

On a drizzly summer day in 1783, French peasants near Annonay were startled to see a globe sailing through the sky toward them. Many of the frightened people thought it must be the moon, suddenly detached from its place in the firmament. When the sphere finally settled to earth, and news of what it actually was raced across the countryside to Paris, all France—and the world—hailed the event as a great scientific triumph.

Throughout the eighteenth century, wits and satirists had had fun treating aerial navigation as an amusing fantasy and a dream of idiots. But it was an age of reason, also, in which serious students and

In the contemporary French print, opposite, the Montgolfiers' first balloon is shown rising above Annonay, bringing consternation and delight to the assembled villagers.

investigators carefully pondered the phenomena of nature. Science had become a religion, and anyone with an inquisitive mind was enrolled in the cult.

In the exciting atmosphere of inquiry, it was not surprising that someone at last would conclude that ascending smoke might be able to lift man from the earth. Late in 1782 the notion occurred to Joseph Montgolfier, the forty-two-year-old son of a French provincial paper maker.

A brilliant and impatient man, Joseph enlisted the interest of his brother Etienne, five years younger and the more methodical of the two. Working without publicity, the brothers succeeded in sending aloft small silk bags filled with hot air. That was in November, 1782. They next experimented with larger vessels, and on June 4, 1783, invited a group of observers to witness their

first public demonstration—the ascension that frightened the peasants.

Not even the Montgolfiers understood the principle that made their balloon rise. The lifting power of smoke was attributed to electricity—the rage of the day—or to a mysterious gas that science had not yet discovered. But there was no doubt that the Montgolfiers had harnessed the force—whatever it was.

Within a month, the scientific community of Paris was agog with excitement. Everyone wanted to meet the brothers from Annonay and witness for himself the newest example of man's progress. The Academy of Sciences invited the Montgolfiers to repeat their demonstration in Paris, and the brothers accepted the summons. But before they could send a second balloon aloft, another man, working from a different principle, had duplicated their success.

47

Man Goes Aloft

Spurred by news of the Montgolfiers' success, Faujas de Saint-Fond, an eminent French geologist, raised a subscription in the summer of 1783 to finance further aeronautical work. His bid to conduct research was immediately accepted by J.A.C. Charles, whose experiments in various fields of physical sciences had gained him some renown.

Charles did not know that the Montgolfiers had used smoke in their balloon, but he was aware of the lifting power of hydrogen, which for the past seventeen years had been known to be lighter than air. Foreseeing the difficulty of containing the gas in a porous envelope, he turned the problem over to two mechanics, Anne-Jean and M.-N. Robert. Within a short time, they fashioned a small, rubber-coated, silk balloon, and on August 27, 1783, Charles sent it aloft filled with hydrogen.

There were now two methods for ascensions, and the stage was being readied for man's first aerial trip. By mid-October, 1783, Etienne Montgolfier, having successfully demonstrated his hot-air balloon to the French Academy of Sciences and King Louis XVI, was conducting captive ascents with a passenger—a bold young doctor named Jean François Pilâtre de Rozier.

The first free flight in the Montgolfiers' hot-air balloon finally occurred on November 21 when two men went aloft. The daring pioneers, Pilâtre de Rozier and the Marquis d'Arlandes, received the acclaim of Paris. But Charles and his hydrogen-filled balloon were right behind them. On December 1, with M.-N. Robert as passenger, Charles too made a successful flight, bettering by far the distance and time in the air set by his competitors.

Charles's first unmanned balloon came to an ignominious end when frightened Frenchmen, among whom it descended, attacked it with pitchforks. Startled by the rush of escaping hydrogen, they tied the balloon to the tail of a horse that dragged it to shreds on the country roads.

Pilâtre de Rozier (above) and the Marquis d'Arlandes soared five miles across Paris rooftops during their historic first free ascent in a hot-air balloon. Their gorgeously-decorated vessel, trailing a plume of smoke from its fire grate, is seen at left as it would have appeared from the home of Benjamin Franklin, an eyewitness.

Some 200,000 Parisians turned out to see J.A.C. Charles (above) and M.-N. Robert make the first ascent in a hydrogen balloon. Waving flags to the assembled multitude, the two aeronauts are pictured at right at the moment of their departure from the Tuileries. Their two-hour voyage took them some thirty miles from Paris.

England
To France
By Air

*In this water-color version of the first
balloon crossing of the English Channel,
an unknown artist tried to capture the
thrill of the historic flight. The aerostat that carried Jean-Pierre Blanchard
and Dr. John Jeffries from Dover to Calais on January 7, 1785, only fourteen
months after man's first ascent in a balloon, had the oarlike devices pictured
(hopefully to help steer the balloon), but
not the opened parachute beneath the
envelope—although Blanchard had used
a similar device in his earlier ascents.*

Up in the Clouds

Even before Blanchard's epochal Channel flight, the excitement of ballooning was spreading across Europe.

Italy was the first country after France to witness an ascension, when Paolo Andreani went up in a hot-air balloon near Milan on February 25, 1784. The following July, four Austrians unintentionally made the first aerial voyage over Vienna when the cord holding their captive balloon suddenly snapped.

Vincent Lunardi, a young Italian adventurer noted for his good looks and dashing charm, made the first ascent in England on September 15, 1784, and seemed genuinely surprised that so many young ladies courageously offered to accompany him on subsequent voyages. Nineteen days later, on October 4, James Sadler, whose aeronautical career was to last until 1815, became the first English balloon pilot.

Attempting to cross the Channel on June 15, 1785, Pilâtre de Rozier fell to his death when his ill-conceived combination of the hot-air and hydrogen balloons burst into flames. But even this first aerial fatality did not dampen popular interest in the spectacle of ballooning.

The indefatigable Blanchard did most to foster the mania. During the summer and fall of 1785 he made the first ascents in Holland, Germany, and Belgium. Later he was the first aerial voyager in Switzerland, Poland, and Czechoslovakia.

When the French Revolution plunged all Europe into turmoil after 1789, Blanchard traveled to the New World with his balloon and introduced the new sport to America.

AMERICAN ANTIQUARIAN SOCIETY

Waving a flag decorated on one side with the Stars and Stripes and on the other with the French Tricolor, the veteran balloonist Jean-Pierre Blanchard made the first ascent in the United States on January 9, 1793. The picture at left, illustrating Blanchard's account of the event, shows the ship's anchor which acted as ballast, but not the small dog who came along as company.

The first woman balloon passenger anywhere was a Madame Thible, who went up in a montgolfière at Lyon on June 4, 1784. One observer noted that "she seems to have shown much greater courage" than her male companion, a painter named Fleurant. During the voyage, shown below in a contemporary water color, the lady sang a comic-opera aria, "Oh, to travel in the clouds."

CABINET DES ESTAMPES, BIBLIOTHÈQUE NATIONALE

Three was a crowd on June 29, 1785, when Mrs. Letitia Sage became the first Englishwoman to dare an ascent. Despite J. F. Rigaud's depiction of the historic moment (left), the balloon could not lift the trio, and the gallant Vincent Lunardi, in uniform, let Mrs. Sage and her companion, George Biggin, ascend alone.

THE GRAND REPUBLICAN BALLOON,

Intended to convey the ARMY OF ENGLAND *from the* GALLIC SHORE,

For the Purpofe of exchanging French Liberty! for Englifh Happinefs!

Accurately copied from a PLAN prefented to the EXECUTIVE DIRECTORY,

BY CITIZEN MONGE.

EXPLANATION OF THE REFERENCES.

A A A. The Balloon.
B. A Pedeftrian Statue, in the Head of which is the Obfervatory.
C. The Light Houfe.
D. The Grand Gallery.
E. Pipes to let out the Inflammable Air.
F. Aerial Officers on the look out.
G. The Ship.
H. The Helm.

I. The Lodge of the Helm-Keeper.
K. The Hofpital.
L. The General's Houfe.
M. The Grand Aeroftatic Pipe.
N. The Sails.
O. Rope Ladders to which the Ship is fastened.
P. Apartments for the Officers.
Q. Grand Magazine of Combuftibles.
R. Small Wings for Ornament.

S. The Water Clofet.
T. Ordinaries and Coffee Houfes.
U. Gallery for mounting Guard.
X. A fmall Balloon to ferve as a Boat.
Y. Telefcope.
Z. A Cannon for Signals.
No. 1. A Tent for the Infpector of the Cordage.
No. 2. Tents for the Aerial Navigators and Pumpers.

The Balloon Goes to War

In June, 1793, with most of Europe united against it, the French Republican government took the unprecedented step of adding an air arm to its military forces. The new organization would make use of captive balloons from which "observers, placed as advanced sentries high in the air, could observe the movements of the enemy."

On April 2, 1794, the first company of French *aérostiers* was formed under the command of Colonel Jean-Marie-Joseph Coutelle. Exactly two months later, Coutelle made his first military ascent at Maubeuge, a besieged city some 125 miles northeast of Paris.

Impressed by the distress which the balloon caused the enemy—and by the lift in morale it gave to their own forces—the French created a second company of balloonists.

During the German campaign of 1796, the first unit was taken prisoner and its balloon sent as a prize to Vienna. But the following year Napoleon employed balloon observers during his siege of Mantua in Italy. When he took a balloon corps to Egypt in 1798, its equipment soon fell into the hands of the enemy, and the balloonists were employed in other fields for the remainder of the campaign. Returning to France early in 1802, they received notice that their corps had been disbanded.

The elegant 1798 English satire of French balloons at left carries such Republican conveniences as a suspended water closet (S), a hospital (K), coffee houses (T), an aerial dinghy (X), and guillotine (center).

54

Colonel Coutelle remained aloft for nine hours during the Battle of Fleurus on June 26, 1794 (above). His observations contributed to a victory that forced the enemy to retreat from Belgium.

A wildly imaginative scheme for invading England (under, on, and over the Channel) is shown in the 1803 print below. Note the wind blowing the balloons one way and the kites another.

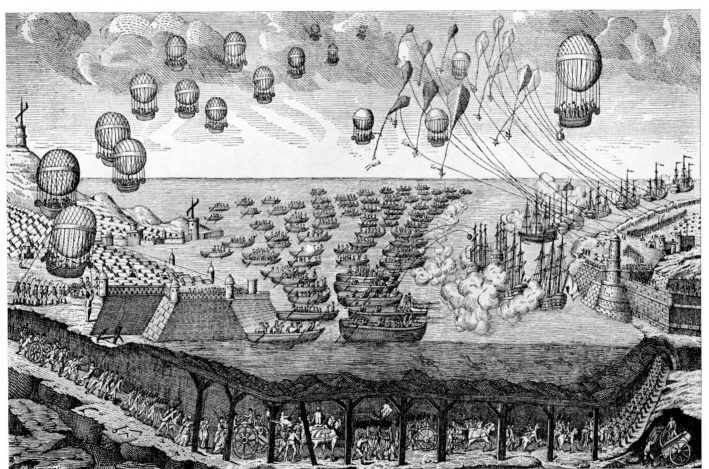

All the Rage

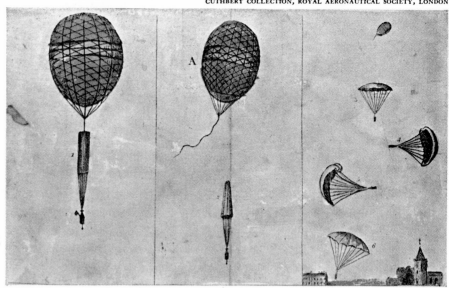

The military debut of the balloon led men to consider other uses for the new invention. Without the ability to steer, however, it seemed ill-suited for commercial transportation or for any other practical function of government or business.

And yet balloons had become a rage. They offered thrills and amusement—both to those who sailed them and to watching multitudes. Painted and decorated with flags and gaudy embellishments, they provided the basis for increasingly spectacular displays that included fireworks, ascents on horseback, and parachute drops. Their lovely shapes inspired fashion designers, and their fashions, in turn, gave cartoonists a new source of merriment. But more important, they gave the public for the first time a feeling of familiarity with the air— once considered unattainable.

André-Jacques Garnerin made the world's first parachute descent on October 22, 1797, in Paris. Five years later he repeated the feat in London, as shown (step-by-step) above.

Cords operated from the basket of the balloon flotilla at right, an 1824 French innovation, were supposed to lower the smaller balloons to give direction to the gaudy vessel.

In 1798 the French aeronaut Tétu-Brissy, who had made the first nocturnal balloon voyage thirteen years earlier, gained whatever honor was attached to the world's first equestrian ascent (below). The doubtless surprised animal suffered greatly from the cold.

Green and Wise

Two of the nineteenth century's most celebrated aeronauts—Charles Green in England and John Wise in America—shared a desire to make the first transatlantic balloon flight.

Encouraged by the success of his record-breaking flight to Germany (right), Green proposed an aerial journey to America in a balloon equipped with propellers operated by clockwork and with a guide rope to regulate ascent and descent. Green spoke knowledgeably of westerly air currents, yet he never made the attempt. Instead, he devoted his last public years to completing an astonishing number of ascents—five hundred before he retired in 1852 at the age of sixty-seven.

Despite setbacks like the 1859 crash (opposite page), Wise never gave up his dream of flying to Europe. Still attempting to set endurance records at seventy-one, the Pennsylvanian disappeared over Lake Michigan in 1879 in a tragic end to his forty-four-year career.

REPETITION
OF THE
DOUBLE ASCENT!
UNDER THE DIRECT PATRONAGE OF HER MAJESTY.
Royal Gardens, Vauxhall,
Grand Day Fete,
Wednesday, Aug. 30, 1837.

The most Extraordinary Attraction!
ASCENT OF THE
Royal Nassau Balloon!

Charles Green's best-known journey—480 miles from London to the German Duchy of Nassau—was made on November 7-8, 1836, in the giant striped balloon pictured above over the Medway River in southeastern England. One of the loveliest balloons ever to grace the skies, it was called the Nassau after the flight and was used by Green to publicize his later ascents, as the poster at left shows.

Hoping to prove that a west-to-east cross-ing of the Atlantic was feasible, John Wise and three companions set out from St. Louis on July 1, 1859, in a balloon optimistically named the Atlantic. *The nearly disastrous end of the 804-mile journey at Henderson, New York, is pic-tured—somewhat inaccurately—in the old print below, with the balloon whirling down like a "maddened elephant through a jungle." (The lifeboat shown dangling beneath the car had been jettisoned over Lake Ontario.) The distance record set on this nineteen-hour voyage, however, remained unbroken for half a century.*

Charles Green

John Wise

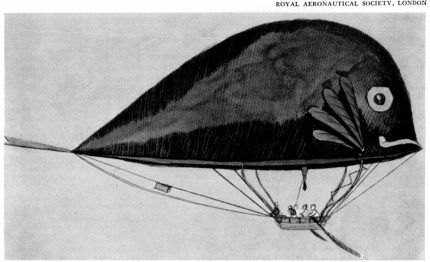

The dolphin-shaped balloon (right) with painted eyes and gills, a pair of oars, and a sliding box of sand for ballast, was the first proposal for a dirigible in England. The scheme was suggested in 1816 by two Swiss armorers in London, S. J. Pauly and Durs Egg, and was known as "Egg's Folly."

In 1785 Lieutenant J.-B.-M. Meusnier of the French corps of engineers conceived the elliptical airship that appears below in the inventor's own drawing. Meusnier's advanced design—never executed—included a rudder and three propellers, as well as an anchor for effecting safe landings.

Power and Ability to Steer

From the beginning the usefulness of the balloon depended on providing it with dirigibility. By late 1783 the cafés of Paris were buzzing with suggestions for supplying direction and movement to aerostats. Most of the plans, though—as one of the Robert brothers noted—seemed designed only to reveal the ignorance of the inventors.

Yet on January 24, 1784, a French physicist, M.-J. Brisson, proposed the elongated balloon shape that eventually was to be used in successful dirigibles. That summer the Roberts, who had helped Charles with his first hydrogen balloon, constructed a cylindrical vessel. Five parasol-shaped oars of blue taffeta, whose opening and closing were intended to propel the vehicle, proved ridiculously inadequate; and, after two unsuccessful trials, the Roberts sensibly abandoned their project.

Other efforts to achieve dirigibility with sails, paddle wheels, flapping wings, and oars served only to prove to the experimenters that such methods were unrealistic—if not totally ludicrous. In March, 1785, the Academy of Lyon received 101 entries in a contest for the best dirigible design. So impractical were they all that the prize was not awarded.

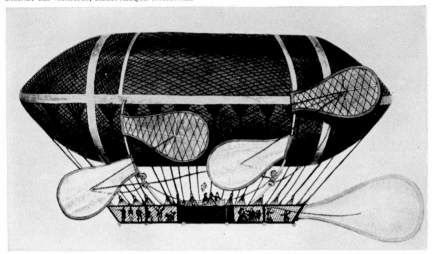

The Comte de Lennox's cigar-shaped airship (left) was exhibited in London during the summer of 1835. The Eagle, as the impractical contrivance was incongruously named, had four paddles on each side, to be manned (it is feared) by aerial galley slaves in a cabin amidships.

The absurd notion of achieving directed flight by harnessing birds to an airship cropped up as late as 1835. Thomas S. Mackintosh, designer of the flying hull below, preferred hawks for the task, or better yet eagles "if they could be tamed —but perhaps strong pigeons would do."

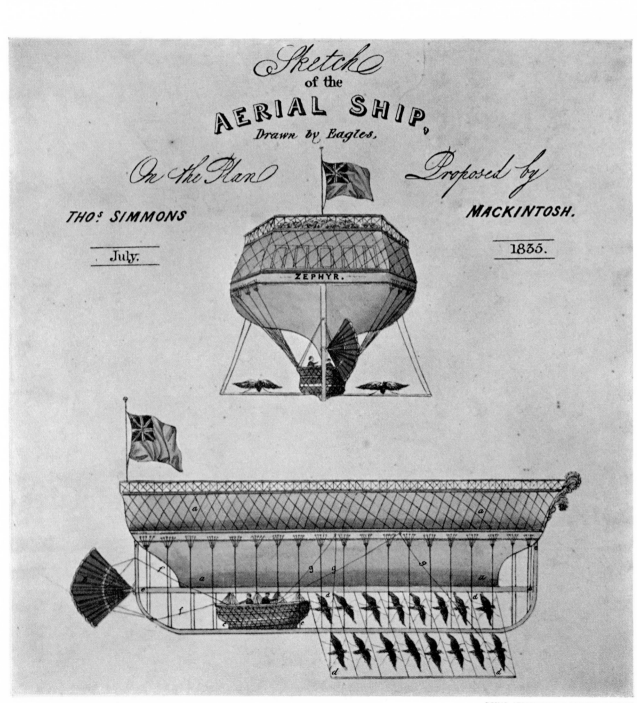

Sketch of the AERIAL SHIP, Drawn by Eagles.

On the Plan Proposed by

THOS SIMMONS MACKINTOSH.

July. 1835.

ZEPHYR.

HISTOIRE CHRONOLO- GIQUE DE L'ARÉOSTATION
Musée de tout le Monde
Juillet 1855
Bureaux rue de la Victoire 3

An Italian caricaturist, using balloonists as symbols of nationalism, depicted (from left): John Bull astride a fish; a Frenchman dropping diplomatic protests; a Russian using tear-shaped stones to hold down his giant balloon; a militaristic Prussian atop a cannon; an Austrian weighted with provinces; an indolently reclining Turk; a capricious Italian with a parrot; and the traditional unhappy Dane.

Balloons in Fun and Fancy

Infinitely the most magnificent and astonishing discovery made . . . perhaps since the Creation," wrote one enthusiast five years after the first balloon had soared into the air. The excitement of the new sport continued to capture the public fancy through the nineteenth century. And for those who scoffed, the balloon—inflated as it was by hot air and sometimes falling straight back to earth again—was a rich subject for satire.

Especially popular were engravings and lithographs of the airships. Practically the entire history of ballooning up to then is included in the 1853 French lithograph on the opposite page. At the top (neatly splitting the title) is the Montgolfiers' first unmanned aerostat of 1783; and at the bottom right, a three-balloon "aerostatic locomotive," designed in 1850 by Ernest Pétin.

Also included are: L.-B. Guyton de Morveau's winged balloon of 1784 (second row, third from left); Tétu-Brissy's 1798 ascent on horseback (fourth row); and a fishlike design of 1850 by Pierre Jullien (hovering over the water). The viewer's morbid taste is satisfied with renditions of no fewer than twelve aerial disasters, while the preponderance of French creations reflects the fact that the country of the balloon's origin long dominated its history.

The 1784 Spanish print at right satirizes ballooning with a bullfight high in the air.

Thaddeus Lowe claimed that his aerial observations of Confederate movements during the Civil War Battle of Fair Oaks, May 29 and June 1, 1862, narrowly averted a Federal disaster. The photograph of an ascent at left reveals the patriotically-decorated gondola of one of Lowe's balloons rising above Union tents in Virginia.

In the sketch below, made from Lowe's balloon over Maryland on December 8, 1861, Rebel camps and batteries are seen across the Potomac River in Virginia. The artist, Colonel William F. Small, emphasized that this was an aerial observation by including the balloon in the drawing, which he submitted to General Joseph Hooker.

The painting at right shows a dramatic moment of the Franco-Prussian War, as Léon Gambetta, leader of the French provisional government, prepares to quit besieged Paris in a balloon on October 7, 1870. The second balloon, carrying stranded Americans, accompanied Gambetta on his daring flight to French-held territory.

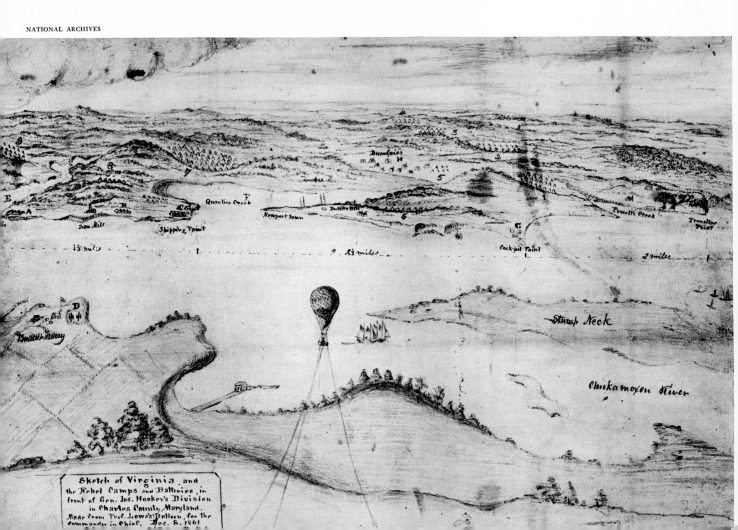

Military Use In America and France

On April 20, 1861, a New Hampshire meteorologist, Thaddeus S. C. Lowe, went up in a balloon in Cincinnati and came down in South Carolina—where he was arrested by secessionists as a Union spy.

Lowe was released as soon as he proved that his flight was a scientific venture and had nothing to do with the Civil War. But two months later he was in Washington, urging the Federal Government to employ military observers in captive balloons.

In a demonstration ascent on June 18, Lowe dispatched to President Lincoln the world's first air-to-ground telegraph message. Lincoln was impressed and soon afterward authorized the creation of an army balloon corps with Lowe in command.

Patriotic Southern women donated silk dresses for a balloon corps for the Confederates, but only the North actually employed a unit during the war. For two years, Lowe's observers hovered over the smoke and roar of battlefields in Virginia, trying to play the role of eyes for the Union armies. Their assistance did not seem worth the expense, however, and when Federal commanders in the field showed little interest in continuing the use of balloons, the North abandoned its air arm in 1863.

The experience of the French during the Siege of Paris in the Franco-Prussian War of 1870-71 was an entirely different one. On September 23, 1870, only four days after German troops completed their encirclement of the French capital, a balloon soared aloft from Paris, flew over the Prussian lines, and landed safely in French-held territory fifty-five miles to the northwest.

Thereafter the French used balloons effectively throughout the siege to maintain contact between the surrounded city and the provinces. Workshops in the capital's railroad stations built balloons at assembly-line speed, and of the sixty-six that were constructed and flown out of Paris during the four-month siege, only six were captured by the Germans, and two others blown out to sea and lost.

The balloons carried more than one hundred persons out of Paris. In addition, they took to the provinces 2,500,000 letters and many carrier pigeons that later flew back to the city with messages reduced on microfilm.

Fairground and Carnival Days

A huge captive balloon, built by Henri Giffard, was the sensation of the Paris Exposition of 1867. Thrill seekers bought tickets and took rides, experiencing the exhilarating adventure of rising high into the air over the exposition grounds.

The following year Giffard took his attraction to London; and for the next forty years in both Europe and America balloon ascensions were an indispensable feature of almost every fair, carnival, and exposition. Few, if any, of the captive balloons equaled the record of 35,000 passengers carried by a Giffard aerostat at the 1878 Exposition in Paris. But over the years, fairground ascensions spread an interest in flight among thousands of people who previously had viewed the subject with skepticism or indifference.

After the turn of the century new thrills were added by free balloonists who awed carnival-goers with stunts and record ascensions. By 1913 balloonists had remained aloft for eighty-seven hours, made flights of nearly 2,000 miles, and gone as high as 35,000 feet.

By that time, the new achievement of flying with wings had overshadowed lighter-than-air ascensions. But many airplane pilots had received their aerial baptism in balloons, and others had first had their imaginations fired by the thrill of ballooning at an exposition or county fair.

RIGHT: *Balloonists often highlighted their acts with stunts like the cannon-launched parachute descent promised in this poster.*

LEFT: *In the early 1900's a balloon vied with a roller coaster at Columbia Gardens, a Butte, Montana, amusement park.*

Miami County FAIR!
Paola, Kansas!
Remember the Dates!

PROF. MONTZ BOZARTH'S

Great CANNON Act!

Fired From a Cannon!

This Great Act will be performed for the first time on the grounds of Miami County Agricultural and Mechanical Association, during the Fair at

PAOLA,
September 29, 30, Oct. 1 and 2, 1896.

NOTE:—Prof. Bozarth is the inventor and positively the only man who has ever performed this Great Act. The Monster Balloon is inflated, the cannon, being eight feet long, is attached and then loaded with powder, the Parachute is carefully folded and placed in the cannon and used as wadding of the charge; a fuse is then lighted, and while in mid-air the cannon is discharged. You see nothing but the cannon during the ascent, and next see the Aeronaut and Parachute Flying Through Space with the Swiftness of a Rocket. The above illustration is from a photograph taken on the experimental trial, April 3d, 1893.

A Polar Tragedy

On July 11, 1897, a balloon rose from the barren shores of Spitsbergen, bounced above the gray waves of the Arctic Ocean, and disappeared into the northern skies. It was the start of an audacious attempt to reach the North Pole in a free balloon—an adventure with a tragic ending, details of which only came to light thirty-three years later.

The project was conceived in 1894 by a forty-year-old Swedish engineer, Salomon August Andrée. Financed in part by Alfred Nobel, the inventor of dynamite and founder of the Nobel prizes, Andrée had a balloon built for himself in France that was capable of retaining its gas for thirty days.

After an abortive attempt to launch the aerial assault on the North Pole in 1896, Andrée and two young companions, Nils Strindberg and Knut Fraenkel, reached Spitsbergen by boat the following May. Difficulties with the balloon, as well as foul weather, delayed them for six weeks, but on July 11 they finally soared away on their great adventure.

A message brought by a carrier pigeon and a letter in a buoy, found later, told of the first two days in the air. The rest was silence, unbroken for thirty-three years.

On August 6, 1930, Norwegian explorers on White Island, some three hundred miles east of Andrée's starting point, stumbled on a silent Arctic camp. There they found the frozen bodies of the three balloonists, together with undeveloped films.

Andrée's pitiful diary and the developed pictures, some of which are seen on these pages, told what had happened: three days out of Spitsbergen, the trio had come down on the ice. After abandoning their balloon and enduring the hardships of a two-and-a-half month trek, they had established the camp in which they had finally perished.

Andrée's balloon, above photographed at Spitsbergen as it set off for the North Pole on July 11, carried sails and trailing guide ropes, two inadequate navigating devices that the explorers hoped would help them maintain a direct course to their goal

In the Arctic sky the balloon did not have enough ballast to dump when ice formed on the envelope. After three days of bumping across the frozen sea, the men landed (below) four hundred miles from Spitsbergen, but five hundred from the Pole

Above is one of the expedition's haunting ghostly photographs, taken in 1897, but not developed until 1930. Fraenkel (left) and Strindberg stand over a polar bear they have shot—a happy addition to their food supply during their march over the ice.

The view below is of the explorers' first camp, established where the balloon landed. Facing starvation, they finally set off to try to reach help. At a subsequent camp on White Island, the three men huddled together for warmth and, one by one, died.

Dirigibles

In the first years of the twentieth century several men finally mastered the ability to steer engine-powered balloons. Among the best-known of the dirigible builders—who included Count Ferdinand von Zeppelin in Germany, the Lebaudys in France, and Thomas Baldwin in the United States—none was a better showman than Alberto Santos-Dumont, the heir to a Brazilian coffee fortune.

Santos-Dumont's intriguing cigar-shaped aerial runabouts were familiar sights in Paris, skimming over rooftops and darting back and forth above the boulevards. His machines seemed little more than sports vehicles in the air, and his contributions to the development of the dirigible were outdistanced by those of Zeppelin. But his flashy feats (like flying from Saint-Cloud to the Eiffel Tower and back) helped arouse interest in the dirigible as a potential means of aerial transportation.

TRANSPORTATION LIBRARY, UNIVERSITY OF MICHIGAN

NATIONAL AIR M

ARCHIV RÖMER

Count Ferdinand von Zeppelin gave his name to the giant rigid dirigibles which he pioneered with flights over Lake Constance in the summer of 1900. Wearing a white cap (at left, above) the 73-year-old German inventor was photographed in 1911 in the gondola of a later airship, the Schwaben. At right, leaning on the rail, is his renowned disciple Hugo Eckener, being tested as a dirigible pilot.

WILLIAM J. HAMMER COLLECTION, IBM

n the photograph above, all eyes are on
antos-Dumont, as he stands poised in the
wicker basket of one of the airships he
built in France between 1898 and 1905. In
906 he turned to heavier-than-air machines, and though his technical contributions were few, he was the first man in Europe to achieve powered flight with wings.

The long tapered dirigible at left was built
in 1902 by the French industrialists Paul
and Pierre Lebaudy. Driving the rubber-
ized balloon was a motor capable of speeds
up to 30 miles per hour. In 1903 the Lebaudy airship completed several long-distance flights to demonstrate the practicability of powered, lighter-than-air flight.

The famous balloon pilot Roy Knabenshue,
pictured at right, flew America's first successful dirigible, the California Arrow,
at the 1904 St. Louis World's Fair. Resembling Santos-Dumont's non-rigids, the
airship was built by Captain Thomas S.
Baldwin of the U.S. Army and was powered
by an engine designed by Glenn Curtiss.

ALOFT IN BALLOONS

It Rose With Majesty

The Marquis d'Arlandes was the world's first flying passenger. A bare five months after the Montgolfiers publicly demonstrated the ascent of an unmanned balloon, the Marquis accompanied J.-F. Pilâtre de Rozier on a flight over Paris and wrote the following account of man's first free hot-air balloon flight.

We went up on the 21st of November, 1783, at near two o'clock, M. Rozier on the west side of the balloon, I on the east. The wind was nearly northwest. The machine, say the public, rose with majesty . . .

I was surprised at the silence and absence of movement which our departure caused among the spectators, and believed them to be astonished and perhaps awed at the strange spectacle . . . I was still gazing, when M. Rozier cried to me—

"You are doing nothing, and the balloon is scarcely rising a fathom."

"Pardon me," I answered, as I placed a bundle of straw upon the fire and slightly stirred it. Then I turned quickly, but already we had passed out of sight of La Muette. Astonished, I glanced at the river.

"If you look at the river in that fashion you will be likely to bathe in it soon," cried Rozier. "Some fire, my dear friend, some fire!"

We travelled on . . . dodging about the river, but not crossing it.

"That river is very difficult to cross," I remarked to my companion.

"So it seems," he answered; "but you are doing nothing. I suppose it is because you are braver than I, and don't fear a tumble."

I stirred the fire, I seized a truss of straw with my fork; I raised it and threw it in the midst of the flames. An instant afterwards I felt myself lifted as it were into the heavens. . . .

At the same instant I heard from the top of the balloon a sound which made me believe that it had burst. . . . As my eyes were fixed on the top of the machine I experienced a shock, and it was the only one I had yet felt. The direction of the movement was from above downwards. . . .

I now heard another report in the machine, which I believed was produced by the cracking of a cord. This new intimation made me carefully examine the inside of our habitation. I saw that the part that was turned towards the south was full of holes [from sparks], of which some were of a considerable size. . . .

I took my sponge and quietly extinguished the little fire that was burning some of the holes within my reach; but at the same moment I perceived that the bottom of the cloth was coming away from the circle which surrounded it. . . .

I then tried with my sponge the ropes which were within my reach. All of them held firm. Only two of the cords had broken. . . .

We were now close to the ground, between two mills. As soon as we came near the earth I raised myself over the gallery, and leaning there with my two hands, I felt the balloon pressing softly against my head. I pushed it back, and leaped down to the ground. Looking round and expecting to see the balloon still distended, I was astonished to find it quite empty and flattened. . . . I saw [Rozier] in his shirt-sleeves creeping out from under the mass of canvas that had fallen over him. . . . we were at last all right.

A Hopeful Prediction

The first manned ascent of a hydrogen balloon was made by J. A. C. Charles and M.-N. Robert at Paris on December 1, 1783. An eyewitness to the event was the American minister to France, Benjamin Franklin, who speculated on the invention's future in a letter written the following January to a friend in Vienna.

It appears, as you observe, to be a discovery of great importance, and what may possibly give a new turn o human affairs. Convincing sovereigns of the folly of wars may perhaps be one effect of it, since it will be impracticable for the most potent of them to guard his dominions. Five thousand balloons, capable of raising two men each, could not cost more than five ships of the line; and where is the prince who could afford so to cover his country with troops for its defence as that ten thousand men descending from the clouds might not in many places do an infinite deal of mischief before a force could be brought together to repel them?

Two Pessimists

Man's ability to soar in balloons was not hailed by all. The two critical letters below exemplified some of the voices of fear and uneasiness that were raised in dissent.

Were I an absolute legislator, I would, therefore, make it death for a man to be convicted of flying, the moment he could be caught; and to bring him down from his altitude by a bullet sent through his head or his carriage, should be no murder. Philosophers would call me a Vandal; the scholar would say that, had it not been for me, the fable of Daedalus would have been realised; and historians would load my memory with reproaches of phlegm, and stupidity, and oppression; but in the mean time the world would go on quietly, and if it enjoyed less liberty, would at least be more secure.

William Cowper
December, 1783

How posterity will laugh at us one way or other! If half-a-dozen break their necks, and balloonism is exploded, we shall be called fools for having imagined it could be brought to use: if it should be turned to account, we shall be ridiculed for having doubted.

Horace Walpole
June, 1785

Help From Washington

When the French balloonist Jean-Pierre Blanchard rose above Philadelphia on January 9, 1793, to make the first flight in the United States, he carried with him this passport:

The bearer hereof, Mr. Blanchard a citizen of France, proposing to ascend in a balloon from the city of Philadelphia, at 10 o'clock A.M. this day, to pass in such direction and to descend in such place as circumstances may render most convenient —These are therefore to recommend to all citizens of the United States, and others, that in his passage, descent, return or journeying elsewhere, they oppose no hindrance or molestation to the said Mr. Blanchard; And that on the contrary they receive and aid him with that humanity and good will which may render honor to their country, and justice to an individual so distinguished by his efforts to establish and advance an art, in order to make it useful to mankind in general.

George Washington

Blanchard's account of his adventure tells how the passport came in handy.

My ascent was perpendicular, and so easy that I had time to enjoy the

A 1785 portrait of Jean-Pierre Blanchard

TISSANDIER COLLECTION, LIBRARY OF CONGRESS

different impressions which agitated so many sensible and interesting persons, who surrounded the scene of my departure, and to salute them with my flag, which was ornamented on one side with the armoric bearings of the United States, and on the other with the three colors, so dear to the French nation. . . . I turned my eyes towards the immense number of people which covered the open places, the roofs of the houses, the steeples, the streets and the roads over which my flight carried me in the free space of the air. What a sight! . . . For a long time could I hear [their] cries of joy . . .

I was at a perpendicular height of 200 fathoms, when I felt a somewhat stronger breeze spring up, which carried me in an easterly direction towards the Delaware: here I met a numerous and thick flock of wild pigeons: they seemed to be much frightened. Alas! it was never my intention in traversing the ethereal regions to disturb the feathered inhabitants thereof . . .

At $10^h.35^m.$ being now in a much more rarefied fluid, and the force of the inflammable gas having increased in proportion to its dilatation, the aerostat was soon raised to [its] highest elevation . . .

Being now fully master of all my ways, I opened the valve of the balloon, and the aerostatic equilibrium was soon broken, but in a manner as exactly graduated and as uniform as that which regulated my ascent. . . .

I soon found myself at the height of about 80 feet above the surface of the ground; I reached it like a bird in full flight; the flexible limbs of the trees around me gave way to the strong pressure of my apparel; I landed at last and set my foot on ground at $10^h.56^m.$ A.M. . . .

With the compass in my hand I formed already plans how to effect my return, after I should have secured my apparatus against accidents, when I heard a noise which informed me of the presence of some person near me. . . . I spied him and enjoyed his whole surprise, when he saw through a tuft of trees such a monstrous machine, balancing on itself, and sinking in proportion as the spirit wherewith it was animated left it. He seemed to be frightened, and I was afraid he would go away again. I let him hear my voice, inviting him to draw near . . . Recollecting that the exhilarating juice of the grape was always amongst mankind the happiest sign of friendship and conciliation, I shewed him a bottle of wine. . . . I then drank, first, and he followed my example. Becoming soon familiar he assisted me in my operations; when another countryman armed with a gun, came to the spot. . . . The first countryman then . . . spoke to the new-comer, and persuaded him to draw near with confidence. Come hither, said he . . . he has a certificate from our Washington, he has shewn it to me; but as I cannot read, come here and read it. Whilst these picturesque scenes were acting, I saw two women and several men on horseback arrive. . . . I could not, nor did I know how to answer all the friendly questions which they asked me; my passport served me instead of an interpreter. In the midst of a profound silence was it read with a loud and audible voice. How dear the name of Washington is to this people! with what eagerness they gave me all possible assistance, in consequence of his recommendation!

Eyes for an Army

The French Republican Army, defending the French Revolution against a coalition of European powers, was the first to use the balloon in combat. The historic event, which took place at Maubeuge, in June, 1794, was described by Colonel Jean-Marie-Joseph Coutelle.

I received the order next day to go with utmost speed to Maubeuge, and propose to General Jourdan the employment of an aerostat for his army.

. . . The officer to whom I delivered my order could not understand my mission . . . and still less an aerostat in the middle of the camp. He threatened to have me shot, as a suspicious character, before listening to me; but ended by relenting and complimenting me on my devotion. . . .

After a trip to Paris—where he conducted experiments and organized an Aerostatic Corps—Coutelle returned to Maubeuge.

My first care was to select the spot, construct the kiln, find firewood, and arrange everything. . . I then rose as often as ordered by the General, with an officer of the Staff, to examine the works of the enemy, his position, and his forces.

We observed his daily progress, till, on the fifth day, a 17-pounder, masked in a ravine within easy distance, fired at the balloon as soon as it rose above the ramparts. The ball passed over our heads, the second was so near I thought the aerostat was perforated, the third fell below us. When I gave the signal to haul down, my company did it with such vigour, that only two more shots could be fired. . .

[Another time] I was at more than two hundred and thirty yards from the ground, when three successive squalls knocked me to the ground with such force that many of the bars that strengthened the bottom of the car were broken. On each occasion the balloon rose with such force and rapidity that thirty-two men at each rope were dragged some distance. It is therefore clear that had the ropes been fixed to anchors they would have broken. . . .

The rocking is troublesome, and increases with the force of the wind, and sometimes prevents the use of glasses; but I must remark that one can see the movements of infantry, cavalry, and artillery with the naked eye; and . . . I could count the pieces on the redoubts and ramparts without any extraneous assistance.

A Near Disaster

On October 1, 1812, Britain's pioneer aeronaut, James Sadler, attempted to cross the Irish Sea from Dublin to Liverpool. The following extract from his narrative begins when Sadler, already within sight of his goal, had been driven back to sea by contrary winds.

It was some considerable time before I . . . observed any prospect of assistance . . . I descended lower, and it was with much pleasure I discovered a Vessel which by signals, gave me to understand she intended on me descending to afford me aid; I at the same time discovered two others to leeward . . . it being near Six o'Clock, and accordingly permitting a part of the Gas to escape, I fell between the two Vessels . . .

As the Car touched the Sea, the Wind which had risen with the Evening acting on the Balloon swept it along . . . I was dragged along through the Sea, now agitated by the increasing breeze which swelled almost into *a gale*—this however had but little effect, and I found myself reluctantly compelled to weaken the buoyancy of the Balloon by reducing the quantity of Gas, I accordingly opened the Valve and the Car immediately sunk . . . in this perilous situation I supported myself for a short

James Sadler, the first English aeronaut

74

me by hanging to the Cane Hoop .. [and] was frequently plunged under water by the rolling of the Balloon, being able with difficulty to keep my head at intervals so long above the surface as to prevent suffocation, but even thus circumstanced did not lose the recollection that however dangerous the clinging to the Balloon, it was still on it my ultimate safety must depend . . .

Immersed in the waves and entirely exhausted, it was but at intervals I caught a glimpse of the Vessel, and .. called out as loud as my feeble state admitted of, to run the bowsprit of the Vessel through the balloon; fortunately my directions were heard and instantly obeyed, the greater part of the Gas was immediately expelled, and the violent motion of the Balloon subdued, a rope was then thrown out from the Vessel for me to seize on, which I was fortunate enough to do, while under water and rather instinctively than otherwise to coil round my arm . . . after being dragged thro' the waves for a length of way, I was at last got on board with much difficulty, after having been in the water for at least half an hour, being quite exhausted, nearly insensible, and *almost lifeless.*

Nothing Is Impossible

Edgar Allan Poe's fictitious account of a transatlantic balloon crossing briefly deceived a gullible public when it was printed by the New York Sun on April 13, 1844. These excerpts are from Poe's invented journal, which he ascribed to Monck Mason, an Irish writer, musician, and aeronaut.

Saturday, April the sixth . . . we commenced the inflation this morning at daybreak; but owing to a thick fog, which encumbered the folds of the silk and rendered it unmanageable, we did not get through before nearly eleven o'clock. Cut loose, then, in high spirits, and rose gently but steadily, with a light breeze at north,

The Sun's headline of Poe's 1844 hoax

which bore us in the direction of the British Channel. . . . At half-past eleven, still proceeding nearly south, we obtained our first view of the Bristol Channel; and, in minutes, were out at sea. . . . We were all now anxious to test the efficiency of the rudder and screw, and we put them both into requisition forthwith, for the purpose of altering our direction more to the eastward, and in a line for Paris. . . . [Then] an unforeseen accident occurred which discouraged us in no little degree. The steel rod connecting the spring with the propeller was suddenly jerked out of place . . . and in an instant hung dangling out of reach, from the pivot of the axis of the screw. While we were endeavoring to regain it, our attention being completely absorbed, we became involved in a strong current of wind from the east, which bore us, with rapidly increasing force, towards the Atlantic. We soon found ourselves driving out to sea at the rate of not less, certainly, than fifty or sixty miles an hour . . . It was now that Mr. Ainsworth . . . [proposed] that we should take advantage of the strong gale which bore us on, and in place of beating back to Paris, make an attempt to reach the coast of

North America. . . . It is needless to say that a very short time sufficed us to lose sight of the coast. . . . We kept on in this manner throughout the day, with no material incident, and, as the shades of night closed around us, we made a rough estimate of the distance traversed. It could not have been less than five hundred miles, and was probably much more. . . . The wind was from the east all night, and gave us the brightest omen of success . . .

Sunday, the seventh . . . This morning the gale, by 10:00, had subsided to an eight or nine knot breeze (for a vessel at sea), and bears us, perhaps, thirty miles per hour, or more. . . . We have an abundance of gas to take [us] across this small pond, even should the voyage last three weeks. I have not the slightest fear for the result. The difficulty has been strangely exaggerated and misapprehended. I can choose my current, and should I find *all* currents against me, I can make very tolerable headway with the propeller. . . .

Monday, the eighth . . . The wind has been blowing steadily and strongly from the northeast all day; and fortune seems bent upon favoring us. . .

Tuesday, the ninth . . . One P.M. *We are in full view of the low coast of South Carolina. The great problem is accomplished. We have crossed the Atlantic—fairly and easily crossed it in a balloon! God be praised! Who shall say that anything is impossible hereafter?*

"I Saw the Enemy Form . . ."

In his unpublished memoirs, now in the archives of the Institute of Aerospace Sciences in New York, Thaddeus S. C. Lowe recounted the use of his captive balloons by the Northern army in the Civil War. This passage describes the Battle of Fair Oaks, May 31-June 1, 1862, during the Peninsular Campaign.

From eleven o'clock, until dark, on the 29th of May, the enemy commenced to concentrate their forces in front of Fair Oaks, moving on roads entirely out of sight of our pickets, and concealing themselves as much as possible in and behind woods where none of their movements could be seen except from the balloon. The following is one of my reports on that day:

"My last ascent was made at sundown which discloses the fact that the enemy have this afternoon established another camp in front of this point . . . They seem to be strengthening on our left opposite this place."

On that night or the following morning, General McClellan ordered the reserves to be moved up to support General Heintzelman in case of an attack, which took place just as this was accomplished. Had not our forces been concentrated, it is very evident that our left or that portion of our army behind the Chickahominy would have been driven back and in consequence, the whole army routed. . . .

On the 31st of May, at noon, I ascended at Mechanicsville and discovered bodies of the enemy and trains of wagons moving from Richmond toward Fair Oaks. I remained

in the air watching their movements until nearly two o'clock when I saw the enemy form in line of battle, and cannonading immediately commenced. . . . I saw we were facing a great battle . . .

I made an observation that showed that the Confederates were marching to attack our troops on the right bank of the Chickahominy before the completion of the bridge would permit those on the left bank to join them. This would mean the destruction of our army. I descended immediately and sent off the most important dispatch of any during my whole experience in the military service. . . .

On receipt of [the report] General McClellan sent express orders to General Sumner to have the bridge across the Chickahominy completed as soon as possible and to cross with his corps at the earliest possible moment and support General Heintzelman. This was accomplished just in time . . . [and] I ascended to a height of a thousand feet and there witnessed the Titanic struggle. The whole scene of action was plainly visible and reports of the progress of the battle were constantly sent till darkness fell upon the grand but terrifying spectacle.

"30 Lbs. Per Passenger"

In 1863 the famous French photographer Félix Tournachon (popularly known as Nadar) compiled for passengers in his huge balloon, Le Géant, a set of rules that make modern air-travel regulations seem simple.

Every traveller on board the *Géant* must take, before mounting, knowledge of the present rules, and engage himself upon his honour to respect them . . .

From the departure to the return there shall be only one command, that of the captain. That command shall be absolute. . . .

Every passenger declares, at the time of ascending, that he carries no inflammable materials. . . .

Nadar and an admirer in a studio pose

On landing, he must not quit the balloon without permission . . .

Silence must be absolutely observed when ordered by the captain.

Victuals and liquors must be deposited in the common canteen, of which the captain alone has the key and who regulates the distribution thereof. Passengers have no claim to victuals and liquors except when on board.

The duration of the journey is not limited. The captain alone decides the limitation; the same judgment decides, without appeal, the putting down of one or more travellers in the course of the voyage.

All gambling is expressly prohibited.

It is absolutely forbidden to any traveller to throw overboard ballast or any packet whatever.

No passenger can carry up with him luggage exceeding 30 lbs. in weight, and occupying more space than any ordinary travelling-bag.

Except in very rare cases, of which the captain alone shall be judge, it is absolutely forbidden to smoke on board, or on land within the vicinity of the balloon.

Civil War balloonist Thaddeus S. C. Lowe

The Siege of Paris

The role of balloons in the siege of Paris during the Franco-Prussian War, 1870-71, was recounted by a French journalist and amateur balloonist, Wilfrid de Fonvielle, whose book, Adventures in the Air, *was published in 1877.*

It took some time to convince the Parisians that their beautiful city could be blockaded; they hoped against all hope that postal runners would be able to slip through the bands of the Uhlans. But when the sad truth became an undeniable reality, M. Rampont [postal director] took the necessary measures with admirable promptness. Scarcely ten days sufficed for M. Eugène Godard to deliver over his first balloon. The manufactory was at first established at the Orléans Station, but latterly at the station of the Eastern Railway. The sight of these graceful globes tinted in striking colours rendered the deserted arches gay. The balloons were arranged in regular lines along the arrival platforms, and served in a measure to people these solitudes. Another manufactory was organised by Jules Duruof at the Northern Station. But ten days are a prodigious delay when it is a question of putting the capital of a country into communication with the rest of the state. . . .

Duruof did not hesitate an instant to brave the fire of the Prussians with an old balloon leaking at every seam. An order arrived in the evening, and next morning at eight o'clock the *Neptune* soared above the *buttes* of Montmartre. Duruof perceived that his only chance of safety lay in the force of the impulse with which he started. He therefore launched his balloon like a projectile which issues from a monster mortar. The *Neptune* described a parabola like that of a bombshell whose descent had been miraculously prolonged. By sacrificing seven hundredweight of ballast, the descent took place about nineteen miles from the Place St. Pierre, in the Department of Eure, not far from the Prussians, but still beyond their range. A true son of Paris, Duruof could not let the opportunity escape of enlivening a situation so terrible. He threw *cartes de visite* down upon the heads of the enemy, who, furious at seeing the blockade thus forced, saluted the *Neptune* with a salvo of artillery, and a rolling fire of musketry. . . .

Louis Godard received as a supplement to his ballast a number of packets of the *Officiel* newspaper, and of the principal journals published in Paris. Scattered in profusion all along the route, these sheets were as eagerly collected as if they had been celestial manna descending from the yet pure heavens.

"Have I Won?"

On October 19, 1901, Alberto Santos-Dumont set out in his primitive little airship to capture the French Aéro Club's 100,000-franc Deutsch prize for the first round-trip flight from Saint-Cloud to the Eiffel Tower within thirty minutes. This thrilling event is a high point of the famous Brazilian air pioneer's autobiography, My Airships.

The official start took place at 2.42 P.M. In spite of the wind striking me sidewise, with a tendency to take me to the left of the Eiffel Tower, I held my course straight to that goal. Gradually I drove the air-ship onward and upward to a height of about 33 feet above its summit. In doing this I lost some time, but secured myself against accidental contact with the Tower as much as possible.

As I passed the Tower I turned with a sudden movement of the rudder, bringing the air-ship round the Tower's lightning conductor at a distance of about 164 feet from it. The Tower was thus turned at 2.51 P.M. . . .

On my way to the Tower I never looked down on the house-tops of Paris: I navigated in a sea of white and azure, seeing nothing but the goal. On the return trip I had kept my eyes fixed on the verdure of the Bois de Boulogne and the silver streak of river where I had to cross it. Now, at my high altitude of 492 feet and with the propeller working at full power, I passed above Longchamps, crossed the Seine, and continued at full speed over the heads of the Commission and the spectators gathered in the Aéro Club's grounds. At that moment it was eleven minutes and thirty seconds past three o'clock, making the time exactly twenty-nine minutes and thirty-one seconds.

The air-ship, carried by the impetus of its great speed, passed on as a racehorse passes the winning-post, as a sailing yacht passes the winning-line, as a road racing automobile continues flying past the judges who have snapped its time. Like the jockey of the racehorse, I then turned and drove myself back to the aérodrome to have my guide rope caught . . .

I cried: "Have I won?"

And the crowd of spectators cried back to me: "Yes!"

Alberto Santos-Dumont before an ascent

CHAPTER 3

Testing a monoplane glider, Otto Lilienthal, Germany's great air pioneer of the 1890's, soars from his man-made hill near Berlin.

LEARNING TO FLY

Throughout the nineteenth century, while balloonists struggled with the problem of dirigibility or control, a dedicated handful of pioneers—and an engaging throng of crackpots, too—clung to the conviction that man's true destiny in the air was to fly with wings. These visionaries usually worked alone and endured endless setbacks and disappointments. Some lost their reputations, and a few, their lives. Most of them failed even to understand the problem they were attempting to solve, but now and then one would contribute something essential to the slowly rising tide of knowledge. However, few bothered to find out what their predecessors had done, and as a result, progress was agonizingly slow.

In 1783, when word of the Montgolfier brothers' wonderful flying globe leaped across the Channel, no one in all England was more thrilled than a bright-eyed nine-year-old named George Cayley. Like countless other small boys, he began experimenting delightedly with paper balloons and lighted candles. With other youngsters the excitement soon faded, but George Cayley was different.

In his teens he experimented with small contra-rotating propellers made of feathers stuck in corks and driven by a whalebone bow—a helicopter device that had been invented a few years before in France. And, like Leonardo, Cayley studied the birds.

In 1804 he built a whirling-arm device that enabled him to study the air pressure on a one-foot square plane set at various angles of incidence. Later, experimenting with small and full-size gliders, he found that setting the wings at a slight dihedral (or shallow V-shaped) angle to each other gave lateral stability, and that a tail plane set behind the main wings was necessary for longitudinal stability.

By the end of the first decade of the nineteenth century George Cayley had completed his basic researches and published his conclusions in scientific papers that laid the foundation of all modern aerodynamics. "The whole problem is confined within these limits," he wrote in 1809, "*viz.*—to make a surface support a given weight by the application of power to the resistance of air." The steam engines of his day were too heavy to be used in flying machines, but when it came to understanding the action of air pressure against an inclined plane, this inquisitive young Yorkshireman was far ahead of his time.

He knew that the secret of winged flight lay in the nature of air itself. He knew that this mixture of gases offers resistance to objects moving through it, that its density can vary, that its particles can be stirred into invisible currents or eddies. He knew that for millions of years this mixture had kept aloft bats and birds and insects—and he believed that some day it would support human beings as well.

He believed this because he watched it support his gliders. A small model that he built and flew in 1804 had had a wing area of only 154 square inches, but in many respects it was the first true airplane device in history. It consisted of an ordinary diamond-shaped kite fastened to a light pole, set at an angle of about 6 degrees. The tail assembly, with vertical and horizontal stabilizers, was attached to the pole by a universal joint so that it could be set at any angle. "It was very pretty," Cayley noted, "to see it sail down a steep hill, and it gave the idea that a larger instrument would be a better and safer conveyance down the Alps than even a sure-footed mule."

Larger ones he did build, both monoplanes and triplanes. One of his notes mentions a glider that in 1849 lifted a ten-year-old boy "off the ground for several yards on descending a hill." In 1853, according to a story told years later by his granddaughter, Cayley coaxed his reluctant coachman into making a trial run in a glider that lifted him across a shallow valley and set him down in a cloud of dust. "Please, Sir George," that outraged retainer is said to have shouted, "I wish to give notice. I was hired to drive, and not to fly!"

Cayley's inquiring talents were not confined to manned flight. He invented, among other things, the caterpillar tractor, automatic signaling devices for railroads, and a self-righting lifeboat. But in aeronautics his reputation is monumental. The long shadow he cast reaches all the way to the Wright brothers.

An Englishman who grew up in the age of steam carried on the work that Cayley began. William Samuel Henson worked in the lace trade at Chard, in Somerset. He had seen the first public railroad become a reality in England and had watched the first steam-powered ships cross the Atlantic. Thus, when Henson decided to build a flying machine in 1841, he looked to steam as the means of propulsion.

Henson was fully aware of Cayley's experiments, for in 1842 when he patented his plans for an "Aerial Steam Carriage," he followed many of Cayley's ideas. His design called for a monoplane with a wingspan of 150 feet, a tail plane shaped rather like a bird's tail, a vertical rudder, and a tricycle landing gear. This surprisingly modern-looking craft was to be powered by two steam-driven pusher propellers. This was Henson's brilliantly original concept. He was the first to envisage the modern propeller-driven airplane.

A full-size version of the *Ariel*, as the machine was called, never would have flown; for one thing, the weight of the steam engine alone would have made flight impossible. But it was the first rational and detailed concept of a powered airplane, and the inventor deserved a more sympathetic hearing than he got. By 1847 Henson, assisted by his friend John Stringfellow, had completed and tested a model with a twenty-foot wingspan. But when it proved incapable of anything more than a descending, powered glide, Henson gave up in disgust, married, and emigrated to America.

The next year, working alone, Stringfellow built another, smaller model based on Henson's designs. With a tiny steam engine driving two 4-bladed pusher propellers, his little monoplane seems to have achieved some sort of part-glide, part-powered flight after releasing itself from a launching cradle suspended on a wire. But it was clear that steam could be used successfully at this stage on small models only; and "finding nothing but pecuniary loss and little honour," Stringfellow gave up his experiments for the next twenty years.

With Stringfellow's withdrawal, the initiative shifted to France. In 1857 Felix Du Temple, a French naval commander, patented a design for a powered airplane that showed several improvements over Stringfellow's model; it had a forward-mounted tractor propeller that pulled it through the air and wings set at the dihedral angle that Cayley had recommended. A small model powered first by clockwork and later by a steam engine took off and flew successfully about 1857 or 1858, the first fixed-wing machine to raise itself unaided from the ground. Later, about 1874, Du Temple built a full-size machine with a tractor propeller driven by a hot-air engine. In an attempted take-off down an inclined ramp, it may have left the ground with a young sailor aboard. If so, it was the first powered, man-carrying leap, or hop. A similar claim was made for a steam-driven airplane built by a Russian naval captain, Alexander F. Mozhaiski, and launched down a long ramp near St. Petersburg in 1884 with I. N. Golubev as pilot.

In 1866 aviation achieved respectability with the founding of the Aeronautical Society of Great Britain. At its first meeting that year an assemblage of its dignified and serious members listened attentively to a report by F. H. Wenham, a marine engineer whose observations of bird flight in Egypt had led him to the study of aerodynamics. His paper was to prove a milestone in the development of aviation. After much experimentation with models Wenham had been able to prove that a cambered (slightly arched) wing was better than a flat surface, and that the lift exerted by such a wing moving at an angle inclined to the wind was derived mainly from the front portion of the wing. He went on to demonstrate that a long narrow wing exerts more lift than a short wide one. Since wings long enough to provide a markedly greater lift might prove unmanageable, Wenham proposed that several shorter wings, placed one on top of another, be substituted as a means of achieving the desired lifting area. It was this proposal that pointed the way to the development of the modern biplane.

Wenham also went on to become the first man to use a wind tunnel for experimentation with wing shapes. It is known today that an airplane's lift results less from the pressure of air against the underside of the wing than from the negative pressure or suction above the wing, where the air is thinned as it rushes over the arched wing surface. Cayley had grasped this principle as early as 1809, but it was not established as a scientific fact until a few years after the first successful powered flight.

Intrigued by Wenham's paper, John Stringfellow once more tried his hand at model airplane building. Following Wenham's lead and Cayley's published recommendation of a multiplane type, Stringfellow designed a model triplane which, although it was not successful, attracted much attention at the exhibition staged by the Aeronautical Society at the Crystal Palace in London in 1868.

In the decade between 1870 and 1880 a brilliant and tragic figure appeared in France. Alphonse Pénaud first read everything he could find on the subject of aeronautics. Then the imaginative young man built and flew beautifully balanced models of helicopters, ornithopters, and airplanes powered by twisted elastic bands. He had not read Cayley when he built his first *planophore*, as he called his little airplane, but he gave the wings a dihedral angle at the tips, and he set his tail assembly some distance behind the main wings at a negative angle. The combination gave his model both lateral and longitudinal stability. With a twisted rubber band spinning the little pusher propeller, the planophore flew more than forty yards in eleven seconds.

In 1876 Pénaud patented a design for an amphibious aircraft that showed a variety of brilliant innovations. These included a single control column to move both rudder and elevators (the first joy stick), retractable landing gear, and a glass cockpit canopy. Power was to be supplied by two tractor propellers, with the engine enclosed in the fuselage. But there was no suitable engine available, and at the age of thirty, discouraged and depressed by the skepticism and ridicule that pioneers must endure, Alphonse Pénaud took a revolver and put a bullet through his marvelous brain.

When Pénaud died in 1880, lack of lightweight power was still thought to be the major barrier to winged flight. Most would-be fliers assumed—a little too readily as it turned out—that if something would just boost them into the air, they would know what to do when they got there. The result was an endless series of theories and proposals. Some thought that electricity might be the answer; others turned hopefully to compressed air. Still others sought a solution in jet propulsion, using steam rockets, "vaporized petroleum oil," and so on.

As the nineteenth century drew to a close, two men came close to powered flight, and both relied on steam. The first was Sir Hiram Maxim, an opinionated, American-born inventor who transferred his citizenship to Britain. The second was a French electrical engineer named Clément Ader.

When he turned to aeronautics, Maxim was already rich and famous as a result of earlier inventions, notably the machine gun that bears his name. After many experiments with wing shapes and propellers, he laid out a half-mile railroad track at his estate in Kent and on it proceeded to build a giant flying machine powered by two enormous steam-driven propellers that at full throttle developed an unheard-of 360 horsepower. The main wing of the huge craft was 110 feet long and 4 feet wide; the total wing surface was more than 4,000 feet.

Maxim was interested only in measuring lift and thrust; he was not really interested in flying at all. To keep his monster down, he added extra wheels on outriggers that would engage secondary wooden guard rails if the machine rose more than a few inches.

In 1894, with his white beard whipping in the wind, the pompous little inventor drove his machine along the track, gradually increasing steam pressure until, despite a total weight of three and a half tons, it actually lifted clear of the track and broke through the restraining guard rails. Faced by the prospect of losing control altogether, Maxim shut off the steam, and his creation came to a stop, slightly damaged. At that point, apparently having done what he set out to do, Maxim gave up. "Propulsion and lifting," he announced brusquely, "are solved problems; the rest is a mere matter of time." His sweeping statement did not even mention the third requirement of successful flight: control in the air.

In 1889, five years before Maxim's effort, a French electrical engineer, Clément Ader, completed a bat-winged, steam-powered machine, which he christened the *Eole*. In 1890 he tested it and claimed that he left the ground in this odd-looking contrivance for a distance of about 164 feet. Later, with some financial backing from the French army, he made and tested other machines. At the 1897 trials of his *Avion III*, official observers noted carefully that it never left the ground. The War Ministry withdrew its backing, and Ader gave up in disgust.

In their preoccupation with the mechanics of propulsion and the dynamics of lift, men like Maxim and Ader contributed relatively little to the art of flying, as such. Maxim talked of controlling airplanes in free flight with gyroscopes and of steering them by varying the speed of the propellers. But he totally lacked the vision and the touch of poetry that were to become the hallmark of the true airman. Ader, who had watched and admired the effortless soaring flight of vultures in Africa, nevertheless patterned his lifting surfaces on a wing-flapping creature, the bat. In the end, it was only when man began to imitate the birds that glide or soar on rigid wings that he truly learned to fly.

In 1881 Louis-Pierre Mouillard, a Frenchman who lived in North Africa, published a treatise on bird flight that was greatly to influence subsequent students of gliding. Mouillard had no great success with the fixed-wing gliders he constructed to amuse himself.

But his insistence in his book, *The Empire of the Air,* that a bird can "sail indefinitely upon the wind without further flapping his wings" encouraged other men to attempt gliding experiments.

The greatest of these birdmen was Otto Lilienthal, Germany's first and most brilliant contributor to the conquest of the air. As a child enviously watching the storks that were common in his native Pomerania, Otto became obsessed with the idea of flight. He read widely but accepted nothing until he had verified it himself. In 1891, when he finally began building a glider, his purpose was clear. He wanted to master the art of flying so that when a suitable means of propulsion was ready to be added to wings, man would be ready too.

Lilienthal's early gliders were monoplanes with cambered wings and a fixed tail plane. The pilot dangled like a marionette from these fragile craft, head and shoulders above the wings, body and legs below. It was by shifting weight, swinging hips and legs forward or back, or from side to side, that the operator achieved some degree of control.

Near Berlin, Lilienthal constructed a conical hill of earth so that he could take off downslope and into the wind, no matter which way it blew. Looking like an athletic mountain climber in his heavy shoes and close-fitting cap, this daring and methodical German radiated a burning intensity as he sought the secrets of controlled flight. Between 1891 and 1896 he made over 2,000 glides, some of them covering several hundred feet. Photographs of his flights appearing all over the world excited great admiration and led other adventurous souls to experiment with gliders.

By 1896 Lilienthal was ready to attempt powered flight. He had constructed a glider with flapping wing tips, and to power it he had built a small motor that operated on compressed carbonic acid gas. On August 9, in one of his standard gliders, he made what should have been a routine glide. The weather was blustery, and a gust of wind suddenly pitched his craft sharply upward. The glider stalled and crashed to earth from about fifty feet, breaking the great pioneer's back. He died the next day.

The influence of Lilienthal can hardly be overestimated. He was the first to demonstrate beyond question that, with or without power, the air could support a man in winged flight. To those who tried to follow where he led he was both an inspiration and a warning. If his life proved that man could indeed imitate the birds, his death was a somber reminder that the air is an alien element and that man would have to master his wings before he could fly with confidence and safety. The price he paid to fly was the highest. But one feels he paid it gladly.

Directly inspired by Lilienthal's early flights, a young Scotsman, Percy Pilcher, had built his first glider in 1895. Before testing the *Bat,* as he called it, he went to Germany to meet the man who knew more about gliding than anyone else in the world. Lilienthal listened patiently to the eager young man's questions, let him try out his new biplane glider, and gave him much useful advice.

The news of Lilienthal's fatal crash in 1896 must have been a blow to Pilcher, but he did not let it deter him. When his original *Bat* did not prove satisfactory, he rebuilt it, adding the tail plane that Lilienthal had recommended. In rapid succession he built three more gliders: the *Beetle;* the *Gull;* and the *Hawk,* a highly successful machine fitted with a wheeled undercarriage. In the *Hawk,* during the summer of 1897, he set a gliding distance record of 250 yards.

By now Pilcher was ready for powered flight. Still no suitable lightweight engine was available, and so he decided to build his own. Designed to produce 4 horsepower, it was to drive a small pusher propeller. All through the year 1898 he worked on it.

Early in 1899, at a meeting of the Aeronautical Society in London, Pilcher met Lawrence Hargrave, an unassuming Australian who, since 1884, had been experimenting in Sydney with every kind of mechanical flight. In 1887 Hargrave had devised the first rotary engine, a compressed-air motor in which the cylinders revolved around a stationary crankshaft. In 1893 he had invented the box kite, whose cellular construction—two cells arranged in tandem—made it by far the most stable kite flown up to that time.

Hargrave knew that in the box kite he had a basic structure that could easily be adapted to gliders or airplanes. When he displayed two of his kites in London and read a paper on them, he fascinated Pilcher. The young Scotsman borrowed the kites, tested them himself, and incorporated some of their features into a new triplane glider.

Late in September, 1899, Pilcher scheduled a demonstration of the new glider and the *Hawk.* When rain soaked both machines, he decided to fly only the well-tested *Hawk.* He was soaring steadily, some thirty feet off the ground, when a tail-plane brace snapped. The *Hawk* flipped over in the air, crashed, and Pilcher was fatally injured. His death was a tragic blow to aviation, for he was a great natural flier.

Octave Chanute, a warm, delightful man already in his sixties and one of America's most successful civil engineers, was captivated by Lilienthal's gliding experiments. A careful and devoted student of aeronautical history, he first attracted attention with a series of magazine articles called "Progress in Flying Machines." Published in 1894 in book form, this was the first factual and trustworthy history of man's attempt to fly and one of the great classics of aviation.

By 1896, Chanute was designing his own gliders, using his knowledge of bridge building to add structural strength to them. He was aided by another engineer, A. M. Herring, who acted as pilot. What Chanute was after was automatic stability—a built-in device that would cause his machine to right itself in the air. On the sand hills fringing windy Lake Michigan he tested glider after glider with rear-positioned tail planes like Lilienthal's. His 1896 biplane glider was his best, but his designs also included a triplane and even a five-winged model. None of these gliders had control surfaces; in all of them the pilot had to rely on body movement for control. But Chanute's experiments with gliders were not nearly so important in aviation history as his subsequent role as collector and disseminator of information.

Of all these early trail blazers one of the most controversial, and surely one of the most unlucky, was Samuel Pierpont Langley. This distinguished astronomer, the director of the Smithsonian Institution, was well into his fifties when the lure of the air gripped him. He began by making elastic-band-propelled models based on Alphonse Pénaud's little aircraft. Then, in 1889, a little aero steam engine designed two decades earlier by John Stringfellow was presented to the Smithsonian. Studying this historic curio, Langley realized that better steam engines could be built and decided that he could build them.

In 1891 he constructed the first of his model "aerodromes," as he called them. The steel frame was too heavy; it would not fly. For the next five years Langley doggedly kept building models, trying to solve the power-to-weight problem. Finally, in 1896, he produced a steam-driven model—a sort of double monoplane with wings set in tandem—that flew for three quarters of a mile and then came down only because the fuel gave out.

This success did not bring Langley the acclaim he deserved. On the contrary, he was criticized and ridiculed for wasting his time with such useless toys. But he refused to be discouraged.

With dwindling funds and almost no encouragement, he had little hope of finding money to construct a full-size, man-carrying aerodrome. But in 1898 the United States went to war with Spain, and suddenly the War Department showed considerable interest in a controllable, power-driven airplane. As a result, Congress granted Langley $50,000 and asked him to go ahead and build such a machine.

Langley was now convinced that a gasoline engine offered more promise of powered flight than steam. He went to one manufacturer after another, asking for an engine that would deliver 12 horsepower and weigh only one hundred pounds. When these requirements proved too formidable, he turned the problem over to his gifted assistant, Charles M. Manly.

A frail, bespectacled little man, Manly chose an engine designed by Stephen Balzer of New York. Balzer's engine was of a radically new type, with the cylinders arranged around a crankshaft. Most of the parts, even the sparkplugs, had to be made by hand. Manly hoped that this radial gasoline engine might produce 20 horsepower. Actually, when finally tested, the five cylinders of the little power plant (it weighed only 125 pounds) produced 53 horsepower—an amazing achievement for the time.

The aerodrome itself followed Langley's favorite design—a monoplane with two main wings in tandem and a tail plane and vertical fin behind. To launch the device he decided to use a catapult, which he mounted on a houseboat in the Potomac River.

Before attempting a full-scale version, he built a quarter-size model which flew successfully, the first time a gasoline engine had actually driven an airplane. In October, 1903, he was ready for what he confidently believed would be the first sustained, man-carrying, heavier-than-air flight in history.

At noon on October 7, with Manly at the controls, the engine was started. It ran perfectly: the twin propellers hurling back columns of air, the 730-pound machine straining for release.

The next day a reporter for the Washington *Post* told the remainder of the story. "A few yards from the houseboat were the boats of the reporters, who for three months had been stationed at Widewater. The newspapermen waved their hands. Manly looked down and smiled. Then his face hardened as he braced himself for the flight, which might have in store for him fame or death. The propeller wheels, a foot from his head, whirred around him one thousand times to the minute. A man forward fired two skyrockets. There came an answering 'toot, toot,' from the tugs. A mechanic stooped, cut the cable holding the catapult; there was a roaring, grinding noise— and the Langley airship tumbled over the edge of the houseboat and disappeared in the river, sixteen feet below. It simply slid into the water like a handful of mortar. . ."

Langley believed that some part of the machine had fouled the launching gear. It should have been a warning to him to abandon the catapult altogether and to set his machine on wheels as Pilcher had done with the *Hawk*. But ignoring the jibes and caustic comments, he grimly salvaged the aerodrome, repaired it, and on December 8 tried again. Again the catapult fouled the aerodrome; again it crashed ignominiously into the river; and again Manly was pulled out, dripping but unhurt.

This second failure crushed even Langley's stalwart spirit. The press of the country, reflecting the curious sadism with which crowds had greeted aeronautical failures since the days of the Montgolfiers, broke into a chorus of jeers.

But the cynicism of the critics was ill-timed. Just nine days after Langley's second and final failure, on a bleak North Carolina beach a powered airplane ran along a track, sailed into the air, wavered along for twelve seconds, then settled onto the sand. While the world was still laughing at Langley, the Wright brothers had flown.

Langley was a great pioneer, but—like Maxim and Ader—he was too concerned with power plants and wing surfaces. It was not enough. The line of endeavor that finally resulted in victory did not go through these ground-based engineers; rather it went through those men who had not only mechanical ingenuity but also the skill, imagination, and daring to seek, first of all, control in the air through gliding experiments: through Lilienthal, Pilcher, and Chanute to the Wright brothers.

Where there are heroes there are usually legends, but the story of the Wright brothers is as straight and unadorned as a hoe handle. Sons of a United Brethren bishop, they grew up in Dayton in the days when the Republican Party, the veterans of the Grand Army of the Republic, and the various denominations of the Protestant church were the forces to be reckoned with in Ohio.

The Wrights were a close-knit family, five children in all, with Wilbur and Orville the two youngest sons. They were taught early in life to be patient, painstaking, and methodical where any kind of effort was concerned. These qualities, plus a superb creativity and a magnificent integrity, were to bring them ultimate success in a field where so many more highly educated men had tried and failed.

In later years the Wrights traced their interest in aeronautics to a toy helicopter that their father had brought home in 1878 when Wilbur was eleven and Orville seven. "A toy so delicate," they wrote, "lasted but a short time in the hands of small boys, but its memory was abiding."

As they grew older the brothers experimented with toy helicopters of their own. Tiring of this, they turned to kite flying as a hobby. This was just for sport; like most sons of ministers, they had to earn a living. Together they produced a small newspaper, worked for a while as printers, then turned to bicycle repairing and manufacturing and built up a small business that was to finance their ventures into aviation.

During the 1890's they were fascinated by Lilienthal's work with gliders and shocked by his death. In 1899, having heard of Langley's experiments with steam-driven models, they wrote to the Smithsonian and asked for a list of the best books on flying. Among those recommended was Octave Chanute's *Progress in Flying Machines,* which so impressed the brothers that Wilbur wrote a letter to Chanute that marked the start of a warm friendship. Throughout their trial-and-error years his friendship and encouragement meant much to the lonely experimenters at Kitty Hawk.

Wilbur's initial letter to Chanute expressed dissatisfaction with the Lilienthal gliding technique and listed his own observations of bird flight. Buzzards, he pointed out, seemed to maintain their balance chiefly by twisting the dropped wing; the increased air pressure on that wing restored the bird to level flight.

This trick of "wing warping," borrowed from the birds, was the first of two great Wright techniques that were to lead to much greater control of gliders—and ultimately, to airplanes. They built a box kite five feet long and found that by warping the wing tips through four controlling strings, they could make it responsive to control from the ground.

From the start the Wrights realized that there were three essential problems facing anyone who aspired to sustained mechanical flight: wing shape and resulting lift; the whole tricky and relatively unexplored business of balance and control in the air; and the satisfactory application of power to a tested wing shape. They also knew that to solve the control problem they had to get up in the air and practice as Lilienthal had done. It was with these things in mind that they began the construction of their first glider.

This was a biplane with a horizontal elevator in front, no tail unit, and wing tips that could be warped by means of cords operated by the pilot or worked from the ground. It was, in essence, a big kite, and the brothers knew they would need a lot of wind to fly it. They wrote to the Weather Bureau in Washington and were advised to try the beaches of North Carolina, where the winds swept in from the sea and there was plenty of open space.

In October, 1900, the brothers assembled this first glider at Kitty Hawk. Though they made a few glides in it, lying prone on the lower wing, there was seldom enough wind for man-carrying experiments and they had to content themselves with flying it as a kite.

Consequently, when they came back the next summer with a second glider, they had enlarged both the wing area and the curvature of the wings. This time they set up a camp at Kill Devil Hills, four miles south of Kitty Hawk. During the summer Octave Chanute, now nearly seventy, made the first of several visits to see what these young bicycle makers were up to. He gave them praise and encouragement, which they needed. Their second glider had many faults, and Wilbur in particular was depressed. "Nobody will fly for a thousand years!" he said gloomily.

In their approach to the basic problems of flying, the Wrights differed sharply from some of their predecessors. Maxim and Langley had sought "automatic equilibrium" in their aircraft, with the pilot in the relatively passive role of driver of the machine. The Wrights decided to abandon this concept and build an intentionally unstable—and hence much more "flyable"—airplane in which the pilot's skill would be the key factor in control. Therefore, they gave the wings of their glider no dihedral, but relied on wing warping for lateral control and on the lever-operated front elevator for longitudinal control.

In this second Wright glider, the wires that controlled the wing warping were attached to a cradle in which the operator lay. If he wished to bank to port, he swung his hips and the cradle to the left. This tightened the cable attached to the outer strut of the starboard wing, warping the rear edge of the wing downward, whereupon increased air pressure would make the wing rise. At the same time, an auxiliary cable would give the port wing an up-warp that tended to lower it. This simultaneous down-warp on one side and up-warp on the other was an important feature of the Wright system.

What the Wrights really learned that second summer on the windy beach was how much they still did not know about aerodynamics and how much of the information on which they had been basing their work was inaccurate. "Having set out with absolute faith in the existing scientific data," they commented at a later date, "we were driven to doubt one thing after another, till finally, after two years of experiment, we cast it all aside."

Back at Dayton, they built a small wind tunnel six feet long and sixteen inches square. In it they began testing dozens of miniature wings. Comparing the lift of square and oblong surfaces, they rediscovered the importance of the "aspect ratio" of a wing—that is, the ratio of its length to its width. They learned what Wenham had discovered in England four decades earlier—most of the lift derived from a cambered wing comes from the front portion, and therefore a long narrow wing (*i.e.*, a wing of high aspect ratio) provides more lift than a short wide one. They also found errors in the wind-pressure tables of Lilienthal that they had been using.

They built their new knowledge into a third glider, which they constructed with wings that were less curved and had an aspect ratio of six to one instead of three to one. They kept the forward elevator but added fixed vertical fins at the rear. When they tested this glider in September, 1902, it flew magnificently. In two months at Kitty Hawk the brothers made almost a thousand glides, some of them covering six hundred feet or more.

The glider seemed to have only one serious fault. They were able to fly it in winds up to 35 miles per hour, but they found that sometimes when the wings were warped the glider did not turn as desired. Instead of turning, the raised (down-warped) wing would pull back, and the machine would go sliding down into the sand with its dropped (up-warped) wing shooting out ahead. Or else, when they tried to correct this by reversing the warping, the lowered wing would hang behind, causing the machine to go into a sudden spin.

Orville realized, finally, that in such cases increased air resistance was retarding the down-warped wing, slowing it down instead of allowing it to advance in a banked turn. Something had to be done to maintain the bank and take the machine around smoothly. It was Orville who suggested that they make their fixed rear fins into a single movable rudder and Wilbur who thought of interconnecting the rudder controls with the warping controls so that air pressure against the rudder would automatically counteract the drag of the down-warped wing.

This linkage of warp and rudder controls was the second of the two great Wright techniques that were to lead to success in the air. With their forward elevator the brothers could rise or descend. With wing warping and rudder synchronized they could turn smoothly to left or right or restore horizontal balance. By the time they returned to Dayton in October, 1902, they had solved the major problems of control in the air. Now all they needed was a power plant to keep them going.

Like Pilcher and like Langley, the Wrights found no lightweight gasoline engine on the market. Building one would have been a formidable challenge for almost anyone except these supreme engineering geniuses. The four-cylinder water-cooled power plant they designed and built weighed over two hundred pounds. But by now the brothers were sure of their calculations as to power and load. They were confident that the 12 horsepower produced by their simple engine would move their new flying machine forward fast enough to allow the wings to lift it into the air.

In addition to their work with wing models in the wind tunnel, the Wrights had also made a careful study of propellers. Almost no serious research had been carried out in this field; even the action of marine propellers was little understood. The Wrights found this their most difficult job. "What seemed at first a simple problem," they wrote later, "became more complex the longer we studied it."

But in the end they designed and built propellers that were far more efficient than either Langley's or Maxim's. These were driven by a pair of long bicycle chains connected to the engine. To counteract torque—the twisting force of the revolving propellers—they made them revolve in opposite directions.

In September, 1903, the Wrights crated up their new machine and shipped it to Kitty Hawk. But a series of mishaps caused delays. The bicycle sprockets kept slipping on the propeller shafts. They solved this finally by melting tire cement into the threads. A tubular shaft cracked; Orville had to go back to Dayton to make a new set. Finally, in mid-December, they were ready.

It has been stated that in its historic first flight the Wrights' machine was boosted by a crude catapult. This is not true; it took off under its own power. Like its predecessors, the 1903 flying machine was fitted with skids for landings on soft sand. The launching device consisted of a light wooden rail about eight inches high. On this rail ran a little trolley with a crossbeam fixed to it. The skids were placed on the crossbeam, and a wire held the machine back until the engine was running at full throttle. Then the wire was released, airplane and trolley went running smoothly down the track until—hopefully—the machine was airborne, leaving the trolley behind. The track, which was in sections, could be laid out on level ground, facing into the wind.

By December 12 preparations were complete, but the brothers had to wait two days for a sufficiently strong breeze. They tossed a coin to see which of them would make the first attempt, and Wilbur won. The breeze had freshened, and they decided that if they laid the track down the slope of a dune, their machine might gain enough speed to take off.

They had invited the people of the neighborhood to be on hand, but few braved the chilly December wind. And those who came were disappointed. With Wilbur at the controls, the flying machine went clattering down the track, rose too steeply, stalled, and fell back into the sand.

Three days later, with the damage repaired, they tried again. This time the wind was so strong that they laid the track on a level stretch of sand. Again they hoisted the prearranged signal to alert the Life Saving Station down the beach, and five men arrived to help them move the heavy machine from its hangar.

By now the wind was blowing more than 20 miles per hour, whipping the sand from the top of the dunes. Orville fitted himself, face down, into the cradle on the lower wing. Slowly he brought the engine up to full power. The restraining wire was released. The trolley moved down the track, slowly, then faster, Wilbur running alongside. Near the end of the track, Orville raised the forward elevator. The machine rose. For twelve seconds it surged forward against the wind. Then, 120 feet from the launching track, it settled back onto the sand. It was 10:35 A.M. on December 17, 1903. The ancient dream was a reality at last.

Three more flights were made that morning. The final one, with Wilbur at the controls, was an extraordinary effort lasting fifty-nine seconds. In that time he covered 582 feet over land, but, since it was bucking a stiff wind, the plane actually flew half a mile through the rushing air—a feat that was to remain unequaled by anyone except the Wrights themselves for almost four years.

After the last flight a gust of wind caught the machine, tumbled it over, and damaged it severely. But the Wrights had their triumph. Lilienthal and Pilcher had glided; Maxim had left the ground; Ader had hopped. But as Orville wrote later, his flight was "the first in the history of the world in which a machine carrying a man had raised itself by its own power into the air in full flight, had sailed forward without reduction of speed, and had finally landed at a point as high as that from which it started."

Back in Dayton their father received a telegram from North Carolina, that, despite minor inaccuracies and telegrapher's misspellings, summed it all up:

SUCCESS FOUR FLIGHTS THURSDAY MORNING ALL AGAINST TWENTY ONE MILE WIND STARTED FROM LEVEL WITH ENGINE POWER ALONE AVERAGE SPEED THROUGH AIR THIRTY ONE MILES LONGEST 57 SECONDS INFORM PRESS HOME CHRISTMAS

OREVELLE WRIGHT

A message of fewer than forty words—but it marked a turning point in human history.

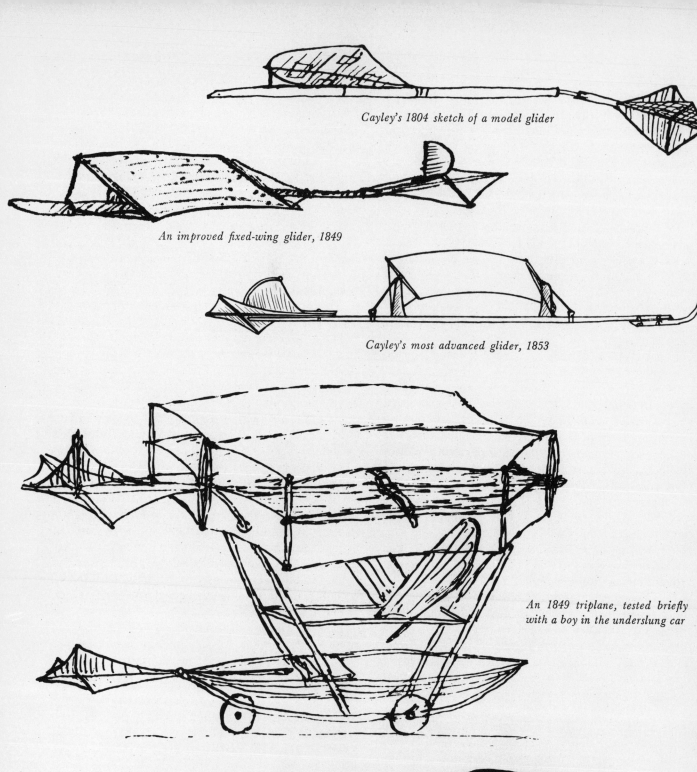

Cayley's 1804 sketch of a model glider

An improved fixed-wing glider, 1849

Cayley's most advanced glider, 1853

An 1849 triplane, tested briefly with a boy in the underslung car

Cayley's 1852 design for a man-carrying glider

George Cayley: Father of Aerial Navigation

Sir George Cayley, precursor of winged flight, as painted in 1841 by Henry P. Briggs.

In 1809-10 *Nicholson's Journal,* a British technical periodical, published three articles "On Aerial Navigation." They marked the first solid step taken by man on a path that would lead, ninety-four years later, to powered flight with wings. The author, Sir George Cayley, had begun his aerial experiments in 1796, when, at the age of twenty-three, he built a helicopter device of cork and feathers. From then until his death in 1857 at the age of eighty-three, the problem of manned flight—and possible solutions to its many aspects—were never long out of his mind.

By 1809 Cayley had designed, built, and flown several small fixed-wing gliders—and one full-size but unmanned one—which were revolutionary departures from the flapping-wing devices favored by his predecessors. The conclusions he drew from his experiments regarding wing surfaces, control systems, aerial stability, and air pressure were incorporated in his 1809 essay. Often reprinted and widely read throughout the nineteenth century, Cayley's study of aerodynamics had an enormous influence on later inventors.

The brilliant Yorkshire baronet did not rest with this achievement; and the developing changes of his fixed-wing glider designs from 1804 to 1853 can be seen on the opposite page. Nor did he confine his research to airplanes.

In 1816 he published the first of four papers on airships, proposing an elongated dirigible powered by steam-driven propellers. More clearly than any of his contemporaries, he realized that the larger the dirigible, the larger would be the percentage of its total lift available for carrying useful loads. And, in 1843, still inventive at seventy, Cayley designed a helicopter whose rotating blades could be converted into fixed wings for forward flight.

The lack of a lightweight engine was one barrier to Cayley's dream of achieving powered flight. But no serious student of aerodynamics who followed him could ignore his pioneering work.

William Samuel Henson

John Stringfellow

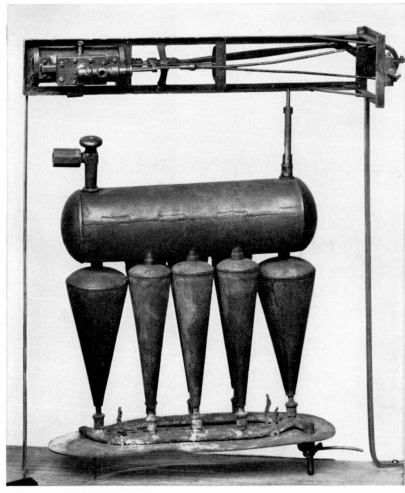

The trim little steam engine above was designed by John Stringfellow for his 1848 model airplane. That craft, already a relic when the photograph at right was taken, had a wingspan of ten feet, a fan-shaped tail, and twin four-bladed propellers. It was incapable of sustained motion, but its brief trial glide in London was once regarded as the first powered flight of an unmanned flying machine.

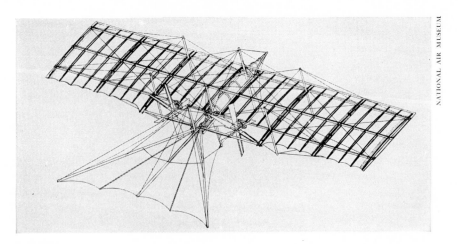

An 1842 drawing shows the cambered wing structure of Henson's aerial locomotive.

90

Henson and Stringfellow

George Cayley's suggestion for a fixed-wing airplane influenced William Samuel Henson, the English lace manufacturer and aviation enthusiast, who, in 1842, applied for a patent on a "Locomotive Apparatus . . . for conveying Letters, Goods, and Passengers from Place to Place through the Air . . . "

Henson's monoplane contained one far-sighted innovation: twin pusher propellers to be powered by a steam engine enclosed in a fuselage below the wings. He had already tested his design with clockwork-powered models, but the inadequacy of his steam engine plagued his further experiments. Working with a fellow industrialist and engineer, John Stringfellow, Henson built and tested a large model of the aerial steam carriage. But when it failed to accomplish anything more than descending glides after it had left an inclined ramp from which it was launched, Henson abandoned the project.

A smaller model, built by Stringfellow in 1848 (above) was also unsuccessful; and the locomotive in the sky remained a dream recorded in fading photographs and models that became dusty museum curios.

91

Aerial
Steam Carriage

To finance the building of his giant steam-powered airplane, Henson tried to organize an "Aerial Transit Company" in 1843. In addition to this imaginative view of the flying steam carriage over London, many other widely-published illustrations showed the Ariel—as Henson called his machine—in effortless flight over China, India, and the pyramids of Egypt. Such grandiose and premature announcements subjected the inventor to great ridicule when his scheme collapsed, but the publicity had gone far to condition even a skeptical and indifferent public to the idea of fixed-wing, propeller-driven aircraft.

The inspiration of the albatross is revealed in the photograph above of Le Bris's second glider, built in 1868. The needle-nosed craft, mounted on a cart for launching, had a movable tail and arched wings patterned after those of the sea bird.

Below are Du Temple's patent drawings for his 1857 powered airplane, showing its tractor propeller and the slight dihedral of the wings (top), the swept-forward wing shape and tail plane (center), and retractable landing gear (bottom, right).

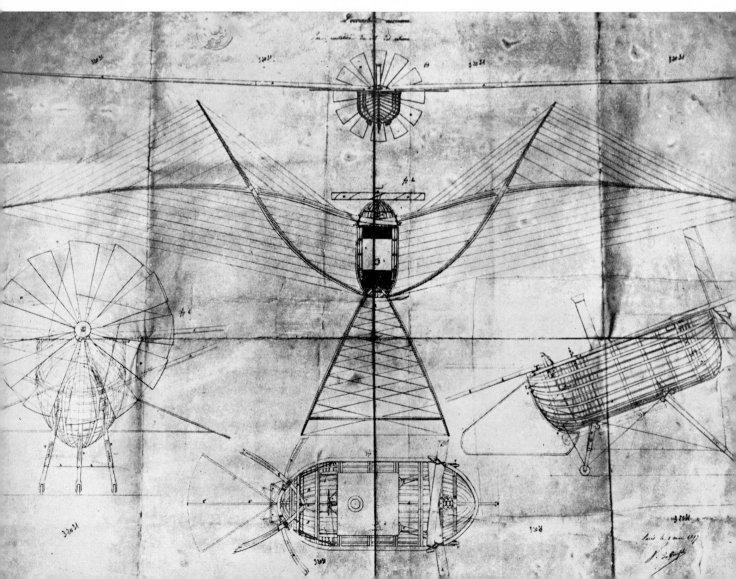

French Progress

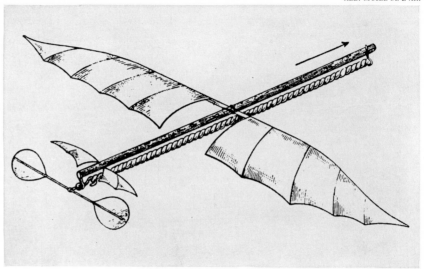

A decade after the failure of String-fellow's model airplane in 1848, two French seamen helped reassert their country's lead, first established by the Montgolfiers, in the race to conquer the air. One of them, Felix Du Temple, based his work on scientific knowledge and scored two notable firsts; the other, Jean-Marie Le Bris, took a bold, empirical approach to the problem—and had less luck.

Before patenting a design for an airplane on May 2, 1857, Du Temple tested a scale model that rose into the air under its own power—the first airplane device ever to do so. Its propeller stopped in mid-air, but its wings, acting as a parachute, sustained the craft until—in the words of Du Temple's brother—the airplane settled to the ground on its wheels as a bird flutters down to land on its claws. A full-size machine, built by Du Temple in 1874 and launched down a ramp, briefly carried a sailor through the air.

The seemingly effortless soaring of the albatross had fascinated Le Bris, Du Temple's brave contemporary, during his long years at sea, and the man-carrying glider he built in 1856, not surprisingly, took the shape of a giant bird with a wingspan of fifty feet. A system of pulleys and levers adjusted the wings to various angles of incidence. Launched from a horse-drawn cart, the device completed one short glide over a quarry. On a subsequent trial Le Bris lost control of his vehicle and fell, breaking a leg. Ten years later, he built another glider, but when it was destroyed during a preliminary, unmanned test, Le Bris gave up his courageous attempts to imitate the birds. Later, at the age of sixty-two, he served in the Franco-Prussian war. In 1872, having survived the perils of the sea, the air, and land warfare, Le Bris was waylaid and killed by highwaymen.

When a hip disease prevented him from following his father's naval career, twenty-year-old Alphonse Pénaud (right) turned to aviation in 1870 and began experimenting with model airplanes powered by twisted rubber bands. One of his model "planophores," similar to the one shown in the drawing above, was flown publicly in Paris on August 18, 1871. With its raised wing tips and negatively positioned tail plane, incorporating a vertical rudder (not shown), it achieved inherent stability. In 1876 Pénaud patented the design below for an amphibious airplane with retractable wheels; but with no suitable engine to drive its twin propellers, it was never built. Four years later, the depressed inventor, at age thirty, committed suicide.

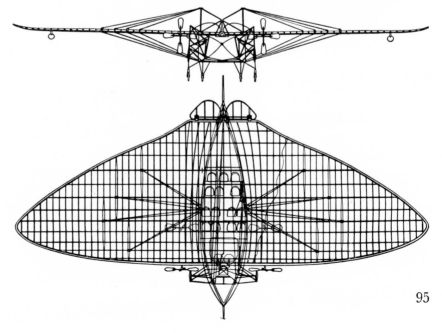

95

Thomas Walker's 1810 ornithopter, as illustrated in this drawing, would work as easily as a bird flapping its wings—if only the operator would pedal hard enough.

Ornithopters
and Helicopters

Despite the contributions of men like Cayley, Henson, and Pénaud, optimistic dreamers continued experimenting with ornithopters. Flapping-wing devices had been discredited by G. A. Borelli in 1680; but—though failure was predictable—patents were still being granted for such machines two centuries later.

In 1784 two Frenchmen, Launoy and Bienvenu, had demonstrated the lifting possibilities of two pairs of contrarotating steel blades made to spin about a vertical shaft by releasing a tightly-wound cord. This deceptively simple device bore the germ of the helicopter. About 1825 an Englishman named David Mayer built a full-size, man-powered helicopter and unblushingly described its failure to rise above the ground as "very flattering, if not perfectly successful." W. H. Phillips flew a model, steam-powered helicopter in 1842; and subsequent inventors never lost sight of this potentially profitable line of aerial experimentation.

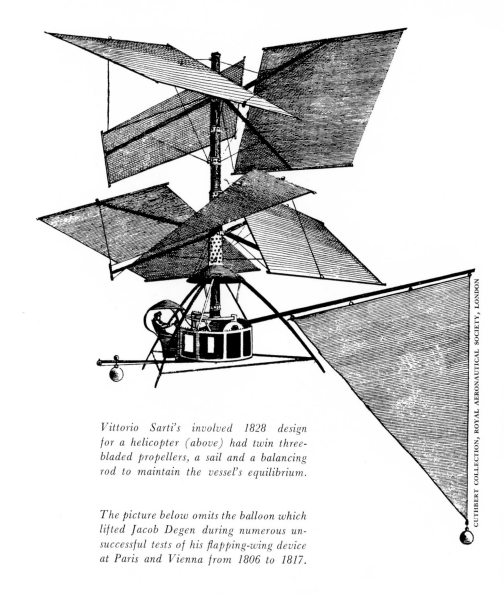

Vittorio Sarti's involved 1828 design for a helicopter (above) had twin three-bladed propellers, a sail and a balancing rod to maintain the vessel's equilibrium.

The picture below omits the balloon which lifted Jacob Degen during numerous unsuccessful tests of his flapping-wing device at Paris and Vienna from 1806 to 1817.

To take his rapid-sequence photographs, Etienne-Jules Marey (right) made multiple exposures on a single photographic plate. The results produced remarkable records of flying birds, like the two above, that first enabled man to study the motions of wings in detail. From his pictures, Marey learned that even large-winged birds used wing beats of slight motion, and that a large wing surface met a correspondingly strong resistance from air currents.

98

Some Lessons
From Nature

Contributions to aviation knowledge sometimes came from unexpected sources; and a new idea, helpful to aviation, sometimes also led to technological advances in other fields.

Hoping to find the answer to heavier-than-air flight by studying the motions of birds, Alphonse Pénaud, about 1873, proposed using a new method of instantaneous photography to record the actions of birds' wings in flight. A contemporary French physiologist, Etienne-Jules Marey, had already embarked on a lifetime's study of muscular movement in men and animals. Putting Pénaud's idea into practice, Marey illustrated his 1873 treatise *Animal Mechanism* with rapid-sequence photographs of birds that corrected centuries of misconceptions based on fallible human vision; and later students of aviation turned repeatedly to his pathfinding work.

Marey himself went on to the study of aerodynamics and, in the 1890's, constructed a wind tunnel. He photographed the action of wind against various shapes, and his methods, in time, contributed to the start of a brand-new field—motion pictures.

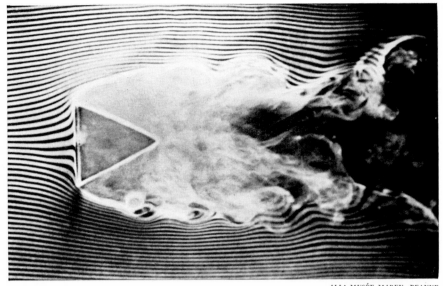

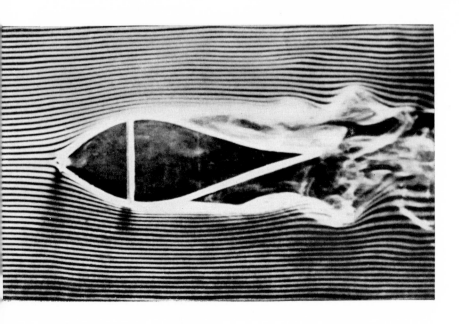

The first wind tunnel for aviation research was built in 1871 by two Englishmen, F. H. Wenham and John Browning. Two decades later Marey studied air flow by photographing the smoke displaced in a wind tunnel by bodies of different shapes. A blunt object (top, above) and inclined planes (center) deflected the air stream to cause a turbulent wake. But a streamlined shape (left) produced an even flow of air and less disturbance in the wake.

Though they look inebriated, the dog, men, and chickens above are actually enjoying the phenomenon of weightlessness during their adventurous trip from Florida to outer space, as described almost one hundred years ago by Jules Verne in From the Earth to the Moon.

100

Fictional Flight

Slow scientific progress has never hampered visionary writers who, through the ages, have gone beyond the inventors to create their own flying machines. Even with successful aviation almost in sight, late-nineteenth-century authors continued to expand on the popular theme of flight, and none did so more persuasively than Jules Verne, the French master of science fiction.

A diligent researcher as well as a prolific writer, Verne spiced his adventure stories with enough technical details to make them sound almost convincing, even today. His first great success, *Five Weeks in a Balloon,* published in 1863, capitalized on current interest in the attempt to achieve dirigibility. But this was a comparatively tame effort for the seemingly clairvoyant Verne, who went on to envision helicopters, artificial satellites, and space capsules.

His 1865 tale, *From the Earth to the Moon,* took three men, prophetically launched in a conical projectile from the Florida coast, through weightlessness into orbit around the earth's satellite. Five years later he rescued his heroes from permanent oblivion in a sequel, *Around the Moon,* which brought the space vehicle back to earth, where it was retrieved after landing in the ocean.

The gay, eye-catching poster above, advertising an 1898 musical farce, seems to promise an airship flying over New York City—an offering that would sorely tax a producer, even with today's elaborate stage devices and greater aviation knowledge.

At left is the cover of an 1893 edition of the Frank Reade Library, a popular adventure series for boys. The intrepid hero made a six week's flight over the Andes in this improbable airship, supported by nothing more than billowing sails, powderpuff propellers, and what appears to be a giant lampshade—technical absurdities that were immaterial to devoted young readers looking to dime novels for little more than escapism.

101

The glider in which Otto Lilienthal dramatically posed before an 1896 experiment (above) had movable wing tips operated by a small carbonic acid gas motor, a strange reversion to the ornithopter principle. Published reports of his theories and photographs of his daring trial flights inspired a whole school of glider pilots.

Wilbur and Orville Wright built their first glider in 1900. On October 10, 1902, Wilbur was photographed (left) in the sophisticated biplane glider used during their third season of trials at Kitty Hawk. They made nearly 1,000 flights in this machine, which, with its movable control surfaces, foreshadowed their 1903 airplane.

Like the Wrights, Octave Chanute was influenced by Lilienthal; but, unlike them, he followed the German's lead in relying on the shifting of the pilot's weight for control. Too old at sixty-four to fly himself, Chanute tested his 1896 glider (right) on Lake Michigan's shore with a fellow engineer, A. M. Herring, acting as pilot.

Mastering the Glider

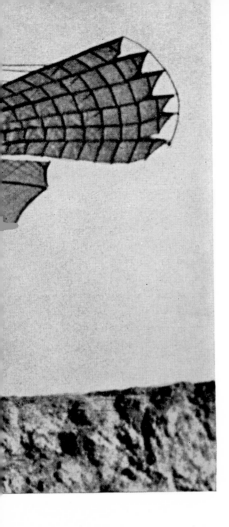

Most of the men working on the problem of winged flight concentrated on the design and construction of large, unwieldy flying chariots, which they hoped to force into the air simply by adding a suitable lightweight engine. It was rather like attaching wings to an automobile in the belief that it would become airborne if driven fast enough.

Only the more clear-sighted aerial pioneers understood that there was another, closely related problem: control in the air. The first man to do anything about this problem was Otto Lilienthal, the pioneer German airman, who blazed a new trail in the sky in 1891 by building and flying the first of several successful gliders.

Lilienthal's death in an 1896 gliding accident shocked the aviation world, but by then there were others to carry on his important work. A young Scottish engineer, Percy Pilcher, perhaps Lilienthal's greatest disciple, was on the point of adding power to his gliders, when, in 1899, he too met death in an aerial mishap.

The gliding career of John J. Montgomery, a science teacher at Santa Clara College in California, also ended in tragedy. Montgomery is said to have experimented with gliders on his family's ranch near San Diego about 1883. Twenty years later, still interested in aviation, the Californian proposed launching manned gliders from a balloon. After several trials of this method, an assistant, Daniel Maloney, died in the crash of a Montgomery glider on July 18, 1905. In 1911 Montgomery himself was killed when one of his later models was upset on take-off.

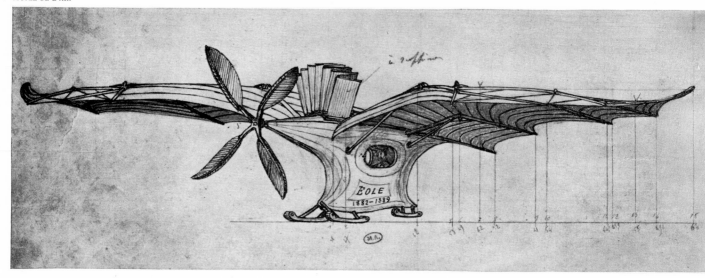

In 1890 Clément Ader made a short, inconclusive hop in the bat-winged craft which appears above in the inventor's own sketch. His Avion III, an unsuccessful 1897 model financed by the French army, had the sole distinction of having its name become the French word for airplane.

Wilhelm Kress, an Austrian piano maker-turned-inventor, built this giant flying machine with three wings set in tandem, twin propellers behind the second wing surface, and rear elevator and rudder in 1898—and placed it on two sheet-aluminum floats for launching from water or snow. Although it capsized and was wrecked while taxiing on a lake prior to a 1901 take-off trial, Kress's float plane was the first full-size airplane to utilize a gasoline engine.

Powered Machines

Several ambitious aerial projects of the late nineteenth and early twentieth century created an erroneous impression that the problem of winged flight was all but solved. The notion was sometimes fostered by the prestige of the inventor himself, or by the implied endorsement of government financing, as in the case of Samuel Pierpont Langley. Working partly with War Department funds, the eminent astronomer and Secretary of the Smithsonian Institution built a full-size "aerodrome" that failed miserably in two 1903 trials.

Eleven years later, Glenn Curtiss, a rival of the Wrights, secretly modified the machine and retested it with limited success. The Smithsonian announced that Langley's invention had been the first airplane capable of sustained, man-carrying free flight, an untenable position it maintained until 1942.

At left, the white-bearded, sixty-nine-year-old Samuel P. Langley encourages his assistant and pilot Charles M. Manly (equipped with a compass on his knee) just prior to the first unsuccessful attempt to achieve powered flight on October 7, 1903. In its second and final trial on December 8 (above), Langley's "aerodrome," again launched from a Potomac River houseboat, is seen falling apart and dropping into the water.

Two acting as one—even in the firmness of their stride: Orville (with mustache) and Wilbur Wright

On the Brink
of Success

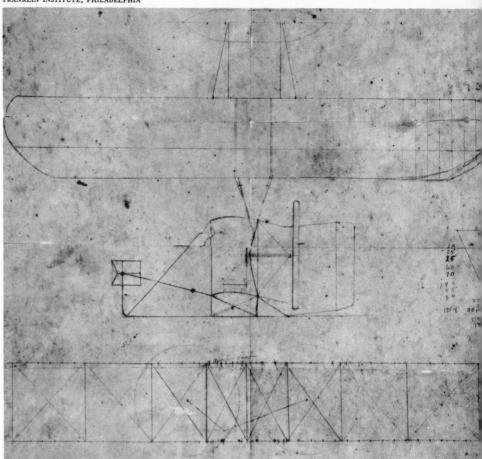

Wilbur Wright was only thirty-two in 1899 when he and his brother Orville, younger by four years, began reading everything available on aviation. Intuitively scientific in method, they worked out new formulas where they found the old ones inadequate; with unflagging patience they tested each new theory in three seasons of gliding experiments at Kitty Hawk.

By the end of October, 1902, they knew the answers to most of the problems that had prevented men from flying with wings, and only needed power to convert their gliders into airplanes. Weary from their two-month outing in North Carolina, they returned to Dayton, Ohio. As they set about to build a power plant for their airplane during that winter and spring, the routine work of making bicycles for the summer trade dropped forever from their minds. The two brothers were standing on the threshold of history.

The detailed three-view sketch of the Wrights' successful 1903 flying machine above was drawn on brown wrapping paper and carries marginal notations in Wilbur's handwriting. The photograph below of the untried airplane standing outside the Kitty Hawk "hangar" was taken on November 24, 1903, twenty-three days before its historic first flight.

The First Powered Flight

Just prior to the first successful trial o
their flying machine on December 17, 1903
Orville Wright rigged a camera with it.
lens trained on the end of the starting rai

and asked John T. Daniels of the Kill Devil Life Saving Station to click the shutter if the machine rose. Then he eased himself down into the operator's prone position. Wilbur ran alongside to steady the wing once it left its resting position on the benchlike object in the center foreground and, as the world's first powered, man-carrying airplane rose into a stiff head wind at 10:35 A.M., fell back (at right) to stare in triumph and wonder at the miracle he and his brother had worked.

In Their Words...

THE USE
OF WINGS

The Scientific Approach

George Cayley's essay "On Aerial Navigation" formed the basis of the modern science of aerodynamics. The following is an extract from his historic paper, the result of a decade of research and experimentation, first published in England in 1809-10.

. . . the scheme of flying by artificial wings has been much ridiculed, and indeed the idea of attaching wings to the arms of a man is ridiculous enough . . . The flight of a strong man by great muscular exertion, though a curious and interesting circumstance . . . would be of little use. I feel perfectly confident, however, that this noble art will soon be brought home to man's general convenience, and that we shall be able to transport ourselves and families, and their goods and chattels, more securely by air than by water, and with a velocity of from 20 to 100 miles per hour. To produce this effect it is only necessary to have a first mover, which will generate more power in a given time, in proportion to its weight, than the animal system of muscles.

. . . it is perfectly clear that force can be obtained by a much lighter apparatus than muscles . . . we may be justified in the remark that the act of flying . . . requires less exertions than from the appearance is supposed. . . . the many hundreds of miles of continued flight exerted by birds of passage . . . [and] the perfect ease with which some birds are suspended in long horizontal flights, without one waft of the wings, encourages the idea that a slight power only is necessary. . . .

All [the] principles upon which the support, steadiness, elevation, depression, and steerage of vessels for aerial navigation depend have been abundantly verified by experiments both upon a large and small scale. Last year I made a machine having a surface of 300 square feet, which was accidently broken before there was an opportunity of trying the effect of the propelling apparatus, but its steerage and steadiness were perfectly proved, and it would sail obliquely downward in any direction according to the set of the rudder . . . Even in this state, when any person ran forward in it with his full speed, taking advantage of a gentle breeze in front, it would bear upward so strongly as scarcely to allow him to touch the ground, and would frequently lift him up and convey him several yards together.

The best mode of producing the propelling power is the only thing that remains yet untried towards the completion of the invention. . . .

In combining the general principles of aerial navigation for the practice of the art, many mechanical difficulties present themselves which require a considerable course of skilfully applied experiments, before they can be overcome. But to a certain extent, the air has already been made navigable, and no one . . . can doubt the ultimate accomplishment of this object. . . .

A Poet's Voice

For I dipt into the future,
  far as human eye could see,
Saw the Vision of the world,
  and all the wonder that would be;
Saw the heavens fill with commerce,
  argosies of magic sails,
Pilots of the purple twilight,
  dropping down with costly bales;
Heard the heavens fill with shouting,
  and there rain'd a ghastly dew
From the nations' airy navies
  grappling in the central blue;
Far along the world-wide whisper
  of the south-wind rushing warm,
With the standards of the peoples
  plunging thro' the thunder-storm;
Till the war-drum throbb'd no longer,
  and the battle-flags were furl'd
In the Parliament of man,
  the Federation of the World.

Alfred Lord Tennyson
"Locksley Hall," 1842

110

"Suitable Paddle Wheels"

In 1842 the English inventor W. S. Henson patented his design for an "aerial locomotive." The machine, as this excerpt from the patent specification reveals, introduced the modern idea of a propeller.

The Invention relates, first, to the constructing of locomotive machinery and apparatus for conveying letters, goods, and passengers from place to place through the air; and secondly, to improvements in constructing steam boilers for the generating of steam to give motion to locomotive machinery in the air. . .

Now, the first part of [my] Invention consists of an apparatus so constructed as to offer a very extended surface or plane of a light yet strong construction, which will have the same relation to the general machine which the extended wings of a bird have to the body when a bird is skimming in the air; but in place of the movement or power for onward progress being obtained by movement of the extended surface or plane, as in the case with the wings of birds, I apply suitable paddle wheels or other proper mechanical propellers worked by a steam or other sufficiently light engine, and thus obtain the requisite power for onward movement . . . and in order to give control as to the upward and downward direction of such a machine, I apply a tail to the extended surface, which is capable of being inclined or raised, so that when the power is acting to propel the machine, by inclining the tail upwards, the resistance offered by the air will cause the machine to rise on the air; and, on the contrary, when the inclination of the tail is reversed, the machine will immediately be propelled downwards . . . to guide the machine as to the lateral direction, I apply a vertical rudder or second tail, and according as the same is inclined in one direction or the other, so will be the direction of the machine.

. . . it will be evident that the principal objects to be considered in the construction of such a locomotive machine are lightness with strength in respect to the machine itself, and lightness with respect to quantity of power offered by the engine employed . . .

"Stepping-Stones to Success"

F. H. Wenham summed up his experiments in a paper that he read at the first meeting of the Aeronautical Society of Great Britain in 1866. His aviation classic suggested, among other things, that a multiplane wing would provide greater lift than a single wing.

Having remarked how thin a stratum of air is displaced beneath the wings of a bird in rapid flight, it follows that in order to obtain the necessary *length* of plane for supporting heavy weights, the surfaces may be superposed or placed in parallel rows, with an interval between them. A dozen pelicans may fly, one above the other, without mutual impediment, as if framed together; and it is thus shown how two hundred weight may be supported in a transverse distance of only 10 ft.

CULVER PICTURES, INC.

Francis Herbert Wenham

In order to test this idea, six bands of stiff paper 3 ft. long and 3 in. wide were stretched at a slight upward angle in a light rectangular frame, with an interval of 3 in. between them, the arrangement resembling an open Venetian blind. When this was held against a breeze, the lifting power was very great; and even by running with it in a calm it required much force to keep it down. The success of this model led to the construction of one of a sufficient size to carry the weight of a man. . . . This was taken out after dark into a wet piece of meadowland one November evening, during a strong breeze, wherein it became quite unmanageable. The wind acting upon the already tightly stretched webs, their united pull caused the central boards to bend considerably, with a twisting, vibratory motion. During a lull, the head and shoulders were inserted in the triangle, with the chest resting on the base board. A sudden gust caught up the experimenter, who was carried some distance from the ground, and the affair, falling over sideways, broke up the right-hand set of webs.

In all new machines we gain experience by repeated failures, which frequently form the stepping-stones to ultimate success.

A Science-Fiction Machine

Jules Verne's 1886 tale, The Clipper of the Clouds, *excited the imagination of readers with a vision of flight. This translation by Karen Termohlen contains a strangely prophetic description of a huge, imaginary helicopter, the* Albatross.

Robur believed that the simpler his apparatus the better; propellers were all that was needed for his flying machine. Some kept the machine suspended in air while others drew it along under conditions that were superbly suited for speed and safety. . . .

The platform was a framework one hundred feet long and twelve feet wide, like a ship's deck with a projecting prow. Below was a solidly-built hull which enclosed the engines, stores, tools, and provisions of all sorts, including the water tanks. . . . There were three deckhouses, whose compartments were used as cabins for the crew or as machine rooms. The bow contained the galley and quarters for the crew; located in the stern were an engineer's cabin and a saloon, above which stood a glass house for the helmsman, who directed the vessel . . . Beneath the hull was an arrangement of flexible springs to soften the jolt of landing—though this was hardly necessary, so skilled was the engineer at mastering the movements of his machine.

Above the deck rose thirty-seven vertical axes, fifteen on each side, and seven, more elevated, in the center. One could almost say that the *Albatross* was a clipper with thirty-seven masts. But instead of sails each mast bore two horizontal propellers . . . which rotated at prodigious speeds. Each axis moved independently of the others; also, each axis turned in the opposite direction from its alternate . . . Thus, while rising on the vertical column of air, the propellers were stabilized against horizontal resistance. . . . Fore and aft were two 4-bladed driving propellers, set on horizontal axes. . . .

Robur decided not to obtain power from steam or other vapors, nor compressed air or other elastic gases, nor those explosive mixtures which produce mechanical motion. He chose electricity, that agent which one day will be the soul of the industrial world. Furthermore, he needed no electro-motor to produce his electricity, but simply batteries and storage cells. What elements composed these batteries, what acids activated them?—only Robur knew. Equally secret was the construction of the storage cells. What made up the negative and positive plates? No one knows. The engineer was careful—and quite sensibly, too—not to patent his invention.

Imitate the Birds

In The Empire of the Air, *published in 1881, the French pioneer Louis Mouillard urged experimenters to master the art of soaring. His proposals, taken up by others, were to lead in time to final success with powered machines.*

I hold that in the flight of the soaring birds *(the vultures, the eagles, and other birds which fly without flapping)* ascension is produced by the skillful use of the force of the wind, and the steering, in any direction, is the result of skillful maneuvers; so that by a moderate wind a man can, with an airplane, unprovided with any motor whatever, rise up into the air and direct himself at will, even against the wind itself.

Man therefore can, with a rigid surface and a properly designed apparatus, repeat the exercises performed by the soaring birds in ascension and steering, and will need to expend no force whatever, save to perform the maneuvers required for steering.

The exact shape of these airplanes need not be discussed . . . for it will be seen . . . that there are scores of shapes and devices which can be

Mouillard, watching birds in Egypt

employed, but all forms of apparatus, however dissimilar, must be based upon this idea.

"A Matter of Practice"

In 1893 Otto Lilienthal, the great German glider pilot, described his early experiments—and summed up his optimistic hopes for the future—in a paper titled "The Carrying Capacity of Arched Surfaces in Sailing Flight," from which the following selection has been taken.

I have now reached the close of a series of experiments during which I had set myself a definite task. This was to construct an apparatus with curved carrying surfaces which should enable me to sail through the air, starting from high points and gliding as far as possible—that is to say, at the least obtainable inclination; and to do this with stability and safety even in winds of medium strength. . . .

The mere discovery that with arched wings supporting forces are evolved which permit soaring to be performed with little effort is far from being the final invention of flying. The successful practical utilization of this important phenomenon in air resistance is going to demand a considerable amount of ingenuity. . . .

I had come to the conclusion that a particular class of difficulties was next to be overcome. In trials with movable wings, in the building of steam air ships, in experiments with mechanical birds of all kinds, I had found out how hard it is to maintain a *stable* equilibrium in the air and to counteract the "whims" of the wind.

For this reason I gave up for the time being motor mechanisms altogether, and limited myself to the simplest form of flight, namely, gliding downward in an inclined direction. . . .

There can be no doubt, in my opinion, that by perfecting our present apparatus, and by acquiring greater skill in using it, we shall

Otto Lilienthal

hieve still more favorable results
ith it, and finally succeed in taking
ng sails even in rather strong
inds. . . .

Of course it will be a matter of
ractice to learn how to guide such a
ying machine . . .

Actual trial alone can decide this
uestion, as we must let the air and
e wind have their say in the matter.

relude to Power

spired by Lilienthal, the Scottish
gineer Percy Pilcher experimented
ith gliders and, like Lilienthal, was
lled in a gliding accident before he
uld try powered flight. He made
is statement in an 1897 lecture in
ublin.

he object of experimenting with
aring machines is to enable one to
ave practice in starting and alight-
g and controlling a machine in the
r. They cannot possibly float hori-
ontally in the air for any length of
me, but to keep going must neces-
rily lose in elevation. They are ex-
llent schooling machines, and that
all they are meant to be, until
wer, in the shape of an engine
orking a screw propeller, or an en-

gine working wings to drive a machine forward, is added; then one
who is used to sailing down a hill with
a simple soaring machine will be able
to fly with comparative safety.

Nothing Is Insuperable

Octave Chanute's Progress in Flying
Machines, *published in 1894, was a
startling summation of how much
man had already learned about
heavier-than-air flying.*

. . . the mechanical difficulties are
very great; but it will be discerned
also that none of them can now be
said to be insuperable, and that material progress has recently been
achieved toward their solution.

The resistance and supporting
power of air are approximately
known, the motor and the propelling
instrument are probably sufficiently
worked out to make a beginning; we
know in a general way the kind of
apparatus to adopt, its approximate
extent and required texture of sustaining surfaces, and there remain to
solve the problems of the maintenance of the equilibrium, the guidance, the starting up, and the alighting, as well as the final combination
of these several solutions into one
homogeneous design.

In spite of continued failures, it is
my own judgment . . . that, once the
problem of equilibrium is solved,
man may hope to navigate the air,
and that this will probably be accomplished (perhaps at no very distant
day,) with some form of aeroplane
provided with fixed concavo-convex
surfaces, which will at first utilize the
wind as a motive power, and eventually be provided with an artificial
motor. . . .

No experiment with a model can
be deemed quite conclusive until the
same principles have been extended
to a full-sized apparatus capable of
sustaining a man, and until this has
been exposed to all the vicissitudes of
actual flight. It will readily be discerned that a less achievement than

this would not prove an adequate
performance, and that no matter
how well a model might behave in
still air, there would still remain the
question as to how it would behave
in a wind, and how it was to solve
the problems of starting up and of
alighting.

. . . In other words, a flying machine to be successful must be at all
times under intelligent control, and
the skill to obtain that control may
be acquired by utilizing the impulse
of the wind, thus eliminating, for a
time at least, the further complica-
tions incident to a motor.

. . . let us hope that the advent of
a successful flying machine, now only
dimly foreseen and nevertheless
thought to be possible, will bring
nothing but good into the world;
that it shall abridge distance, make
all parts of the globe accessible, bring
men into closer relation with each
other, advance civilization, and
hasten the promised era in which
there shall be nothing but peace and
good-will among all men.

*Among those students of flight who
found inspiration in Octave Chanute's commentary were Wilbur and
Orville Wright.*

Octave Chanute

113

The Wrights

The climactic episode of the invention of the airplane is nowhere revealed in more fascinating detail than in The Papers of Wilbur and Orville Wright, *edited by Marvin W. McFarland and published in 1953. The following excerpts, sketching the Wrights' progress until their first triumphant flight, start with part of a letter of introduction written by Wilbur to Octave Chanute from Dayton, Ohio, on May 13, 1900.*

For some years I have been afflicted with the belief that flight is possible to man. My disease has increased in severity and I feel that it will soon cost me an increased amount of money if not my life. . . .

My general ideas of the subject are similar to those held by most practical experimenters, to wit: that what is chiefly needed is skill rather than machinery. The flight of the buzzard and similar sailers is a convincing demonstration of the value of skill, and the partial needlessness of motors. It is possible to fly without motors, but not without knowledge & skill. This I conceive to be fortunate, for man, by reason of his greater intellect, can more reasonably hope to equal birds in knowledge, than to equal nature in the perfection of her machinery. . . .

I make no secret of my plans for the reason that I believe no financial profit will accrue to the inventor of the first flying machine, and that only those who are willing to give as well as to receive suggestions can hope to link their names with the honor of its discovery. The problem is too great for one man alone and unaided to solve in secret.

On September 23, 1900, Wilbur wrote from Kitty Hawk, North Carolina, to his father Bishop Milton Wright.

I have my machine nearly finished. It is not to have a motor and is not expected to fly in any true sense of

the word. My idea is merely to experiment and practice with a view to solving the problem of equilibrium. I have plans which I hope to find much in advance of the methods tried by previous experimenters. When once a machine is under proper control under all conditions, the motor problem will be quickly solved. A failure of motor will then mean simply a slow descent & safe landing instead of a disastrous fall. In my experiments I do not expect to rise many feet from the ground, and in case I am upset there is nothing but soft sand to strike on. I do not

Wilbur Wright

intend to take dangerous chances, both because I have no wish to get hurt and because a fall would stop my experimenting, which I would not like at all. The man who wishes to keep at the problem long enough to really learn anything positively must not take dangerous risks. Carelessness and overconfidence are usually more dangerous than deliberately accepted risks.

Back in Dayton, on November 16, 1900, Wilbur again wrote to Chanute.

In October my brother and myself spent a vacation of several weeks at

Kitty Hawk, North Carolina, experimenting with a soaring machine. . .

Our plan of operation was for the aeronaut to lie down on the lower plane while two assistants grasped the ends of the machine and ran forward till the machine was supported on the air. . . . The man on the machine then brought the machine slowly to the ground, so slowly in fact that the marks of the machine could be seen for twenty or thirty feet back from the point where it finally stopped. . . . And although in appearance it was a dangerous practice we found it [was] perfectly safe and comfortable except for the flying sand, and the machine was not once injured although we sometimes landed at a rate of very nearly thirty miles per hour. The operators did not receive a single bruise. . . . We found no difficulty in maintaining fore-and-aft balance. The ease with which it was accomplished was a matter of great astonishment to us. It was so different from what the writings of other experimenters led us to expect.

The following summer the Wrights were again in North Carolina. Wilbur Wright's diary for Tuesday, July 30, 1901, reads:

We have experimented safely with a machine of over 300 sq. ft. surface in winds as high as 18 miles per hour. Previous experimenters had pronounced a machine of such size impracticable to construct and impossible to manage.

On September 18, 1901, Wilbur addressed the Western Society of Engineers in Chicago. His speech, titled "Some Aeronautical Experiments," included the following comments.

The person who merely watches the flight of a bird gathers the impression that the bird has nothing to think of but the flapping of its wings. As a matter of fact this is a very small part of its mental labor. To even mention all the things the bird must keep in mind in order to fly securely through air would take a considerable part of the evening. . . . The bird has learned [his] art . . . so thoroughly that its skill is not apparent to our sight. We only learn to appreciate it when we try to imitate it. Now, there are two ways of learning how to ride a fractious horse: one is to get on him and learn by actual practice how each motion and trick may be best met; the other is to sit on a fence and watch the beast a while, and then retire to the house and at leisure figure out the best way of overcoming his jumps and kicks. The latter system is the safest; but the former, on the whole, turns out the larger proportion of good riders. It is very much the same in learning to ride a flying machine; if you are looking for perfect safety, you will do well to sit on a fence and watch the birds; but if you really wish to learn, you must mount a machine and become acquainted with its tricks by actual trial.

On October 23, 1902, at the Kill Devil Hills near Kitty Hawk, Orville wrote to his sister Katharine.

The past five days have been the most satisfactory for gliding that we have had. In two days we made over 250 glides. . . We have gained considerable proficiency in the handling of the machine. . . .

Hearing of the Wrights' progress, Chanute wrote to Wilbur from Chicago on December 9, 1902.

I think you had better patent your improvements. How far do you think of carrying on aeronautical work?

A week later Wilbur replied from Dayton.

It is our intention next year to build a machine much larger and about twice as heavy as our present machine. With it we will work out problems relating to starting and handling heavy weight machines, and if we find it under satisfactory control in flight, we will proceed to mount a motor.

On June 24, 1903, Wilbur again addressed the Western Society of Engineers in Chicago.

By long practice the management of a flying machine should become as instinctive as the balancing movements a man unconsciously employs with every step in walking, but in the early days it is easy to make blunders. . . . As yet we consider ourselves little more than novices in management. A thousand glides is equivalent to about four hours of steady practice,

Orville Wright

far too little to give anyone a complete mastery of the art of flying. Progress is very slow in the preliminary stages, but when once it becomes possible to undertake continuous soaring advancement should be rapid. Under special conditions it is possible that this point is not so far away as might be supposed.

Back at Kill Devil Hills, Wilbur wrote to Chanute on October 16, 1903.

We are expecting the most interesting results of any of our seasons of experiment, and are sure that, barring exasperating little accidents or some mishap, we will have done something before we break camp. . . . I wonder what our luck will be.

On Thursday, December 17, 1903, man's long dream of flight came true. Orville's diary records the event.

When we got up a wind of between 20 and 25 miles was blowing from the north. We got the machine out early and put out the signal for the men at the [Life Saving] station. . . . After running the engine and propellers a few minutes to get them in working order, I got on the machine at 10:35 for the first trial. The wind at this time was blowing a little over 27 miles. . . . On slipping the rope the machine started off increasing in speed to probably 7 or 8 miles. The machine lifted from the truck just as it was entering on the fourth rail. Mr. Daniels took a picture just as it left the tracks. I found the control of the front rudder quite difficult on account of its being balanced too near the center and thus had a tendency to turn itself when started so that the rudder was turned too far on one side and then too far on the other. As a result the machine would rise suddenly to about 10 ft. and then as suddenly, on turning the rudder, dart for the ground. A sudden dart when out about 100 feet from the end of the tracks ended the flight. Time about 12 seconds. . . At just 12 o'clock Will started on the fourth and last trip. The machine started off with its ups and downs as it had before, but by the time he had gone over three or four hundred feet he had it under much better control, and was traveling on a fairly even course. It proceeded in this manner till it reached a small hummock out about 800 feet from the starting ways, when it began its pitching again and suddenly darted into the ground. The front rudder frame was badly broken up, but the main frame suffered none at all. The distance over the ground was 852 feet in 59 seconds.

115

CHAPTER 4

In a Deperdussin like the one in which he set the 1912 world speed record (108 m.p.h.), the French aviator Jules Védrines leaves Cala

OFF WE GO!

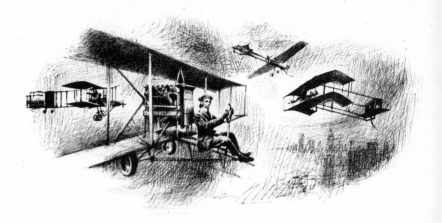

In many ways, of all the breathless aviation decades that have passed since Kitty Hawk, the first remains the most vivid. It begins in obscurity and silence, and perhaps in the cold statistics of aeronautical achievement it has the least to offer. But in adventure and excitement, color and romantic episode, it stands alone.

One reason may be that while the number of people involved was small, the extent of their daring seemed limitless. In the perilous air decade before the First World War, to leave the comfortable earth on fragile wings demanded a blend of courage and curiosity, dedication and daring, fanaticism and fatalism. Regardless of nationality, these early fliers seemed linked as a fraternity accepting a common challenge. Most of the small band knew one another. Fierce rivalries flared among them, but there were few jealousies and little pettiness. When one of them failed and died, as many did, each felt the loss of a fellow adventurer who could never be replaced.

Perhaps it was because all of them faced a single great adversary, and all of them knew it. From the beginning many noble themes have been woven into the fabric of flying: man against gravity, man against distance, man against time. But the basic theme of the early years was as old as the oldest flying legend: man against death. Each of the first fliers understood that the air was an alien element into which man ventured only at his peril. Far from shrinking from the challenge, they welcomed it. They played a dangerous game for the excitement of it—and accepted without bitterness the consequences of losing.

The beginnings of that decade were strangely quiet. In his triumphant telegram of December 17, 1903, Orville Wright requested his father in Dayton to "inform press" that powered flight with wings was achieved at last. Before Bishop Wright could do so, a Norfolk, Virginia, newspaper published a fragmentary and misleading account, based on a pirated copy of the telegram. To counteract further garbled reports, the Wrights issued a statement to the Associated Press on January 5, 1904. But the nation's press was skeptical and unmoved. Editors were weary of claims that had proved false and of flying machines that did not fly. Consequently, those papers that did print the dispatch ran it without comment, and news of the greatest aerial achievement of all times was greeted with appalling indifference.

The apathy was to last, incredibly, for more than four years. So little known was the Wrights' accomplishment that in October, 1906, when the irrepressible Alberto Santos-Dumont wavered off the soil of France, standing bolt upright in a clumsy tailless biplane, he was convinced that he was the first man in history to fly with powered wings.

The Wrights are popularly believed to have been secretive and averse to publicity. This might have been the case in later years, when they felt that competitors were trying to steal their invention, but it was not so at first. If anything, they were anxious to show the world what they had done. In the spring of 1904 they invited the press to watch a demonstration of a new and improved version of their flying machine.

They were now using a cow pasture near Dayton for their work. Unfortunately, on the day the press showed up, a combination of unfavorable wind conditions and engine trouble made flying impossible. The next day, when a few persistent reporters came back, the engine failed on take-off, and the machine sat down abruptly. After that, the press lost interest.

The Wrights stoically accepted the fact that they had more work to do. They were off the ground, but

118

just barely. The low power and unreliability of their engine made them resort to an assisted take-off, using a catapult device consisting of a tall derrick with a weight attached to their machine by a long rope. Control in the air was still primitive and difficult, and it was not until September 20 that Wilbur was able to make a circular flight. On November 9, he celebrated the election of Theodore Roosevelt by circling the field four times in a three-mile flight that lasted a little over five minutes.

The next year—1905—the Wrights designed and built another larger and improved flying machine, which proved capable of turning, banking, doing figures of eight, and flying for distances that were astonishing. The problem of stalling on tight turns in their restricted practice field was overcome when the brothers learned to put the nose down and pick up additional speed, which gave greater controllability. They also unlinked their rudder controls from their wing-warping controls, thereby gaining much greater flexibility in their handling of the airplane. By the end of the summer they were making flights that ended only when their fuel was exhausted—as on October 5, when Wilbur flew for more than thirty-eight minutes and covered more than twenty-four miles.

At this point, almost two years after their initial success, the Wrights were still the only human beings who had achieved powered flight with wings. And yet, they still failed to receive the acclaim and encouragement that their accomplishment should have brought them. In January, 1905, the brothers had offered their invention and scientific knowledge to the War Department, which flatly rejected three separate overtures without even bothering to investigate. Discouraged by the cold reception and by troubles with the Patent Office, Orville and Wilbur settled on a policy of secrecy to ward off costly litigation with potential imitators. In 1906 they built no new planes and for two and one-half years did not even fly.

Hoping to find more interest among European governments, the Wrights crated one of their machines and took it abroad in 1907. No one there, however, would agree to pay their asking price of $250,000 for a machine which they were unwilling to demonstrate until a contract had been signed; and the brothers came home, leaving the flying machine sitting forlornly in its crate at Le Havre.

By this time the work of the Wrights had been the subject of considerable discussion, debate, and even imitation among European aeronautical pioneers, particularly in France. First word of their activities crossed the ocean as early as 1902 when Octave Chanute, that tireless disseminator of information, began a correspondence with Captain Ferdinand Ferber of the French army. Ferber had been making and testing gliders since 1899, following, without much success, Lilienthal's example. When Chanute gave him some information about the Wrights' experiments, he started building "Wright-type" gliders. Since the specifications Chanute sent were not complete, Ferber's imitations were failures, which led him to conclude—erroneously—that the Wrights were not making significant progress.

In April, 1903, Chanute came in person to lecture at the Aéro Club in Paris. What was intended to be no more than a routine progress report became a turning point in the development of European aviation. The old man told of his own gliding experiments and described the Wrights' 1902 glider in considerable detail, not omitting the key fact that rudder and wing-warping controls were operated simultaneously. By these revelations Chanute was handing French fliers a blueprint for success, and his words spurred a few of them to new efforts.

Of these, the most important were Robert Esnault-Pelterie, a gifted engineer, and Ernest Archdeacon, a wealthy automobile and balloon enthusiast. These men had already encouraged another engineer, Léon Levavasseur, to build a powered, birdlike, single-wing airplane, which, though it did not fly, pointed the way to later successful monoplanes. In 1904, to test the Wrights' design, Esnault-Pelterie attempted to copy their 1902 machine, and Archdeacon also built a "Wright-type" glider. Lacking complete specifications, they were unsuccessful and asserted that the reports of the Wrights' achievements were unfounded.

Esnault-Pelterie also came to the conclusion that wing warping was unsatisfactory and dangerous. This led him to the invention of the aileron. He fitted two "independent horizontal rudders" to the wing tips of a second "Wright-type" glider that he constructed in 1904, but this glider had no great success either because of other shortcomings.

By now new names and faces were appearing on the French aviation scene. An energetic, hawk-nosed manufacturer of automobile headlights, Louis Blériot, began to "occupy himself passionately with problems of aviation." Someone had conceived the idea of mounting a glider on floats and towing it behind a fast motorboat. So Blériot and Archdeacon ordered a pair of float gliders from a young architectural student who was also a glider pilot, Gabriel Voisin.

Voisin's float gliders kept the forward elevator and biplane configuration of the Wrights, but they also incorporated Hargrave's box-kite principle with a tail unit consisting of two large cells. This, again, reflected European preoccupation with built-in stability as opposed to the Wrights' emphasis on "flyability." These gliders had only limited success, but their design was most influential where early European biplanes were concerned—especially since Voisin and his brother Charles became, before long, the first professional airplane builders. Among the early buyers of their biplanes were two men whose names were soon to become famous, Henri Farman and Léon Delagrange.

In 1906, having built and flown twelve small dirigibles, Alberto Santos-Dumont turned his attention to heavier-than-air flight. In building his airplane, he set the box-kite wings at a pronounced dihedral, relying for power on an Antoinette engine made by Levavasseur and for control on another box-kite cell placed so far out in front that the machine—in such flight as it achieved—looked as if it were flying tail first.

After testing this creation, suspending it under one of his dirigibles, the little Brazilian set out to capture the Archdeacon prize of 3,000 francs for the first person to fly twenty-five meters (about eighty feet). On October 23, 1906, at Bagatelle, in Paris, he managed to leave the ground for nearly two hundred feet; two weeks later, on November 12, again at Bagatelle, he flew 722 feet to win the French Aéro Club's prize for the first flight of one hundred meters. He thus achieved the first heavier-than-air, powered, man-carrying flights in the Old World. All Europe was electrified. Almost no one believed that 4,000 miles away, in Ohio, the air had already been conquered.

In 1907, having had little luck with biplanes, Blériot decided to experiment with powered monoplanes. That year he built three, all different. The third one—a direct ancestor of the monoplane as we know it today—had large forward wings, an enclosed fuselage, and tail unit comprised of a rudder and combined elevator and ailerons ("elevons"); and made five short flights before it crashed on landing.

In America, the Wrights were finally facing some home-grown competition. A young motorcycle racer named Glenn Curtiss had become interested in aeronautics. Lean, adventurous, obsessed with engines and speed, he typified the breed of men that was emerging to share in the conquest of the skies.

When he was not setting motorcycle speed records, Curtiss was building lightweight engines for Thomas Baldwin's dirigibles. So successful were these that Curtiss attracted the attention of Alexander Graham Bell, the aging inventor of the telephone. In October, 1907, Bell, Curtiss, and others formed the Aerial Experiment Association and began building airplanes with features borrowed from both the Wrights and the Voisins.

Their third airplane, the *June Bug,* attracted far more attention and acclaim than the Wrights had ever received. On July 4, 1908, Curtiss flew it more than a mile before several hundred people at Hammonds-

port, New York—the first wholly public flight in America. The *June Bug* was fitted with wing-tip ailerons. This soon brought Curtiss into historic conflict with the Wrights, who considered any form of movable wing section to be an extension of their wing-warping idea. Though previously generous in giving help to any amateur flier who asked for it, they sued Curtiss for infringing their patent. The issue, bitterly fought through the courts, was finally settled in favor of the Wrights.

Meantime in England such pioneers as S. F. Cody, J. W. Dunne, and A. V. Roe were struggling to lift themselves into the air. Cody, an American-born adventurer who fascinated the British by dressing like an Arizona sheriff, built a biplane for the War Office that was called officially *British Army Aeroplane No. 1.* At Farnborough, on October 16, 1908, he made the first powered flight in Great Britain. He kept on flying until 1913, when he was killed.

Like Cody, Dunne was employed at the Government Balloon Factory at Farnborough, designing and building flying machines. He was something of a mystic who later wrote a best seller called *An Experiment with Time.* In 1907 he added an engine to a revolutionary tailless biplane glider with swept-back wings, a configuration he thought might solve the elusive goal of built-in stability. Lack of an adequate power plant held him back, and through 1908 he made little more than powered hops.

A. V. Roe, a former Merchant Navy officer, was experimenting with both biplanes and triplanes. He crashed so often that at one point he was prosecuted as a menace to public safety, but he went on to found the Avro Company, whose planes distinguished themselves in both World Wars.

The important year 1908 saw the complete vindication of the Wrights both at home and abroad. In February the U. S. Army finally accepted their bid to build an airplane for military use. The machine, said the Army, would have to be able to carry two men and fuel for 125 miles and fly at least ten miles nonstop at an average speed of 40 miles per hour. The next month, the brothers sold their French patent rights to a syndicate for $100,000. This meant that Wilbur would have to go to France to demonstrate the machine that was still crated there, while Orville worked at home to carry out the commitment to the United States Government.

Since neither brother had flown for well over two years, they went back to Kitty Hawk to regain their skill with their 1905 machine, slightly modified. The changes allowed them to fly sitting up, instead of in the uncomfortable prone position, which had minimized air resistance but had given them painful cricks in the neck. They were still using a catapult device for launching and, unlike Curtiss and the European pioneers, still preferred skids to wheels.

In May Wilbur sailed for France, where he was met with unconcealed skepticism from both the public and the press. But on August 8, when his machine slid easily down its track and into the air, the critics were silenced, and European fliers astounded. Where they had been forcing their clumsy machines to become grudgingly airborne through engine power, here was this soft-spoken American darting and soaring like a bird. "Marvelous!" cried the press. "Glorious! Sensational!" "We're beaten," confessed Delagrange. "We don't even exist." The chorus of cheers went on and on, while Wilbur set record after record. Blériot conceded instantly that the Wright biplane was far superior to any European machine—a generous admission from a man now wedded to monoplanes. Looking to the future, an Englishman, Major B. F. S. Baden-Powell, made a memorable pronouncement: "That Wilbur Wright is in possession of a power which controls the fate of nations is beyond dispute."

During the rest of the year Wilbur stayed in France, revolutionizing European aviation and captivating everyone with his modesty, good humor, and willingness to share his knowledge and skill. He tried —not always successfully—to avoid banquets and speechmaking. "I only know," he said on one such occasion, "of one bird, the parrot, that can talk, and it doesn't fly very high."

At home Orville finally broke through the barrier of governmental and public apathy that had surrounded the Wrights' remarkable accomplishments. His series of test flights for the Army at Fort Myer, Virginia, dumfounded official Washington. On September 3, flying solo, he demonstrated his new two-seater with brilliant success, banking effortlessly around the parade ground while the spectators below "went crazy." In the following days he repeatedly broke his own endurance records. But on the last day of the test series, September 17, tragedy overtook him. During a flight with a passenger, Lieutenant Thomas Selfridge, a twenty-six-year-old West Pointer who had worked with Curtiss and Bell in the Aerial Experiment Association, a cracked propeller led to a chain reaction of mechanical failures, and the plane crashed. Orville was badly injured, and Selfridge was killed, the first man to lose his life in an airplane. Within ten months, however, Orville was flying again at Fort Myer, and by the end of July, 1909, he completed the tests, demonstrating a new machine that easily met the Army's requirements.

This year, 1909, was even more memorable than 1908. Dr. Henry W. Walden designed, built, and flew the first American monoplane. J.T.C. Moore-Brabazon became the first British subject to fly in Britain. The first flights were made in Canada, Austria, Sweden, Rumania, Russia, Turkey, and Portugal; and Europe continued to heap honors on the Wright brothers. In October the Crown Prince of Germany presented a diamond and ruby stickpin to Orville after he had made the first flight of over 1,000 feet in elevation. Returning to America, Wilbur thrilled over a million New Yorkers with their first sight of an airplane when he flew up the Hudson River from Governors Island to Grant's Tomb during the Hudson-Fulton celebration. But, earlier in the year, the first flight across the English Channel had already given aviation a tremendous boost.

The *Daily Mail* of London had offered a prize of £1,000 to the first aviator to fly the Channel, and a handsome half-English, half-French airman, Hubert Latham, set out to capture it. Latham was a chain-smoking daredevil who had taken up flying because he feared he had tuberculosis—and preferred a sudden death (he said) to a lingering one. Strangely, his health seemed to improve with every crash. In the end he was killed hunting big game in Africa—by a wounded buffalo.

He made his first Channel attempt from Sangatte, not far from Calais, on July 19. His slender Antoinette monoplane, designed and built by Léon Levavasseur, had flap-type ailerons and a 50-horsepower engine. This engine failed when Latham was about a third of the way across the Channel. Fortunately, his Antoinette floated nicely, and Latham, calmly puffing a long cigarette, patiently waited for rescue by a French destroyer that had been ordered to trail him. M. Levavasseur, a more-than-interested spectator, immediately ordered that another plane be made ready.

After Latham's failure, Louis Blériot decided to make the same attempt in his latest monoplane. He set up headquarters at Les Baraques, a few miles nearer Calais. Bad weather held him up until Latham had time to return with his new Antoinette to his base at Sangatte.

Now began a nerve-racking vigil in which each flier kept one eye on the weather and the other on his rival. On Saturday night, July 24, Latham went to bed leaving strict orders to be called at 3 A.M. if the wind dropped. The wind did drop, but Latham's friends let him sleep serenely on.

Louis Blériot, however, was wakeful. A burn on his foot was troubling him. At 2:30, noticing that the wind had slackened somewhat, he climbed into an automobile, drove to the field where his plane was sheltered in a tent, and had it brought out and made ready. For the next half hour he hobbled around on his crutch, watching the night sky. At 3:30, in the cool, pre-dawn grayness, he took off and flew a couple of circles to test his three-cylinder, 25-horsepower Anzani engine.

This engine had a tendency to overheat. Now it seemed to be running smoothly, so Blériot landed before the overheating process could begin. "Replace the fuel," he said to his mechanic. "In ten minutes I start for England."

It was 4:35 when he took off and pointed his tractor propeller out over the choppy Channel. Latham's friends, watching from a distance, had assumed that Blériot was merely making practice hops. When they saw him head out to sea, they rushed to wake their airman, who struggled into his flying clothes and had his Antoinette brought out. But, by now, the wind was too strong, and Latham could not take off.

Blériot had no compass, no instruments of any kind. He sat hunched over the controls, the air stream from the propeller whipping past his helmeted head. On he flew, holding to what he hoped was the right course, until he saw the great chalk face of Shakespeare Cliff rising from the sea. A cross wind had pushed him to the east; he was nearer Deal than Dover. He swooped down to a rough landing near Dover Castle, almost at the spot where Blanchard and Jeffries had started their cross-Channel balloon flight in 1785. He had covered the twenty miles in thirty-seven minutes.

Two days later, Latham made his second attempt, but his engine failed again and he crashed into the sea less than a mile from the English coast, this time cutting his face rather badly.

Blériot was lionized and feted; Latham was hailed as a gallant and courageous loser. Certainly France was now far ahead in the game, with airplane builders like the Voisins, Henri Farman, Levavasseur, Esnault-Pelterie, and Blériot, and such daring airmen as Latham, Delagrange, Ferber, Lefebvre, Paulhan, and others. Santos-Dumont was also still active; his latest aircraft was the smallest monoplane yet. Christened the *Demoiselle,* it had a wingspan of only eighteen feet and a two-cylinder engine. Some wag remarked that it looked like an infuriated grasshopper, but the little man flew it with his customary skill and gusto.

If a date can be selected when this wonderful new sport of flying came of age, it was probably the fourth week of August, 1909, when the first great air meet was held at Reims, France. The Wrights were not there, but some of their aircraft were—and virtually every other aviation pioneer was on hand.

It was a colorful and exciting week. The first day the field was so soggy that some of the fliers could not get off the ground. Those who did, took off with great gobs of mud clinging to their wheels.

Blériot covered one leg of the speed course and was forced down with grit in his carburetor. Latham, his face still scarred from his Channel plunge, flew airplane *No. 13* and also had engine trouble. Lefebvre recklessly braved a stiff wind to circle the six-and-a-quarter-mile course in nine minutes.

Day after day records were set and then broken. Piloting a new biplane of his own design, Henri Farman won the endurance prize with a flight of more than three hours. He also thrilled the crowd by carrying two passengers. This airplane combined many of the best features of both the Wright and Voisin types and became very popular.

Glenn Curtiss also had a new biplane, derived from his famous *June Bug.* Brown-faced and intense, he captured for America the speed prize offered by New York *Herald* publisher James Gordon Bennett, averaging a marvelous 43 miles per hour. Latham flew as high as he could and claimed the dizzy altitude of 1,200 feet. The judges awarded him the prize, but said he had been no higher than 500 feet.

No one was killed, though there were close calls. On the last day Delagrange's propeller flew apart in mid-air, and he was lucky to make a forced landing without serious injury. Henri Fourneau wrecked his airplane, but walked away from it; so did Louis Bréguet. Blériot was badly burned. He tried to set a new speed record; a fuel line broke and caught fire, and the gas tank exploded.

Despite such mishaps, there was a spirit of excitement and adventure, of freshness and enthusiasm, that people long remembered. Before Reims the practicality of flight was in doubt; after Reims it was a demonstrated fact.

Contemporary reports of the Reims meet speak constantly of "aviator's luck" or of the "charmed lives" of the fliers. And indeed, as had been the case with the very first balloonists, a kind of beginner's luck did seem to prevail. Between 1891, when Lilienthal's first glider flew, and the Reims meet, only four men had been killed in heavier-than-air accidents— three of them in gliders. But with no safety devices of any kind, not even seat belts, this record could not long be maintained. Lefebvre was killed in a Wright machine soon after Reims. Ferber died two weeks later in a Voisin crash. Within a few months, flying a Blériot, Delagrange fell to his death. Altogether, in 1910, thirty-two men were killed—grim notice that the air would not easily forgive man for conquering it.

Even so, 1910 was another year of progress. In January, the first international air meet in the United States was held at Dominguez Field, Los Angeles. The setting was 6,000 miles from Reims, but the cast of characters was familiar. Glenn Curtiss, this time carrying a passenger, topped the speed that had won him the Gordon Bennett trophy in France and set a new world's record of 55 miles per hour. Louis Paulhan, a French pilot soon to become world-famous, set an altitude record of 4,165 feet. People came from hundreds of miles to view such marvels.

The London *Daily Mail* shrewdly realized that the glamour of flying could be converted into paying circulation, a theory amply proven by Blériot's Channel flight in pursuit of a *Mail* prize. As early as 1906 it had offered a prize of £10,000 to the first person to fly from London to Manchester, a distance of almost two hundred miles, in twenty-four hours. Not to be outdone, one competitor made its own offer: £10,000 to the first person to fly to Mars and back within a week; another gaily offered £10,000,000 to anyone who could fly five miles out from London and back again. But the *Mail's* offer was a serious one, and after the Reims air show it was inevitable that within weeks, or months, some of the birdmen, as they were beginning to be called, would be after it.

The first long-distance, cross-country airplane race in history, then, took place in England in April, 1910. It was followed breathlessly by hundreds of thousands of people, and even more than Blériot's flight served notice upon the world that aviation was no longer a dream or a madman's sport, but a new and revolutionary form of travel.

At dawn on April 23 a handsome young Englishman, Claude Grahame-White, set out from Park Royal in an effort to win the *Daily Mail* prize. His Farman biplane was powered by a Gnome rotary engine producing 50 horsepower with a pusher propeller. Grahame-White flew for two hours and landed, half-frozen, at Rugby, a record-breaking cross-country flight of eighty-five miles.

After refueling and thawing himself out, he took off again and got as far as Lichfield, more than halfway to Manchester, before a combination of gusty winds and engine trouble forced him to abandon his attempt to beat the twenty-four-hour deadline. Next day the wind flipped his Farman over, damaged it, and the disappointed airman had to take it back to his base near London for repairs.

By Wednesday, April 27, Grahame-White was ready for another attempt. But now a foreign competitor had appeared in the person of Louis Paulhan, fresh from his triumph at the Dominguez meet in Los Angeles. Paulhan, who also flew a Farman, had had it shipped to Hendon, near London. All that day he was busy assembling it, with the help of Henri Farman himself. At 5 P.M. it was ready, and without even a trial flight the Frenchman announced that he intended to take off and fly as far as he could before darkness set in. This he proceeded to do, following a special

train that had been chartered to guide him, and he got as far as Lichfield before the long twilight ended.

Grahame-White, meanwhile, having reached the conclusion that it was too windy to fly, had settled himself for an afternoon nap. But when word came at six o'clock that Paulhan had started, he flung himself into his Farman, took off despite the wind, and flew some sixty miles before darkness forced him down. This left him still fifty-seven miles behind his rival, and in a frantic effort to close the gap he decided to risk an almost unheard-of thing: a night take-off. At 2:30 the next morning, despite his friends' protests, he soared away from a field feebly illuminated by automobile headlights and vanished into the dark.

By this time the whole country—and indeed much of the world—was wild with excitement. On the route to Manchester people sat up all night hoping to catch a glimpse of either flier. French and British newspapers put out extras. Bulletins were posted in New York and Berlin.

Grahame-White, who knew that a landing in the dark could be fatal, was having his problems. "A great difficulty presented itself in not knowing in the darkness whether I was ascending or not . . . but I soon became accustomed to watching closely the movements of my elevating plane, which was silhouetted before me against the sky. . . . On I flew. The weirdness of the sensation can scarcely be described. I was alone in the darkness with the roar of my engine in my ears."

A friend had agreed to shine his automobile headlights on the wall of an inn on his line of flight. Grahame-White managed to spot this primitive air beacon, then picked up a freight train and followed it into Rugby.

When the Englishman landed he was only a dozen miles behind Paulhan, who had just left Lichfield. But no one appeared to help him in his struggle against a fierce wind on the ground, and his Farman was nearly wrecked for the second time. Meanwhile Paulhan flew straight to Manchester, where a huge crowd cheered him deliriously.

The growing list of accomplishments in the air made for an era of wonderful achievement and sometimes wonderful nonsense. Backyard airplane builders began to appear everywhere, putting together weird-looking contraptions, few of which ever left the ground. In England, Moore-Brabazon, holder of Pilot Certificate No. 1, took a pig for a ride in order to put an end to the old ironic expression of unlikelihood, "when a pig can fly." In France, the first women pilots were publicized. In America, barnacled admirals stirred slightly when a young civilian pilot, Eugene Ely, flew his Curtiss off the deck of a cruiser at Hampton Roads, Virginia, on November 14, 1910. Two months later he performed the considerably more difficult feat of landing on a wooden platform built over the afterdeck of the U.S.S. *Pennsylvania*. Curtiss himself continued to make news, flying down the Hudson River from Albany to New York to win a prize of $10,000 offered by the New York *World*.

Engines and air frames improved, and so did performance. At Boston Harbor, in September, 1910, a huge crowd watched British and American fliers compete for prizes totaling almost $100,000. England's Grahame-White won the speed race—and $10,000—with a flight around Boston Light. Later he took his Farman to Washington and astonished the populace by landing and taking off from a street alongside the White House.

Both Curtiss and the Wrights by now had established flying schools, and the number of pilots was slowly rising. Future generals and admirals were learning to fly, including Benjamin D. Foulois, Frank Lahm, Thomas Milling, H. H. Arnold, John H. Towers, and Marc Mitscher. Harry Houdini, the great magician, was one of the first showmen to exploit the publicity value of airplanes; in 1910 he was flying his own Voisin from one theatrical engagement to another. In October of that same year at St. Louis ex-President Theodore Roosevelt eluded his aides and went for an aerial ride, alarming his pilot, Arch Hoxsey, by refusing to hold on—he was too busy waving with both hands.

This was also the beginning of an age of daredeviltry in the skies, when a handful of young adventurers thrilled crowds by performing seemingly impossible stunts in their flimsy kites. Curtiss and the Wright brothers had formed exhibition teams that toured the country, giving small-town America its first glimpse of the fledgling airplane. At fairgrounds, race tracks, and farm pastures all over the country, crowds watched in shuddering expectation to see if these madmen would tear the wings off their planes—and sometimes they did just that.

The most spectacular of the stunters was Lincoln Beachey, a dirigible pilot who joined Curtiss in 1910. He promptly wrecked two planes, but went on to become, in Orville Wright's opinion, "the greatest aviator of all." Neatly dressed, with celluloid collar and jeweled stickpin, Beachey on the ground looked as sedate as a deacon, but in the air he was a wild man. He could—and did—scoop handkerchiefs from the airfield with his wing tip. He liked to seesaw along a row of hangars, sticking a wing casually into each one as he flew by, and he enjoyed flying under bridges. In 1911 he set an altitude record of 11,600 feet by the simple expedient of filling his gas tank to the brim and

climbing until he ran out of fuel, whereupon he sailed down to a graceful dead-stick landing.

In 1913 a French stunt flier, Adolphe Pégoud, made the loop the loop famous. Chagrined because he had not thought of it first, Beachey became a fanatical looper, often attempting it at suicidally low altitudes. Death was more patient with him than with many of the other early stunt fliers, but in 1915 at the San Francisco Exhibition the wings of his plane collapsed, and he was hurtled into San Francisco Bay. More than 50,000 people saw Beachey's death dive.

By the end of 1910 the range of airplanes was increasing dramatically, thanks more to pilot persistence than to any built-in reliability. Flights were made from Florida to Cuba, and over the Swiss Alps. In the United States, in 1911, Calbraith P. Rodgers made the first transcontinental flight.

But a far more significant American achievement of that year was the introduction, by Glenn Curtiss, of the first practical seaplane. To make water-based takeoffs and landings possible, Curtiss simply fitted a large float beneath the center section of his standard landplane and added smaller auxiliary floats to the wings.

By the beginning of the second decade of the century there were some 350 certified pilots in France. Great Britain ranked next with about sixty. Then came Germany, Italy, and Belgium, with the United States a poor sixth. Important new names in airplane design were being heard from: Sopwith, de Havilland, Vickers, Bristol, Handley Page in England; Sikorsky in Russia; Fokker in Holland; Deperdussin in France. Within a few years war was to etch these names deeply into men's minds.

While aviation was spreading its appeal, lighter-than-air travel was by no means forgotten. During the first decade of the twentieth century, ballooning made a come-back as a sport, and the Gordon Bennett races for free balloons attracted much attention. But more importantly, in France the Lebaudy brothers after 1902 sponsored a series of successful dirigibles, which proved the practicability of powered airship flights. In England, keeping an uneasy eye on the shifting balance of power in Europe, the government also experimented with airship building. But by far the most spectacular developments in lighter-than-air craft came from Germany, where Count Ferdinand von Zeppelin was building the great dirigibles that bore his name.

Zeppelin's first dirigible, launched in 1900, had reached a speed of about 16 miles per hour in some of its trials. The *LZ-2 (Luftschiff Zeppelin 2)*, built in 1905, was equipped with much more powerful engines but was wrecked by the wind after completing only two voyages. But now the government was becoming interested. After the *LZ-3* had made several successful flights, Zeppelin was told that the German army would buy an airship if it could fly for twenty-four hours and make a round trip of 435 miles from her base to an assigned goal.

On August 4, 1908, Zeppelin's newest dirigible, the *LZ-4,* set out to pass the twenty-four-hour test. After an eleven-hour journey, an engine failure compelled the airship to land. Repairs were soon completed, and it ascended a second time, only to be forced down again by further motor trouble. During this second stop for repairs the craft was struck by a squall and dragged along the ground until it exploded in a sheet of flame. Zeppelin and his aides were in despair, but the catastrophe roused the German people to such a pitch of patriotism that within a few weeks they had contributed nearly $1,500,000 to a Zeppelin fund. The government thereupon decided to accept the *LZ-3* and launched a great airship-building program that lasted until the closing days of World War I.

By 1910 public confidence in dirigibles had risen to a point where the first aerial passenger service became possible. Zeppelin himself piloted his craft, the *Deutschland,* on her maiden voyage. She was wrecked a few days later, but four sister ships continued to carry passengers for the next four years without loss of life. These civilian airships were comfortably fitted with carpets and wicker armchairs; cold lunches and wine were served aloft, and thousands of passengers bought tickets to sail in comfort through the skies at about 45 miles per hour.

But it was a risky form of travel. Hydrogen was just as explosive as it had been in Pilâtre de Rozier's day and the huge bulk of the dirigible made it vulnerable to storms and high winds. Zeppelin's fourteenth airship, which had been assigned to the German navy, was wrecked over the North Sea and the crew of thirteen drowned. Three weeks later his eighteenth ship exploded in mid-air, killing its crew of twenty-five. Of the twenty-six dirigibles that Zeppelin built by 1914 more than half came to a violent end.

American experience with airships was not much happier. In 1907 Walter Wellman, a journalist and explorer, set out to fly over the North Pole in the *America,* a much smaller dirigible than the giant Zeppelins. He took off from Spitsbergen on September 2. Bad weather forced him to land on the ice, deflate the airship, and salvage what he could. Another attempt in 1909 was equally unsuccessful.

When Admiral Peary's dash to the Pole with dog-sleds destroyed the novelty of Arctic exploration for him, Wellman decided to rebuild the *America* and attempt to fly the Atlantic. He increased her length, gave her two engines, and added a detachable lifeboat

to her equipment. He also devised a steel guide rope that weighed two tons, with drums of gasoline spaced at intervals as extra ballast. He called it an "equilibrator," certainly a classic misnomer. With a crew of six and a small gray cat as a mascot, he set out from Atlantic City on October 15, 1910.

Almost from the beginning nothing went right. Eighty miles out one engine quit. At night the hydrogen contracted and the dirigible descended so low that it was almost rammed by a schooner. The next morning when the wind rose, the "equilibrator" began to jump from wave crest to wave crest, threatening to shake the gondola loose from the gas bag. Finally, after an erratic flight of several hundred miles, the weary airmen sighted a steamer, and Wellman decided to abandon ship. Valving hydrogen, he descended as low as he dared and released the lifeboat. As the *America* soared away, the "equilibrator" struck the little boat and stove in one side, but all hands were saved, including the cat.

Despite such episodes, the faith of lighter-than-air men in their fragile craft was virtually indestructible. The engineer of the *America,* Melvin Vaniman, put months of work into building another dirigible, the *Akron,* with which he planned to succeed where Wellman had failed. But in July, 1912, on a trial run near Atlantic City the *Akron* burst into flames in mid-air and the crew of five was killed.

Less than ten years had now elapsed since "the miracle at Kitty Hawk," but already airplane designers were beginning to dream of transoceanic flight. In 1913 a landplane piloted by Roland Garros, a French musician-turned-pilot, flew 453 miles across the Mediterranean in less than eight hours. In Russia Igor Sikorsky was designing giant multi-engine airplanes capable of carrying as many as fifteen passengers, and the precursors of all large multi-engine craft.

In 1914 the *Daily Mail* offered a prize of $50,000 for the first successful nonstop transatlantic flight, and the directors of the Panama-Pacific Exposition offered three times that much for the fastest round-the-world flight in less than ninety days. Airmen were eager to meet the challenge. In America Rodman Wanamaker commissioned Glenn Curtiss to build a trimotor seaplane for the transatlantic attempt. The flight, he announced, would be made in July.

But the flight was not made in July. In the struggle to conquer the air—from the very beginning—death had been man's great adversary. This had given flying its intensity, its honesty, its innocence. Now death was to have an ally in the skies, and that ally was man himself.

On June 28, 1914, the age of innocence in the air came to an end. The pistol shots at Sarajevo ended it.

Towed by a racing motor boat, the float glider built by Gabriel Voisin for Ernest Arch-deacon (above) rose from the Seine for a flight of nearly 500 feet on June 8, 1905. On July 18, testing a similar glider built for Louis Blériot, Voisin was dumped into the water. Undiscouraged by the mishap, he and his brother Charles later that year set up the world's first airplane factory near Paris to produce in time the pusher-propeller biplanes that set European standards up to World War I. In March, 1907, Léon Dela-grange made a short hop (below) in one of the first two machines built by the Voisins.

Europe Flies

When news of the Wrights' gliders crossed the Atlantic in 1902 and 1903, Ferdinand Ferber, Robert Esnault-Pelterie, and Ernest Archdeacon unsuccessfully tried to build imitations in France. Unwilling to concede that America had the lead in winged flight, European aviation pioneers generally discounted further reports from the United States.

Wilbur Wright flew a distance of twenty-four miles in October, 1905, but Alberto Santos-Dumont's far more modest flights a year later (above) were nevertheless acclaimed in Europe as the world's first. By early 1908 Henri Farman and Léon Delagrange were making flights of more respectable distances in Voisin airplanes, but aviation in Europe still lagged behind that in America.

Santos-Dumont's awkward biplane, the 14-bis, looked like a tailless goose with an outstretched neck, but in it the Brazilian made Europe's first heavier-than-air, powered flights in 1906: 197 feet on October 23, and (pictured above) 722 feet on November 12.

The prophetic single-wing airplane below—also the first equipped with pneumatic tires—was built in 1906 by Trajan Vuia, a Hungarian living in Paris. Though unsuccessful, Vuia's machine led Blériot to adopt the monoplane configuration in his 1907 models.

The Big Year

In 1908 the Wright brothers ended two and a half years of secrecy to make public flights that won for them the overdue plaudits of an amazed world. Their sudden triumph was scored on two continents.

Wilbur made his public debut in France on August 8, while Orville began tests for the U.S. Army at Fort Myer, Virginia, on September 3. Although an accident cut short Orville's flights, Wilbur continued to astonish European observers with performances in France.

The record for European fliers that year was set by Henri Farman on October 2, but his twenty-five-mile flight failed to equal marks already set by the Wrights. Wilbur completed his European trials on December 31 with a seventy-seven-mile flight lasting two hours and twenty minutes—an achievement that Europe was unable to surpass for eight months. And the first European to fly for over an hour, Paul Tissandier, did so in a Wright machine.

OPPOSITE PAGE: *Orville Wright circles the Fort Myer parade ground on September 9, 1908, making the world's first flight of over one hour. He was seriously injured and his passenger, Lieutenant Thomas Selfridge, killed in the September 17 crash (below), which ended the 1908 Army trials.*

ABOVE: *Wilbur Wright's airplane is taken from its hangar at Hunaudières racecourse near Le Mans, France, where it was first flown. Later, at Camp d'Auvours, Wilbur made 104 flights, setting endurance and altitude records that proved his invention's superiority to European models.*

Glenn Curtiss

Unlike the Wrights, who preferred to work alone, Glenn Curtiss enjoyed the stimulus of team work. His first plane, the *June Bug,* was built for the Aerial Experiment Association, a research organization founded in late 1907 by Alexander Graham Bell. Flying this plane on July 4, 1908, Curtiss won the *Scientific American*'s prize for the first public flight in America of over one kilometer.

Curtiss captured the prize a second time on July 17, 1909, with a fifteen-mile flight in another plane built for the Aeronautical Society of New York. Then, on May 31, 1910, the dynamic young aviator retired the *Scientific American* trophy with a spectacular flight down the Hudson River from Albany to New York.

Curtiss's contributions to aviation went far beyond record-breaking flights. Late in 1910 he established a flight training school near San Diego, California, where the first U.S. Navy pilot, Lieutenant Theodore G. Ellyson, learned to fly. For over two years Curtiss had been experimenting with float planes, and on January 26, 1911, he launched his first practical hydroplane at San Diego. In May, impressed by the designer's further achievements, the U.S. Navy ordered its first two planes from Curtiss.

CULVER PICTURES, INC.

USAF, NATIONAL ARCH

Curtiss scored his first triumph with a 5,000-foot flight in the June Bug *on July 4, 1908, above. The Wrights later won a court case in which they charged that the movable wing tips infringed their patents.*

At right, Curtiss demonstrates the military potential of his seaplane by landing near the U.S.S. Pennsylvania, *anchored in San Diego harbor, on February 17, 1911. After the plane had been hoisted on and off the ship by crane, Curtiss returned to his base.*

Alexander Graham Bell, Curtiss's mentor in the Aerial Experiment Association, built the honeycombed structure at left—a "tetrahedral kite," which was tested on frozen Lake Keuka, New York, in 1909.

BLÉRIOT
DOUVRES
25 juillet 1909

Blériot's historic Channel flight inspired works of art like the dramatic (but slightly inaccurate) tapestry above. In the midst of admiring crowds, the beaming aviator was soundly bussed by his wife (opposite page).

Hubert Latham, pictured at right in his Antoinette, was Blériot's closest rival. His July 19 attempt to fly the English Channel ended in the failure shown at far right.

132

Blériot Flies the English Channel

By mid-1909 French airplane builders were closing the gap in aviation development between America and Europe that Wilbur Wright's stunning 1908 flights in France had revealed. Nothing dramatized the European resurgence more than the first flight across the Channel, made by Louis Blériot on July 25, 1909.

Blériot had built his original monoplane in 1907; although he steadily perfected the design in subsequent models, the No. XI monoplane in which he set out from Calais was still a frail, unproved aircraft. The resolute Frenchman was determined, however, that the honor of the first winged Channel flight should come to his country—just as Blanchard's balloon crossing had brought glory to France 124 years earlier.

"For ten minutes," he recalled of the tense moments after he had left the French coast, "I was alone, isolated, lost in the middle of the foamy sea, seeing nothing on the horizon, not even a boat. . . . These ten minutes seemed long to me, and, truly, I was happy to catch sight of . . . a gray line which detached itself from the sea . . . It was the English coast."

Among the first persons to greet Blériot after his landing near Dover were British officials who went through the solemn ritual of a customs inspection. In London, 120,000 people flocked to see his airplane; and orders for monoplanes deluged the elated Frenchman.

Perceptive observers saw the flight as a grim portent of the future. "The day that Blériot flew the Channel," the British aviator Sir Alan Cobham later wrote, "marked the end of our insular safety, and the beginning of the time when Britain must seek another form of defense besides ships."

133

Men and Machines

Many new figures—some destined to play important roles in the future of flying—appeared on the European aviation scene in 1909 and 1910.

Paced by Blériot, Farman, and Levavasseur, France held the lead over other countries in air progress, but England was now moving to catch up. Many of Britain's first pilots went to France for flying instruction, and the work of early British builders often reflected the influence of French designs. Frederick Handley Page's successful 1910 monoplane was derived from Blériot's famous model, and Geoffrey de Havilland's first practical airplane, built that same year, was patterned after a Farman. Impressed by his design, the British government hired de Havilland as its first official test pilot and designer.

A. V. Roe, the youthful British designer pictured above in his 1909 triplane, called his creations "avroplanes." He built the first enclosed cabin airplane in 1912; another model, his 1911 biplane, led to the famous Avro 504 trainer of World War I

A former artist and automobile racer, Henri Farman (right) was Europe's first successful pilot. Through 1908 he continued to modify a box-kite biplane that the Voisins had built for him, and in 1909 he began producing his own influential planes

ABOVE: *S. F. Cody sits in the biplane in which he won the first British military aviation competition in 1912. Four years earlier the American-born aviator had made the first flight in England.*

At left is the two-rotor helicopter built in 1907 by Paul Cornu. Tested in France on November 13, it managed to lift a man off the ground, but practical helicopters were still thirty years away.

OVERLEAF: *German interest in flying was focused on Count Zeppelin's great airships, one of which is pictured above Lake Constance in 1909, a year before passenger service was started.*

The Aero Club of America sponsored
Glenn Curtiss as the official United States
entry at Reims. In the photograph above
Curtiss is seen rounding the pylon to win
the first Gordon Bennett Trophy with a
clocked speed of 47.65 miles per hour
for the fastest two-lap flight around the
course. Second-place Louis Blériot later
pushed the speed record up to 47.85 miles
per hour in the fastest single-lap flight.

Government and military officials from
several countries came to enjoy the sport
at Reims, and left convinced that the airplane had an important future. The white-
bearded gentleman to the left of the ominous sign on the official box is French
President Armand Fallières. Another spectator was Lloyd George, the future British
Prime Minister in the First World War.

Reims Air Meet

Apart from its success as a social gathering and a grand spectacle," an observer noted of the Reims air meet of August 22-29, 1909, "[the event marked] an awakening to the world of the practicability of human flight."

So rapid was aviation's progress in 1909 that scarcely a month elapsed between Blériot's daring solo flight across the English Channel on July 25 and the opening of the French tournament in which more than thirty planes were entered. The Wrights had just completed their second series of Army trials at Fort Myer and did not attend, but six of their planes flown by European pilots competed with the best designs of European builders.

There were many stars at the meet, including Henri Farman, who set a distance record of 112 miles. His feat of carrying two passengers easily around the six-mile course also proved that the airplane was no longer merely a sports vehicle for a lone pilot.

MUSÉE DE L'AIR

AMBULANCE

ABOVE: *Silhouetted against a murky sky, one of Léon Levavasseur's Antoinettes, flown by Hubert Latham, sets the Reims altitude record of 508 feet.*

Buzzing horses and diving at the stands, Eugène Lefebvre (below) was the Reims clown. One week later, he became the first pilot killed in a crash.

139

FAMOUS AIRPLANES: 1903-1914

WRIGHTS' FIRST PLANE (U.S.) 1903

SANTOS-DUMONT 14-BIS (FR.) 1906

VOISIN-FARMAN (FR.) 1907

CURTISS JUNE BUG (U.S.) 1908

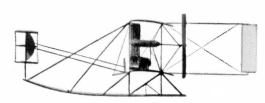

WRIGHT "A" (U.S.) 1909

BLERIOT NO. XI (FR.) 1909

SANTOS-DUMONT DEMOISELLE (FR.) 1909

LEVAVASSEUR ANTOINETTE (FR.) 1909

HENRI FARMAN III (FR.) 1909

CURTISS (U.S.) 1910

WRIGHT "B" (U.S.) 1910

NIEUPORT (FR.) 1910

CURTISS TRIAD (U.S.) 1911

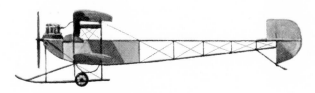

AVRO BIPLANE (BR.) 1911

VICKERS FE-6 (BR.) 1913

MORANE-SAULNIER TYPE "L" (FR.) 1913

DEPERDUSSIN (FR.) 1913

SOPWITH TABLOID (BR.) 1913

SIKORSKY GRAND (RUSSIA) 1913

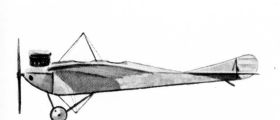

RUMPLER TAUBE (GER.) 1913

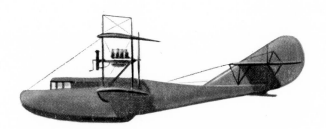

CURTISS AMERICA (U.S.) 1913

FARNBOROUGH BE-2 (BR.) 1913

MARTIN "TT" (U.S.) 1914

DRAWN FOR AMERICAN HERITAGE BY JOHN T. MC COY

Belmont: 1910

America's top aviation event of 1910 was the international air meet held the fourth week of October at Belmont Park. Crowds of up to 25,-000 people came to the New York race track to watch daily contests.

The meet reached a breathless climax on October 30 with a $10,000 elapsed-time race between Belmont and the Statue of Liberty, a round trip of thirty-three miles. By 3:30 P.M., England's debonair Claude Grahame-White had completed the circuit in 35 minutes, 21 seconds. Having wrecked his own plane, the American flier John B. Moisant borrowed a French machine and set out a few minutes past 4. When Moisant returned shortly after 4:30, everyone assumed that he had not completed the course.

The announcement that Moisant had done so—and beaten Grahame-White's time by 43 seconds—brought charges of technical violations, and the tourney ended in controversy.

ABOVE: *The popular Claude Grahame-White captured the Gordon Bennett Trophy at Belmont on October 29 by flying his Blériot twenty laps around the three-mile course at a 61-mile-per-hour speed. Alfred LeBlanc of France was flying 68 miles per hour when he ran out of gas.*

LEFT: *Crowds at the tournament were fascinated by the spectacle of different types of planes performing in the air simultaneously. The spectators are seen watching some of the latest models, including (from top) a Wright, a Farman, a Blériot, an Antoinette, and another Farman.*

RIGHT: *Almost disguised by his helmet and goggles, Orville Wright poses at the controls of the "Baby Grand," the Wright entry in the Gordon Bennett race at Belmont. Orville tested the plane at 70 miles per hour, but Walter Brookins, a member of the Wright exhibition team, smashed it during the take-off for the speed contest.*

Cal Rodgers's meandering transcontinental route of 1911 (avoiding the worst mountains) is traced on the map at right. The first coast-to-coast flight took forty-nine days to complete. But with sixty-nine stops—many of them not scheduled, and twenty-three in Texas alone—the aviator logged only eighty-two hours, four minutes in the air during the 3,220-mile journey.

With a cigar—that became his trademark —clamped in his mouth, and a scar from a previous accident showing on his forehead, Cal Rodgers presented the picture of the daring aviator as he was buttoned into his flying clothes. The layers of sweaters under his jacket provided little protection against the icy cold during his cross-country trip in the open-seat biplane.

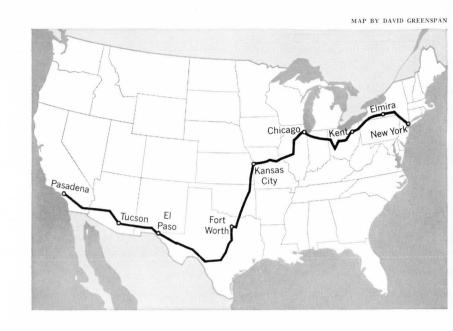

Across America

Late in 1911 William Randolph Hearst offered a $50,000 prize for the first coast-to-coast flight across America. With little chance of meeting Hearst's thirty-day deadline, but determined to reach California anyway, Calbraith P. Rodgers, a rangy motorcycle racer with only sixty hours of flying experience, took off from New York on September 17.

Rodgers had christened his specially-built Wright biplane the *Vin Fiz*, after a soft drink made by his commercial sponsors; and a three-car train carrying his wife and mother, mechanics, and $4,000 worth of spare parts followed—and sometimes led—him as he doggedly crossed the nation in a series of short hops. Pushing his fragile aircraft to the limit of endurance, he reached Pasadena on November 5—nineteen days too late to qualify for the prize.

ABOVE: *Aides rush to extricate Rodgers from the wreckage of his plane after one of the nineteen crashes that marked his halting progress westward. The* Vin Fiz *was repaired so many times that at journey's end only the rudder and a single strut of the original frame remained. Cal himself completed the trip with his leg in a cast.*

BELOW: *People waited in suspense all along Rodgers's route, and even pasture landings like this one had its spectators. At Pasadena a crowd of 20,000 hailed the successful completion of the flight and draped the modest airman with a flag. During an exhibition flight four months later, he crashed into the Pacific and was killed.*

An unusual, but impractical, design of 1910 had wings of fluttering airfoils.

Backyard Builders

By 1910 aerodynamic principles tested by the Wrights, Curtiss, Farman, and Blériot were more or less standardizing the basic shapes of planes; and anyone who wanted to fly could imitate their proven designs. Nevertheless, many persons who had caught "the flying bug" worked on their own ideas and turned out a stream of weird and wonderful contraptions which they hoped would bring them fame and fortune. Most of these machines were unflyable and remained in the backyards and empty fields in which they were built. Strange as they seem today, they are a testament to the many unremembered pioneers whose energies and dreams, though doomed to failure, were an important part of the early feverish, do-it-yourself days of aviation.

Having fashioned graceful wings, this 1909 inventor seems stumped by the power problem.

MUSÉE DE L'AIR

A Kansas creation, perhaps inspired by a water tank.

A French model of 1908 resembled an aerial vegetable shredder.

ARCHIV RÖMER

This 1910 English machine could have been a precursor of modern mobile sculpture.

A "flying saucer" of 1911 had an elaborate circular wing structure and went nowhere.

Aviation's greatest stunt pilot was Lincoln Beachey, shown in the contemporary photomontage above flying under the Niagara Falls bridge after spanning the famous cataract on June 28, 1911. Races between airplanes and automobiles were also popular in flying's first decade. Below, Ruth Law Oliver, in a Curtiss, keeps pace with a speeding racing car.

Exhibition Fliers

In the years before 1914, teams of exhibition fliers thrilled crowds across America with aerial stunts, set new records of speed and endurance, and —in the case of the Curtiss and Wright teams—promoted the aircraft of rival builders. At Belmont Park in October, 1910, John and Alfred Moisant enrolled a group of French and American aviators to tour the United States and Mexico.

Flying during those years was also something of a family affair; Matilde Moisant, John and Alfred's sister, was the second American woman to win a pilot's license. In 1912, sixteen-year-old Katherine Stinson learned to fly; and later her two brothers, Edward and Jack, and her sister, Marjorie, set up a flying school in Texas.

148

The aviator with a chestful of medals at right is
Art Smith, whose exhibition flights in Japan helped
popularize aviation there. Below is Arch Hoxsey,
one of the "Heavenly Twins" (with Ralph Johnstone) of the Wright team. Hoxsey and Johnstone
were killed within a month of each other in 1910.

America's first licensed woman pilot was Harriet Quimby
(above), who was also the first woman to fly the English
Channel. A teammate of Lincoln Beachey in the Curtiss
group was the nerveless Charles K. Hamilton (left). "We
shall all be killed if we stay in the business," he said, but he
was one of the few of the stunters to die a natural death.

149

Growing Up

The military potential of the airplane, though underrated, was not entirely overlooked in the first years of the twentieth century. The French decided to buy war planes in 1909 but were not sure whether to assign them to the artillery or the engineers. Great Britain's Royal Flying Corps was established in April, 1912.

After the U.S. Army had purchased a flying machine from the Wrights on August 2, 1909, the brothers trained the first Army pilots, Lieutenants Frederic E. Humphreys and Frank P. Lahm. A third young officer, Benjamin D. Foulois, was about to solo when the airplane—the Army's sole machine—was damaged on November 5. Humphreys and Lahm were transferred back to their original units, and Foulois was sent to Fort Sam Houston, Texas—to complete his training on his own!

LEFT: *Foreshadowing the aircraft carrier, Eugene Ely lands on the cruiser* Pennsylvania *on January 18, 1911; he had made the first ship take-off two months earlier.*

The Wrights' triumph was an event of our own times, and "In Their Words" now records the legacy of many persons still alive. From this chapter on, unless otherwise noted, the material in these sections is all from personal interviews made in the United States and Europe for this book by the Columbia University Oral History Research Office, and is published here for the first time.

In Their Words . . .

EARLY BIRDS

"The Grandest Sight"

Although streetcar passengers and other citizens of the Dayton area were aware of the Wrights' experiments at Huffman Prairie in 1904, no accurate account of their activities was published until January, 1905. The first eyewitness report by a man who understood the significance of the Wrights' achievement appeared, oddly, in a Medina, Ohio, magazine called Gleanings in Bee Culture. *Its publisher, A. I. Root, wrote the account after watching the first circular flight in history on September 20, 1904.*

Dear friends, I have a wonderful story to tell you—a story that, in some respects, outrivals the Arabian Nights fables . . . God in His great mercy has permitted me to be, at least somewhat, instrumental in ushering in and introducing to the great wide world an invention that may outrank electric cars, the automobiles, and all other methods of travel. . .

I am now going to tell you something of two boys . . . who love machinery, and who are interested in the modern developments of science and art. Their names are Orville and Wilbur Wright, of Dayton, Ohio. . . . I found them in a pasture lot of 87 acres, a little over half a mile long . . .

It was my privilege, on the 20th day of September, 1904, to see the first successful trip of an airship, without a balloon to sustain it, that the world has ever made, that is, to turn the corners and come back to the starting-point . . . there was not another machine equal to such a task as I have mentioned, *on the face of the earth* . . .

The machine is held until ready to start by a sort of trap to be sprung when all is ready; then with a tremendous flapping and snapping of the four-cylinder engine, the huge machine springs aloft. When it first turned that circle, and came near the starting-point, I was right in front of it; and I said then, and I believe still, it was one of the grandest sights, if not the grandest sight, of my life. Imagine a locomotive that has left its track, and is climbing up in the air right toward you — a locomotive without any wheels, we will say, but with white wings instead, we will *further* say—a locomotive made of aluminum. Well, now, imagine this white locomotive, with wings that spread 20 feet each way, coming right toward you with a tremendous flap of its propellers, and you will have something like what I saw. The younger brother bade me move to one side for fear it might come down suddenly; but I tell you, friends, the sensation that one feels in such a crisis is something hard to describe. The attendant at one time . . . said he was shaking from head to foot as if he had a fit of ague. His shaking was uncalled for, however, for the intrepid manager succeeded in righting up his craft, and she made one of her very best flights.

"Everybody Was Excited"

Wilbur Wright's epochal flights in France, in 1908, started a new era for European aviation. Ross Browne, an American who was employed at the time by Louis Blériot, tells of those dramatic days.

The newspapers in Paris were calling Wilbur Wright a fourflusher, and they said that he was bluffing, that he wasn't going to fly. [Roland] Garros told me he asked Blériot, "What's the matter with Wright? Why doesn't he fly?" Blériot said, "He knows what he's doing."

Sure enough, in August he decided he was going to fly it. We all got on a train and went to Paris and drove to the race track where Wright was. We met Wright, and Blériot was all excited. He looked over the machine and he felt the wings. Mr. Wright showed him how the warping was going, and everything.

To make a long story short, he got into the machine that afternoon, got off into the air, and made a beautiful circular flight. You should have seen the crowd there. They threw hats and everything. The Voisins were there, and Delagrange, and, oh, practically everybody in the country who was interested in flying. Everyone was excited, and now, of course, the newspapers said what a marvelous man he was.

Everybody was excited. That was the impetus to all flying. Everybody was interested, it seemed, overnight. Blériot was just tickled to death. He said, "I'm going to use a warped wing. To hell with the aileron!" He was just like a young boy, really.

Wright was very helpful to Blériot. They got along marvelously well—they respected each other and liked each other. You could tell.

All this time Blériot had his mind set on flying the Channel, and he was working toward that end. Well, Latham tried it and came within ten miles of the English coast, so old Blériot couldn't get there quick enough. We packed up, put the machine in a boxcar, and went to a little town called Les Baraques. We got that thing all ready, and on July 25, 1909, Blériot flew. In thirty minutes he landed in Dover.

Well, he was wined and dined, but he couldn't get back quick enough. "Come on, I've got to have more power, I've got to have more power,"

he'd say. You see, he only had a 25-horsepower motor. The first week telegrams and orders started coming in. The mechanics were holding their heads: "What are we going to do?" They were getting mechanics from everywhere. And, you see, there were no air mechanics; they were taken from automobile factories, practically all of them.

Anyhow, Blériot put the XI aside until he had "more power, more power." "I'm going to get a Gnome," he said. So the seven-cylinder rotary motor was shipped down to him. I think Garros told me it cost around four or five thousand dollars. It was the most beautiful thing you ever saw in your life, and Blériot was tickled to death. He couldn't get into the machine fast enough. Anyhow, they got the motor in and he made a flight. He could go at least 15 miles per hour faster than with the old Anzani.

The only trouble that I ever could see with it was that they used castor oil for lubrication, and that would fly back in your face; and, oh, that castor oil was miserable to get off.

England's First Pilot

J. T. C. Moore-Brabazon, later Lord Brabazon of Tara, learned to fly in France and then became the first Englishman to fly an airplane in his own country.

I went over to France in 1908 and got a Voisin machine. Being very distrustful of the Antoinette engine which Farman had used, I put in a Belgian engine called a Vivinus because I thought it would be more reliable. That engine was scarcely man enough for the job. It would only climb if I went without my coat, without my boots, and with only a half gallon of petrol. And under those conditions, in 1908, I did flights of up to five hundred yards at Issy-les-Moulineaux, near Paris.

Down at Châlons-sur-Marne I fitted up an eight-cylinder E.N.V. en-

J.T.C. Moore-Brabazon

gine, and this was powerful enough. I did flights of over a kilometer frequently. I then took the machine back to England, and on May 3, 1909, I made a flight at Isle of Sheppey in my Voisin, which ranks as the first flight ever made in England by an Englishman.

I flew, I suppose, half a mile at about forty feet. The Voisin machine had no side control, you know. The left wing started going down, and the only way to restore that was to turn around to the right so as to accelerate the wing that was down. Well, when I turned the wheel for the rudder, I found that nothing happened because the pin had gone from the shaft. There was nothing to do but land as quickly as I could at an angle of 45 degrees. Well, that, as you can imagine, busts a machine very much. The engine was at the back, and it shot past me, luckily, and didn't catch fire. But I was pinned down to the ground by a lot of wires. I have a keen recollection of the fact that my two Irish terrier dogs had chased this machine. They were licking my face in the middle of the wreckage which was rather odd.

Later that year, the Short brothers built me a machine rather like those

153

of the Wrights'. With it I won the Michelin Cup, and also the *Daily Mail* prize for the first flight in an English machine. It was launched on a rail, and it was difficult to fly.

Pitching was the worst thing. There was no stabilizing plane on it at all. You were always sort of busting about the whole time. That was very disturbing, especially as you were sitting out on the front wing—nothing underneath you and nothing to hold you in. Very insecure. Very alarming, I always found, when you got up to any height at all. The side planes were operated by my feet; the rudder, by my left hand; and the elevator, by my right. It was very difficult, really. I don't know how we did it.

Flying for the Wrights

To publicize their planes both the Wrights and Glenn Curtiss organized exhibition teams of fliers in the United States. Frank Coffyn was an original member of the first Wright brothers' exhibition team.

My first solo was on the infield of the Indianapolis Motor Speedway on June 14, 1910. I was scared to death. Wilbur Wright, who was a very thoughful and wonderful character, held on to the right wing. In those days we had to put the plane

CULVER PICTURES, INC.

Frank Coffyn

on a starting rail with a crosspiece on a skid, and the only control we had of the engine was the advancing and retarding of the magneto.

Wilbur ran along, holding the wing so I could get up enough speed to get off the starting rail. In my excitement I'd forgotten to advance the spark on the magneto, and I just plunked on the ground, much to my embarrassment. But later on that afternoon I tried it again and was able to get off.

I had planned to follow the contour of the race track, but I suddenly realized that there wasn't any track below me! I had forgotten to bank the plane and I was just slung out sideways. But I corrected that and flew out to the end of the infield track; that was the only way I could get down without smashing up the plane. Everybody was furious with me because I'd landed it so far away. We had to truck the plane back to the starting rail.

There were five of us who were called the Wright exhibition team— Walter Brookins, Arch Hoxsey, Al Welsh, Ralph Johnstone, and myself. We were under a two-year contract to fly for the Wrights, and I was the only one of the five who completed the contract. Johnstone, Hoxsey, and Welsh were all killed during that time.

Most of the accidents were caused by stalling the planes flying too slowly. Hoxsey got caught in the downdraft of a grandstand, crashed into the crowd, and killed ten or fifteen people. But I was fascinated by flying, and I felt that I knew the structural limitations of the plane. I did my flying in a careful manner.

We'd fly around the race track, or the field, or wherever we were, and go up a couple of thousand feet, or something like that. Then we'd do some figure eights. In those days it was a very extraordinary kind of flying. There were always great crowds to see us fly, and they were a great nuisance in a way. When we'd come

down, they'd rush out on the field and take souvenirs off of the plane— pieces of the fabric. They gave us a lot of trouble. They got so excited!

We flew at fairs and at aviation meets. The Wright Company gave us a base salary of twenty dollars a week, and fifty dollars a day for every day we flew. In those days I was able to make six or seven thousand dollars a year because they kept me busy and I was able to fly without cracking up. The Wright Company never let us keep any of the prizes we won. The company kept them, and we just got our fifty dollars a day. No bonuses, nothing. It was a sore point with us because the Curtiss Company allowed their pilots to keep 50 per cent of all the prizes they won. We used to get furious about it, but it didn't do us any good. The Wrights wouldn't let us have it.

An Incident With MacArthur

General Benjamin Foulois was one of America's earliest flying officers. After preliminary training from the Wrights in 1909, he joined an Army unit in San Antonio. The following incident, which occurred in Texas in 1911, is taken from an Air Force Historical Foundation interview.

About this time the government was having its fuss with Mexico, as usual . . . and troops from all over the country moved in there and occupied just about 95 per cent of the drill ground [at San Antonio], which left me just a rectangular section about five hundred or a thousand yards long and about five hundred yards wide to do all my flying in . . . [One day] I came in to land, and . . . there was a battery of artillery filing right straight across the field. Well, that disconcerted me a little bit, and I pulled on and went on over the battery, cut my engine, and started to land. I hit the ground [at around 50 miles an hour], and I just touched the ground and went into the air again—up about twenty or twenty-

154

Army flier Benjamin Foulois

ive feet. I was headed straight for
row of tents—the Engineer camp
here right in front of me.

The head tent at that time was
occupied by a young lieutenant of
he Engineers named Douglas Mac-
Arthur. Well, I had the choice of
wrecking the tent or wrecking something else, and while I didn't know he
was in the tent at the time . . . I
turned right down along parallel to
the tents at about twenty or thirty
feet out in front of them. Right
smack in front of me was a horse and
buggy . . . before I could lose my
running speed I hit Mr. Horse right
smack in the chest. He went back on
his haunches and I swear that horse
actually looked at me with the most
astonished expression on his face.

Well, as I started to scramble out
of the plane and do a little cussing
about it, Mr. Horse got back on his
haunches and he whirled, over went
the wagon, and he went hell–bent for
election across the field. When this
happened somebody back behind me
said, "Benny, what in hell are you
trying to do down there?" . . . hearing this, MacArthur came sticking
his head out of the tent and wanted
to know what I was doing. I said,
"Well, it was a choice between your
tent and that horse. . . . Horses and
men are expendable down here, but
government property like tents, etc.,
I'd have to pay for before I knew it."

"Please, a New Machine?"

*The father of United States Marine
Corps aviation was Lieutenant Alfred A. Cunningham, who first flew
in August, 1912, after less than three
hours' instruction. A few months
later he addressed the following plea
to Captain W. I. Chambers, officer-
in-charge of Naval aviation.*

My Machine, as I told you and Mr.
Towers probably told you, is not in
my opinion fit for use. I built it from
parts of the Burgess F and Wright B,
which are not exactly alike and nothing fitted. I had to cut off and patch
up parts and bore additional holes in
beams in order to make them fit. The
engine bed, made by Burgess, was
not exactly square with the front
beam, so the engine had to be
mounted a little out of true (with
reference to the engine bed). I have
made over 200 flights in this machine
and recently, in spite of unusual care
of myself and men, something seems
to vibrate loose or off a majority of
the flights made. One of the propeller
shafts is the same one used with the
Cyro motor in the old machine. It is
the only left-hand shaft here. While
the engine runs smoothly, it does not
deliver nearly as much power as
when it was newer, and even then, it
did not have enough power to fly

Lieutenant Alfred A. Cunningham

safely in any but smooth weather. It
is impossible to climb over a few hundred feet with a passenger. The
whole machine has just about served
its usefulness, and I would like very
much to have a new machine of the
single propeller type. Lt. Arnold, of
the Army, after seeing the machine
run and examining it, said that none
of the Army fliers would go up in it.
Will you kindly let me know what the
prospects are for my getting a new
machine.

Selling Aviation

*Beckwith Havens began his aviation
career as Glenn Curtiss's first airplane salesman. He sold no planes,
but became a flier and from 1911 to
1913 toured the country as one of the
best-known pilots of the Curtiss Exhibition Company.*

I once had a one-day date in Enid,
Oklahoma, on a Sunday. The flight
was put on by a newspaper there.
The editor met me at the train and
took me to his house for lunch. He
told me that they had had J. A. D.
McCurdy there the year before, but
due to the high winds he hadn't been
able to fly. Then he said, "You know,
our people just don't believe it's possible to fly." With that, a gust of
wind slammed the front door wide
open and blew a picture right off the
wall. I thought, "Oh, Boy, am I going to have trouble here!"

We went out to the field where
they had set up a kind of bleachers
right on the prairie. A big crowd began to gather, with the usual thing;
they were kind of skeptical, and there
was booing and so on. The wind was
pretty high and I thought, "This is
going to be rough."

In that kind of situation we used
to try to stall because the wind usually would go down toward sundown.
To kill time, and also to see if there
were any gopher holes that might
trip me up, I started to walk away
from the grandstand. Also, I wanted
to get away from all those people

hooting at me and making me nervous. I got out aways and heard a horse galloping after me. It was the sheriff in a buckboard behind a calico pony. He was in a buckboard because he only had one leg—he'd had a leg shot off in a gun fight. He pulled his pony back so that he slid up alongside me, looked down at me, and said, "Son, are you going to fly?"

I said, "Yes, sir," and he said, "Git in here." Back we went at a gallop and pulled up in a sliding stop in front of the grandstand. He got up on his one good leg, hitched his gun belt up, held up one arm for quiet. When the crowd had quieted down a bit, he yelled at the top of his lungs, "Folks, give this boy a chance. This is the last ride he takes before he rides with the undertaker."

With that everybody laughed. That broke the tension. I took off, and everything was all right, so I was a big hero. But that's the way it was. We were out there convincing the skeptics that it was possible to fly heavier-than-air.

"An Agonizing Dilemma"

The memorable aviation year of 1913 saw many long-distance flights, including the first nonstop crossing of the Mediterranean Sea. Roland Garros, a French aviator, covered the 453 miles from the French Riviera to Tunisia in less than eight hours. In this excerpt from his previously unpublished diaries, Garros describes some anxious moments of that flight.

The first hour went by so happily that my sensations, at first acute, mellowed. Everything sang confidence: the surrounding calm, the even hum of the motor, the soft slipping of the wings through the fresh air. Behind me, the Esterel Mountains, almost obliterated, still marked the place from which my friends' good wishes followed me. To my left, Corsica was so clear it seemed next door . . .

Roland Garros

Suddenly, a sinister sound of breaking metal. The whole plane shook. I thought I was lost. Yet the motor continued to turn, with a regular "knock" that reverberated through my body. Instinctively I aimed toward land—an hour's flight away. On the hood a hump appeared; the metal was punctured, and drops of oil seeped through and were thrown into my face by the wind. Obviously one of the motor parts had come off. Why didn't it stop?

Much anxiety in the next few moments. But excessive fright subsides quickly . . . I had reduced my motor speed to the minimum. The machine seemed suspended in space.

An hour went by. Finally I sighted Ajaccio. It was up to me to end the adventure. But that would have been deplorable. "It'll hold out for a few minutes yet—as far as Sardinia," I thought. "There, I'll have two hours over land and can survey it comfortably . . . "

The trip continued without incident. I became accustomed to the terrible vibrations. Over Sardinia I ran into air currents and a head wind that slowed me. The sky lost its clarity and cloud masses forced me to drop from

1,500 to about 800 meters. Tim went by. There was Cagliari. A agonizing dilemma: would I land o go on? I was almost an hour behin schedule; my fuel reserves were ex hausted . . . Above all, I had a moto that had been running for five hour minus one of its parts.

I scanned the ground for my me chanic's signals. The sun was blind ing; I saw nothing. Besides, I hadn' yet made up my mind. To land wa to mutilate this crossing, to spoil : dream . . . I'll never forget that mo ment of hesitation. A mysteriou force, stronger than my reason and my will power, carried me along to ward the sea.

The Greatest Showman

The legendary Lincoln Beachey wa America's greatest stunt pilot, thrill ing audiences throughout the coun try with breath-taking loops an dives. Hillery Beachey, himself ar early dirigible and airplane pilot, re calls his brother's spectacular career

My brother first flew a plane in the winter of 1910. He got into a plane and his big trouble was that he wanted to stick it right up into the air. There wasn't enough power to do it and she stalled—she'd lose

The great (and natty) Lincoln Beachey

156

peed, come down on her tail, and reak up. He broke up several of 'urtiss's planes in Los Angeles. Curss was afraid to look—just turned way when he first saw him fly.

Lincoln's main stunt was to come own headfirst, to make a vertical ive from 5,000 feet with his motor hut off, and land exactly where he anted to.

I remember once in Dallas, Texas, e made two landings from this dive f his, and each time he came down ithin a foot of the other. He used o dive over a race track, and he'd ome to the starting wire and dive nder it, and not hit the ground or he wire either.

I've seen him come down from ,000 feet, straight down, and take oth hands off the wheel and hold hem out, and let the plane come out f it itself.

In 1912 Curtiss and Wright had oth sold planes to the Army, and heir specification was that they had o make a figure eight in a certain mount of space. They were flying he Wright plane a little shorter than he Curtiss. Curtiss asked my brother o go down there and show them how hey could fly. My brother went down nd took his hands off the wheel and, o hands, flew shorter—a smaller igure eight—than anybody had ever lown before. The next day he got a etter from the Army asking him not o fly an airplane at any Army field gain. Why not? Well, Army fliers night try to emulate him, and kill hemselves.

My brother wanted speed, that's he main thing. And, he wanted to e a showman. I remember seeing im make a landing on the backtretch of a race track where there vere trees hanging over the track. He'd level off on one side, then turn nder the trees to make his landing. That was somewhere in the Middle Vest where William Jennings Bryan vas talking. I think they both got a housand dollars a day, Bryan and Lincoln Beachey.

"Good Luck, Young Feller"

Ruth Law Oliver, one of the early woman fliers, was a star attraction at fairs and exhibitions. She also set several altitude and long-distance records, one of which she describes.

I had been flying for several years, just making these exhibition flights in and around single spots—a few miles here, a few miles there. I had a great desire to take off and go somewhere in flight, never having done it. Well, in 1916 there was a lot of excitement about long-distance flying. So I brought my exhibition plane to the Curtiss factory. They put overhangs on the upper wings to give it more lift and extra tanks for gasoline. Where we normally carried eight gallons of gas, I could carry fifty-three. We figured that with fifty-three gallons I could break Victor Carlstrom's long-distance record [in the United States], which was about 490 miles.

We took the plane to Chicago, and I left Grant Park there at four o'clock in the morning. It was then November 19. I was sitting out in front and it was pretty cold. We had put on a little aluminum shield to cover my feet and limbs. I had heavy chauffeur's fur-lined gloves, a mask of leather that I could just look through, and several layers of clothing—leather coat on the outside and leather breeches. So I didn't look any more like a woman than anything at all. A man, a workman with his lunch pail, came hurrying over, stretched out his hand, and said, "Well, good luck, young feller. I hope you make it." I guess his good wishes helped me because I did make it. I flew nonstop to Hornell, New York—512 miles in five hours and forty minutes.

The Geodetic Survey had supplied me with maps covering the route, great big maps. I couldn't handle those in an airplane so I had to cut strips out about eight inches wide and paste them on a strip of thin cloth. Then the boys at the Curtiss

Ruth Law Oliver

factory made what they call a map box. It was a box with two rollers similar to the rollers in a camera. So I fastened the strip of map on those rollers—it had a glass top. Having no instrument panel, I had to tie it to my left knee so that I could reach it and turn the map to keep the area under me all the time in view.

I didn't get lost at all. The only thing that caused me considerable concern, outside of being cold, was that flying over Cleveland I looked back—the oil gauge was back of me on the radiator—and there was no pressure. But I thought, "I might as well keep going 'cause I can't land here." The motor kept right on going until I got to Hornell. The weather was fine, though cold; and I had a following wind, so I was able to fly at a hundred and some odd miles an hour. That assisted me in making the record.

The next morning I went on to New York City and landed at Governors Island, twenty-seven hours after I had left Chicago. The New York Central Railroad people came out and said, "You see, New York Central is still the fastest time between Chicago and New York, only twenty-two hours!"

157

CHAPTER 5

ÉTABLISSEMENT CINÉMATOGRAPHIQUE DES ARMÉES

An unusual air photograph of the early part of the war shows a French pilot and observer awaiting combat over the Champagne front

WORLD WAR I

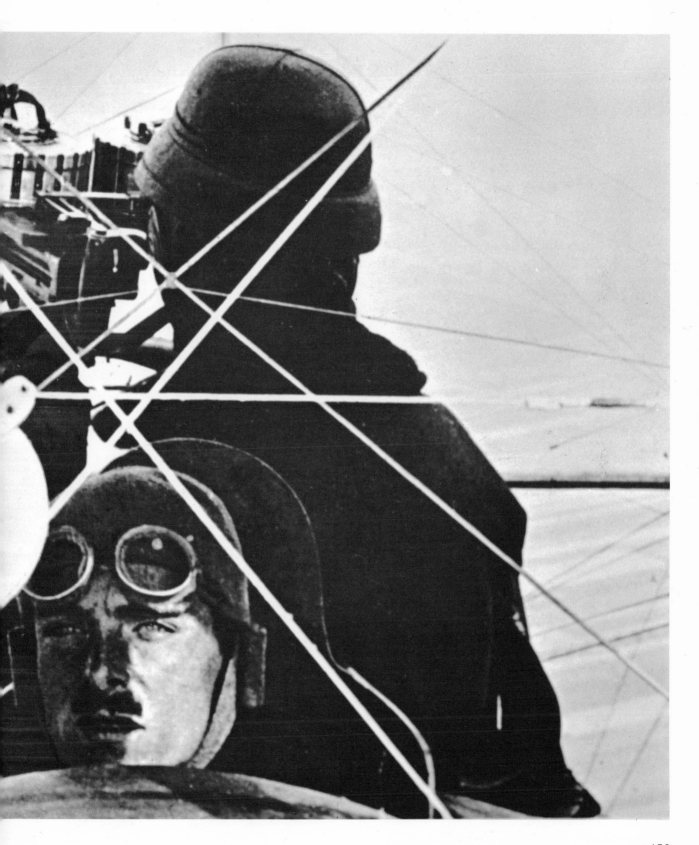

At the outbreak of war in 1914, the airplane was still a toy, though potentially a deadly one. Planes had been built that could fly at speeds of over 125 miles per hour. Others could reach altitudes of 25,000 feet, or fly nonstop for more than a thousand miles. These were highly-specialized aircraft: high performance in one area usually ruled out capability in others. But it was inevitable—with war acting as a spur to technology—that the airplane would emerge from its first conflict not only a more sophisticated machine but also a highly versatile weapon.

As always, there were those who shrank from the pain of a new idea. In 1910, for example, the British War Secretary announced serenely: "We do not consider that aeroplanes will be of any possible use for war purposes." Others, including even the Wright brothers, took the optimistic view that the airplane—seeing all and knowing all—would actually abolish war. "When my brother and I built and flew the first man-carrying flying machine," Orville sadly wrote in 1917, "we thought that we were introducing into the world an invention which would make further wars practically impossible."

But in every major European country during the prewar years a few realists struggled against government inertia and lack of funds to develop warplanes that they felt certain would be needed. As a result, when hostilities began, the adversaries were fairly evenly matched: roughly 1,200 German combat planes to 1,000 for France and Britain.

The British, who had organized the Royal Flying Corps in 1912, had varieties of the BE-2, a steady and reliable reconnaissance biplane made by Captain Geoffrey de Havilland, a designer and test pilot who later went on to found his own aircraft company. His plane could carry two men, guns, and a camera at speeds up to 75 miles per hour and stay up for three hours. The English also had the Avro 504, which they soon began to use for light bombing, and the Bristol Scout and the Sopwith Tabloid, single-seater planes capable of speeds of over 90 miles per hour. The French had similar types, notably the Morane-Saulnier monoplane and the Nieuport biplane for scouting, and the slower Farman "pusher" biplane for observation. Germany had several different heavy biplanes for artillery spotting and reconnaissance, and for scouting adopted the Albatros biplane and the Taube ("Dove"), a monoplane whose swept-back wings had given it its name.

The war began in August, 1914, and, as the visionaries had foreseen, planes were in it from the beginning. When the British hurried Lord Kitchener's little expeditionary force to France, thirty-seven combat planes went with it. Only one of them had a machine gun. On his own initiative one of the British pilots, Lieutenant L. A. Strange, mounted a Lewis machine gun on a French Farman and on August 22 attempted to chase an enemy aircraft. The German got away from him because the Farman could not rise above 3,500 feet. Deciding that the weight of the gun was the main reason for this shortcoming, Strange's commander ordered him to leave such weapons to the infantry where they belonged.

The principal use of planes by both sides at first was for observation of the enemy's positions and activities, and the demand was for slow, stable aircraft from which fliers could study and photograph the ground. For a time this concept guided official thinking; the German High Command actually tended to restrict production of the faster planes because greater speed made good camera work difficult. Few of the observation planes carried arms; if an Allied spotter met a

German reconnaissance plane, the pilots were quite likely to wave companionably to each other and go on about their business.

There were a few attempts at bombing, but they were crude and ineffective. Only weeks after the war began a German lieutenant hand-dropped two 4-pound bombs, while he was flying over the outskirts of Paris. Another pilot, in what was probably the first attempt at psychological warfare from the skies, dropped a note tied to an old cavalry boot stating that the German army was at the gates of Paris and urging the people to surrender.

As the war progressed, the Allies too began to use bombs, sending some planes over German-occupied Brussels. The first long-range strategic strike in history came in November, 1914, when the British daringly sent three Avro 504's to bomb the Zeppelin sheds at Friedrichshafen, on Lake Constance in southern Germany. Little damage was done to the Zeppelin base and one of the British planes was downed, but the surprised Germans retaliated by forming a bombing squadron which they called the "Ostend Carrier Pigeons." By January, 1915, they were raiding Dunkirk, France, behind the Allied line, flying in formation and—surprisingly—flying at night.

Inevitably, single-seater scouts of both sides were given the assignment of driving off enemy bombers and reconnaissance planes. But for months their armament remained incredibly primitive. Late in July, 1915, Captain Lanoe Hawker of the Royal Flying Corps took off in his Bristol Scout armed with a cavalry carbine mounted on the starboard side of the fuselage and pointed at an outward angle so that the bullets would clear the propeller. Over the Ypres salient, flying with one hand and firing with the other, Hawker attacked three German two-seaters in succession and shot down two—an exploit considered so remarkable at the time that he was awarded England's highest military decoration, the Victoria Cross.

Such accurate deflection shooting from a moving platform at a moving target was beyond the marksmanship of most gunners. What was needed was a gun that could fire straight forward so that the whole airplane could be aimed at the enemy, thus eliminating one of the variables. Ironically, a device to enable a machine gun to fire through a rapidly spinning propeller had been patented in England before the war and sent to the War Office, where it vanished in the fogs of officialdom. The French had also tried the idea and abandoned it, mainly because the gun they used was not satisfactory.

In February, 1915, Roland Garros, the famous French pilot who had been the first man to fly across the Mediterranean in 1913, mounted a forward-firing automatic rifle on his Morane monoplane close behind the propeller. The rear of the propeller was armored with triangular steel plates designed to deflect such bullets as might hit it. It was a potentially suicidal device, but Garros went into battle with it and within sixteen days had scored five victories over Germans who did not bother to take evasive action when they saw him coming at them straight on. Garros thus became the first Allied "ace" of the war, acquiring a name that was already widely used in France to describe an outstanding performer in any field of endeavor. The advantage that Garros gained with his forward-firing gun lasted until April 19, 1915, when engine trouble forced him to land behind enemy lines. Both the pilot and his plane were captured (Garros eventually escaped), and the armored propeller was closely examined.

Early in the war the Germans had been wise enough to employ a brilliant Dutch airplane designer named Anthony Fokker. Now, with Garros's captured plane in their hands, the Germans called Fokker from his factory at Schwerin, where he was building his first warplane, the *Eindecker* [monoplane] *I*. They showed him the Garros device and told him to duplicate it, or come up with something better.

Fokker, who had never seen a machine gun at close range, returned to Schwerin with the propeller from the captured French plane and a standard German Parabellum machine gun. His solution of the problem was essentially a simple one. Garros had fired through his propeller blades at random—a kind of airman's Russian roulette, since a bullet at any time might strike the flier's own propeller. Fokker realized that the firing of the weapon must be synchronized with the revolving of the propeller blades; this he did—in two days' work—by connecting the gun and engine with a rod-and-lever mechanism which allowed the gun to fire only at safe intervals. This "interrupter gear" was far from foolproof (later, the German ace Max Immelmann shot off his own propeller twice while using it), but Fokker installed it on one of his own monoplanes and demonstrated it successfully to a group of German officers.

The skeptical military men insisted that Fokker personally test the weapon in action. Under protest—as a Dutchman he was technically a noncombatant—Fokker took off from a front-line airfield a few days later, got a French Farman in his sights, and then abruptly decided that, as he later said, "the whole job could go to hell . . . I had no wish to kill Frenchmen for Germans. Let them do their own killing!"

This the Germans were eager to do. The first Fokker Eindecker equipped with the new interrupter gear went to Lieutenant Oswald Boelcke, a schoolteacher-turned-pilot who was then Germany's leading ace. The second went to Lieutenant Max Immelmann, who shot down the first plane at which he fired.

Immelmann, whose moody arrogance contrasted sharply with Boelcke's sunny amiability, was already famous for an aerial combat maneuver that bore his name, a half-roll at the top of a steep climb in which the controls were momentarily reversed—the elevators acting as rudder, and the rudder as elevators. Actually, this "Immelmann turn" had been known to stunt fliers before the war. But the "Eagle of Lille," as Immelmann was called, remained the idol of Germany until his death in 1916.

Thanks to Fokker's ingenuity, the Germans were dominant in the air for several months. In an effort to halt the "Fokker scourge," as the Allied press soon began calling it, the British stepped up production of planes with pusher propellers, like the Vickers Gunbus, in which the gunner could fire forward. After several of their pilots had shot themselves down using the Garros deflector device, the French tried mounting a machine gun on the top wing of their Nieuports and firing over the propeller. It gave them a clear forward field of fire but slowed down their fighters by increasing drag. Meanwhile, no Allied reconnaissance plane dared to fly without heavy escort. On February 7, 1916, one British BE-2 survey plane alone was assigned an escort of no less than twelve fighters.

The Germans were so jealous of their secret weapon that they forbade pilots flying Fokkers equipped with the new gear to cross into enemy territory. But in April, 1916, one hapless German, lost in a fog, landed by mistake behind the Allied lines. The plane was captured, the gun examined, and the device instantly copied for Allied use. Later a much more efficient hydraulic synchronizer was introduced by the British.

In time new Allied war aces began to make a mark: Georges Guynemer and Jean Navarre for France; Lanoe Hawker and Albert Ball for England. Guynemer, a frail-looking youngster suffering from tuberculosis, was shot down seven times before he finally disappeared on a mission in 1917. Navarre, who wore a woman's silk stocking for a helmet, was a wild and impulsive fighter. On one occasion, when Zeppelins were reported over Paris, he took off clutching a butcher knife "to disembowel the monster." Closer inspection revealed the monster to be nothing more than a cigar-shaped cloud. Badly wounded in 1916, he did not recover for two years.

In November, 1916, Hawker went down under the guns of Manfred von Richthofen, who was to become the top-ranking ace of the war. In a savage, dramatic battle the two men fought from 10,000 feet down to 150 in plain view of the troops in the German and British trenches. Finally a bullet from Richthofen's red Albatros creased Hawker's skull, and the unconscious pilot crashed to his death.

Albert Ball, a dreamy-eyed youth who raised rabbits and vegetables around the airfield to keep his mind off the war, was a deadly killer in the air. He ran his score up to forty-four victories before—like Guynemer—he disappeared. One version of his death is that, having developed a casual habit of buzzing a church tower in German-occupied territory to see what time it was, he was shot down by a machine gun that the enemy had cunningly planted in the tower.

Ball believed in closing in on an enemy plane almost to the point of collision before opening fire, a tactic used by most of the great air fighters. When Richthofen, then an unknown, first met Oswald Boelcke, he asked him how he had achieved his string of victories. Boelcke smiled. "I fly close to my man," he said, "aim well, fire, and then he falls down."

There was more than that to air combat, and Boelcke knew it. He made detailed studies of airplanes, their capabilities, strengths, and weaknesses. He hand-picked his pilots and painstakingly taught them combat tactics: deflection shooting, use of cloud cover, decoys, wind direction, attacks from out of the sun or from the enemy's blind spots. It was Boelcke who first suggested that fighters be formed into attack squadrons instead of being limited to escort duty. It was he who organized and trained the "flying circus" that Richthofen later took over, and it was he who on June 23, 1916, shot down Victor Chapman, the first American airman to die in the war. Chapman was one of the original members of the Lafayette Escadrille, a volunteer unit of American fliers fighting under the French flag.

Boelcke seemed immune to enemy bullets, and his squadron-mates considered him invincible in the air. But on October 28, 1916, in an attack on two British de Havillands, Erwin Bohme, one of his best pupils, brushed the wing of his plane against Boelcke's. The Albatros fell out of control and Boelcke was killed. Even his enemies were saddened. The Royal Flying Corps flew over his grave and dropped a wreath inscribed to "our brave and chivalrous foe."

The adjective was not ill-chosen; there *was* chivalry in air combat in those days. The risks were so appalling—wings could come off in a dive, a single bullet could turn a gasoline tank into an inferno—that fliers felt a kinship that transcended nationalism.

For the fighter pilots war in the air was strangely intimate. Often, thanks to the personal insignia emblazoned on most planes, they knew exactly who their opponent was, and air duels were often likened to clashes between armored knights of medieval romance.

Occasionally a victor would spare his adversary's life. A story is told that when Guynemer and the German ace Ernst Udet met in 1916, they fought for eight minutes—until Udet's guns jammed. The Frenchman flew close, watched the German hammering futilely at his useless weapons, waved a sympathetic hand, and flew away. Udet survived two combat parachute jumps in World War I to become a high-ranking Luftwaffe officer under Hitler—and eventually a suicide.

Many pilots unafraid of bullets were terrified of fire. The pack parachute had been invented by an American showman before the war, and spotters in observation balloons were equipped with chutes packed in leather tubes. But no Allied pilots and—until near the end of the war—few Germans carried them. The excuses were both cruel and stupid. It was claimed that parachutes were not sufficiently reliable to justify mass production and that if pilots had them, they might be tempted to bail out without a fight. As a result, numerous lives were lost unnecessarily. It was not unusual for airmen to jump from blazing planes, preferring quick deaths to being roasted alive.

By the summer of 1916 the Fokker Eindecker was obsolescent, inferior to the Nieuport and to two new Allied fighters, the British Sopwith Pup and the French Spad, whose initials stood originally for *Société pour la Production des Appareils Deperdussin* and later, when Blériot took over production, for *Société pour Aviation et ses Dérivés*.

It was clear, now, to the high command of both sides that to attain air supremacy was to blind the enemy. Great air battles raged over Verdun and the Somme salient, but neither side was able to maintain a decisive advantage; the tide of victory ebbed and flowed as Allied and German designers produced new and more effective weapons. Tracer bullets made their first appearance in air combat in July, 1916, when the bloody struggle on the Somme was at its height. Fighter planes began to be armed with rockets to shoot down observation balloons. The first crude flying bombs were discussed and some experiments were made, but none was ever flown operationally.

Decisions regarding the most effective use of available aircraft began to plague the top commanders. Unable to match the air power massed by the Germans for the assault on Verdun, the French ordered their planes to attack the German rear in other sectors. Anguished cries from field commanders for air protection put so much pressure on the German General Staff that they sacrificed their air supremacy over Verdun—and the fortress did not fall.

The war in the air was not limited to the western front. In the south, Austrians fought Italians in the skies, and a fiery Italian officer named Giulio Douhet

got himself court-martialed for criticizing his superiors' failure to exploit air power properly. In the east, the Russians tried to make up for inferior equipment and organization with suicidal courage. Their first victory was scored less than a month after the war began—and by an unarmed plane. When his airfield was raided by three German planes, Captain P. N. Nesterov took off in a French Morane and deliberately rammed the German leader. Both planes crashed and both pilots were killed. A. A. Kazakov, the top-ranking Russian ace with seventeen victories, also destroyed his first Albatros by ramming it with the undercarriage of his own fighter. With the collapse of the Russian war effort in 1917, he joined the British fighting in northern Russia.

A. P. de Seversky, the most famous Russian naval flier, was shot down on his first night-bombing flight early in the war and lost his right leg when the bomb his seaplane was carrying exploded. Later, with special permission from the Czar, he returned to active service and became Chief of Fighter Aviation for the Baltic area. In fifty-seven operational flights he shot down thirteen German planes and proved that a missing leg was no handicap. He was in the United States when the Bolsheviks seized power in 1917 and he remained in America to continue a distinguished career as a test pilot, aircraft designer, and tireless advocate of air power.

Though seaplanes and flying boats never received the publicity or acclaim that was showered on land-based fighters, they were widely used by both sides for reconnaissance, bombing, and torpedo attack. In May, 1915, a British patrol seaplane warned Admiral Beatty of the approach of the German fleet at Jutland, and by the end of the war the British had developed long-range seaplanes that could cross the North Sea and kill Zeppelins patrolling the German coast.

Bombers, too, evolved rapidly from the first slow reconnaissance two-seaters whose primitive missiles were hand grenades, steel-tipped darts, or sometimes simply bricks. The effective British light bomber, the de Havilland DH-4, was replaced in later years by the DH-9 and the DH-9A, which could carry a bomb load of 450 pounds under the wings. For a heavy bomber Great Britain had the Handley Page 0/400, a twin-engine machine that could carry 1,800 pounds of bombs; the Germans relied mainly on the Gotha, which had similar performance. By the end of the war the British had produced a number of giant four-engine bombers capable of carrying 7,500 pounds of bombs. They were designed to bomb Berlin and were ready to do so when the Armistice was signed.

Probably the single most significant aeronautical innovation that appeared during the war came from a

German engineer, Hugo Junkers. In 1915 Junkers produced an all-metal monoplane with a fully-cantilevered wing—no external struts or bracing. The cantilever idea was applied with great success to the excellent Fokker fighters of 1917 and 1918.

While revolutionary advances were being made in Europe, aviation in the United States was lagging badly. Almost no progress had been achieved in the development of military aircraft. For three years after the Army had accepted its first Wright machine in 1908, that lone airplane had been the United States air force. Each year the Signal Corps had tried in vain to get additional aviation funds. Not until March, 1911, was money finally appropriated for the purchase of five more planes.

By the end of 1913, of the twenty-eight aircraft purchased by the Army, nine had crashed. Of some forty Signal Corps officers trained as pilots, eleven had been killed. The survivors grew restless and dissatisfied with what they considered indifference and poor leadership in the higher echelons. Feeling that they had nothing to lose, they stated their grievances in a sharply-written round-robin letter and fired it off to Washington. This out-of-channels maneuver did not endear them to the top brass. The infuriated Chief Signal Officer described the fliers as "deficient in discipline and the proper knowledge of the customs of the service and the duties of an officer." It was an accusation that was to go echoing down through the years.

When tension arose along the Mexican border in 1914 and 1915, detachments of the 1st Aero Squadron were sent to Texas. In March, 1916, after the revolutionary leader Pancho Villa crossed the Rio Grande and killed seventeen Americans, eight planes were assigned to General John J. Pershing to aid in his pursuit of the Mexican. As things turned out, it was the planes that needed help; battered by dust storms, windstorms, and snowstorms, unable to fly over the Mexican mountains, they were finally given the meek task of carrying messages.

By April, 1916, only two Army airplanes were left and these were declared unfit for service. The fiasco prodded Congress into appropriating $13,000,000 for the expansion of military aviation, but the lawmakers were soon to learn that dollars could not be converted into aircraft overnight. Of the 366 machines ordered in 1916, only sixty-four were delivered—and most of the manufacturers who were under contract simply could not build the planes and asked to be relieved of the assignment.

When America entered the war on April 6, 1917, the Aviation Section of the Signal Corps had 131 officers, most of them pilots; about one thousand enlisted men; and fewer than 250 aircraft. This in itself was frightening, but the over-all picture was worse. There was only one airplane plant—Curtiss—that could be called a factory; the rest were hardly more than shops. There were perhaps a dozen aeronautical engineers of sound reputation, but none was even remotely qualified to design an up-to-date fighting airplane. Tight censorship in Europe had prevented such knowledge from crossing the Atlantic, and the Allies had steadfastly refused to allow American air observers in Europe to visit the fighting fronts.

The deficiencies were not recognized at first. Within days after the American declaration of war, military missions were arriving from Europe clamoring for planes. Grandiose plans and dazzling promises were made. One program called for "22,625 airplanes, plus 80% spares and 44,000 engines"—this from a nation that had produced fewer than a thousand planes in the thirteen years since Kitty Hawk. The original plans also promised 263 American squadrons in action by June, 1918. But when the war ended in November, only forty-five American squadrons were at the front, and not a single American-designed combat plane had been used in the fighting.

Inevitably, the goals had to be scaled down, with much recrimination, faultfinding, and bitterness. One decision, made fairly early, was to mass-produce only a few well-tested types of aircraft. Curtiss was given a large order for its JN-4D's and for flying boats. The JN-4D, better known as the Jenny, became the standard training plane. The British DH-4 was selected for American mass production; later, the Handley Page 0/400 bomber and a three-engine Caproni bomber were also built in the United States. But only the DH-4 was produced in quantity, nearly 5,000 being turned out by the end of 1918.

These DH-4's and the Handley Page 0/400's were powered by Liberty engines, America's most significant technical contribution to the air war. Two automobile engineers, Jesse G. Vincent and J. G. Hall, who also had some experience with aircraft power plants, are often credited with designing the Liberty engine during one forty-eight-hour session in a Washington hotel room. Actually, a number of engineers from private industry and the government contributed ideas to the project. The initial design, presented at the end of May, 1917, called for a V-8 engine with light steel cylinders that would deliver up to 300 horsepower. Within a month, the first handmade engines were ready for testing. When the eight-cylinder engine did not prove sufficiently powerful, the Liberty was redesigned for twelve cylinders, raising the output to 400 horsepower. Mass-produced, this engine became the backbone of American military aviation and remained so until the mid-1920's.

All advanced training of American flying personnel was carried out in Europe, where experienced instructors and combat aircraft were available. About 2,500 American pilots received this advanced training, most of them in France. It was not until April, 1918—a full year after the United States' entry into the war—that American fliers were in combat and even then they had to fly French planes.

For the last seven months of the war, however, the Americans carried an ever-increasing share of the aerial offensive. Their first daylight bombardment squadron began operations in June, 1918. Next month, reorganized as the First Brigade under command of Colonel William Mitchell, the Americans were given responsibility for a sector of the front in the Chateau-Thierry area. Here, outnumbered by more experienced German squadrons, they met their first fierce opposition and suffered fairly heavy losses.

Billy Mitchell, the American commander, was a flamboyant falcon of a man. Son of a Wisconsin senator, he had enlisted as a private in the Spanish-American War and later served as a Signal Corps officer in the Philippines and Alaska. In 1915, when he was thirty-six years old, he took up flying and was in Europe as an observer when the United States declared war on Germany. He was the first pilot wearing an American uniform to fly over the enemy lines. His reports on the Allies' conduct of the war were so thorough and penetrating that his selection as combat commander was assured.

Mitchell was greatly impressed by the British air strategist, General Hugh "Boom" Trenchard. Trenchard conceived of the airplane as an offensive weapon that could, if properly exploited, play the decisive role in any war. He told Mitchell that heavy bombing could wreck the Ruhr and cripple the German war machine, but added dryly that this was difficult to achieve when the bombers were at the beck and call of ground commanders. Concentration of air power was the essential thing. Massive air formations responsible only to air commanders were the key to victory. The age of the individualist in the air, Trenchard insisted, was over.

Mitchell's imagination soared even higher than Trenchard's: he dreamed of a great airborne assault in which an entire American infantry division would be lifted over the stalemated trenches, "ten men in each plane," and dropped by parachute behind the unsuspecting enemy. There, as he visualized it, ground-strafing Allied planes would hold off the Germans until the paratroopers could organize and launch their attack.

When the war ended, such an air-drop was actually being planned for the winter of 1919. But in the spring of 1918, when Mitchell first conceived of it, the Germans were far from beaten in the air. In June, 1918, the best of all the Fokker designs—and probably the best fighter plane of the war—reached the front: the Fokker D-7. The new German Pfalz 12's and Albatros D-5's were almost as good.

By early summer American names were being added to the list of aces. Lieutenant Eddie Rickenbacker, a former automobile racing driver now with the 94th Aero Squadron, scored his first victory on April 29 and his sixth on May 30. During June he was hospitalized by an ear infection and was out of action through July and August. But in September and October he shot down twenty more and ended the war with a total of twenty-six.

Perhaps the most colorful American combat flier was Frank Luke, the "balloon buster from Arizona." A strange combination of shyness and aggressiveness, he antagonized some of his fellow pilots by his boastfulness and contempt for authority. But no one ever questioned his courage. Five times he brought his plane back so full of holes that it had to be retired from combat, and, by late September, he was the leading American ace. But his refusal to obey orders became so intolerable that on September 29 his commanding officer told him that he would be grounded until he could learn the rudiments of discipline.

Angered, Luke took off in his French Spad without permission and headed for enemy territory. An order was issued for his arrest, but it was never put into effect. Late that afternoon, having refueled at a forward field, Luke flew over an American balloon headquarters and dropped a note: "Watch three Hun balloons on the Meuse. Luke." He destroyed the first, was wounded badly in shooting down the second, but kept on and brought the third down in flames. He then strafed German troops in the village of Murvaux before something—probably faintness from loss of blood—forced him to land. Surrounded by German soldiers, who called on him to surrender, he fought with his pistol until rifle fire killed him. For such gallantry—however undisciplined—he was awarded posthumously the Medal of Honor, the only World War I airman so honored while fighting was still going on.

In the years that have passed since the end of this "war to end wars," the legend has taken root that the men who fought in the skies were somehow different from those who fought on land and sea. Perhaps this was true. The aces had to be men of great skill and valor. They had to possess superb vision and lightning-quick reflexes. They had to have that marvelous mixture of geometry and prescience that makes a deadly marksman—or they did not long survive.

But individually they were so different that no generalization fits them all. Some were war-lovers who killed with ferocity and satisfaction. Others killed equally well, but always with regret. Some were sportsmen who despised the twisted rules of the game. There were hunter-killers like Richthofen, who presented himself with a silver cup after every victory. There were God-fearing teen-agers like Albert Ball, who assured his parents in his letters that he always remembered to say his prayers—and who died before he was twenty. There were cool, calculating perfectionists like René Fonck, France's top-ranking ace who ended the war with an official score of seventy-five enemy planes. There were fanatics like France's Charles Nungesser and Germany's Rudolf Berthold, who carried into battle wounds that would have hospitalized lesser men. There were Willy Coppens, the Belgian ace, who once —incredibly—landed on a German observation balloon and took off again, and the great Canadian ace, Billy Bishop, who won the Victoria Cross for attacking an enemy airfield singlehanded. Where such men were concerned there was no common denominator except courage and a pair of fragile wings.

Each warring nation praised and publicized her pilots in different ways. In France anyone who shot down five enemy planes became an ace, and aerial exploits were given wide publicity. The sterner Germans doubled the requirements; not until a flier had scored ten victories was he hailed as a *Kanone*. Britain took the traditional tight-lipped attitude that heroism should not be unduly publicized; a hero's war record was made public for the first time at the solemn occasion of his decoration. American headlines were full of brilliant feats in the air.

All the combatants had fairly strict requirements for verification of victory claims—three eyewitnesses were usually necessary. As a result, many of the great aces on both sides undoubtedly scored more kills than their records show.

Despite the legendary accomplishments of the aces, air power during the first three years of the struggle was more romantic than decisive. Reconnaissance was the most important function and it became steadily more efficient as coordination with the ground forces improved and more effective cameras were developed. But static trench warfare tended to reduce the value of air observation. So did camouflage. Besides, night movement of troops could easily be carried out unobserved. For twelve hours out of every twenty-four the airplane was blind.

Tactical use of the airplane—ground strafing, artillery spotting, and troop support—was limited by vulnerability to ground fire, although armored planes made their appearance early in the war. If the pilot were brave and determined, considerable damage could be done. Ernst Udet was once credited with destroying a British tank, diving on the armored giant six times until it went out of control and turned over. But low-level strafing was a hazardous business. A German infantryman's random bullet brought down Edward Mannock, Britain's highest-ranking ace. Francesco Baracca, top-ranking Italian ace, was killed while machine-gunning Austrian trenches.

Until late in the war strategic bombing from airplanes was generally too inaccurate and too sporadic to be effective. But from the outset, the Allies were highly apprehensive about the German dirigible fleet. The English knew that both Count Zeppelin's monsters and the somewhat smaller Schutte-Lanz airships had the range and lift to carry impressive bomb loads to any point in the British Isles. The only defensive measures in the early months of the war were air strikes against the Zeppelins' home bases—ineffective with the primitive bombers then available—and blackout of targets at night. As the struggle lengthened, exaggerated claims of damage done in England by the Zeppelins gave the German people an unjustified sense of optimism. But far from destroying British morale, the damage wrought by these giants of the sky tended to anger the victims and harden their will to resist.

Most of the Zeppelins that raided England belonged to the German Naval Airship Service, whose commander was Peter Strasser, a man of great courage and ability. Strasser was convinced that the primary mission of his airships was scouting—sea patrol and spotting for the German navy. He tried to send two or three Zeppelins aloft each day on twelve- to twenty-hour patrols over the North Sea. But such searches were at the mercy of the weather. A cross wind of more than 12 miles per hour made it impossible for the big ships to leave or enter their hangars.

The first raids against England were limited to minor attacks on coastal areas, but by August, 1915, "squadron raids" on London had begun—always at night and always in the dark of the moon. The most daring and successful Zeppelin commander was Heinrich Mathy, who made 120 war flights, including thirteen raids against England. He took the *LZ-13* over London on September 8 and dropped some two tons of bombs, setting fires that did $2,500,000 worth of damage in the most destructive raid of the war.

By the summer of 1916 British planes were armed with incendiary and explosive ammunition. Early in September, one of these night fighters shot down a German army airship in flames. Three weeks later two other airships that tried to attack the capital were brought down. On October 1 Mathy himself perished when his airship was hit over England.

By this time the Kaiser was convinced that the raids should be halted. Strasser and his supporters argued that the Zeppelin raids kept at home English forces needed on the western front. Airships capable of reaching greater altitudes, they pointed out, would be immune to the punishing blows of the Royal Flying Corps. Modifications enabling the Zeppelins to fly at altitudes up to 20,000 feet were introduced in 1917, but they brought new problems of inefficient engine performance and oxygen starvation to the crews.

In the last mass raid of the war, made on October 19, 1917, eleven Zeppelins reached England, but only seven returned safely to Germany. Three months later five more ships were lost in a series of explosions at the Ahlhorn Zeppelin base. Two more were destroyed on the ground the following July when seven British Camels from the carrier *Furious* hit the Zeppelin sheds at Tondern, near the Danish border—the first time carrier-based airplanes had attacked a land-based target.

Still Strasser refused to concede defeat. On August 5, 1918, he led five Zeppelins against England. His flagship was the new *LZ-70,* a giant that had recorded speeds of 82 miles per hour on her trial runs. The British had heavily-armed aircraft ready and waiting. Before she could even reach the English coast, the *LZ-70* went down in flames under the guns of a DH-4. With Strasser's death, the Zeppelin organization virtually disintegrated.

In September, 1918, a month after Strasser's death, the great drive against the Saint-Mihiel salient was under way. To support this offensive nearly 1,500 Allied warplanes, including day and night bombers, observation squadrons, and more than 700 fighters, were assembled under the command of Billy Mitchell, now a brigadier general. For the first time the outnumbered Germans were put on the defensive and kept there. About a third of the Allied air force was used to support ground troops, while the rest carried out long-range bombardment or sought to whittle down German fighter strength. Always sensitive to rear-area attack, the Germans tried desperately to halt the Allied bombers but often found themselves

trapped and outnumbered by Allied fighters. On October 9, when the Germans tried to launch a counterattack in the Meuse-Argonne area, the Allies smashed at their concentration points with two hundred bombers escorted by over one hundred fighters. From this operation, probably the largest raid of the campaign, only one American aircraft failed to return. Five weeks later, the war was over.

At the Armistice, despite a painfully slow start, American front-line air strength consisted of 740 combat airplanes, almost 800 pilots, and 500 observers. Losses in seven months of increasingly violent fighting had been 289 planes and 48 balloons, as against confirmed claims of 781 enemy aircraft and 73 balloons destroyed by American air fighters.

Despite these impressive statistics and the enduring legend of heroism left by the air fighters of World War I, it is impossible not to categorize this first sustained military use of air power as more spectacular than effective. No airplane or dirigible, for example, ever succeeded in sinking or seriously damaging a surface warship. No war industry was ever put out of action by bombing. In no major engagement was victory ever won or lost exclusively by air power—or lack of it. Giant technical strides were made in aviation; but looking back now through the keyhole of history, it is the men who are most vividly remembered and not the machines.

Through most of World War I infantry was still the queen of battles and artillery was king. But only in the closing weeks of the struggle—as hundreds of Allied bombers hammered German troop concentrations, railroad junctions, and supply depots; as swarms of Allied fighters battered down aerial opposition and made daylight movement of enemy troops more and more difficult—did it become evident that a new military doctrine was being forged on the iron anvil of war. Ground commanders varied in their degree of perceptiveness, but during the furious fighting of September and October that led to Germany's collapse this precept was written in blood and fire for those who had eyes to see: *If you hold the air, you cannot be beaten; if you lose the air, you cannot win.*

The Storm Breaks

As World War I began, the visions of air-minded prophets soared above the realities of contemporary aviation. General Ruffey of the French Third Army dreamed of an independent, offensive air force of 3,000 planes, though at the time France and Great Britain combined could bring only 220 combat-ready machines to the western front to oppose Germany's 260. And, with only about a dozen aircraft factories on each side, it was unlikely that these numbers could be rapidly increased.

At the outset the novel air war in an uncrowded sky was fought with chivalry. The catalyst of war would change both the planes and the men.

With businesslike stride, a German unit (above) walks a small observation balloon to its launching site in a hayfield. The canvas gondola at the balloon's stern carried aloft two military observers—usually to a height of about 2,000 feet. The balloons were held to the ground by cables, and when attacked were quickly winched in. Because of their heavy fighter protection, the big gasbags were sometimes considered to be tougher game to hit than airplanes.

A flimsy-looking biplane (left) built by Aerowerke Gustav Otto in Johannisthal, Germany, starts a clattering take-off from a board runway in August, 1914. By the war's start, Germany's Imperial Air Service had stipulated that all new biplanes must provide space for a pilot and observer, as well as bomb racks and fittings for cameras. Government purchasers also demanded planes with 100-horsepower engines and a minimum top speed of 65 miles per hour.

Zeppelins in War

The notion that dirigibles were useful only for reconnaissance was short-lived. Although scouting remained the primary function of airships, Peter Strasser, commander of the German Naval Airship Service, outfitted Zeppelins for bombing raids.

Filled with highly combustible hydrogen, and with their flights severely hampered by adverse weather conditions, the ponderous ships in the sky were far from ideal bombers. If the delicate balance of ballast and lift was upset, Zeppelins would soar to heights where lack of oxygen and extreme cold incapacitated the crew. Also during "valving off"—the release of gas which enabled the dirigible to lose altitude—Zeppelins were especially vulnerable to incendiary fire.

Strasser armed the gondolas below the balloon and the platform on the bow with machine guns, but the airships were almost defenseless against attack from above. To lessen the chance of outright explosion, he had the Zeppelins built with many separate gas compartments. Nevertheless, dirigible commanders were often so unnerved by the sight of another Zeppelin in their squadron plummeting in flames that they would abandon the objective, drop out their bombs, and quickly run for home.

Despite the risks, Zeppelins in 159 sorties over England dropped 220 tons of bombs, causing damage worth $7,500,000. By 1918, however, excessive losses to Allied firepower had all but ended the raids of the awesome airship-bombers.

The only known photograph of a Zeppelin armada in action (left) was taken from the LZ-11 during the August 9, 1915, raid over England. Gordon Crosby's painting at right captures a moment of triumph for R. A. J. Warneford—and one of terror for the doomed crew of the LZ-37, reduced by the British flier's gunfire to a plunging inferno.

Over the Front

During the Allied retreat from Mons in August and September, 1914, aerial reconnaissance played an important role for both sides. From then on, a determined struggle began to dominate the air and keep enemy observers out of the sky.

The new air fight raged with increasing intensity. Soldiers in muddy trenches and shellholes watched the dogfights over the lines and cheered the planes of their own fliers, many of whom they knew by name. When an ace fell, even the enemy felt the loss—a gallant contender had departed from an arena of sportlike combat.

ARCHIV KRUEGER

LEFT: *Possibly the greatest military aviator until his accidental death in October,
1916, was Germany's Oswald Boelcke, seen
being helped into his flying jacket. A
brilliant organizer and teacher, he inspired
other German fliers like von Richthofen.*

RIGHT: *This aerial photograph, the only
one known of a combat kill in World War
I, shows a French plane falling in flames
over the front. Pilots who fell to their death
behind enemy lines were often treated
respectfully and buried with full honors.*

BELOW: *The observation role of the airplane is dramatically revealed by this low-
altitude shot of German infantrymen
scampering out of their trenches at the
Somme in 1916. Observers reported such
movements to the ground commanders.*

A Caudron biplane drops smoke fuses to illuminate the positions of enemy infantry at the Battle of Verdun in 1916.

In his scene of Sacy-le-Grand airfield, Farré depicted the quieter side of aerial warfare: training and maintenance.

War's outbreak brought the French artist Henry Farré home from Buenos Aires. Volunteering as an aviator, he served two years in a bombing squadron. As the Army Museum's artist delegate, he re-created the air war's novel drama on these canvases.

Second-ranking French ace Georges Guynemer, flying a Spad, sends two German aviators hurtling from their burning plane.

A French FBA hydroplane, bombing from less than two hundred feet, destroys a German submarine in the North Sea, 1916.

OVERLEAF: *Farré's painting shows a Nieuport 11 "Bébé," bearing the Indian-head insignia of the Lafayette Escadrille, diving to strafe the German-held town of Chaulnes, France, in 1917. Pilots often used up ammunition this way before heading home.*

The Americans Get Ready

A famed Lafayette Escadrille member, Raoul Lufbery—third-ranking American ace —poses in his Nieuport (above), as two sergeants stand by with the lion cub "Whiskey" on a French airfield. Below, three of the group's original members, James McConnell, Victor Chapman, and Kiffin Rockwell, enjoy relaxation in off-duty hours.

OVER THERE: Impatient with U. S. neutrality, a number of Americans volunteered for service with the Allies during the first years of the war. By April, 1916, so many of them were in French aviation that France authorized the formation of a squadron of American fliers under Captain Georges Thenault.

Two lion cub mascots, "Whiskey" and "Soda," epitomized the flair and bravado of the group, called the La-fayette Escadrille. Within a month, on May 20, 1916, Kiffin Rockwell scored the squadron's first victory; and courageous and skillful fliers like William Thaw, Norman Prince, and James N. Hall soon added more triumphs.

The unit became a nucleus for 180 American volunteers serving in 93 French squadrons. Nearly a third of them were killed, but they accounted for 199 German planes.

OVER HERE: In March, 1911, when Congress voted $125,000 for the Army Signal Corps air branch, just one military training plane existed in the United States: Lieutenant Foulois's dilapidated Wright at Fort Sam Houston, Texas. As more planes became available, mishaps increased, and the accidents hurt the cause of those who sought more money for military craft. Finally, in July, 1914, the Army purchased both Wright and Curtiss models, improved by Grover C. Loening, and a new "TT" trainer designed by Glenn Martin.

Naval aviation, meanwhile, had been prodded by men like Washington Irving Chambers and Artemus Gates. But their efforts had little better success against public and governmental apathy.

Because of this indifference, the United States, when it finally entered the war in April, 1917, ranked fourteenth among world air powers.

The punitive expedition against Pancho Villa in 1916 gave U.S. aircraft a nearly fatal combat baptism. Curtiss planes, like the one shown above, could neither fly above the 12,000-foot-high mountains nor withstand Mexico's desert temperatures. The photograph below of a trainer being hauled out for testing at College Point, New York, captures prewar America's casual, shirt-sleeve approach to air power.

179

A fiercely patriotic poster calls young Americans to a new military role. Such appeals made thousands of sudden converts to aviation.

In the War

Although lack of planes, pilots, airfields, and technicians restricted American war efforts at the outset, U.S. instructors gave 15,000 American pilots their preliminary training in this country. Advanced instruction was conducted abroad, and the 1st Aero Squadron, under Major Ralph Royce, arrived in France in September, 1917. In April, 1918, Lieutenants Alan Winslow and Douglas Campbell scored the first American victory. Some U.S. fliers like Elliott White Springs and Clayton Knight flew part of the time or throughout the war with British squadrons, and others, including Fiorello LaGuardia, who led a bomber group, served in the Italian theater.

American Air Service commanders in France—Mason Patrick, William Mitchell, Benjamin Foulois, Frank Lahm, and Thomas Milling—organized and led the last big air battles of the war.

Training accidents were frequent, and often freakish—as witness the embarrassing landing of a Curtiss Jenny at right. By August, 1918, fliers like those of the U. S. 148th Squadron, taking off from Dunkirk in Camels (below), were combat veterans.

PETER M. BOWERS COLLECTION

FAMOUS AIRPLANES: 1914-1918

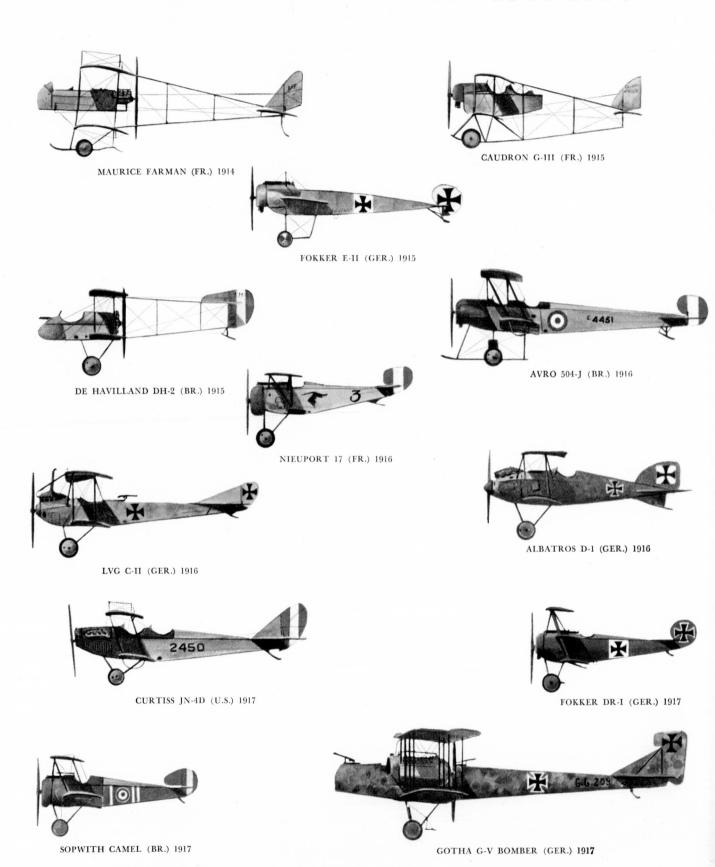

MAURICE FARMAN (FR.) 1914

CAUDRON G-III (FR.) 1915

FOKKER E-II (GER.) 1915

DE HAVILLAND DH-2 (BR.) 1915

AVRO 504-J (BR.) 1916

NIEUPORT 17 (FR.) 1916

LVG C-II (GER.) 1916

ALBATROS D-1 (GER.) 1916

CURTISS JN-4D (U.S.) 1917

FOKKER DR-I (GER.) 1917

SOPWITH CAMEL (BR.) 1917

GOTHA G-V BOMBER (GER.) 1917

BRISTOL F-2B (BR.) 1917

SPAD 13 (FR.) 1917

BREGUET 14 (FR.) 1917

SE-5 (BR.) 1917

FOKKER D-VII (GER.) 1918

HANDLEY PAGE 0/400 (BR.) 1917

JUNKERS D-I (GER.) 1918

AMERICAN DH-4 (BR.-U.S.) 1918

LOENING M-8 (U.S.) 1918

NAVY-CURTISS F-5L (U.S.) 1918

Leergewicht: 2740 kg.
Nutzlast: 1235 kg.
zul. Gesamtgewicht: 3975 kg.

Auf rechter Seite aufsteigen

Trial by Fire

Behind the drama of dogfights and dawn patrols, aviation was rapidly learning many new lessons to leap ahead faster during the war than it had ever done before.

Technological developments were piled one upon another. European and American manufacturers, responding to military appeals for planes and engines with improved performances, dropped old models and labored around the clock to produce revolutionary new designs. Specialized aircraft were developed for bombing, pursuit, and attack.

Navies shaped aviation to their own needs. The American Navy produced, besides its ace David Ingalls, two future statesmen, Robert Lovett and James Forrestal, whose World War I experience with planes served the nation well in later years.

ABOVE: *A French pilot, on his way to combat, took this photograph, showing beyond his wing the Nieuport fighter of France's third-ranking ace, Charles Nungesser. Nungesser, one of the war's most often wounded pilots, carried a coffin, skull, and crossbones insignia on his plane (see page 187).*

RIGHT: *A German Hansa-Brandenburg W-29 seaplane strafes a stricken English Curtiss flying boat in 1918. The W-29 appeared in the last months of 1917. A highly-maneuverable monoplane with a top speed of 110 miles per hour, it was heavily armed with two synchronized Spandau machine guns mounted alongside the engine.*

LEFT: *A German gunner, sucking on an oxygen tube and garbed for high-altitude flight, mans his machine gun on a giant Gotha G-IV bomber. These twin-engine, pusher planes mounted the war's only gun cockpit on the tail assembly. Gothas could carry 1,500 pounds of bombs but, like all World War I bombers, did little damage.*

The Fraternity
of the Brave

Romantic writers have often likened the aces of World War I to chivalric knights. Their trade held them together, and though they were as diverse as any other group of men, they looked upon themselves as a special breed of fighters, different from the soldiers and sailors below.

Those who survived did so principally because of luck and also because they combined with their daring a deadly skill that marked them as the new men of war, flying free and brave above all obstacles.

Manfred von Richthofen (2nd from left, beside Anthony Fokker)
Top German Ace: 80 victories

Ernst Udet
German: 62 victories

Raymond Collishaw
British Naval Ace: 60 victories

Billy Bishop
Top Canadian Ace: 72 victories

Edward Mannock
Top British Ace: 73 victories

Charles Nungesser
French: 45 victories

René Fonck
Top French Ace: 75 victories

Frank Luke, Jr.
American: 21 victories

Eddie Rickenbacker
Top American Ace: 26 victories

The photograph above shows the fiery end of two German observation balloons shot down in February, 1918. The German habit of sending up a second balloon as the first one fell accounts for the pair's proximity.

Bristol F-2B fighters, like the group flying over the Alps at right, were used in modified version by the RAF until 1932. Before war's end, Britain had built 3,101 of these "Brisfits," as they were nicknamed.

The Allied Edge

After the summer of 1917, the sheer numbers of Allied craft began to overwhelm the German air forces. Sopwith Camels, Spads, and SE-5's appeared in such quantity that the Germans—to maintain any offensive position—were forced to combine their *Jastas* (fighting units originally composed of no more than fourteen planes) into large squadrons.

The Allied edge in production was matched by a new Allied sense of how to organize and use air forces. In August, 1917, General Jan C. Smuts completed a report on British air organization that led to the formation, on April 1, 1918, of the Royal Air Force. General Hugh "Boom" Trenchard then organized the Independent Air Force with a mission of long-range bombing, a development that came too late to make a real showing in this war—though Trenchard's ideas were to carry forward powerfully to World War II.

At the time of the last German offensive, in March, 1918, the British had 1,232 planes in France. And still production was expanding; by war's end, eight months later, the RAF had 1,799 planes at the front. The Americans, too, overcame their initial unpreparedness and by the Armistice were producing DH-4's in the United States at the rate of 1,100 per month. Conversely, the Germans built 4,000 planes fewer in 1918 than in 1917.

The growing might of the Allied air fleets and their control of the sky were not the most critical factors in the war, but they did undermine the Germans' will to fight.

In the last two air offensives of the conflict, the Allies employed formation flying, strategic bombing, and saturation attack. Aviation had traveled an immeasurable distance from the days when gentlemen on reconnaissance missions waved to one another in friendly greeting.

FIGHTING IN THE SKIES

"Some Were Lucky"

The outbreak of World War I created a hectic demand for new planes of greater capabilities. T.O.M. Sopwith, builder of several famous British fighters, including the Camel, recalls the pressure on designers in the conflict's early days.

When we started the First World War, there were no fighters. The small, rather high-performance—for their day—aircraft that we were building were really built as scouts. From scouts they developed into fighters, literally—from going up with rifles and revolvers to the day when we learned to fire through the propeller.

Development was so fast! We literally thought of and designed and flew the airplanes in a space of about six or eight weeks. Now it takes approximately the same number of years.

From sketches the designs went to chalk on the wall. Until about the middle of the war there was no stressing at all. Everything was built entirely by eye. That's why there were so many structural failures. We didn't start to stress airplanes at all seriously until the Camel, in 1917.

Flying in those days was empirical. We really weren't structural engineers at all. It was a constant gamble, in a way. We just flew by the light of nature. Some of us were lucky and some of us weren't.

Chased by Fokkers

William Sholto Douglas, later a World War II Marshal of the RAF, was one of the early British fliers. The following incident occurred in 1915 when the air above the western front was dominated by German Fokkers.

I was sent out on reconnaissance in a BE-2C with one other aircraft to escort me. When we got out nearly as far as Cambrai, there were about half a dozen of these Fokkers dancing about in the sky in front of me. My escort was shot down more or less straightaway, and I had a very lively half hour dashing about the sky with these people after me.

I afterwards discovered that one of the six pilots flying these Fokkers was [Oswald] Boelcke and another was [Max] Immelmann, and so recognize that I was fairly lucky to get away with it. I was chased right down to the ground and had to hedgehop back to our side at about five hundred feet or even lower. can remember dodging around trees with these people trying to dive on me. But they weren't able to dive so well because I was so close to the ground that they were apt to dive into the ground.

I got hit in the engine coming back over the lines. I had climbed up to about eight hundred feet to get back and then dived over the lines and I got properly peppered from the front-line trenches, of course. Got my engine hit and came down about a mile behind the British front-line trenches.

"Fear in His Eyes"

French ace Alfred Heurtaux (twenty-one victories) recalls the excitement of air combat and days of flying with his friend Georges Guynemer France's second greatest ace (after Fonck), who scored fifty-four victories before he was killed.

As an observer early in the war I was only baggage. We crashed the first time—no bullets, just a bad pilot. We crashed the second time, and the third time we crashed from about three hundred feet. Not because of the Germans, but because of the pilot. That was why I asked to become a fighter pilot. I went to the commander and said that I didn't mind getting killed, but I preferred to do it myself. So he sent me to the training field, and I learned to fly.

In June, 1916, I went to the Cigognes [Stork] squadron. We used very old Nieuports. The engines were worn out—the wings also. I was the youngest pilot in the squadron so I got the worst plane. But in that first one I shot down five German planes, so I took command of the squadron by the end of July, a month and a half after joining it.

I think one of the most dramatic incidents was near Peronne, a small city near a river. First I killed the pilot. The observer was in the rear shooting at me with a machine gun. When the pilot was killed, the observer held up his two hands and I remember his expression, the fear in his eyes. I will remember it always. He was killed in the crash—he had no chance to escape.

[Georges] Guynemer was a good friend of mine and we flew often together. When we were flying together, it was impossible to get near the Germans because we had big storks on our planes and the Germans knew exactly who the pilots were. They were always flying from us. They did not want to attack when Guynemer and I were both there. So we said we must go alone. We both wanted to be the first and finally we threw dice. I was the winner so the next day I went up.

Heurtaux, as painted by Henry Farré

The meeting place was always at four thirty in the afternoon near Peronne—every day we knew exactly where to meet the Germans. But I was shot down in fifteen seconds—bullets in my engine. So I put down and got back to the squadron. Guynemer was laughing at me, but he went the next day and was shot down too. I went the next day and was shot down again. On the fifth day I went very high and waited for the Germans at nearly 5,000 feet. They shot at me, and I was flying in very short circles. I could see their bullets piercing my wings when I turned. But finally they had no more bullets, and I started to fire and shot down two of the five. Guynemer shot down two more the next day, and we never saw the fifth one again.

I was twenty-three years old. All of us were very young. Everyone was in good spirits, and there was a feeling of camaraderie. It was like a sport. But in 1917, when several were killed, the mood changed. None of the old pilots was left.

The Lure of Clouds

Victor Chapman, an American student in Paris, volunteered for the French Foreign Legion when the war began. After service in the trenches, he transferred to French aviation, became one of the original members of the Lafayette Escadrille, and was the first American pilot killed in combat. He wrote the following in a letter home a few weeks before his death on July 23, 1916.

Everyone says they get tired of flying, "It's monotonous." I don't see it, but on the contrary, an infinite variety is this, when there is a slight sprinkling of clouds. Clouds are not thin pieces of blotting paper; but liquid, ceaselessly changing steam. I played hide-and-seek in and out of them yesterday; sometimes flat blankets like melting snow on either side below me, or again, like great ice floes with distant bergs looming up,

Victor Chapman, shortly before his death

and "open water" near at hand, blue as a moonstone cloud, floating full, for all the world like a gigantic jellyfish (those that have red trailers and a sting).... Some have many feathery, filmy points and angles, others are rounded and voluminous, with cracks and caverns in them. These are all the fair-weather, fleecy clouds; for there are the lower, flatter, misty ones, and the speckled, or mare's tail clouds, above which one never reaches. There are such a lot of trumpet-shaped and wind-blown clouds this evening that I should like to go out and examine them; but it's a bore for my mechanic, and I doubt if I could go high enough to warrant crossing the lines.

Night Bombing

Almost from the beginning of the war, planes were used for aerial bombardment. Cy Caldwell, a Canadian with a night-bombing squadron of the Royal Flying Corps, reminisces about their effectiveness.

Looking back, I can say I don't think we did any good. I think we scared a lot of people, and kept a lot of German troops awake when they should have been getting their rest. But as for damage done, I think it was quite negligible. After all, to drop two 112-pound bombs of TNT —that's a pretty miniscule effort, is it not? We usually dropped them on places like railroad stations. The idea was to disrupt communications. As we only dropped them twenty or twenty-five miles over the lines, what were we bombing? We really were bombing a bunch of poor Belgian and French civilians.

We made one or two raids on a place called Gontrode, which was near Ghent, and we were supposed to hit Zeppelin hangars there and blow up Zeppelins. We never succeeded. Some of us didn't find the places, and those that did just dropped their bombs and went off. They didn't destroy any Zeppelins. That was the beginning of bombing, and it was very ineffectual.

The bombsights were simply a little wire arrangement and the observer was supposed to peer through these wires. As his pilot flew him up to the target, when the two wires, top and bottom, came in line, he was supposed to pull the chain and away went the bombs. Oh, there was no doubt about it, they all hit the ground. No question about that. But what they hit we never knew.

The antiaircraft was very inefficient, but it did frighten you. After all, you're up there sitting there, and you have searchlights on you, and you feel that you're just like a bird flying through a lot of shot. But it's a very big sky, you know.

A Kill for Richthofen

Before his death on April 21, 1918, the top ace of the war, Germany's Manfred von Richthofen, shot down eighty enemy planes. One of his victories, scored during a fight with a British flier in April, 1917, is described in this excerpt from T. Ellis Barker's translation of Richthofen's autobiography.

Suddenly one of the impertinent Englishmen tried to drop down upon

Manfred von Richthofen

me. I allowed him to approach me quite near, and then we started a merry quadrille. Sometimes my opponent flew on his back and sometimes he did other tricks. He was flying a two-seater fighter. I realized very soon that I was his master and that he could not escape me.

During an interval in the fighting, I assured myself that we were alone. It followed that the victory would belong to him who was calmest, who shot best, and who had the cleverest brain in a moment of danger.

Soon I had got him beneath me without having seriously hurt him with my gun. We were at least two kilometers from the front. I thought he intended to land, but there I had made a mistake. Suddenly, when he was only a few yards above the ground, I noticed how he once more went off on a straight course. He tried to escape me. That was too bad.

I attacked him again, and to do so I had to go so low that I was afraid of touching the roofs of the houses in the village beneath me. The Englishman defended himself up to the last moment. At the very end I felt that my engine had been hit. Still I did not let go. He had to

fall. He flew at full speed right into a block of houses.

There is little left to be said. This was once more a case of splendid daring. The man had defended himself to the last. However, in my opinion, he showed, after all, more stupid foolhardiness than courage. It was again one of the cases where one must differentiate between energy and idiocy. He had to come down in any case, but he paid for his stupidity with his life.

American Unpreparedness

Prior to its entry into the war, the United States gave little attention to its own air strength despite the lessons of Europe. This frustrating period was recalled by one of the Army's first flying officers, General Thomas DeWitt Milling.

None of the things for which the airplane was used [in Europe] had been missed by us right at the beginning. We didn't have equipment that could do anything to speak of, but the reason for that was that we didn't have money to go into any development.

The Signal Corps made sacrifice after sacrifice. For instance, we got so little money appropriated that time and time again General [James] Allen would take Signal Corps money and use it for aviation. No other branch was interested in it. Most of the people in the ground branches just looked down upon it; they didn't think it was of any use.

The situation had gotten so bad in 1916 they finally decided to give us some money. That's when the business was going on at the [Mexican] border, and there was a big hue and cry throughout the country. So they appropriated about $13,000,000— a huge sum. We didn't have the personnel to use it, or anything. If that money had been distributed over the previous five or six years, we'd have been somewhere by that time. That began the expansion of this country for World War I.

Thank You, and Good-by"

America's leading ace, Eddie Ricken-backer, who scored twenty-six victories with the 94th Aero Squadron, had a hard time getting to the front. His prior assignment was Chief Engineering Officer at a training school at Issoudun, France.

I'd been trying to get out of that place. I wanted to go to gunnery school. "Tooey" [Major Carl Spaatz] didn't think I should: he figured that I was indispensable and therefore I should stay there.

On New Year's Day [1918], another chap and I went on a little trip in a Nieuport. They were putting on a football game there at Issoudun, and a bunch of brass came down from Paris. So when the two of us got back, the football game was going on, and I broke it up stupidly. I mean, I spun down within a hundred feet of the ground and pulled this little thing out, and the next thing I knew, I was on the ground. "Tooey" grounded me.

Well, I made a deal with the head surgeon and went to the hospital with a heck of a cold—you know, the dirty, damp weather. There was a man who was, I thought, qualified to take my job over; I didn't think he could do what I could do at the front or wanted to do or wanted to try. "Tooey" felt otherwise.

When I got out of the hospital, the surgeon had evidently talked to "Tooey" and told him what I was up to—but I *was* really feeling terrible. I went down to see "Tooey," and he handed me my orders for Cazeau [gunnery school]. He said, "I'm on to your little game, and if you feel that way about it, I don't want you around here."

I said, "Thank you, and good-by." The only difficulty in the gunnery training was that they had Frenchmen towing a target with an old biplane. We kids would get up there for practice shots, and we'd dive maybe a hundred yards out. They'd

count the holes you made in it, and that was your record and qualification as far as fighter pilot shooting was concerned. On two occasions I cut the rope just about twenty feet behind the airplane. They went wild!

But I finally got out of there and went to the front.

One for Campbell

Douglas Campbell, also a member of the 94th Aero Squadron, was the first American-trained pilot to shoot down an enemy plane (on April 14, 1918). He recounts his experiences leading to his first kill.

The thing they couldn't teach you, which you learned only by having some luck, was how to see the enemy airplane. The first time I went over the front lines in an airplane was with [Raoul] Lufbery and Eddie Rickenbacker. We flew around for about an hour and a half while the gasoline would last, and it all seemed very dull.

When we got back Lufbery asked us what we saw, and we hadn't seen anything—but he'd seen a couple of groups of German planes not very far away. The secret of seeing them

Campbell with the 94th's insignia

NATIONAL ARCHIVES

was not to focus—just gaze around. Then anything that crossed your field of vision you'd see.

We were supposed to have two machine guns, but in fact I never had more than one gun. The day after I made a patrol on which I was wounded the second gun showed up. I never had the use of it. I always carried a small hammer strapped to my wrist because the Vickers .303 machine gun that we had could jam in about five different ways. Two of the jams—the most frequent ones—could sometimes be corrected by reaching over the windshield and batting on one of the outside levers with a hammer. They jammed quite often. If you got one of the other kind of jams, you might as well give up and leave.

Our first patrol from the Toul airport was a dawn patrol [on April 14]. The weather was foul, about a five-hundred-foot ceiling. They took off—David Peterson, Rickenbacker, and Reed Chambers—and went out over the front, and they couldn't see anything. [Alan] Winslow and I were on alert sitting in one of those wood-frame canvas hangars, in which there was a telephone, and we were playing gin rummy or something at about nine o'clock in the morning. The telephone rang and there was a message that two German airplanes had crossed the line and were heading in our direction.

I took off first and circled the field while Winslow took off, and I was just about to fall in behind him when I saw him shooting his guns. I could see the tracer bullets coming out, and I thought, "What's he shooting here over the town for?" Then I saw that he was shooting at an airplane which had black crosses on it. I'd never seen a German airplane before, but I thought that must be one. Just at that point he went out of sight under my wing, so I tipped up in a sharp turn so I could see how to help him—which was very fortunate because just at that

193

moment the tracer bullets began going past my head from this other fellow up above that I didn't even know was there.

Well, I can't remember exactly what maneuvers took place except that, as I say, the ceiling was only five hundred feet, and I remember that at the beginning he had the advantage, having more altitude than I did. I remember at one point pulling up almost vertical to take a shot at him and then stalling out of that and suddenly discovering that there was the ground coming up at me. But I had room. When I came out of that dive, he was flying in the same direction three hundred feet higher, so I just pulled up and shot at him and he caught fire. I didn't get hit at all that time.

In the meantime, somehow, out of the corner of my eye I'd seen Winslow's adversary land in a plowed field and turn over on his back. I think Winslow put a shot through his carburetor or something and stopped his engine. My adversary, burning, glided down and landed on the other side of our airfield. We came down and landed and discovered we'd been off the ground for only four and a half minutes!

"This Is My Last Day"

Rickenbacker's friend and flying companion in the 94th "Hat-in-the-Ring" Aero Squadron was Major Reed Chambers, an ace who ended the war with six planes and one balloon to his credit.

Our first few rides it was an adventure. And then as we commenced to lose people, and fellows in the other squadrons would be shot down, you developed a feeling that "This is my last day." In fact, Rickenbacker and I, when we would take off on a voluntary patrol, which we did regularly—we'd do our regular missions and then we'd start out again—we'd shake hands and say, "Well, I'll be slapping you in the face with a

Reed Chambers

spade." That was our greeting.

"Rick" wasn't the best pilot in the world; he couldn't put as many holes in a target that was being towed as I could, but he could put more holes in a target that was shooting at him than I could. Rickenbacker's greatest asset was his judgment of distance. He would move right in on them, and he wouldn't shoot until he could see the whites of their eyes. I and many others, we'd start shooting too far away, and our guns would jam or they'd splatter so wide that we didn't get them. But "Rick" rarely missed. He even pulled the wing off an Albatros one time, with his tail skid. And he really worked. He had more official hours over the lines than any other American pilot.

One of the closest calls I had was at Toul. Rickenbacker and I were alone that time, and all of a sudden this antiaircraft burst right under me, and within a matter of a very few seconds my motor jammed—just stopped with a shudder. We were very high, and I headed for our lines and landed right among our 75's, just back of the infantry, with a dead stick. I made a good landing: no trouble at all.

I inspected the airplane. A piece

of shell had gone right through th[e] fins of the front side, and it cut thos[e] steel fins just like you'd take a knif[e] and cut cheese. It had cut the fin[s] and then pushed in to the point tha[t] it seized the piston. On further ex[-] amining the plane, I found that th[e] butt of the shell evidently had com[e] right up under my seat and came ou[t] four inches back of my head. An[d] that was close! However, I wouldn['t] say that I was so terribly frightened[.] I was frightened after I got back o[n] the ground.

"I Couldn't Kill Him"

Open cockpits and modest speed[s] frequently made aerial fighting dr[a-] matically intimate. A moving inci[-] dent of close combat is recalled b[y] Gill Robb Wilson, who flew wit[h] both the French and the America[n] air services.

I was out one day flying as gunne[r] with a friend of mine named Jea[n] Henin. He was kind of a clown, b[ut] a very nice boy; he'd been a ban[k] clerk in Paris. We got into a dogfigh[t] over the Oise canal. I was firing to th[e] rear. Suddenly I felt Henin beatin[g] me on the back, and I could hear hi[m] yelling, "Here, over here! Fire, fire[!"]

I turned around—I had to swin[g] the Lewis guns—and there with h[is] wings locked with ours was a Germa[n] fighter pilot in a Pfalz. I looked rig[ht] down this German's throat. He was [a] man, I would think, about forty-fiv[e] or fifty years old. He had on a blac[k] woolen helmet. How in God's nam[e] he ever got there I don't know. [I] could touch the end of his wing.

I swung the guns on him, and th[e] guy just sat there. He had a mus[-] tache. I can still see him. There wer[e] deep lines on his face, and he looke[d] at me with a kind of resignation. [I] looked over those machine guns [at] that guy, and I couldn't kill him. H[e] was too helpless.

Gradually, he drifted off. I said [to] Henin, "I couldn't kill him." He sai[d,] "I'm glad you didn't."

The Dogfight

George A. Vaughn, a veteran of many aerial battles, was the second-ranking American ace to survive the war. He scored seven victories while he was attached to the Royal Flying Corps and six more with the American Expeditionary Forces.

Most people seem to think a dogfight is just two airplanes going round and round and round for minutes and minutes at a time until one shoots the other down. As a rule, it didn't work out that way because there were so many in the sky that you jumped from one to the other, and two or three of them shot at you, not just one. You shot at four or five—anybody you could get your sights on—and then another one. It was usually just two or three bursts, and then maybe you were on another fellow or maybe somebody was on you this time. That's the way it was.

The atmosphere was more or less a sporting one in those days. I suppose it was the last time that there would really be such a thing as, you might say, hand-to-hand combat in the air. Although we flew in formation, when the actual combat came it was strictly a one-man proposition. Everybody was by himself.

George A. Vaughn

"This Is It, Brother"

Not all World War I pilots were aces. Leroy Prinz, who served with the U.S. 1st Pursuit Group in France, reveals disarmingly that he was often more of a liability than an asset.

In France I crashed and crashed and crashed. I got so I'd pull my throttle clear back and put my hand over my nose because when I landed I'd invariably break my nose. Invariably. I just didn't have the knack of it. I was the only guy in the 1st Pursuit Group who wasn't a hero. The Germans had to shoot *somebody* down, you know.

On my first flight over the lines I was flying number-three position on the left. Well, unless you've been in the air you don't know how blind you can be. I swear, I looked to the left, and when I looked back I was alone. It seemed that the squadron had seen a patrol or something and they'd all gone. Well, I had no more idea where I was than a jack rabbit. And I started thinking, "God, wouldn't it have been wonderful if I'd studied those contour maps? Wouldn't it be nice if I knew something about a motor? What would you do if your machine gun jammed?" I had snuck through, as they say, every bit of training, and here I was alone in the air, and God knows where.

I said, "Well, the first thing I'll do is climb high. If anybody gets me, it will have to be from below." I finally got that baby up till that altimeter was just wiggling at around 17,200 and shaking like a man with palsy. I didn't understand why I couldn't breathe. There was no such thing as an oxygen mask, and nobody'd ever told me about this. I was gasping, trying to catch my breath, and my motor was spluttering. I thought, "Oh well, I'm going to fall to pieces. This is it, brother."

I finally got the compass and it pointed in the opposite direction to what I was going. I turned around, made a long gradual glide, and came to a cloud bank. Lo and behold, there was a silhouette—a plane in front of me. I thought, "Oh, this is nobody else but Richthofen." I didn't stop for combat; I just pulled both guns and let him have it.

Then I was on my long glide, and all of a sudden I saw tracer bullets going by my wing. Brother! I didn't know who was on my tail, but I put that baby into a dive, and I dove and dove, and pretty soon I ran out of gasoline. I made my usual landing in a field and smashed the be-jesus out of this Nieuport. As usual, my nose was smashed, too.

When I came to, they were Yanks! They took me back to Toul and I reported to Major [Harold] Hartney. I said, "I've been up in combat, sir. I lost the patrol and on my return I attacked an enemy aircraft. I don't know how I could have missed it. Then as I was flying along, I was attacked by a squadron of German planes, and my motor was conking out so I took a long dive and landed."

He said, "Very interesting. Well, I'll tell you something. Two and a half hours ago you passed over this field going hell-bent for election." I'd missed my own field!

And at that, Johnny Wentworth walked in and he said, "And let me tell you something, the next time you take a shot at me in the air I'll really shoot you down!" All I had done was to get lost, shoot at my own man, and crash another plane. I never lived down that phony report.

Later General Billy Mitchell invited us up to headquarters, and he sent for me.

"I want to see the insignia on your collar," he said.

I said, "Well, it's U.S. A.S.S.C. That's regulations, sir."

He said, "I thought you might have an Iron Cross up there. You are the damndest ace the Germans have. I'm going to ground you for a while so we can build up the air force."

CHAPTER 6

First of the fearless wing walkers was Ormer Locklear (above on a Curtiss Jenny), who was killed while filming a movie in 1

THE TWENTIES

At the end of hostilities in 1918, aviation, like many a war hero, found itself abruptly unemployed. Surplus warplanes, ill-suited for civilian use, were dumped on the market at a fraction of their original cost, leaving manufacturers with little demand for new aircraft. Military airfields, too, were deactivated rapidly, resulting in a shortage of landing fields that further discouraged production; why build planes when there were no facilities to handle them?

In addition, where flying was concerned, a curious psychological reaction set in. During the fighting the airplane had been heroic and glamorous, but now grim associations of violence and death clung to it. There was in the American public's mind an added sense of humiliation and uneasiness about the country's failure to "darken the sky with clouds of planes." Almost a billion dollars had been appropriated for the purpose, yet General Billy Mitchell had come home raging that as a combat commander he had received exactly 196 American warplanes—and none had ever been flown in combat. Where had the money gone? Was it true that the DH-4 was obsolete even when American production of it had been ordered? Why had the United States tried to fit American engines to European air frames instead of building its own planes from scratch?

The country worked off its frustrations in typical fashion: a series of investigations that captured a few headlines but proved essentially nothing. America quickly forgot the questions of the past in its glorious enjoyment of the present, for these were the golden twenties.

In 1920 a wholesale reversion of military personnel to peacetime rank was ordered, striking a blow to service fliers' pride, prospects—and pocketbooks. And those American pilots who tried to make aviation a career in civilian life did so at considerable sacrifice. "What's the most dangerous thing about flying?" someone once asked Dick Depew, a war pilot-turned-barnstormer. "The risk," growled Depew, "of starving to death."

Even so, a lot of adventurous young men were willing to chance it. Flying war-surplus DH-4's and Curtiss Jennies, and sleeping in open fields under the wings of their weather-beaten craft, they hopped from town to town, from carnival to county fair, giving exhibitions of stunting, wing-walking, parachute jumping—anything that would attract a crowd. Then from the audience, they hoped, a few brave souls would hesitantly step forward to go for a ride at prices that averaged about fifty cents a minute.

No nervous groundling who tried it ever quite forgot the heart-thumping assortment of sensations that came from being strapped into an open cockpit: the bewildering array of gadgets; the oily, unfamiliar smells; the shattering roar of the engine; the rush of wind over the mud-speckled windscreen; and the stomach-shriveling first steep bank. The wild-eyed passenger would glance backward to see if the pilot had lost his mind—or perhaps had tumbled out—and would receive a reassuring nod from the goggled, helmeted creature of the sky. Then followed a gradual relaxing and the soaring exultation of actually *flying*, of becoming a member—however humble—of one of the most exclusive fraternities in the world.

These flying gypsies were remarkable men. Casual and rakish though they looked, they were often skilled mechanics and almost always first-rate pilots. They had accidents and forced landings, but they usually managed to survive. In addition, they treated their customers with an honesty and a friendly good humor that did much to recapture the public's interest in planes and restore its faith in the future of aviation.

And they brought romance back to flying.

As the years passed, some of the barnstormers abandoned their dangerous and unpredictable way of life for more prosaic jobs. Others went back into the Army or Navy so that they could continue to fly at government expense. A few hoarded their money, set up flying schools, or undertook the first tentative efforts to haul freight or passengers that led, in some cases, to the eventual establishment of commercial airlines.

In Europe passenger-carrying airlines had sprung up immediately after the war. The defeated Germans, of all people, were first to enter the field; the Deutsche Luftreederei was operating between Berlin, Leipzig, and Weimar less than three months after the Armistice. By the end of 1919 both the British and the French had organized London-to-Paris service. Having fled to Holland, the energetic Tony Fokker was busy setting up new factories, and KLM—the Dutch airline—was started that same year.

America, with its special problems of terrain and distance, got off to a slower start. In August, 1919, a company called Aero Limited was organized to fly vacationers and summer commuters from New York to Atlantic City. Soon afterward, observing the melancholy changes wrought by the new Prohibition Act, Aero Limited moved its headquarters to Miami and began ferrying thirsty Americans to various oases in the Bahamas. Another company with the same objective was the Aeromarine Sightseeing and Navigation Company, operating between Miami and Havana.

In those days the carrying capacity of commercial planes was so limited that passenger revenues alone could not cover operating costs. Recognizing this, most European countries were paying subsidies to their fledgling airlines. The French government, for example, contributed up to 1,000 francs of each commercial pilot's annual pay. It took the British a little longer to learn the lesson. Not until April, 1924—after the failure of several independent airlines in that country—was Imperial Airways formed, with a government subsidy to sustain its operation. In America opponents of such subsidies warned that they invariably led to excessive governmental control and tended to stifle private initiative. But it was obvious that without some help, private operations could not succeed. The solution in this country, eventually, took the form of government airmail contracts to private airlines.

Beginning in 1918, however, the United States Post Office tried to fly the mail itself. During the war the Army had organized a mail run between Washington, Philadelphia, and New York. Before hostilities ended, the Post Office Department took over with seventeen planes of its own, and with pilots recruited mostly from civilian instructors at Army bases.

Almost at once plans were made for a mail route from New York to Chicago over the storm-plagued Allegheny Mountains. By the summer of 1919 mail pilots were flying this "graveyard run" in open-cockpit, rebuilt warplanes under incredible conditions: no radio beams, no weather stations, no blind-flying instruments, not even lighted air beacons. Carrying the mail over the mountains was fully as hazardous as combat flying. Of the first forty pilots hired by the Post Office Department, thirty-one were killed before the operation was turned over to private airlines.

Despite its misfortunes in the east, the Post Office gradually pushed its operations westward and opened new routes, letting a few contracts to private fliers. In Seattle, an enterprising aviator, Edward Hubbard, persuaded postal authorities to let him run the airmail across Puget Sound to Victoria, British Columbia. He made his initial flight in 1919 in a pontoon-equipped biplane, the first aircraft built at the new Seattle factory of William E. Boeing, an air-minded member of a wealthy lumber dynasty.

In the public mind, these tentative commercial airlines and the beginnings of airmail were overshadowed by the first dramatic transatlantic flights. Soon after the end of the war, the United States Navy decided to demonstrate the range and power of its new Curtiss flying boats by sending three of them under Commander John H. Towers to England via Newfoundland, the Azores, and Portugal. On May 6, 1919, the *NC-1* (Navy Curtiss-1), *NC-3,* and *NC-4* left Newfoundland on the first leg of the transoceanic journey. The *NC-1* became lost in the fog and landed some two hundred miles west of the Azores, where her crew was picked up and the plane abandoned. The *NC-3,* skippered by Towers, landed on seas so rough that she could not take off again. With no aid in sight, Towers masterfully half-sailed, half-taxied the plane, by now severely damaged, the final 205 miles to the Azores—a tour de force of navigation.

From the start the *NC-4,* under the command of Lieutenant Commander Albert C. Read, proved faster —and luckier—than her sister ships. Fog blanketed the sea near the Azores, but she made it to Horta without difficulty, covering the 1,380 miles at an average speed of 74.8 knots. From there she went on triumphantly to Portugal and England.

This feat still left the London *Daily Mail's* 1913 offer of £10,000 for the first nonstop flight between the British Isles and the New World unclaimed. More than 1,800 miles of stormy ocean lay between Newfoundland and Ireland. Even with a tail wind, a loaded plane could not make much more than 100 miles per hour. Cockpits were still open. Air-to-ground communications were so primitive that radios were frequently discarded to lessen weight.

These hazards did not deter a pair of Britons who tried the nonstop transatlantic flight a month after the trip of the *NC-4*. Captain John Alcock and Lieutenant Arthur Whitten Brown (whose parents were American) had both been prisoners of war in Germany. Flying a twin-engine Vickers-Vimy remodeled bomber, they took off from St. John's, Newfoundland, on June 14, flew for sixteen hours and twenty-seven minutes through appalling weather, and at last claimed the *Daily Mail* prize when they made a crash landing the next morning in an Irish bog.

The last great flight of 1919 was an 11,000-mile race against time from London to Australia. Again a prize was the incentive: £10,000 was offered by the Australian government to any Australian pilot who completed such a flight within thirty days from the start in an all-British-built airplane.

In a Vickers-Vimy biplane similar to the one used by Alcock and Brown, Captain Ross Smith, an Australian war flier, left England on November 12. Reasonably good airfields were available as far as Calcutta, but for the last stages there were virtually no facilities at all. A combination of bad weather and bad luck plagued Smith and his three-man crew most of the way. Yet, twenty-seven days and twenty hours out of England, they landed at Port Darwin—with fifty-two hours to spare—and were able to claim the prize.

These record flights, however, did little to lift military aviation in America out of its postwar doldrums. Yet, ever since the Armistice, the indefatigable Billy Mitchell—who was now Assistant Chief of the Army Air Service in Washington—had been a driving force behind Army air activity. In October, 1919, acutely aware of the publicity received by the Navy for the *NC-4*'s triumphant crossing of the Atlantic five months earlier, he sent seventy Army pilots across the continent in both directions in what was termed an air race. Actually, it was a badly-needed survey flight that pointed up the inadequacy of the nation's air facilities. Mitchell also organized an aerial forest-fire watch on the West Coast, a flying border patrol along the Rio Grande, and urged mass Army flights to Alaska and around the world. In 1920 Captain St. Clair Streett, commanding four DH-4's, successfully executed the Alaskan flight.

Such Army aircraft as the DH-4's, however, had become dangerously obsolete. In a twelve-month period, from midsummer 1920 to midsummer 1921, the Air Service suffered 330 crashes and sixty-nine fatalities. The Army fliers complained bitterly about the de Havillands and called them "flaming coffins." But the mood of the country was one of financial retrenchment and a "return to normalcy." There was little government support for spending money on new military planes.

In the face of official indifference, Mitchell raised his voice with increasing passion. One of his principal arguments, certain to arouse hostility from many Naval leaders, was that the bomber and torpedo plane had rendered surface warships obsolete. Mitchell clamored ceaselessly for a chance to prove that he was right. Publicly, he produced embarrassing magazine articles and gave out uninhibited newspaper interviews calling for a stronger air force. Privately, he expressed his conviction that behind the resistance to his views lurked sinister big business groups interested primarily in the profits to be made from building battleships.

Undoubtedly, Mitchell had courage, energy, and the historic position of being right. But he did not suffer fools gladly, and he had an unfortunate tendency to consider anyone who differed with him a fool. Some of his charges, moreover, were unfair. His statements to the press made it sound as if the struggle were basically between a hidebound Navy and an eager young Air Service. This was not so; many top Navy experts agreed with him.

He was supported strongly by Admiral Bradley Fiske, who as far back as 1912 had pioneered the torpedo plane. Admiral William S. Sims, who had commanded American Naval Forces in European waters during the war, came out flatly for aircraft carriers as opposed to battleships. One of the Navy's most brilliant strategists, Admiral W. F. Fullam, prophesied that "sea power, or fighting power, in the future will be largely dependent upon control of the air."

The same controversy was raging in England. Jack Fisher, who had been a wartime First Sea Lord of the Admiralty, joyously sank his fangs into colleagues who kept clamoring for more battleships. "There is only one thing to do to the ostriches who are spending these vast millions on what is as useful for the next war as bows and arrows," he roared. "Sack the lot." The real battle was not so much between the Navy and the Army Air Service as it was between air-minded and non-air-minded officers everywhere.

Finding his recommendations consistently blocked or ignored, Mitchell felt justified in appealing to Congress or the public over the heads of his superiors. By the beginning of 1921 the uproar he had stirred reached national proportions. Mitchell kept insisting that his bombers could sink any warship afloat—and he kept offering to prove it.

In June and July Mitchell got his chance. The targets were former German warships, anchored some seventy-five miles off the mouth of Chesapeake Bay.

First, Naval seaplanes sank a German submarine, the *U-117*. Next a destroyer and the light cruiser *Frankfurt* went down under a rain of bombs from Army planes. But the critical target was the "unsinkable" dreadnought *Ostfriesland,* which had survived severe mine damage and gunfire at the Battle of Jutland, and was one of the most heavily-armored ships in the world.

Attacks carried out on July 20 by Naval, Marine, and Army fliers with light bombs made little impression on the German giant. The Army's first assault on the morning of July 21, made with 1,000-pound bombs, was equally ineffective. But under Mitchell's fierce prodding, Army Ordnance had developed a new bomb weighing 2,000 pounds, and now, flying at about 2,500 feet, a formation of eight Martin bombers —each carrying one of these giant bombs—sank the pride of the German navy in just twenty-five minutes.

There was a lesson to be learned from the bombing tests, and some high-ranking Naval officers were quick to admit it. "We must put planes on battleships," announced Rear Admiral William A. Moffett, the new Chief of Naval Aviation, "and get aircraft carriers quickly." Within eight months he got his first carrier; on March 20, 1922, the U.S.S. *Langley* was commissioned at Norfolk, Virginia.

By 1921 the Navy had been assigned the principal lighter-than-air mission and was building a great rigid dirigible, the *ZR-1,* in Philadelphia. Although a sister ship being built in England crashed on her final test, Admiral Moffett stoutly reaffirmed his confidence in lighter-than-air craft and announced that work would continue on the *ZR-1,* eventually to be christened the *Shenandoah.*

The hazards of hydrogen-filled airships were brought home to the Navy even more vividly in 1922 when the semirigid dirigible *Roma,* purchased from the Italian government, struck high-tension wires near Langley Field, Virginia, and exploded in a sheet of flame. Eleven men saved themselves by jumping. Thirty-three were lost. After that, hydrogen was abandoned as the lifting agent in American dirigibles. The substitute was helium, an inert gas only slightly heavier than hydrogen that eliminates the risk of fire.

While lighter-than-air men struggled with such ancient problems, Billy Mitchell continued to plot aerial feats that would capture public attention and help buttress his arguments for an independent air force. In May, 1923, after two unsuccessful Army attempts to fly nonstop across the country, Lieutenants John A. Macready and Oakley G. Kelly took off from Roosevelt Field, Long Island, in a single-engine Fokker T-2. Almost twenty-seven hours and more than 2,500 miles later they landed at Rockwell Field, San Diego. Next year, in a heavily-publicized "dawn-to-dusk"

race against the sun, Army Lieutenant Russell A. Maughan streaked from Long Island to San Francisco in seventeen hours, fifty-two minutes. Flying a new Curtiss pursuit plane, he averaged 150 miles per hour, including refueling stops. He landed just at sunset and proudly handed the Mayor of San Francisco a copy of *The New York Times* printed that same day.

While Maughan was racing the sun, three Army airplanes on the other side of the planet were nearing the halfway point in the most ambitious aerial exploit yet undertaken—a mass flight around the world. On April 4, 1924, eight of the Air Service's best pilots had taken off from Seattle in four "world cruisers"—single-engine biplanes designed to fly both as landplanes and seaplanes. Two of them completed the 26,000-mile circuit of the globe at Seattle on September 28.

Such a series of triumphs might have mellowed almost any man except Billy Mitchell, but he was far from satisfied. A tour of Europe had convinced him that German militarism was very much alive, and that the Germans were already planning to exploit air power in a war of the future. A visit to the Far East had also left him highly critical of American defenses, especially at Pearl Harbor. "If our warships there," he wrote, "were to be found bottled up in a surprise attack from the air and our airplanes destroyed on the ground, nothing but a miracle would enable us to hold our Far East possessions. It would break our backs. The same prediction applies to the Philippines . . . "

By now official patience with the self-appointed prophet was wearing thin. "That man," fumed President Calvin Coolidge to Secretary of War John W. Weeks, "has talked more in the last three months than I have in my whole life." The result of Presidential displeasure was that when Mitchell's tour of duty as Assistant Chief of the Air Service ended, he was not reappointed but was sent instead to what his superiors hoped would be the obscurity of an air base in Texas.

In the summer of 1925, partly no doubt in an attempt to counteract Mitchell's criticisms, the Navy sent a seaplane on a hazardous nonstop flight from San Francisco to Hawaii. It also ordered the dirigible *Shenandoah* to make a series of "public relations" appearances in Midwestern states. Both decisions were disastrous. The seaplane, *PN-9 No. 1,* ran out of fuel short of Hawaii, and was forced to land at sea. For ten days Commander John Rodgers and his crew struggled to sail the craft the remaining distance. Suffering from hunger and thirst, they were finally picked up by a submarine within sight of land.

On September 3, 1925, two days after Rodgers had disappeared, the Navy's proud *Shenandoah* was caught in a violent line squall near Marietta, Ohio, and came apart in mid-air, killing fourteen men.

Forty-eight hours after this second disaster Mitchell issued a blistering statement accusing the War and Navy Departments of "incompetency, criminal negligence, and almost treasonable administration" of aviation affairs. He followed this up with a blast calling for an investigation of the "disgraceful" situation by a board to be composed of "representative Americans instead of representatives of the army and navy bureaucracies." By such actions Mitchell made his trial by court-martial inevitable, and his conviction on charges of "insubordination and conduct unbecoming to an officer" a foregone conclusion. When President Coolidge confirmed his conviction on January 25, 1926, Mitchell promptly resigned from the Army.

During the trial itself, public sentiment was with Mitchell. "He has done more for the cause of aviation," wrote Frank Tichenor, editor of *Aero Digest,* "than any other man in the nation's history except the Wright brothers." At the other extreme was Admiral Moffett's furious denunciation of Mitchell as a man "of unsound mind and suffering from delusions of grandeur." In the middle were those inclined to agree with General Charles P. Summerall, who pronounced Mitchell "one of that damn kind of soldier who is wonderful in war and hell in peace."

Perhaps the sharpest indictment that can be brought against Mitchell is that for all his fireworks—and even with truth on his side—he did not get what he was after, namely a strong and independent air force. Far from winning acceptance for his ideas, his tactics tended to alienate the very people who might have implemented his theories. As a result, his prophecies were disregarded, and his contributions outweighed by the bitterness he aroused.

While the Mitchell controversy dominated the headlines, men in the background were working on proposals that would set the pattern of development for military aviation in this country for the next two decades. Nettled by Mitchell's criticism, President Coolidge in September, 1925, appointed a commission to study, among other things, the "best means of developing and applying aircraft in national defense." As chairman of the board he named Dwight Morrow, a partner in the banking firm of J. P. Morgan. On November 30, just after Mitchell had rested his defense and while he was awaiting the verdict of the court-martial, the Morrow Board submitted its report, which flatly rejected some of Mitchell's arguments. Air power, the report noted, was not sufficiently developed to justify creation of an independent air arm; building up a strong air force at the expense of naval armaments, limited by international treaty, would be a disservice to the cause of world disarmament. "The next war may well start in the air," the Morrow Board

glibly predicted, "but in all probability it will wind up, as the last one did, in the mud."

To pacify the less violent military critics of America's defense establishment the Morrow Board suggested that the Air Service be renamed the Air Corps to give it more prestige, but it failed to recommend that its status within the War Department be changed.

The essential provisions of the report were incorporated in the Air Corps Act, passed by Congress on July 2, 1926. This law dutifully changed the name of the Air Service to Army Air Corps, and created the post of Assistant Secretary of War for Aeronautics. Similar provisions were written for the Navy. A more positive aspect of this new legislation was the authorization given to the War and Navy departments to begin a five-year expansion plan. Although lack of funds delayed the start of this program until 1927, the new orders for military planes, in time, assured the development of a domestic aircraft industry.

Along with its study of military aviation, the Morrow Board had considered problems of commercial aviation in America. As far back as 1922, Secretary of Commerce Herbert Hoover had drafted legislation covering this subject, but for three years his suggestions were ignored by Congress. Not until February, 1925, did Congress pass the Kelly Bill "to encourage commercial aviation and authorize the Postmaster General to contract for airmail service." Only private operators with adequate experience and equipment were given consideration and, as an incentive to bidding, they were promised up to four fifths of the revenue derived from the mail they carried. Within two months the Postmaster General had received more than 5,000 inquiries from applicants whose eagerness to gain the rewards obviously exceeded their ability to meet the requirements.

In October, 1925, the Post Office asked for bids on eight small "feeder" routes. Contract Air Mail Route Number 1, between Boston and New York, went to Colonial Air Transport. Colonial's operations were directed by a dynamic, twenty-six-year-old Yale graduate, Juan Terry Trippe, who promptly bought two Fokker trimotor planes capable of carrying six passengers in addition to the mail. National Air Transport received the contract for the Chicago-Dallas-Fort Worth run, and later took over the eastern section of the transcontinental route, from New York to Chicago. The western section, from Chicago to San Francisco, was awarded to the Puget Sound airmail pioneers, William Boeing and Edward Hubbard, who formed Boeing Air Transport and put into service twenty-five new Boeing 40's, which could carry two passengers in an enclosed cabin.

Actually, the first domestic airmail flown by a private airline was carried in planes owned by Henry Ford. Impressed by William Stout's early experiments with thick-wing, all-metal airplanes, Ford purchased five of his single-engine monoplanes and early in 1925 started a freight service between Detroit, Cleveland, and Chicago. Later, when Stout redesigned his plane and powered it with three Wright Whirlwind motors, Ford bought him out altogether and announced that he would carry passengers as well as freight.

Carrying the mail was so much more profitable than carrying people that most airlines with mail contracts made little effort to attract passengers. But small struggling operators who had no mail subsidy had to find cash customers or go out of business. Often these "independents," as they were called, acted as salesmen for new airplanes that were gradually superseding the war-surplus types.

With the spur given to commercial aviation by passage of the Kelly Bill, it became apparent that a greater degree of governmental control and supervision of the air was imperative. Realizing that "the foundation for military aviation was a strong commercial service," Secretary of Commerce Hoover insisted that the Morrow Board give its attention to this problem. The committee's conclusions led, in May, 1926, to the passage by Congress of the Air Commerce Act, which has been called the "legislative cornerstone for the development of commercial aviation in America." The act created a Bureau of Aeronautics in the Department of Commerce, which was authorized to license all American planes and pilots, set up and enforce rules for air traffic, investigate accidents, test new engines and aircraft for safety—in short, assist, guide, and police the development of civil aviation in all possible ways.

During these years of controversy and compromise over the future of military and civilian aviation in the United States, a number of important technological breakthroughs were scored by both European and American scientists. Even before the end of the war, Hugo Junkers was building his first all-metal airplanes in Germany. In 1919, realizing that the corrugated metal being used in airplane construction produced high drag, another German builder, Adolph Rohrbach, began producing planes with smooth metal surfaces—thus originating the modern "stressed-skin" concept in which the covering of the wing adds to its strength and load-bearing capacity.

The cantilevered wing requiring no external bracing had also been pioneered by Junkers in the last years of the war. Further development of this principle by Junkers and by Anthony Fokker, who extended his operations to the United States in the twenties, for the first time brought the monoplane into serious competition with the more familiar biplane, especially in the field of transport airplanes.

Convinced that biplanes wasted too much power overcoming drag, William B. Stout in 1920 designed an unorthodox American monoplane, which he described as "nothing but a wing with control surfaces." A further step toward the flying-wing concept was taken by Vincent J. Burnelli, an American designer who in 1924 built a biplane in which the fuselage enclosing the engine contributed to the wing lift. Meanwhile, the Handley Page slotted-wing device and Orville Wright's invention of the split flap began a long series of control-surface improvements.

These years also saw the introduction or development of such aviation refinements as the pressurized cabin, retractable landing gear, mid-air refueling, reversible and variable pitch propellers, a radio-controlled pilotless airplane, and radial air-cooled engines as a substitute for the heavier water-cooled models. And airplanes were first used for crop-dusting, cloud-seeding, and the gathering of weather data.

"Progress in aeronautics is being made at so rapid a rate," the National Advisory Committee for Aeronautics report of 1923 concluded, "that the only way to keep abreast of other nations is *actually to keep abreast,* year by year, *never falling behind.*" The Committee, composed of distinguished military and civilian air authorities, had been established by act of Congress in 1915 to "supervise and direct the scientific study of the problems of flight, with a view of their practical solution." Conducting its own research at the Langley Memorial Aeronautical Laboratory in Virginia and ceaselessly encouraging and reporting on the work of others, NACA played an increasingly larger role in American aviation up to 1958 when it was reorganized and renamed the National Aeronautics and Space Administration with an exciting new role to play in the developing space age.

The Daniel Guggenheim Fund for the Promotion of Aeronautics, established in 1926, gave aviation another shot in the arm. The air-minded New York philanthropist had founded the School of Aeronautics at New York University in 1925, and his $2,500,000 fund extended the program of aviation education across the country with generous grants that enabled several universities to build experimental wind tunnels. In succeeding years the fund sponsored the Safe Aircraft Competition, encouraged private flying clubs, and endowed a national aeronautical collection at the Library of Congress. A continuing spur to scientific progress, the fund also fostered commercial aviation by urging the development of a practical air transport vehicle, instituting a national program of roof-markings as navigation aids, and setting up the first aeronautical weather reporting service on a model airline operated by Western Air Express between Los Angeles and San Francisco.

In another area, the ultimate decline of the airplane as a military weapon was foreshadowed by the work of an American scientist, Dr. Robert H. Goddard, of Worcester, Massachusetts. On March 16, 1926, Goddard fired the first rocket propelled by liquid fuel. In a treatise published in 1920, he had suggested that it was theoretically possible to send a rocket to the moon; and if the rocket carried a pound or two of photographic flash powder it might even be possible—with a big telescope—to see it hit a dark area on the moon. Far ahead of his time, Goddard received skeptical and often jeering publicity in the United States, and most Americans soon forgot about him. But Germans and Russians read his writings with interest, and in those countries his influence helped shape rocket development that by World War II was ahead of the rest of the world.

Back in the twenties, however, the airplane alone provided the public with enough thrills to appease its hunger for sensation and novelty. And world interest in aviation rose with each new attempt to set records of distance and speed in the air. In 1924 Britain's Alan Cobham flew from London to Rangoon, Burma, and back; the next year he made the round trip from London to Capetown. His pioneering survey flights would one day help to tie the British Empire together in a commercial air network. Lieutenant Commander Richard E. Byrd and his pilot Floyd Bennett earned for America the glory of the first flight over the North Pole on May 9, 1926. Two days later the Norwegian explorer Roald Amundsen crossed the Pole in an Italian-built dirigible, the *Norge*.

On May 22, 1919, seven years before these flights over the Pole, a prize of $25,000 had been offered by Raymond Orteig, a New York hotel owner, "to the first aviator who shall cross the Atlantic in a land or water aircraft (heavier-than-air) from Paris or the shores of France to New York, or from New York to Paris or the shores of France, without stop."

For seven years this prize had gone unclaimed, not because wings were fragile or men lacked courage, but because airplane engines could not be counted on to run continuously for such a distance. But now a new power plant, the 220-horsepower, air-cooled Wright Whirlwind engine, was proving itself unexcelled in lightness, reliability, and efficiency for long distances.

Designed by Charles L. Lawrance, and developed by the Wright Aeronautical Corporation, three of these radial engines had taken Byrd to the Pole. In September, 1926, a tall, slender airmail pilot employed by the Robertson Aircraft Corporation in St.

Louis began to wonder if such an engine might not pull a carefully designed monoplane across the tremendous 3,300-mile arc of land and sea that stretched from New York to Paris.

Twenty-four years old and looking even younger, Charles Augustus Lindbergh had already logged almost 2,000 hours in the air. Ex-barnstormer, wing walker, survivor of emergency parachute jumps, captain in the Missouri National Guard, he had all the flying experience needed, but little money. He took his idea—and $2,000 of his own savings—to a group of businessmen in St. Louis. Hesitantly, they agreed to raise another $13,000 to buy a long-range monoplane equipped with a Whirlwind engine. They had qualms about a single-engine airplane, but Lindbergh convinced them that extra engines simply increased the chances of engine failure. Besides, he pointed out, they could not afford a multi-engine plane.

Other men with greater financial backing had their eyes on the Orteig Prize and the glory that would go with it. Already the French war ace René Fonck had come to grief in an attempt to fly the Atlantic, when his Sikorsky trimotor crashed on take-off at Roosevelt Field, Long Island, killing two members of the crew. A new Fokker trimotor was being built for Commander Byrd, and a Bellanca monoplane capable of carrying two men over the ocean was being made ready by the Columbia Aircraft Corporation. Lieutenant Commander Noel Davis and Lieutenant Stanton Wooster of the U. S. Navy were testing a big Keystone Pathfinder biplane with three Whirlwind engines. In France another war hero, Charles Nungesser, was planning an east-to-west Atlantic crossing with François Coli. Lindbergh and his backers knew there was no time to lose.

When negotiations with Fokker and other leading manufacturers got nowhere, Lindbergh turned to a small, relatively unknown company, Ryan Airlines, Inc., of San Diego. On February 23, 1927, Lindbergh arrived in San Diego, and the next day he wired his St. Louis backers that the California builders could produce the plane, complete with engine, for $10,580. What was more, they thought they could do it in sixty days. For two months he and the small Ryan factory staff worked feverishly on the new plane. Exactly sixty days after the business negotiations had been settled, the *Spirit of St. Louis* was air-borne.

On May 10, with all tests completed, Lindbergh flew nonstop to St. Louis in fourteen hours and twenty-five minutes—a new record from the Pacific Coast. Two days later he was in New York.

Meanwhile, things had been going badly with the big multi-engine ships. Byrd's Fokker had crashed on landing with Fokker himself at the controls, seriously injuring Floyd Bennett. The plane was still being re-paired. Davis and Wooster had been killed when their Keystone crashed in a marsh. On May 8 Nungesser and Coli had disappeared over the Atlantic. Even the Bellanca had been involved in a crack-up.

Reports of weather conditions over the Atlantic were discouraging. For a full week Lindbergh waited. His competitors—Byrd, Giuseppe Bellanca, Clarence Chamberlin—were kind and helpful, but he acquired a permanent distaste for the intrusive tabloid press. Most of the time he spent checking his plane, peeling off every ounce of surplus weight. There would be no radio in the *Spirit of St. Louis,* and no parachute.

On the night of May 19 Lindbergh had planned to see *Rio Rita,* a musical hit. It was raining in New York; the tops of the skyscrapers were lost in mist. On the way to the theater, a call was made to the weather bureau. Now the forecast for the North Atlantic was suddenly more favorable. Forgetting the theater, Lindbergh made plans to leave early the next morning.

At the moment of take-off, conditions were any-thing but favorable—a soft, rain-soaked runway; an overloaded plane; an engine whose tachometer regis-tered 30 revolutions too low; a maddening breeze that shifted from a light head wind to a 5-mile-per-hour tail wind just after the little plane had been placed in position; a propeller set for cruising, not take-off. But something whispered to Lindbergh that he could get his ship off the ground, and he did, clearing a web of telephone wires by twenty feet and vanishing into the misty grayness on a compass heading of 65 degrees —the heading he had worked out for the first hun-dred-mile segment of his great circle route to Paris.

The story of that flight has been told many times, twice by Lindbergh himself. His first account, pub-lished in 1927 and titled *"We",* was a stiff and un-adorned account that gave little but the bare facts. "Being young, and easily embarrassed," he wrote years later, "I was hesitant to dwell on my personal errors and sensations. Also, believing in aviation's future, I did not want to lay bare, through my own experience, its existing weaknesses." In 1953 he told the whole story in a fine book, *The Spirit of St. Louis.*

Twenty-seven hours after take-off, he spotted fish-ing boats, circled low, cut his engine, and shouted futilely, "Which way is Ireland?" Actually, he was exactly on course, and two hours ahead of schedule. Across the southern tip of Ireland he flew, across the south of England, across the Channel. Then the land-ing in the dark at Le Bourget field at Paris, with the huge, stampeding, hysterical crowds. "Everyone had the best of intentions," he wrote with a flicker of humor in *"We",* "but no one seemed to know what they were."

In the days that followed, Lindbergh's stature as a hero grew until it almost blotted out the sun. No one has ever fully explained the outpouring of admiration and affection that came from all over the world. Granted it was a magnificent flight, splendidly marked by simplicity and perfection. Granted Lindbergh's subsequent performance was faultless: he was modest, he was composed, he seemed to have an infallible in-stinct for saying and doing the right thing. Still there had been other great flights, and other personable and modest fliers.

Perhaps it was because something in Lindbergh—his integrity, his courage, his indifference to money, the hint of Puritanism about him, of monasticism al-most—touched the spark of nobility that glows, however faintly, in human beings everywhere, remind-ing them that man's spirit can also soar on wings above materialism, above the dark waters of selfishness.

The symbolism of the flight was irresistible. As Am-bassador Herrick said of Lindbergh, "He started with no purpose but to arrive. He remained with no desire but to serve. He sought nothing; he was offered all."

RIGHT: *Postal officials prepare to load the mail into a Signal Corps Jenny at a field in North Philadelphia. The date was May 15, 1918, the first day of the airmail service between Washington, Philadelphia, and New York. A humiliating mishap marred the day: the pilot assigned to fly from Washington to Philadelphia flew to southeastern Maryland instead. His mail eventually went north by train, an unpropitious beginning for the fledgling U.S. service.*

BELOW: *Passengers don helmets and flying coats before boarding a converted DH-9 bomber for a flight from London to Paris. They paid £21 for the privilege of being squeezed into the uncomfortable, open rear cockpit. The airline, Aircraft Transport and Travel, Limited, was the first to schedule daily flights. The service, which began on August 25, 1919, was an outgrowth of military flights that had carried British officials to the Peace Conference.*

KLM AEROCARTO N.V.

Seeking Work

Aviation, the romantic military branch of the war, found itself regarded as a useless curiosity in peacetime. Barnstormers drew crowds at county fairs in America, and stunt fliers enlivened the movies. Gliding was a popular sport in Europe, and the exploits of the first transatlantic fliers made exciting reading. But to many people, the airplane was a frivolity that could never earn its keep.

Two new developments began to change some minds. In Europe commercial airlines sprang up soon after the Armistice, and although the planes were uncomfortable and expensive, they usually reached their destinations safely.

In the United States airplanes were flying the mail. Scheduled mail flights had been inaugurated even before the end of the war. Delays were frequent, and fatalities high, but routes were expanded, and in February, 1921, the mail was flown from San Francisco to New York for the first time, in thirty-three hours and twenty minutes.

Although it sometimes bit off more than it could chew, the airplane had gone to work.

Although the villain seems to have the upper hand in the movie still above, there is no doubt that the hero emerged victorious. Aerial sequences added drama to many low-budget films, as well as to expensive epics like Wings and Hell's Angels. Below, a glider takes off from a hillside in Germany, where gliding enjoyed a rebirth because of the Versailles Treaty limitations on aviation.

Across the Ocean

Although two successful flights across the Atlantic were made in 1919, transoceanic trips were a perilous business for airplanes. The Navy's *NC-4* flew safely to Europe via the Azores in May, but her two sister ships were forced down into stormy waters by bad weather. In June, fog and ice almost turned Alcock and Brown's nonstop flight into a disaster.

That same summer, however, a dirigible crossed the Atlantic and made it look easy. Britain's *R-34* left Scotland on July 2, and although constant head winds reduced her speed, she reached Mineola, Long Island, four and a half days later (below). Her return trip to England took only seventy-five hours. Lighter-than-air men were jubilant, and the dirigible's reputation for safety and reliability in the next decade rose higher than was deserved.

Captain John Alcock and Lieutenant Arthur Whitten Brown are shown above with a model of their Vickers-Vimy biplane and with the bag of mail they carried on the first nonstop flight across the Atlantic. They left Newfoundland on June 14, 1919, and crash-landed safely in a bog at Clifden, Ireland, sixteen and a half hours later.

The first plane to span the Atlantic was the United States Navy's NC-4, which flew from Newfoundland to the Azores, Portugal, and England. In the artist's conception above, the NC-4 is shown over Drake's Waters off Plymouth Hoe, England.

The Lean Years

The end of war prosperity had brought a critical period to America's budding aviation industry. Seattle's William Boeing assessed the situation in a letter to his staff soon after the Armistice:

"I look for a splendid future in peacetime, but there is going to be a gap of six months to two years when it will be a hard struggle. In the meantime we should keep our shop occupied with other work. Comb the field and see what we might go into. I can suggest showcase work and interior woodwork."

Boeing was correct in his prediction of a doldrums period. But he was overly optimistic concerning the duration. With only a minimum of government military orders and practically no demand for commercial planes, American builders experienced a long period of lean years.

During that time, many of them never stopped dreaming—and working at planning boards. Great names of the future stayed in the business— men like Boeing, Donald Douglas, Lawrence Bell, James Kindelberger, Claude Ryan, Igor Sikorsky, Eddie Stinson, William B. Stout, and Sherman Fairchild. Along with established pioneers like Glenn Curtiss, Glenn Martin, and Grover Loening, they competed for the occasional government order and eagerly sought the rare private sale.

Financing was a constant problem, and shops were often half-empty or temporarily shut down. Sometimes designers left their employers and gambled with shops of their own. In the end, those with staying power and ability who had kept their favorite planes flying, while constantly testing and improving them— were rewarded. As activity picked up, they won bids and expanded operations that, in some cases, boomed eventually into huge plants.

210

Glenn Martin and his staff posed in 1918 in front of the original Martin bomber, the MB-1 (above), which was produced too late for use in World War I. From left to right: Lawrence Bell, Thomas E. Springer, Glenn Martin, and Donald Douglas.

Donald Douglas left Martin in 1920, and with only $600 capital established his own aircraft company in Santa Monica, California (above). The initial model built by Douglas was the Cloudster, the first plane to lift its own weight in payload.

A typical municipal airport in the United States was the muddy Twin City Airport of Minneapolis-St. Paul, Minnesota (left). At the end of 1920 there were only 271 flying fields in the nation, including fifty-seven military and airmail installations.

211

FAMOUS AIRPLANES: 1919-1927

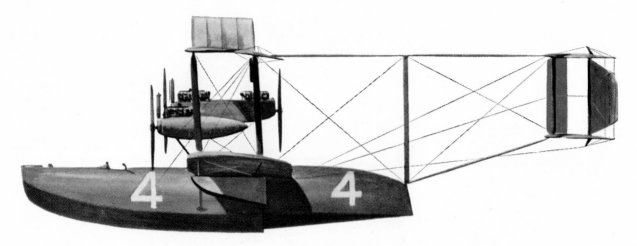

CURTISS NC-4 1919

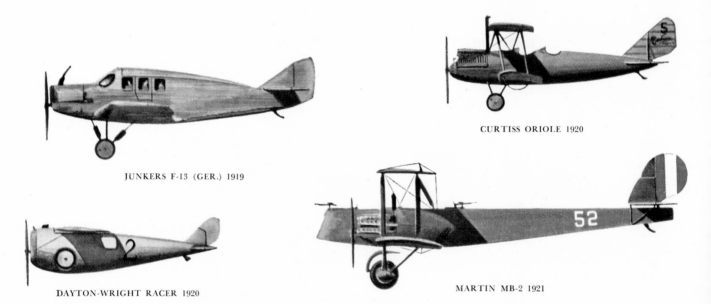

JUNKERS F-13 (GER.) 1919

CURTISS ORIOLE 1920

DAYTON-WRIGHT RACER 1920

MARTIN MB-2 1921

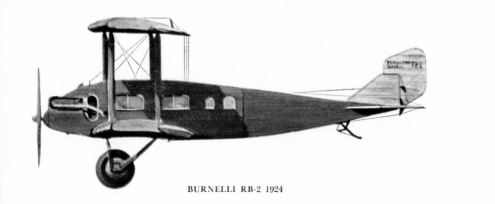

BURNELLI RB-2 1924

TRAVEL AIR 1924

STOUT AT-2 1924

DOUGLAS C-1 1925

CURTISS P-1 1925

RYAN M-1 1926

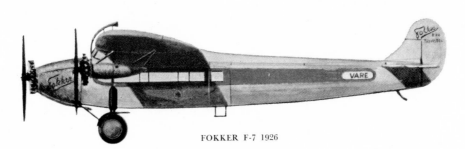

WRIGHT BELLANCA 1926

FOKKER F-7 1926

FAIRCHILD FC-2 1926-27

BOEING F2B-1 1926-27

LOCKHEED VEGA 1927

RYAN SPIRIT OF ST. LOUIS 1927

Ideas that Worked...

...And One that Didn't

The flying boat at the far left was built in Denmark for the Japanese in 1923. The designer was Germany's Dr. Adolph K. Rohrbach, who eschewed the corrugated metal surfaces employed by his contemporaries. His planes featured fully-stressed, smooth metal skins and metal box-spar wings, which added to the wing strength.

The modern helicopter was foreshadowed by Juan de la Cierva's Autogiros, one of which is shown at the left. Although the fuselage and propeller were those of an airplane, lift was provided by four large rotating blades with flapping hinges. The Autogiro, first flown in 1923 in Madrid, needed only a short runway for take-offs.

Gianni Caproni, an Italian designer whose huge triplane bombers were widely used in World War I, came a cropper in 1919 with his gigantic Model 60, the "Houseboat" (below). The unwieldy flying boat, which was built to accommodate one hundred passengers in comfort, weighed more than 30,000 pounds. Its eight 400-horsepower engines could not lift the nine-winged monster, and Caproni abandoned the model.

CULVER PICTURES, INC.

COLLECTION OF PETER M. BOWERS

The French poster (above) advertised the Société Maritime Aérienne's seaplane serv- ice from Antibes on the Riviera to Ajaccio in Corsica. The cost of the round- trip flights, which started in 1922, was 352 francs (about $70) in a twin-engine plane, with a special rate of 288 francs for those willing to fly in a single- engine plane. Below, passengers disembark after an Imperial Airways flight from London to Paris. The plane is an Armstrong-Whitworth Argosy, which carried twenty passengers, each of whom had a window that could be opened during the flight.

Speed and Comfort

Europe's fledgling airlines strug- gled to survive in the early 1920's. The converted bombers being used for passengers were too small for profit, and there were too many air- lines for too few customers.

Government subsidies and more efficient aircraft solved the problem. Following the example of Holland's KLM, Germany and England merged their anemic private airlines into state-supported Lufthansa and Imperial Airways. And multiple-en- gine airliners that could carry up to twenty passengers in their sumptu- ous cabins were designed by builders like Anthony Fokker, Hugo Junkers and Frederick Handley Page.

Passenger totals for the world's airlines, excluding China and Rus- sia, soared from 5,000 in 1919 to 434,000 a decade later in 1929. It was not yet self-supporting, but avia- tion had become a big business.

The luxurious interior of the French Farman 180 featured overstuffed chairs, indirect lighting, and a mahogany bar with a brass rail to hang on to in bad weather. The twin-engine biplane was put into service in 1929 by Lignes Aériennes Farman.

217

A phosphorus bomb, dropped from a Martin MB-2 explodes over the U.S.S. Alabama *(above) in one of the tests conducted in 1921.*

Billy Mitchell

Naval officers were stunned when General Billy Mitchell's bombers sank the supposedly impregnable *Ostfriesland* on July 21, 1921. Some wept openly as they watched the huge German battleship go down under a quick and deadly hail of 2,000-pound bombs.

Diehards pointed out that the ship was neither defended nor moving when it was attacked, and the joint Army and Navy report of the event, signed by General John Pershing, stated that the battleship was still the "bulwark of the nation's sea defence." But Mitchell had tasted victory, and he became even more uncompromising in his crusade for a stronger air corps.

Mitchell's appointment as Assistant Chief of Air Service was due to expire in 1925, and he determined to make the most of his tenure. He exposed the vulnerability of American cities with a series of mock air attacks, and he proved again, in further demonstrations at sea, that battleships were no match for bombers. Mitchell knew that the future of air power rested on civilian as well as military support and understanding, and so he set out to reawaken the nation's interest in aviation.

General Mitchell, in a Morse pursuit plane (above), ordered some of his pilots to drop their bombs in the water around the Ostfriesland. The impact of the underwater explosions shattered the ship's hull and sank her in twenty-five minutes (below).

Army Triumphs

Under Mitchell's ceaseless prodding, U. S. Army Air Service pilots smashed world records and made flights that pressed both men and planes to the limit of endurance. Most spectacular were the first nonstop flight across the continent made in 1923 by Lieutenants John Macready and Oakley Kelly, and the round-the-world flight of 1924. But there were other triumphs too.

In September, 1922, Lieutenant James Doolittle became the first person to fly across the United States in less than a day. With only one stop, he flew from Florida to California in twenty-one hours and twenty minutes. In May, 1923, Lieutenant H. G. Crocker raced from Texas to Ontario, Canada, in less than twelve hours nonstop. And in June, 1924, Lieutenant Russell Maughan beat the sun from New York to California, as he flew 2,670 miles in less than twenty-two hours, including refueling stops.

Speed records fell as men like Maughan, H. R. Harris, Ralph Lockwood, and Cyrus Bettis—all Air Service lieutenants—increased the performance of their planes. And endurance records toppled when a pioneering aerial refueling device helped Lieutenants Lowell Smith and John Richter to remain aloft for more than thirty-seven hours in August, 1923. Each month saw new Army Air Service successes—and new ammunition for Mitchell's crusade.

The first nonstop flight across the United States was made in May, 1923, in the huge Fokker T-2 monoplane at left. Lieutenants John Macready and Oakley Kelly, who had failed in two earlier attempts to fly across the continent from west to east, flew from Long Island, New York, to San Diego, California, in twenty-six hours and fifty minutes. They covered 2,520 miles at an average speed of 94 miles per hour.

Chances of success seemed slim when eight round-the-world fliers left Seattle, Washington, in four Douglas World Cruisers on April 6, 1924 (above). But other nations were attempting the journey, and the United States had to try. Before the month was over, the flagship Seattle *crashed into an Alaskan mountainside. Nevertheless, the remaining planes, commanded by Lieutenant Lowell Smith, continued across the northern Pacific. By June 2 they had reached Kagoshima, Japan, where they were given an enthusiastic welcome by 50,000 flag-waving Japanese (left). All three planes then flew safely across Asia and Europe, but a faulty oil pump caused the* Boston *to be abandoned at sea during the flight to Iceland in August. The* Chicago *and the* New Orleans *went on across the North Atlantic and returned triumphantly to Seattle on September 28, after flying 26,345 miles in under six months.*

221

Rear Admiral William A. Moffett (right), who became the first chief of the Navy's Bureau of Aeronautics in 1921, was an ardent supporter of naval air power. He led the campaign for aircraft carriers, and believed that the bulk of the nation's air strength should be kept at sea. Billy Mitchell, on the other hand, felt that carriers were as vulnerable to bombing as were battleships, and he also criticized Moffett's lighter-than-air program. The two became bitter enemies, and Moffett called Mitchell a man of "unsound mind."

The Navy Flies

American Naval aviation was partially eclipsed in the 1920's by the more sensational exploits of the Army Air Service pilots. Nevertheless, progress was made in adapting aviation to the Navy's mission.

Naval pilots and engineers pioneered in the refinement of aerial torpedoes, air-cooled radial engines, all-metal airplanes, and catapults for launching planes from ships. An accurate high-altitude bombsight was developed for the Navy by Carl Norden. Seaplane tenders were put into service, and the first aircraft carriers were built. Despite these advances, and the fact that Navy pilots broke many records, some Naval leaders were criticized, often unfairly, for inefficiency and shortsightedness. To counteract any impatience with Naval progress, two highly-publicized flights were ordered in 1925. The first, a nonstop flight to Hawaii, was a failure. And two days later, the second, a good-will tour by the dirigible *Shenandoah,* ended in disaster.

Planes were launched from cruisers and battleships by a turntable catapult (above), first tested successfully in 1921 by Commander Holden C. Richardson. Early models were powered by compressed air, but gunpowder was used later. In October, 1922, Lieutenant V. S. Griffin made the first carrier take-off for the U.S. Navy.

America's first aircraft carrier, the U.S.S. Langley (left), was commissioned in March, 1922. The flight deck of the converted collier was only 534 feet long and 64 feet wide, and her facilities were primitive. But she served her purpose as a test ship, and remained in service until sunk by the Japanese early in World War II.

The Navy's attempt at a nonstop flight from California to Hawaii failed when Commander John Rodgers's PN-9 No. 1 (right) ran out of fuel after 1,841 miles of flight. The crew fashioned a sail from the wing fabric, and sailed for 450 miles before they were rescued ten days later. Rodgers was killed in a plane crash in 1926.

The Death of a Dirigible

The Shenandoah, *pride of the United States Navy, came to a violent end on September 3, 1925. Caught in a line squall during a tour which was—ironically— meant to improve the Navy's public rela-*

ons, the airship was driven upward by e storm to an altitude of 3,150 feet. She en plummeted to within 150 feet of the ound, only to be pushed up again to 700 feet. Unable to withstand the abuse,

the Shenandoah ripped apart in the air near Marietta, Ohio.

The forward section, piloted as a free balloon by Lieutenant Commander Charles Rosendahl, came down safely. But the main

control car plunged to the ground. Among the fourteen men killed was the Shenandoah's commander, Zachary Lansdowne, who had been a passenger aboard the R-34 when it crossed the Atlantic in 1919.

Great Air Races

Competition for two coveted racing trophies gave tremendous impetus to aviation in the 1920's. Pitting nation against nation, and the Army against the Navy, the Schneider and Pulitzer Races capitalized on the natural rivalries of the fliers to encourage technological progress.

The Schneider Trophy Race, established in 1913 by Jacques Schneider of France, was open to seaplanes of all nations. The first pure racing planes appeared in the 1923 contest which the United States won with a Curtiss CR-3, the first plane to fly with a metal propeller. Its pilot was Lieutenant David Rittenhouse of the Navy, whose speed was 177 miles per hour. Each subsequent Schneider Race was marked by innovations in designs and engines, culminating in the great Supermarine aircraft, forerunners of the Spitfire fighters of World War II. British pilots, flying Supermarines at speeds up to 34. miles per hour, won the Schneider Race three consecutive times, and retired the trophy in 1931.

The Pulitzer Races were first held in 1920, when the Pulitzer brothers of St. Louis donated the trophy to spur the progress of American aviation. From that first year, when Lieutenant Corliss Moseley of the Army beat out thirty-six other entries in a Verville-Packard racer, to 1925, when Lieutenant Cyrus Bettis won with a record-breaking 24. miles per hour, the Pulitzer Races excited the imagination of American designers and pilots, and gave a new competitive spirit to the growing aviation industry.

Winner of the first Pulitzer Race with speed of 156 miles per hour was a Verville-Packard 600 racer, shown banking over pylon at left. Second was a Thomas-Morse pursuit plane, piloted by the World War I ace Harold Hartney. The race was held at Mitchel Field, Long Island.

A highlight of the 1922 Pulitzer Race, held near Detroit, Michigan, was the first public demonstration of retractable landing gear. Spectators were thrilled when the pilots of two Verville-Sperry pursuit planes, one of which is shown at left, cranked up their landing gear; but the wheel wells of the planes were uncovered and the resultant drag slowed down the craft. The race was won by a Curtiss biplane flown by Lieutenant Russell Maughan at a record-breaking speed of 205 miles per hour. Below, Major Mario de Bernardi of the Royal Italian Air Force stands up in his Macchi M-39, with which he won the 1926 Schneider Trophy Race held in Virginia.

A smiling Jimmy Doolittle stands proudly on a pontoon of the R3C-2, the Army Curtiss biplane which he flew at 235 miles per hour to win the 1925 Schneider Trophy. The same plane, with wheels instead of floats, had won the Pulitzer Race earlier that year. It was the last biplane to win the Schneider Trophy; monoplanes dominated all future contests. At right, a Supermarine S-5 is wheeled out for a test flight prior to the 1927 Schneider Race. The streamlined Supermarines, which beat out all competitors in the last years of the Schneider Races, were designed by R. J. Mitchell, whose innovations led to the great British fighters of World War II.

Over the Pole

Shortly after midnight on May 9, 1926, a Fokker trimotor, the *Josephine Ford*, took off on skiis from a snow-packed runway at King's Bay, Spitsbergen. Commanded by Richard E. Byrd, and piloted by Floyd Bennett, the plane flew across the forbidding arctic waste toward the North Pole.

Navigation without landmarks of any kind was perilous, and tension was increased by the discovery that one of the engines was leaking oil. But the plane stayed aloft, and the pilots kept their bearings. At 9:02 A.M. they became the first men to fly over the top of the world.

Sixteen hours after take-off, they returned triumphantly to King's Bay. Among those who greeted them was Roald Amundsen, the Norwegian explorer, who himself was to fly over the Pole in the dirigible *Norge*, three days after Byrd's success.

Amundsen congratulates Byrd, in furs, after the first Polar flight (above). When Byrd first arrived at Spitsbergen, his ship could not dock because of ice. A raft ferried the partly disassembled plane to shore (below).

The Norge, *shown over Spitsbergen, carried a crew of sixteen over the North Pole on May 12, 1926, and then flew 2,200 miles to Teller, Alaska. Aboard were Roald Amundsen and Lincoln Ellsworth, who had failed in a 1925 attempt to fly over the Pole, and Umberto Nobile, the airship's designer.*

229

Early on the morning of May 20, 1927, the Spirit of St. Louis *was towed by a truck from Curtiss Field, Long Island (above), to adjoining Roosevelt Field, which had a smooth runway. As the airplane was hauled backward through the rain, Lindbergh thought the scene looked "more like a funeral procession than the beginning of a flight to Paris." But a beginning it was; at 7:52* A.M. *he made a successful take-off.*

Parisian police tried to hold back the ecstatic crowd at Le Bourget airport when Lindbergh landed (above), but their efforts were futile. The mob broke through the barricades and while some ripped pieces of fabric off the Spirit of St. Louis *as souvenirs, others dragged Lindbergh from the cockpit and carried him away on their shoulders. Enthusiastic crowds also greeted Lindbergh in Brussels and in London.*

230

"We"

At first, Charles Lindbergh was too busy to think of sleep. Pleased with his successful take-off, he checked his instruments carefully and followed the geography of the land below him on his maps. And he discovered unexpected sources of annoyance. Clumps of mud, for instance, had been thrown onto the wings during take-off. Lindbergh had been ruthless in eliminating excess weight; how ironic that uninvited chunks of dirt should now add to the plane's load.

By the fourth hour of flight, his body began to cry for rest. But there were squalls over Nova Scotia to buffet the plane and shake him back to alertness, and later, over the hazy Atlantic, there were ominous ice cakes on which to concentrate. During the twelfth hour, he flew low over St. John's, Newfoundland, and saw the weather-beaten faces of men on the ground looking up at him in amazement.

North America was behind him now, and Lindbergh flew on through fog and darkness. When he shined his flashlight on the wing, he saw that there was some icing. But sleep was still his deadliest enemy. He cupped his hands into the slipstream to direct the icy wind against his face; he stamped his feet and bounced up and down in his seat. And sometimes, during the endless night, he had to hold open his eyelids with his thumbs.

Then it was morning. Lindbergh settled his plane low over the turbulent ocean. He knew that the land he saw was a mirage, and he continued onward as if in a daze. In the twenty-sixth hour he saw a porpoise, and then birds, and later, boats. Excitement conquered his need for sleep. He flew over Ireland and, now fully awake, on toward France and into the pages of history.

In Their Words . . .

FLYING FOR LOVE

"There Was a . . . Bang"

European commercial airlines, starting up in 1919, provided jobs for many World War I fliers. Alan Campbell Orde, a British pilot, recalls the days of transition from war to commercial flying.

An RAF communication flight had been started at Hendon [near London] for the purpose of flying important persons about. I was posted to it at the end of 1918.

This was cross-Channel, from London to British Army headquarters in France, and later on to Paris when the Peace Conference came up. This I believe was really the inception of the commercial flying that we started later.

We had to find our way from one place to another mostly by sight and contact flying, and, of course, in those days we had a great deal of engine trouble, which caused the forced landing to be a fairly common occurrence.

I continued in this work until toward the end of 1919, when British air transport started. Many of us in my squadron were offered jobs in one of the two original companies on the London-Paris route. I should have gone back to the university, but I couldn't face, somehow, leaving the thing I'd started and become so interested in. I couldn't resist the temptation to sign up with Aircraft Transport and Travel, Limited. Of course, we were using the same equipment, the DH-4 and DH-9, converted for carrying passengers, so we continued to have similar experiences.

For instance, flying in heavy rain on one occasion [from Paris to London], one of the blades of my wooden propeller started to come apart. The fabric coating, which covered the leading edge of one of these blades, had worn through, and the first thing I knew there was a terrific bang and very heavy vibration.

I had to come down on the beach at Le Touquet. We were short of daylight, but my two passengers were very nice. I explained what the trouble was, and one of them said, "I've got a penknife on me. I'll have a go at fixing this thing." So he helped me, and we hacked this loose piece of wood and fabric off the blade and got it started up again. I took off from this sandy beach, and we got across to England while there was still daylight. In those days the passengers took part in the whole thing in very good spirit.

The Sound of the Wires

Without commercial airlines in the United States, American fliers often had to choose between the hand-to-mouth existence of a barnstormer and the dangerous career of flying the mail. Dean Smith was one of the best-known early airmail pilots.

It was the spring of 1920. There had not been a great deal of airmail flying, and the pilots were getting killed almost as fast as the Post Office Department could employ them. So the airmail was considered pretty much a suicide club, and only pilots desperate to fly would join it.

But the pay was excellent. We were soon making from $800 to $1,000 a month, and in the early twenties this was really a tremendous amount of money.

Most of the planes that we flew in those days were biplanes that had bracing wires stretched diagonally to make an X between the struts. We had no instruments to speak of, and we learned to fly by feel. For instance, when gliding in, we learned to listen to the sound of the wires whistling through the air, which increases in pitch as the airplane goes faster, and decreases, of course, as it slows up. If it's whistling pretty loud and shrill, you're going too fast. If it's barely whispering, then you're near a stall.

We had all learned that if we got inside the clouds for any length of time we became confused and felt

232

of us tried to think of ways that might be able to remain oriented. [W]e tried things like bobs on the end [of] a string. I remember one fellow [who] had a half-full milk bottle that [he] thought he could use as a level.

[Of] course, none of these things [wo]rked because of the centrifugal [for]ce involved in any turn. So we [we]re pretty well convinced that you [cou]ldn't fly blind for any length [of] time. However, we all learned [wa]ys to prolong such flying. We got [so] that we could climb up through [clo]uds by feel, by bracing our feet [an]d feeling the wind on our cheeks, [an]d things like that. Eventually, even [th]en, we would get confused and the [pla]ne would stall and spin down.

[T]here were no official weather re-[po]rts at that time, and so we would [try] to locate some farmer to tell us [wh]at the weather was like. A farmer's [id]ea of a weather report was whether [it] was hot or cold, raining or not. [Th]e height of the clouds and the visi-[bil]ity they didn't know anything [ab]out. They would give us some [str]ange responses sometimes: when it [wa]s foggy, they'd say that they could [se]e up to a mile.

[T]he real hardship of flying in [tho]se days was the cold. We had [be]arskin flying suits, but even so, the [col]d, particularly out West, was ter-[rib]le. The planes were drafty, and the [fir]st ones had poor windshields and [ho]les in the bottom around the base [of] the stick where the air would come [b]lowing up, and the temperatures [wo]uld get below zero. Pretty soon, [yo]u'd sit there and you couldn't move [mu]ch. I'm sure this resulted in some [ac]cidents because pilots got so bitter-[ly] cold and so numb, and so obsessed [wi]th the misery that their judgment [wa]s poor. Then we got some heat, [wh]ich helped a great deal. By using [he]at exchanges on the exhaust pipes [we] were able to pipe some warm air [int]o the cockpit. We also improved [th]e windshields and plugged the [ho]les. From then on it was possible to [ha]ve relative comfort.

On the Flying Trapeze

Barnstorming pilots, performing dare-devil feats to entice customers to take rides, sometimes banded together in "flying circuses." Duke Krantz, billed as "The Flying Diavolo," was a stunt flier for the Gates Flying Circus.

We had crowds sometimes of thirty or forty thousand people—tremen-dous crowds. The main thing was, of course, to put on wing-walking shows to draw the people. Then, in between times, we would sell tickets and take the people for rides. Of course, it was very scientifically arranged so that we could load and unload rapidly. One man would pull passengers out from one side of the ship while another man would push them in from the opposite side.

In the beginning, we charged two dollars and fifty cents for a short ride, five dollars for a long ride. If they wanted any stunts at all, it would be an additional five dollars. There was a dollar admission fee for the exhibition, but the stunts were just the attraction to get passengers.

At first we used to sit on the top wing of the plane with our toes underneath, sort of around the straps. But, of course, that was not as spec-

Duke Krantz garbed for aerial stunting

tacular as standing up on top. In order to do that we had to have little secret devices, like having a belt under my sweater that nobody could see. I had cables—full cables, not wires—made up with snaps on them, and they were hidden in the airplane all the time. So when I got up in the air, I would stand up, I would hook the cables to the belt, and take one in each hand. As I reached up, I was snapping these fittings that nobody could see. Then I would straighten up and, with no hesitation at all, stretch out good and tight. The pilot would go into a dive and come around in a loop. That was, of course, one of the spectacular stunts.

The breakaway was quite exciting too. We had a very narrow cable ladder so you could pull yourself up onto the wing. We'd put straps around the ankles and snap the snaps at the end of the cables onto them. At the right time we would dive from the landing gear, head down, swing for a while, then come back up and climb up the ladder.

For plane changes—of course, you had to use two airplanes— the ladder would be attached to the wings of the ship above. I would climb out on the wings of the lower ship and walk out past the outer strut and up on the upper wing, where there was a brace that you could steady your leg against. That was the only thing you could hold on to at all. The upper ship would overtake the lower one with the ladder swinging from its wing tip, and I would reach for the last rung. Then it was only a matter of hanging on, because by that time the other ship was out from under you, leaving you in space. It was quite exciting. One time the ships came too close, and to keep from be-ing hit I threw myself down on the wings and lay with my shoulder over the aileron. The other wing from the upper plane was not more than two feet from my face. By that time they started to separate. I grabbed for the ladder and got hold of the center part of it, but it so happened that the lower end of the ladder got caught between the aileron and wing of the lower plane. There I was, hanging in the middle of the ladder, and they were jerking up and down, trying to get loose. Finally, half of the aileron was torn off the lower ship and I climbed up.

Other stunts that I used to do? I'd go out and hang by my toes through the cross wires. Then I had a trapeze that I attached to the landing gear with a mouthpiece on it, and I used to go down and hang from that by my teeth.

When I made a plane change, I used steel tubing rings and steel cables. One time we had thunderstorm activity, and flying around we accumulated a lot of static. So the minute I made contact I got a terrific shock and almost let go. That was a very close shave.

The Best Plane in Texas

Another source of income, less talked about in the 1920's, is remembered by Ben O. Howard, who went on to become a racing pilot and designer.

The thing that really held up aviation's pants for quite a few years was bootlegging. Other than the barnstormers, only the bootleggers put money into the thing.

An airplane got to the point where it was measured not by how fast it would go or how safe it was but by how many cases it would carry. A bootlegger in Houston gave me my first order to build an airplane. It would carry more liquor than any other airplane in Texas, so I was told.

In those days flying an airplane was a lot different from the way people think about it today. I associate flying with the smell of an OX engine and the put-put sound of it, and wondering if the drift wire is going to break off and go into the propeller, or swing back—and also with a Model T Ford. Model T's in those days would go about 40 miles an

Ben O. Howard in the 1920's

hour. It was not at all unusual for a Model T to pass you in your plane. All of those things sort of run together in your mind.

There was no such thing as aviation gas, of course. We just used regular gasoline. Some of it wasn't too good. We used to put moth balls in our gasoline—supposed to make it run better. Incidentally, we used to run all the gasoline through chamois skin to get the water out because the jets we used in the OX engines were so small that little balls of water wouldn't go through. It was quite a trick to climb through a fence with a ten-gallon milk can full of gasoline and get it hoisted up and poured. Those cans were pretty heavy to get up there without stretching the wires.

Tying the airplane down was another thing—how to tie an airplane so that it would ride out a windstorm. And how to lift the wing. You never jacked an airplane; you got under the wing and lifted it up to the point where you could put something under it to hold it up while you changed the tire or rewrapped a shock cord. You could always tell a pilot by the knicks on his hand—he always had the skin knocked off his hands.

Navigation in those days was, course, following the railroad track Well, following a railroad track is right, providing you know which rection you're going in, and provid also that it doesn't run into the si of a hill. You can't find it on t other side!

Incidentally, you used to get sh at all the time while you were flyi along. Of course, that was duri Prohibition. It was so routine th you really didn't pay much attenti to it: to be flying along and see t little white clusters of smoke and casionally to have a little mark your airplane. In fact, one time I h a wing strut split. I never heard ol revenue agent ever using an airplar but the moonshiners down there the woods thought they did.

Days of the Sick Can

Despite its rapid development, Eu pean commercial flying in the 192 could still be adventurous—as called by Dennis Handover, a Briti airline executive.

On the London-Brussels-Colog service, we were flying largely Dl 34's, which were single-engine a craft carrying eight passengers and crew of two. We didn't have ste ards or anything of that kind. The were no refreshments. I don't thi we even had a lavatory. We had great number of sick cans, howeve flying around unpressurized at l altitudes was very sick-making. Y never got above 2,000 feet becau you didn't dare lose sight of land.

We had a very, very amateur ty of radio telephone. It was one those things that was subject to mospherics. It was a question large of shouting down the micropho and hoping. Very often you could hear whether they had received yo message or not.

I remember it took me very nea a week to get from London to C ogne on one occasion, because had forced landings all over t

ce. But the passengers didn't leave
plane. It was an adventure in
se days. Not like today—if you're
minutes late, there's a row. No,
We stuck to the airplane. It was
t of the fun. They knew, of course,
t it was still pioneering. It was an
nt if you could come back and say,
ve just flown London to Cologne."

rtiss and Martin

ome Hunsaker, one of America's
emost aeronautical engineers since
13, was in charge of aircraft de-
n for the United States Navy from
16 to 1923. He reminisces here
ut two great pioneer builders._

nn Curtiss was a very modest
n. Some of his success perhaps
ne from his modesty, because peo-
always wanted to help him. He
sn't quite sure what he ought to
and people pitched in to help.
nn Martin was always very sure
what he was doing, and didn't
nt help, and didn't get it. And he
s very successful too.

had a very pleasant experience
enever I went up to Curtiss on my
val inspection jobs. We'd never
rd about payola then, and the
ger of having a meal with a con-
ctor. When I went to Hammonds-

Glenn Martin, early in his career

port, I usually stayed in the spare
guest room of Curtiss's house, and
Mrs. Curtiss looked after me. I had
a very pleasant time, stretching my
visit a little longer than necessary in
the autumn because Curtiss loved to
shoot pheasant. Curtiss liked a glass
of wine; he liked to hunt pheasant
with a good dog. Part of the reason
that he decided to retire [after World
War I] to Florida and to experiment
with farming was that he would have
plenty of opportunity to shoot. He
withdrew, again as a modest man,
feeling he'd done about as much as he
could in his art and feeling that the
industry was getting beyond his comprehension. He wasn't an engineer;
he didn't understand what some of
the improvements were. He didn't
understand Wall Street and public
participation in corporations. I think
his withdrawal was a realization that
he was no longer a leader in the art,
and the time had come for him to
step aside.

Martin was a much tougher sort.
He dealt with financial and business
people, and he dealt with the competitive rat race that he got into. My
relations with Martin were never
intimate. He was not the kind of man
that I would spend a holiday with

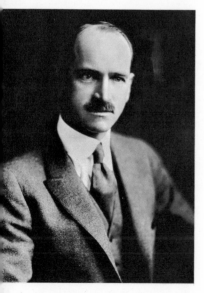

Glenn Curtiss

willingly. He was a little hard to
understand. He was a bachelor, and
he had to live up to his mother's idea
that he was the great man of his
generation.

The Mountains Were High

_Lieutenants John Macready and
Oakley Kelly of the Army Air Service were twice thwarted in an attempt to make the first nonstop flight
across the United States. Macready
describes the second failure (going
from west to east) and then tells of
the third historic try that took them
successfully without a stop from New
York to San Diego, in May, 1923._

On our second attempt we circled
around, used up some gasoline, and
got over the [southern California]
mountains. Then it was a question
of wandering around the United
States. We had to go clear down to
Texas; we couldn't go straight ahead
and get over the [Rocky] mountains.
As each gallon of gasoline was con-
sumed, we'd get a little more elevation, but the mountains were going
up faster than we were. So we'd go
down, follow the low places. Then,
after we got where we could get
across—oh, that was the worst trip!
—it stormed and rained at night.
There was a tornado—people killed
on the ground. We were dodging this
lightning and stuff, getting between
it and the storms. Then, as we got
toward Indianapolis, the engine
wasn't going too good. We knew we
couldn't make New York. We had a
cracked cylinder, so Kelly poured
coffee and soup into the radiator because you have to keep the engine
cooled when the water is leaking out.
We landed on the parade ground at
an Army post at Indianapolis.

Sure, it was uncomfortable. But
here's the thing in a nutshell—
you're in a jam and you've got to get
out of it; you're too darn busy to be
scared.

On our successful flight we took
off from Long Island at about eleven

235

thirty in the morning. It took us about a mile, maybe a mile and a half, to get off, and our wheels were still on the ground when we came to the drop-off from Roosevelt Field to Mitchel Field. We went over the ledge and down. Kelly was taking it off and I was behind. I was wondering, "Is it going to touch the ground? If it does, it's no use." But it maintained its flight and we just got over the hangars ahead. We had to keep from stalling and get just as much climb out of it as we could. Then we were over the water, near Staten Island, getting up around one hundred feet, maybe even a little more than that.

We got across the Alleghenies all right, but it began to get dark around Dayton, and it began to drizzle. You couldn't see anything but the lights of the cars on the highways, and we could only keep our compass from getting entirely out of control by checking it with the highways.

We went over by St. Louis. We didn't see it, but we could see the glow in the sky because it was just misty under the clouds. And then we were over some mountains. As long as you can see some outside fixed point you can balance your plane

John Macready, bundled for high altitude

and everything's O.K. But if you've got nothing, you can't tell if you're upside down or how you are. I was flying then and there'd be times when you wouldn't get any outside point at all in the drizzle. We were over the Ozarks. I knew that if that kept up, I was just going to lose control of that plane. Then there'd be a light, some mountain cabin. Then you find that you're cocked up on the side, but you're still going ahead. When you see that light, you can get yourself adjusted again. In Kansas we came out from under the storm. Then we could see the section lines and we could keep our course.

The impression that you get when you're flying across and you see no lights is that you're alone, and you don't know that anybody's interested. You think you're alone, and of course, we didn't know exactly where we were.

I remember looking down and I thought, "What the dickens are those things on the ground?" Then I realized that we were over New Mexico and those were mud huts of the Indians. When we got out into Arizona we weren't sure where we were. The mountains were getting higher. We couldn't get over them so we had to deflect our course. We were just going over treetops, not very high, I'd say, one hundred feet, something like that. Then we saw a place where we could get through, a break in the mountains, and we came through. We were keeping the general idea of our direction by this compass, which was swinging around loose, and then pretty soon I saw a little town. You can work out a pattern by the way the railroads come in. Then you check it with your map. The town was nothing, but we were located. For the first time during the night we were located, the first time since St. Louis.

Then we were over the Tehachapis and then down over San Diego. Well, as I said, we had the impression that nobody was interested.

Then we came gliding toward No[rth] Island, and we came pretty close o[ver] the U. S. Grant Hotel. We saw [a] bunch of people on top of the h[otel] waving sheets and so forth. We w[ent] on and landed at Rockwell Fie[ld] and, of course, we were pretty ti[red] when we got there.

"Everybody Was a Mechanic"

A second spectacular Army achie[ve]ment was the first flight around [the] world, from April to Septemb[er] 1924. Leslie P. Arnold, one of [the] four fliers who completed the trip, calls the great undertaking.

We started out with four planes, a[nd] two of the four made the compl[ete] trip. The local papers intimated t[hat] there was not much hope that [we] would complete the journey, but [as] we circled over Seattle, I thou[ght] that there was at least a fifty-fi[fty] chance of the planes getting arou[nd] —that is, that at least two wo[uld] make it. I wondered which of [the] others would make it. It ne[ver] dawned on me that I wouldn't.

The airplane was a biplane a[nd] had metal framework covered w[ith] linen; there was a single Libe[rty] engine of 400 horsepower. The ma[xi]mum ceiling was around 8,000 [feet] so we had to fly under things inst[ead] of over them. There was just a sm[all] glass windshield in front of us, pr[ob]ably six inches high and eight[een] inches in width. It was no protect[ion] at all unless you got way up under [it] was nothing to have your should[ers] wet through. They got iced up in [no] time at all.

The Air Force did a beautiful [job] in getting supplies out in advan[ce.] We always knew what each box c[on]tained whether we found it in Alas[ka,] India, or where. Box number o[ne,] for instance, would have a gallon [of] pure alcohol for use with the cool[ing] system of the engine. We used [to] make hot toddies from this—so[me]thing we needed to get the chill [off] after sitting in the open cockpit.

Leslie Arnold during the world flight

Nobody ever touched the planes [b]ut us. If an engine had to be [ch]anged, we changed it. We washed [th]em, babied them, put them to bed. [W]e did everything but sleep with [th]em. After a flight we had a routine [pr]ocedure which we followed. If the [w]ater connection had to be taped or [sh]ellacked, we did that—so we knew [it] wasn't going to fall down on the [ne]xt hop. Everybody was a mechanic [an]d everybody was a flier.

[O]nce we even had to sleep in the [pl]ane when we had a forced landing [in] the jungles of Indochina. We were [fl]ying down the coast when a spray [of] water hit us. We knew that some[th]ing had gone wrong in the engine. [It] began to heat up too much. We [la]nded in the mouth of a river to dis[co]ver that one of the cylinders had [cr]acked. The other boys landed [al]ongside. We had to get a new en[gi]ne, so they took off and went to [To]urane; Lowell Smith and I stayed [in] the airplane, sleeping on the wings. [Fi]nally, out of the darkness came a [S]wedish voice. It was Erik Nelson [an]other one of the fliers]. He had [m]ade arrangements through Stand[ar]d Oil and the local tribes, and we [w]ere towed up the river to the capital [of] the French kingdom of Annam.

It was an interesting ride, with the natives in their sampans towing us. The chief was riding in his sampan with a parasol and with his favorite wives fanning him.

The trip from Iceland to Greenland was the most frightening. We were two planes by that time. Everything was fine for about one hundred miles when we ran into fog and drizzle. We kept circling lower and lower until we were just over the water. There we saw broken ice and drifting icebergs, but we were past the point of no return and we had to keep going. So we plowed through this. The icebergs and the fog are both a dirty gray color, and it was very difficult flying seventy-five or one hundred feet off the water. We would veer off here and there; when you saw one ahead, there was no way to go except up in the fog. Finally we turned to the west and found the shore of Greenland. Then we had one hundred miles of clear weather and again ran into fog. We decided to stay on top this time, and kept our position by the mountain peaks. At last we arrived at a certain peak and thought the harbor should be under us. So we came down through the fog and landed in a nice little harbor. The second plane had not come in, however, and we went about our routine maintenance work, never saying a word. We felt too bad to say anything. But after about half an hour we heard the unmistakable noise of a Liberty engine. Then we had one of the finest parties Greenland had ever seen.

Flying on from Greenland to Labrador, we got halfway across when two of our gas pumps failed— we had to pump the gas by hand. It got tiresome and my arm began to get numb. So I thought the only way to do it was to use a combination of my belt and handkerchief around my neck like a sling and to pull it with my other hand. I did that for close to four hours. It was tiresome, but it beat the hell out of swimming!

Scoring A Beat

Charles "Casey" Jones, World War I pilot, racer, and flying instructor, headed the Curtiss Flying Service, flying newspaper photographs in the days before the wirephoto.

One of the worst times I ever had was in 1925, when Floyd Collins was trapped in a cave in Kentucky. Every day they expected to get him out, and the whole country was excited. I decided to fly to Kentucky myself to get the news photographs.

I got to our field at Garden City, Long Island, before daybreak. But when I got into the airplane, there was no compass in it. Typical of the way they ran things in those days. The mechanics hastily put one in, and I took off. There was an overcast, so I flew over it for about an hour and a half on the compass. Then the clouds started to break, and I came down. By then I should have been over the mountains; instead it was perfectly flat. The compass was better than 90 degrees off: I was east of Philadelphia!

I flew back to the airmail field at New Brunswick, New Jersey, and got them to fix it. Then I started again. It was a terrible day. We didn't used

The veteran "Casey" Jones

to fly on instruments; we used to go under the stuff, and I was dodging mountains all day. I'd flown six or eight hours trying to get across the mountains and couldn't. Finally I came to following this road—having no idea where I was—and I saw a sign on the road: *Moundsville, 14 miles.* Then the road disappeared in fog. I decided I'd had enough for the day, so I landed in a field.

The field was all right, except that somebody had tethered a calf out in the field. There was a little crowbar that they'd tied the rope to, and that crowbar just caught a bit of my landing gear and took a hole out of the side of the fuselage about the shape of a football and three times as large.

Well, I phoned the people I was working for and found that Floyd was still in the cave. So I went into town and got hold of a blacksmith, and we got some plywood and a couple of pieces of metal and went out and patched the hole.

The next morning I went out to the field to take off, but it was very cold and we couldn't start the engine. We had no starters in those days; we had to crank the engine. Luckily there was a fellow there who'd been in the Air Corps during the war, and he was able to swing the propeller. There was also a fellow butchering hogs, and so we got some hot water from him. It was a water-cooled engine, you see, and by putting hot water in it we could start it.

Well, I flew to Moundsville, got the pictures, and flew them to New York. Coming back, I was flying low over the Delaware River; and I knew where the field was if I could follow the river and pick up the Pennsylvania Railroad tracks at Trenton, New Jersey. But I'd forgotten about a bridge, and suddenly it loomed up ahead of me. The only thing I could do was go under it, instead of over it. But then, that wasn't so unusual in those days. I landed in Jersey City, and we got a beat on everybody.

"A Blaze of Glory"

Night flying of the airmail, which the Post Office began as a regular service in 1924, was a hazardous occupation. Leroy Ponton de Arce, who flew the mail from 1925 to 1927 on the Boston-New York route, describes one of his many close calls.

We had no instrumentation of any kind other than the compass, an airspeed indicator, and a tachometer. We had no parachutes or flares or anything of that nature.

I remember pleading for some type of flares, so the operations manager picked up some surplus flares that were used on English planes during the war. Of course, the Fokker Universal was a monoplane, and they mounted these under the wing. Nobody stopped to think that when this thing went off it was right in line with the pilot's eyes.

I was flying one night past Framingham, Massachusetts, and I lost my engine. It was pitch-dark, so the only thing I figured to do was to head for the biggest black spot I could find, which I assumed would be the swamps. I started letting down and I decided then would be a good time to try out these flares. I pressed the button and they went off like a firecracker, and there I sat in a big blaze of glory, absolutely blinded. I couldn't see a thing. I just held her in as easy a glide as I possibly could and wound up in the swamp. The engine sank, but fortunately it hit a stump. The tail was standing almost perpendicular in the air. I climbed out, with my big Teddy-bear flying suit on, and went right up to my neck in water. But I got out all right, and took my mail to the post office.

The next day I remember running into a young fellow who said, "Gee, you fellows are sure expert in the handling of these airplanes. I just don't understand how you maneuver so beautifully." Of course, my chest swelled out a little bit and I said, "Well, that's just routine."

"No, no, that's wonderful," [he] said, "the way you missed those hi[gh]-tension lines down there." I sa[id,] "What high-tension lines?" He sa[id,] "Those high-voltage lines across t[he] swamp." If I'd stood up on the t[ail] I could have hit them, but I did[n't] even know they were there.

Flying in those days, with that ki[nd] of equipment, was 80 per cent l[uck] and 20 per cent ability.

A Flying Seal

On May 11, 1926, Umberto Nob[ile,] Roald Amundsen, and Lincoln E[lls]worth flew over the North Pole [in] the airship Norge. *Unlike Co[m]mander Richard Byrd, who two d[ays] before had reached the Pole in [a] plane and returned to Spitsberg[en,] the crew of the* Norge *flew on acr[oss] the Arctic to Alaska. General Nob[ile] describes the end of the trip.*

The flight lasted three full days. [On] the second day we were flying acr[oss] the hitherto unknown region ly[ing] between the North Pole and Alas[ka.] We had hours and hours of gr[eat] anxiety because of the ice which [be]gan to form almost everywhere [on] the hull and most thickly on the me[tal] parts and the rigging. At times, un[der] the pressure of the wind, pieces of [ice] detached themselves and fell into [the] propellers, which flung them agai[nst] the hull. There were ominous crac[ks,] and my men were kept hard at wo[rk] running from spot to spot to loc[ate] and repair the damage. The stock [of] patching material was almost at [an] end when at last the ice format[ion] stopped just before we reached [the] northern coast of Alaska.

Then, at the beginning of [the] third day of flight, we found o[ur]selves in the middle of a heavy sto[rm] raging over the Bering Straits. T[he] wind was strong and the fog de[nse] and persistent, and in order to ch[eck] our route we were forced to fly un[der] it, very near the ground. Under th[ese] conditions the navigation and ha[n]dling of the ship became very di[fficult]

General Umberto Nobile

ult and dangerous. Time after time peak would surge up through the og, forcing us to climb steeply, in rder to avoid a crash.

These hours of nightmarish flying the fog subjected the crew to a ontinuous nervous tension just when hey were already exhausted by two ong days of flying. At last the fog eased and we found ourselves above ort Clarence, Alaska. The ship, haken by the squally wind, was itching and rolling. Now and again here were flurries of snow. We were ollowing a desolate gray shore, with ills that were even more dreary.

We had enough gasoline to reach Nome, which was only one hundred iles away to the northwest, but hile the gale persisted it would have een madness to go on, with a crew o tired. So I decided to land. Notithstanding the weather conditions nd the fact that we had no help rom the ground, we made an excelnt landing. Five or six Eskimos from he village of Teller were standing round us gaping.

Later, we were told that one of the skimo boys had taken the airship or a flying seal and had rushed houting to his father: "Dad, shoot it own!" But fortunately for us, his ather did not take his advice.

The Lindbergh Epic

Harold M. Bixby, a St. Louis businessman, was one of Charles A. Lindbergh's original backers. He tells of some of the events that preceded the famous flight.

Lindbergh came and asked me to help him raise the money. I was then president of the Chamber of Commerce in St. Louis and treasurer of the Flying Club, and I had my own airplane at the field.

It took him quite a long time to convince me that it could be done. At first I even made my participation contingent upon his purchasing a three-engine airplane. However, he convinced Harry Knight and me that a single-engine airplane was three times as apt to get there as a three-engine airplane. At that time, too, the Wright J-5 had been fairly tested and had broken the endurance record. That proved conclusively that it was capable of continuous flight long enough to take him to Paris. We finally agreed and he went down to buy the *Columbia,* which Chamberlin and Levine eventually flew across.

Of course, the time element was very important. A lot of other fellows —René Fonck, Richard Byrd, Noel Davis—were getting hot and bothered about this flight to Paris. In fact, it was very questionable whether there was really time to do it.

We had a thousand dollars from Albert B. Lambert, and $2,000 from Lindbergh, as well as a thousand from Bill and Frank Robertson, and five hundred from Earl Thompson. We borrowed $10,500 on the endorsement of Harry Knight and me.

Oh, it was a great responsibility, I'm telling you. It could have backfired. People were getting killed every day, and this was just one more chance. Of course, you didn't have to be very smart to realize that Lindbergh was an exceptional pilot. There is no question but what he is one of the greatest pilots this country has ever produced.

Lindbergh came back to St. Louis, of course, and said, "I've failed in getting the *Columbia.* It will be at least another sixty or ninety days before Ryan can build the airplane. Shall I go ahead or not?"

We told him to go ahead and so he took the check out to San Diego. The rest is history.

In California, Ryan Airlines built the Spirit of St. Louis *between February and April, 1927. O. L. Gray, a Ryan installation mechanic who helped work on the plane with Lindbergh, recalled this anecdote in an interview recorded in later years by the Ryan Aeronautical Company.*

I think we'd worked about three weeks on this engine installing it into the fuselage. At that time we had one chain-fall hooked to a rafter to hoist our engine into the fuselage. We had a maintenance man up there removing this chain-fall because we didn't need it any more; the engine was bolted to the fuselage. He dropped either a ten- or twelve-inch crescent wrench out of his pocket onto the number-one cylinder, and broke off one of the little cooling fins, about the size of a quarter. Lindbergh almost cried about that. He thought it over for a while, and I said to him, "We could smooth that out with a file and paint it, and never know the difference." "I'll always know the difference," he said. "We want another engine in there."

I thought he was joking at the time, and that was when somebody spoke up and said, "Why so much perfection in this?" And he said, "Two reasons for that: one is I'm a poor swimmer." —Up to that time I didn't even know what he was going to do with the *Spirit of St. Louis!*— "The other reason is that I've always been taught that perfection in your preparation and planning will assure you of getting to your destination."

He was very happy when we removed that engine and put in another one.

CHAPTER 7

Taking off from Oakland, California, on August 16, 1927, is the Aloha, which won second place in the "Pineapple Derby" to Hawa

THE THIRTIES

The impact of Lindbergh's achievement on American aviation was explosive. From May 21, 1927, onward, men knew that the airplane was actually capable of all that the dreamers and pioneers had claimed for it. It could span oceans, shrink the globe, compress time, unite people with goods and services—or destroy them with bombs and bullets, wherever they might be on earth. Man had truly conquered the air, and it was merely a matter of time—and money—before full-fledged commercial and military air power would come into being.

Like the first four-minute mile in foot racing, the flight broke through an invisible psychological barrier and touched off a whole series of record-breaking performances. Within six weeks of Lindbergh's arrival in Paris, two more planes had spanned the Atlantic. On June 4 Clarence D. Chamberlin, accompanied by his financial backer Charles A. Levine, made a record-breaking nonstop flight of over 3,900 miles from New York to Germany where he was forced down by fog only 118 miles short of his goal, Berlin. On June 29 Commander Richard E. Byrd and a crew of three finally set out for Paris in their Fokker C-2 trimotor, the *America*.

Taking off in the rain, with Bert Acosta and Bernt Balchen as pilots and George O. Noville as radio operator, the *America* followed the trail that Lindbergh had blazed. For much of the distance they flew through fog. Climbing at times as high as 10,000 feet, and steering only by the luminous compass dials, Byrd repeatedly noted in his log: "Impossible to navigate."

The fog lifted briefly as they reached the French coast, but then closed in again. With fuel running low, the fliers' only chance was to make a landing on water. Dropping flares into the ocean, they ditched the big landplane just off the Normandy beach and paddled dejectedly ashore in a rubber boat.

At almost the same time another C-2, the *Bird of Paradise*, was making an even more remarkable flight, from Oakland, California, to Honolulu, Hawaii. The hazard faced by two Army fliers, Lieutenants Lester G. Maitland and Albert F. Hegenberger, was obvious: the slightest navigational error would cause them to miss the islands altogether. They were aided to some extent by a radio beacon—the first use of this device in overseas flight—but their receiver worked only intermittently. Adding to their anxiety was the apparent absence of their food supply, which had actually been put aboard, but had been stowed away so carefully that the fliers could not find it until they had covered the 2,400 miles to Hawaii in twenty-five hours and fifty minutes of faultless flying and navigating.

Again the pioneers did a better job than some of their imitators. In July a pair of civilians, Ernest L. Smith and Emory Bronte, barely made it to the island of Molokai from Oakland before running out of fuel. In August the first transoceanic air race in history took place when James D. Dole, a planter in Hawaii, offered prizes totaling $35,000 for a flight from Oakland to Wheeler Field on the island of Oahu.

The Dole "Pineapple Derby," as it was called, was not one of aviation's more illustrious events. It was not an attempt to advance the science of aeronautics; some of the airplanes entered were little better than homemade crates. There was not even the challenge of a great new adventure; the flight to Hawaii had already been made twice. The chief motives of the contestants were simply publicity and money.

Of the sixteen original entries, two crashed on their way to the small, single-runway airfield at Oakland. Trying to forestall further disasters, the Government inspected the remaining planes and tested the competence of the pilots and navigators. Six planes were eliminated. Of the remaining eight, only one—the *Woolaroc*, a single-engine, Travelair monoplane—carried a radio capable of both sending and receiving. Four of the contestants either crashed on take-off or turned back. Only two of the other four—the *Woolaroc* and the *Aloha,* a Breese monoplane—completed the flight. The others disappeared. An Air Corps search plane that went out to look for them spun into the sea, killing two Army fliers.

The following year, however, in one of the most successful and daring flights of all time, four men conquered the Pacific completely. A pair of Australian fliers, Squadron Leader Charles Kingsford-Smith and Flight Lieutenant Charles P. T. Ulm, were convinced that a flight from the United States to Australia was possible. With limited funds, they came to the United States and for about $15,000 managed to buy a secondhand Fokker trimotor that had been used by Sir Hubert Wilkins for arctic exploration.

With three new Wright Whirlwind J-5 engines, Kingsford-Smith and Ulm carried out a number of preliminary endurance flights. Authorities in Australia, worried by the "Pineapple Derby" disasters, tried to dissuade them from their transpacific plans, and their financial problems seemed endless. But on May 31, 1928, with two Americans, Harry W. Lyons and J. W. Warner, as navigator and radio operator, they took off from Oakland and flew to Hawaii without difficulty. From there they made a spectacular flight of 3,000 miles through head winds, rain, and turbulence to the Fiji Islands. A third hop of 1,762 miles brought them to Brisbane, Australia, on June 9.

Eight days later, the first woman to fly the Atlantic became an international heroine overnight. On June 17, 1928, rangy, tousle-headed Amelia Earhart made a flight from Newfoundland to Wales as a passenger in another Fokker C-2, piloted by Wilmer Stultz, with Louis Gordon as mechanic. When people praised her courage, she demurred. "The bravest thing I did," she said with disarming modesty, "was to try to drop a bag of oranges and a note on the head of an ocean liner's captain—and I missed the whole ship!"

By 1929 transoceanic flights had lost much of their novelty, although the publicity given them helped stir new interest in the airplane as a passenger-carrying vehicle. Commercial aviation in the United States, however, still had a long way to go. In the period 1919-27, European lines had moved ahead of their American counterparts. About 1924 a series of amalgamations of small European pioneer companies had resulted in stronger airlines, such as Aero-Lloyd in Germany, Air Union in France, and Imperial Airways in Britain. Encouraged and partially underwritten by their governments, the lines were energetically pushing air routes around the globe to overseas possessions: the Dutch out of Batavia in the East Indies; the British to India and Australia; and the French down through Africa to Madagascar. American airlines during those years tended to be small, mail-carrying companies with little capacity for (or interest in) passenger travel.

The Lindbergh flight acted like adrenalin in the blood stream of American aviation. In a single year after Lindbergh's flight, applications for pilot licenses in the United States jumped from 1,800 to 5,500. In 1928 the nation's airline operators doubled their mileage, trebled their mail load, and quadrupled the number of passengers they had carried in 1927. And airline stocks boomed. In 1929, before the stock market crash, the public bought aircraft manufacturing securities to the tune of $400,000,000.

Fortunately, technological developments kept pace with the public's quickening interest. In 1927 the famed Lockheed Vega had appeared. Designed by Allan H. Loughead (who used a simplified spelling in his company name) and John Northrop, it was a brilliant adaptation of the Fokker type of high-wing monoplane. Capable of carrying a pilot and six passengers at speeds up to 135 miles per hour for a distance of five to nine hundred miles, it served as America's challenge to the lead in transport design so long held by Fokker and Junkers. In engines, the more powerful 425-horsepower Pratt and Whitney Wasp was replacing the old reliable 225-horsepower Wright Whirlwind. In 1928 the National Advisory Committee for Aeronautics developed an engine cowling that increased air speed with no increase in horsepower, and the following year instrument flying became a reality with Jimmy Doolittle's first completely blind take-off and landing in a trainer equipped with a hooded cockpit. Another development that was to insure safe, practical all-weather commercial flying in the years to come was the introduction in 1929 of the use of two-way voice radio.

But the key factor in the sudden expansion of American commercial flying was the growing awareness of big business that there was money to be made in it— if the necessary mergers were made and the right men given the right kind of backing.

Whenever the magic combination of cash and courage appeared, things happened quickly. In July, 1927, the aggressive and far-sighted Juan Trippe had won a contract to carry mail between Key West and Cuba. Within a year he had secured two more foreign mail contracts to Puerto Rico and the Canal Zone, which meant that his brash young Pan American Airways would be receiving about two and a half million dollars a year in mail revenues alone. Within three years Trippe's Fokker amphibians and Sikorsky flying boats had thrown an aerial loop around South America, "just in time," he liked to say, to keep foreign competition—mainly French and German—from dominating that continent.

After a long, complicated, and often bitter struggle among a welter of rival companies three major transcontinental air systems began to take shape in the United States. In 1929 Lindbergh agreed to lend the enormous prestige of his name to Transcontinental Air Transport, which soon became known as "the Lindbergh line." It offered a combined rail-and-air service across the central part of the nation to transcontinental passengers who could sleep all night in Pullmans while crossing the Alleghenies or the Rockies, transferring to planes over safer flying country. This hybrid form of travel was never a great success. It offered relative safety, but not much in terms of time saving. In October, 1930, Transcontinental merged with Western Air Express to become Transcontinental and Western Air (TWA) and inaugurated an all-air service from coast to coast.

The preceding March, United Airlines, operating between the West Coast and Chicago, had bought out National Air Transport and extended its service to New York. A third great airway system sprawled across the southern section of the nation. Composed of a jumble of minor airlines, this cumbersome organization, American Airways, eventually developed into one of the most profitable lines in the country.

In March, 1929, these three big systems came under the penetrating eye of Walter F. Brown, Postmaster General of the new Hoover Administration. Like his predecessors, Brown felt that the Post Office Department should encourage commercial aviation in the interests of national defense. But he also felt that rapid expansion would never take place so long as government subsidies made it more profitable for the airlines to carry mail than to carry passengers.

Consequently, he sought an amendment to the original Kelly Act that would eliminate the old pound-per-mile rate and pay operators according to how much cargo space they made available. Brown figured that this would encourage the airlines to place orders for larger airplanes; then, if mail did not fill the extra space, the operators would carry passengers rather than fly half-empty. The new proposal, passed as the McNary-Watres Bill, also attempted to reward progressive operators by providing for extra payments to airlines using multi-engine planes equipped with the latest navigational aids. The whole point of the new law, Brown said, was to develop aviation in the

broad sense and to stimulate manufacturers "who would compete with each other and bring their aeronautical industry up to the point where it could finally sustain itself."

This approach meant, inevitably, that when it came to bestowing mail contracts Brown would tend to disregard the small, struggling, independent airlines in favor of the larger companies with better financing and more experienced personnel. After a series of meetings, later known sardonically as the "Spoils Conferences," the big operators did walk off with most of the contracts. Brown's motives were sincere enough, but almost from the start of the Hoover regime the independents were sharpening their knives and looking eagerly at the scalp of the Postmaster General.

When Brown assumed office, all transcontinental mail was being carried by United Airlines over the northern route. The new Postmaster General felt that there should be two other mail routes across the country. Given his preference for strong, experienced airlines, it was no surprise when American Airways won the southern route and TWA, the central route.

In addition to the three big transcontinental routes, a host of independents were competing strongly with one another. This competition, working back to the factories, soon produced some revolutionary aircraft designs. In February, 1933, Boeing brought out a low-wing, all-metal monoplane, the 247, that in many ways was the first modern airliner. It was also a demonstration of the superiority of all-metal construction; the 247 clearly antiquated the part-wood, part-metal planes of the twenties and early thirties. Carrying ten passengers, powered by two Wasp radials, the new plane was designed to fly on one engine if necessary. Cowled engines, appearing for the first time on an airliner, greatly reduced drag. This airplane, derived from the Boeing B-9 bomber of 1931, strongly influenced European designers. The British Bristol 142, the German Junkers Ju-86, and the Heinkel He-111 all owed a debt to Boeing.

Ordinarily such an airplane might have outdistanced its competition for several years, but within a few months an even more remarkable plane was in the skies.

In 1932, like many other corporations battling the Depression, the aircraft manufacturing firm of Donald Douglas had fallen upon lean times. Douglas himself had been passionately interested in aviation ever since 1908 when, as a wide-eyed youngster, he had watched Orville Wright demonstrate his marvelous flying machine for the Army at Fort Myer. Later he had worked as Glenn Martin's chief engineer. In 1921 he had formed his own company, in back of a barber shop in Santa Monica, California.

244

In August, 1932, a query came to Douglas from Jack Frye, vice-president of TWA. Could Douglas build an all-metal, trimotor monoplane capable of carrying a crew of two and at least twelve passengers at a speed of 150 miles per hour and with a cruising range of 1,000 miles? Douglas designers set to work and the result, less than a year later, was the DC (Douglas Commercial)-1.

The DC-1, of which only one was built, was a twin-engine, all-metal, stressed-skin monoplane somewhat larger than the Boeing 247 and slightly faster. It was powered by two Wright R-1820 Cyclone engines which drove fixed-pitch propellers. When the DC-1 was modified into the DC-2, variable-pitch propellers became standard equipment and gave much improved performance. The DC-1 was also equipped with flaps, which made low-speed approach and landing possible. Another important innovation was the long-chord cowling around the radial engines, a vital factor in the DC-1's excellent drag characteristics.

Tests carried out with the DC-1 were so successful that TWA ordered twenty-five aircraft of the same type, with a few changes. Douglas sold these DC-2's, as they were called, for $65,000 apiece, and lost money on the order. But the age of the modern airliner had begun.

The capabilities of both the Boeing 247 and the Douglas DC-2 were dramatically demonstrated to the world in October, 1934, in a race from England to Australia. The Boeing was flown by Colonel Roscoe Turner, the Douglas by a KLM Dutch crew. The 11,000-mile race was won by a de Havilland Comet, a twin-engine military airplane that flew the last two and one-half hours of its run on one engine. But the "sedate" American transports were right behind the Comet. The DC-2 landed at Melbourne just over seventy-one hours after leaving England. The Boeing was third, another Comet racer was fourth, with the other entrants strung out behind. By the end of the year Douglas was turning out ten DC-2's per month. Altogether it produced 220 of these fine aircraft for airlines all over the world.

The year 1934 also saw the appearance of the Lockheed L-10 Electra. Smaller and faster than the Boeing 247 and the DC-2, it carried only eight passengers, but its low operating costs made it popular, and Lockheed built about 150 of them.

By this time American Airways had inaugurated a transcontinental sleeper service, using Curtiss Condor biplanes. These were reliable, but slow; the company wanted a plane that could leave New York at sundown, fly through the night with three or four refueling stops, and land in California the next day. They too brought their problem to Douglas. Trying to stretch the DC-2 to include berths for overnight passengers, Douglas engineers finally came up with a new airplane, the DC-3, that could be used as a twenty-one-passenger day plane or a fourteen-passenger "Skysleeper." The new plane went into service with American on June 26, 1936, powered by two 900-horsepower Wright Cyclone engines. It turned out to be the most successful transport ever built, answering for the first time the three basic requirements of speed, safety, and economy.

One reason for its popularity was its great durability. The multispar construction of wing and tail made the airframe highly resistant to fatigue or structural failure. Some DC-3's flew as many as 70,000 hours without being rebuilt. Carrying more passengers than its predecessors, its operating costs represented a 25 per cent improvement over the Boeing 247, and brought the airline operators much closer to the break-even point. Before the appearance of the DC-3, domestic airlines in the United States were covering less than two thirds of their total costs. The new airplane made it possible for them to cover more than 80 per cent. By 1939 the DC-3 was carrying about three fourths of all domestic air traffic.

While technology was making such spectacular advances, political problems were darkening the aviation horizon. In Washington the Hoover regime had been replaced by Franklin D. Roosevelt's New Dealers. Thirsting for blood, the independent airline operators were clamoring that the recent Republican Postmaster General had been guilty of favoritism in his allocation of mail contracts to the big operators. Not at all averse to pinning charges of misconduct on their political rivals, the New Dealers launched a Senatorial investigation under the chairmanship of Hugo L. Black of Alabama. The findings seemed damaging at the time—although later a court held there had been no discrimination or collusion—and the Administration was prompted to take a drastic step.

On February 9, 1934, President Roosevelt instructed Postmaster General James A. Farley to cancel all domestic airmail contracts and ordered the U. S. Army to fly the mail effective February 19. Believing that the airmail flights would give his peacetime fliers valuable training under emergency conditions similar to war, Major General Benjamin D. Foulois, Chief of the Army Air Corps, promptly accepted the assignment.

The Army agreed to maintain fourteen routes connecting eleven major cities with total daily runs of 41,000 miles. The job, Foulois estimated, would take 500 officers and 148 airplanes; and he had just ten days to prepare for it. Foulois immediately set up airmail headquarters in Washington; divided the country into three zones with zone commanders at Newark, New Jersey, Chicago, and Salt Lake City; asked the National Guard for additional airplanes; ordered Army planes stripped of military equipment to make room for the mail sacks; installed radios and additional navigation aids in these converted planes; and initiated familiarization flights in which Army pilots received training in blind and radio-beam flying. When three pilots were killed during these trials, Foulois strengthened the safety requirements, emphasizing that lives and property would not be sacrificed to keep the mail going.

Commercial operators were skeptical of these preparations—and bitter because they had been cut off from the subsidy that had nourished them for so long. In a last-ditch effort to prove to the public that the job of flying the mail belonged in experienced, private hands, TWA staged a sensational flight on the night of February 18. Flying a brand-new DC-2, rushed to completion just before the fatal deadline, vice-president Frye and Captain Eddie Rickenbacker, now vice-president of Eastern Air Transport, flashed across the country together to deliver the last load of mail from Los Angeles to Newark before noon on February 19. Their time of thirteen hours and four minutes was an unheard-of performance for a transport airplane. The next day the Army took over.

Although plagued by bad weather and hampered by lack of adequate training, the military pilots made a brave try. By March 10, however, ten men had been killed—either in training or actual airmail flights —and Foulois temporarily halted the program. After a thorough inspection of men and equipment, the mail flights were resumed on March 19. As the weather improved, the Army began to do a creditable job. But by now the tide of public opinion was running strongly against the entire unfortunate experiment. By May, the job of carrying the mail was back in private hands.

As a face-saving gesture, Postmaster General Farley —who had never relished his role of Lord High Executioner—decreed that no airline could win a new contract if it had been represented at the so-called "Spoils Conferences" of 1930. As a result, some of the major lines submitted bids with their names slightly changed. American Airways became American Airlines. Eastern Air Transport turned up as Eastern Airlines. Transcontinental and Western Air submitted its bid as TWA, Inc.—apparently all the camouflage needed. On May 8, with hustling Jack Frye flying a powerful new Northrop Gamma, TWA set a new coast-to-coast record, delivering the mail from Los Angeles to Newark in less than twelve hours. Nevertheless, it took the airlines several years to recover

from the financial losses and dislocations that had been caused by the suspension period.

Meanwhile, record-breaking flights had continued; even in the grim years of the Depression the public had not lost interest in them. In 1931 a one-eyed ex-parachute jumper, Wiley Post, and his Australian-born navigator, Harold Gatty, had thrilled the country by flying their Lockheed Vega, the *Winnie Mae,* around the world in eight days, fifteen hours, and fifty-one minutes. Two years later, in July, 1933, Wiley Post's second dash around the world in the *Winnie Mae*—this time alone—furnished the decade with perhaps its most remarkable display of flying endurance. The Sperry Gyroscope Company in the fall of 1932, had perfected an automatic pilot that made it possible for the pilot to relax in the cockpit while the plane flew itself. Equipped with this and other new devices—notably a radio direction finder —Post succeeded in slashing almost a day from his previous record. He was killed two years later in a tragic crash near Point Barrow, Alaska, that also took the life of his flying companion, Will Rogers.

Two months after Post's death, a tall, intense young Texas millionaire named Howard Hughes set a new speed record for landplanes, flying his Hughes *Special* at 325 miles per hour. Three years later, with four companions, Hughes flew a Lockheed 14 around the world in the remarkable time of three days, nineteen hours, and fourteen minutes. Powered by two Wright Cyclones, the plane was a flying laboratory that cost $300,000. Hughes paid all expenses himself. Nor did he claim any special credit. "Please remember," he said, "that I am but one of five persons who made that trip, and being taller than any of them kept getting in the way and making a nuisance of myself. If you must praise anyone, save your shouts for Wiley Post, for by flying around the world alone, in the time he did, and with but one eye, he made the most amazing flight that has ever occurred."

It was an attempted round-the-world flight that cost Amelia Earhart her life in 1937. Unlike Wiley Post and Howard Hughes, who had followed the relatively short northern route, she planned a 27,000-mile flight close to the bulge of the equator. This, she said, would be her last long-distance effort. Flying a Lockheed Electra, with Fred Noonan as navigator, she reached New Guinea late in June. Her next scheduled stop was tiny Howland Island, 2,556 miles across the South Pacific. Noonan was uneasy about his chronometers; he was having trouble setting them accurately. Nonetheless, on July 2 they took off. A United States Coast Guard vessel, the *Itasca,* was stationed near the island. It received radio messages from the plane that told of head winds and heavy fuel consumption. A final fragmentary call seemed to indicate that the Electra was off course, lost. After that, there was silence.

That same year, the most harrowing and spectacular of all air disasters wrote a fiery finish to passenger-carrying airships. On May 6, 1937, nosing down through the sultry dusk to a landing at Lakehurst, New Jersey, the giant Zeppelin *Hindenburg,* largest dirigible ever built and pride of Nazi Germany, exploded in a sheet of flame that killed thirty-five of the ninety-seven persons aboard.

Up to that point, confidence in dirigibles had somehow managed to survive an almost unbroken series of failures and tragedies. The tremendous size of the great ships, their apparent stability, their lack of dependence on fragile wings—these had lent an air of majesty to their flights and had given a false sense of security to those who rode in them.

In 1928, returning to the Arctic, General Umberto Nobile had piloted the dirigible *Italia* to the North Pole, then crashed on the ice pack on his way back to Spitsbergen. Faint radio signals touched off massive rescue efforts. Roald Amundsen disappeared, trying to save his former companion. Finally, after weeks of misery, the survivors were picked up—some by airplanes, some by a Russian icebreaker.

This was just one more link in the chain of lighter-than-air tragedies. In 1930, outward bound for India, the big British dirigible *R-101* crashed in flames in France. Of the fifty-four souls aboard, only six survived. England abandoned her dirigible experiments, but America and Germany kept on.

The German-built *Los Angeles* was retired after a dozen years of docile flying, and the reliable *Graf Zeppelin* made a round-the-world flight in 1929 and later safely ferried passengers across the Atlantic. But these were happy exceptions to a grim rule. In 1933, on her fifty-ninth flight, the American-built *Akron* crashed at sea in a storm off the New Jersey coast. Seventy-three out of seventy-six men aboard were lost, including Admiral Moffett, the Navy's staunchest dirigible enthusiast. Two years later the *Akron's* sister ship, the *Macon,* was wrecked off the California coast. Only two lives were lost—a pair of crewmen who jumped too soon. After the *Hindenburg* disaster, Hitler grounded the *Graf Zeppelin,* and another monster airship under construction—the *LZ-170*—was never allowed to make a commercial flight.

Even before this final tragedy, the advent of the long-range airliner was already robbing the great sky ships of such value as they had. Like the dinosaurs, they fell victim to their own huge bulk and lack of adaptability. After the death of the *Hindenburg,* they became extinct.

One reason Hitler grounded the *Graf Zeppelin* was his intense dislike for her commander, Dr. Hugo Eckener. For years Eckener had been forthrightly urging his passengers to beware of the Nazis. "These madmen are after you," he would say to complacent British or American travelers. "They mean to conquer Europe—yes, the whole world!"

His colleagues would smile tight-lipped smiles, and say that, after all, Herr Doktor was an airman, not a statesman. But the grizzled little German was right. Throughout the turbulent 1930's some of the great powers were preparing for another big war by fighting little wars.

Militaristic nations never lack excuses to justify their aggression. In January, 1932, the so-called "Shanghai Disturbances" touched off a war in Asia. At first the Japanese suffered sharp and unexpected reverses at the hands of the Chinese 19th Route Army. But by sending two aircraft carriers equipped with Nakajima and Mitsubishi fighters, they were able to control the air over the combat zone. The value of this air superiority impressed the Japanese so deeply that they initiated a tremendous program of air-power expansion that continued right up to Pearl Harbor.

Nor were the aggressors in Europe idle. In Italy, after Mussolini came to power, the neglected air force was made autonomous—a policy advocated as early as 1921 by Guilio Douhet. In print and speech this Italian officer had insisted that future wars would be won by those nations that possessed independent air forces capable of carrying out massive bombing of enemy cities (as opposed to selective bombing of industrial targets) in order to cripple an enemy's morale. Douhet's theories were studied by military leaders throughout the world and now, in 1935, were tested with grim results by his own countrymen.

In October Italy invaded the primitive African kingdom of Ethiopia. The Italian Regia Aeronautica promptly went into action. More than three hundred combat airplanes, mostly three-engine bombers, were used to harass the enemy and supply the Italian ground forces. Against virtually no opposition, they tested every weapon in their arsenal, including poison gas—a mode of annihilation which Douhet had stressed in preference to conventional bombs.

The next year, when civil war broke out in Spain, Mussolini sent both fighter and bomber squadrons to aid Franco's rebels. When that fierce and bitter war ended almost three years later, more than seven hundred Italian warplanes had been in action, carrying out some 5,000 bombing missions and claiming a total of 903 Loyalist planes destroyed. The Germans, too, seized the opportunity to test their rapidly expanding

Luftwaffe under combat conditions. In August, 1936, six Heinkel fighters and twenty Junkers bomber-transports were given to Franco; and in November, sending combat personnel to Spain disguised as "strength-through-joy" tourists, the Germans organized the Condor Legion, a miniature air force complete with fighters, bombers, dive bombers, seaplanes, and even antiaircraft batteries.

One squadron of Heinkels was commanded by an aggressive young officer, Adolf Galland, who had learned to fly gliders in "de-militarized" Germany, and who had later been given secret pilot training in Italy. In Spain, Galland's squadron specialized in ground attack, and developed tactics that were later to characterize the *blitzkrieg* against Poland and France. It was found as the war went on that the Heinkels could not hold their own against the fighters that the Loyalists were receiving from the Russians, and they were gradually replaced by the new and deadly Messerschmitt Me-109's.

The war in Spain also saw the first operational use of the Junkers dive bomber, a form of flying artillery that the Germans had developed after studying some early American experiments. In December, 1937, three of these Ju-87A's screamed down upon Loyalist gun positions at Teruel with such spectacular results that the Germans promptly sent more of them into action. These gull-winged "Stukas" were relatively slow and were vulnerable both to conventional fighters and to ground troops seasoned enough to stand firm and shoot at them. But in 1938—as in the early stages of World War II—they were a terrifying and demoralizing weapon.

By 1938 German airplane production was on a wartime basis, and the Condor Legion was methodically testing two new bombers, the Heinkel He-111B-1 and the Dornier Do-17E-1. These flew successfully in unescorted raids against the weakening Loyalists, and led the German High Command to think that they could protect themselves. It was an expensive illusion; the same tactics were to prove disastrous two years later in the Battle of Britain.

Against these Italian and German warplanes in Spain were ranged some of Soviet Russia's best fighting aircraft. As early as October, 1936, twin-engine bombers flown by Soviet "volunteers" were raiding Seville, Granada, and other rebel-held cities. These were SB-2's (SB standing for *Skorostnoi Bombardirovshchik,* or "fast bomber") designed by A. N. Tupolev, who had been turning out planes for the Soviets since 1919. The Russians also poured more than a thousand fighters into Spain, chiefly Ilyushin Il-15's and Il-16's which were equal or superior to most of the Fascist fighters. In the end the Loyalists lost the

war, but the reports sent to Moscow on the performance and limitations of their planes under combat conditions were of great value to Soviet strategists.

Spain was not the only testing ground for the Russians. When fighting again broke out between Japan and China in 1937, Il-15 and Il-16 fighters with Chinese insignia were soon flying against carrier-based Mitsubishi fighters—and holding their own. Russia had long regarded Japan's conquests in China with alarm, and in the summer of 1939 tension along the Mongolian border broke into an unofficial but savage war in which both the Russian and Japanese air forces were heavily engaged. For the first time, the Japanese found themselves up against a strong modern air force and were roughly handled. Only Soviet preoccupation with the growing Nazi menace in the West prevented a major Japanese defeat.

This came as a shock to the Japanese, who had been testing and improving military planes ever since the "Shanghai Disturbances" of 1932. Gradually long-distance bombing had become the province of their naval air force, the army air force being used primarily for ground support. Japanese naval fliers had had to learn some lessons the hard way—as when they attempted an unescorted daylight raid on Hankow in April, 1938, and lost thirty-six out of forty bombers. But gradually they had pushed the defenders inland. By July, 1940, they were sending bombers over Chungking—almost at will. Flying escort on these missions was a new fighter, the Mitsubishi A6-M2 Type O Model 11. This was the famed Zero-Sen. Light, maneuverable, heavily armed, it was so superior to anything else in the skies that the Chinese air force virtually disappeared. By the end of 1941, the only opposition of any consequence was being offered by ninety Curtiss P-40's flown by a group of American volunteers commanded by General Claire Chennault and known as the Flying Tigers.

While the totalitarian nations were testing their warplanes and toughening their pilots in actual combat, the Western democracies were slowly shaking off the military lethargy that had gripped them since the end of World War I.

In the United States the growth of air power had been thrown out of balance by a national policy based on the belief that weapons would be needed only to fight a defensive war against an invader. In such an attack against the United States proper, the Navy would fill its traditional role as the first line of defense, and land-based bombers would provide support by flying out to sea and helping to sink the invader. Air Corps doctrine, based on offensive strategic bombing rather than continental defense, ran opposite to this. But using national policy to justify the building of bombers, Air Corps planners concentrated on the development of a long-range bomber that could, among other things, intercept a hostile fleet far offshore. In the early 1930's this mission was entrusted to twin-engine planes like the Boeing B-9 and the Martin B-10. The B-10, with its enclosed cockpit, gun turrets, and retractable landing gear, was almost as fast as the best pursuit planes, and helped foster faith in the bomber.

Unfortunately, as a result, fighter plane design and production lagged in the prewar days. A few fighter enthusiasts like Chennault protested, vigorously but in vain. The Lockheed P-38, Bell P-39, and Curtiss P-40, designed in 1936 and 1937, were not ready when war broke out in Europe. At that point—September, 1939 —the Air Corps had only obsolescent Curtiss P-36's— and no night fighters at all.

But it did have the most powerful bomber in the world as a result of the vision and persistence of men like General Foulois. In July, 1935, the XB-17, a revolutionary four-engine long-range bomber, designed by Boeing, had been test-flown. In August it made a nonstop flight of 2,100 miles at an average speed of 232 miles per hour, which put it in a class by itself. Even before this, the Air Corps had asked for a bomber with a range of 5,000 miles, capable of flying to Hawaii, Alaska, or the Canal Zone without having to stop en route. This had resulted in the XB-15, an airplane that proved too large for any power plants then in existence. It was not put into mass production, but it was the direct ancestor of the B-29.

Interservice rivalry raised its head in 1938, when the Air Corps, demonstrating its range at halting an enemy offshore, sent a flight of B-17's to "intercept" the Italian liner *Rex* 725 miles at sea. The Navy viewed it as an invasion of an area intrusted to itself as guardian of the sea approaches, and the Air Corps shortly found its combat range restricted to one hundred miles off the coast. In addition it was instructed to limit itself to the number of B-17's completed or on order. The ruling was handed down, incredibly, on the eve of Munich.

The Navy itself was hampered to some extent in building up a carrier force by dissension in its ranks over the value of naval air power. By 1936 the original carriers, the *Langley, Lexington,* and *Saratoga,* had been reinforced by the *Ranger,* the *Enterprise,* and the *Yorktown,* with the *Wasp* under construction. During the mid-1930's, the number of naval aircraft was held to about 1,000, but in May, 1938, Congress authorized the Navy to treble that number.

By this time, too, both Great Britain and France were rearming frantically. The British had been jolted into action in 1935 by Hitler's boast that the Luftwaffe, which had been in existence officially only two weeks, had already attained parity with the RAF. By 1936 Britain had set up a "shadow factory" system, with small plants feeding parts to the great airplane production centers. By 1937 a chain of twenty radar warning stations was being built—a piece of foresight that was to save England. Airfield construction was also stepped up drastically. In the summer of 1938, Chamberlain's appeasement of Hitler at Munich was bitterly criticized, but the year thus bought was invaluable to the RAF. At the time of Munich, Great Britain had only forty-three Hurricane fighters—and three Spitfires—with which to oppose some 1,200 battle-ready German bombers. A year later, the RAF had more than five hundred modern fighters ready to meet the invader.

France, which for years had had the largest air force in the world, was unable to rise to the same challenge. Governmental instability, lack of funds, a sentimental fondness on the part of some commanders for outdated types of aircraft, all acted as a drag on the Armee de l'Air at a time when to delay was to guarantee disaster.

By 1938, awake at last to its own shortcomings and its peril, France was feverishly ordering warplanes from abroad. But before any substantial deliveries could be made, the storm broke. On September 1, 1939, having hitherto used his Luftwaffe mainly for intimidation, Adolf Hitler sent 1,600 warplanes slashing into Poland above his racing panzers. Ahead of the world now lay six flaming years of war.

The first transatlantic airplane passenger, Charles A. Levine, and pilot Clarence Chamberlin (above) posed on June 7, 1927, in front of the Bellanca monoplane that had just carried them 3,911 miles nonstop from New York to Germany. Chamberlin had hoped to win the Orteig prize, but Lindbergh beat him by two weeks.

After Lindbergh

Charles A. Lindbergh's epoch flight to Paris opened a dramatic of long-distance flying. In the twe months following his triumph, thir one planes set out to span the peril Atlantic. Only ten of them s ceeded, and the failures cost twe lives. But neither those disasters similar ones in the Pacific disco aged other pilots who hoped to bre records and attain instant fame.

A few of the aviators who flash across newspaper headlines of the riod are pictured on these and t following two pages. But there w many others. Determined pilots li Charles Kingsford-Smith, Dieudon Coste and Maurice Bellonte, Russ Boardman and John Polando, Jan Mollison and his wife Amy Johns and colorful personalities like Dou las "Wrong Way" Corrigan becan popular heroes and kept aviation the front pages of the world's pre

Many of the transoceanic fligl were foolhardy, but the pilots w had the skill and luck to succe made valuable contributions to avi tion's growth. They spurred the velopment of new planes and navig tional devices. And they made cle to the world that commercial airlir would soon follow the routes th they had blazed across oceans a around the globe.

After a hazardous flight across the Atlantic in 1927, Commander Richard E. Byrd's Fokker trimotor was forced down off the Normandy coast by fog and shortage of fuel. Aboard the plane were, from left above, George Noville, Byrd, Bert Acosta, and Bernt Balchen.

The first east-to-west crossing of the North Atlantic was made in 1928 by Baron Guenther von Huenefeld, Major James Fitzmaurice, and Captain Herman Koehl, seen at right. They flew their Junkers monoplane from Ireland to a crash-landing off Labrador. Eight previous attempts at a westward crossing had cost seven lives.

Amelia Earhart gained sudden fame when she crossed the Atlantic in 1928 as a passenger in a plane flown by Wilmer Stultz. Four years later, she made the first transatlantic solo flight by a woman. Her disappearance over the Pacific in July, 1937, is still a mystery.

Headline Flights

The dangerous 2,400-mile flight from Oakland, California, to Hawaii was first made in June, 1927, by Army Lieutenants Lester Maitland and Albert Hegenberger, shown above taking off in their Fokker trimotor. BELOW: Ruth Elder prepares to fly from Roosevelt Field, Long Island, to Europe in October, 1927. She and George Haldeman crashed near the Azores, but the publicity furthered a movie career for the photogenic Miss Elder.

BELOW: Wiley Post climbs out of the Winnie Ma after his solo flight around the world in 1933. The tr took seven days and nineteen hours, breaking the re ord that he and Harold Gatty had set on a 1931 fligl

left, William Brock and Edward Schlee pose with the Stin-
n monoplane they flew from Newfoundland to Tokyo in 1927.
bove is one of the twelve Savoia-Marchetti seaplanes that flew
om Italy to Brazil in 1931, under the command of General
alo Balbo, who also led a 1933 mass flight from Italy to Chicago.

ABOVE: Masaaki Iinuma and Kenji Tsukagoshi are welcomed
at Croydon, England, in 1937 after a flight from Tokyo in the
Kamikaze ("Divine Wind"). At left, a twelve-motor Dornier
Do-X flies over the Rhine bound on a tour that brought it to
New York in 1931. BELOW: Howard Hughes lands at Floyd Bennett Field, Long Island, after flying around the world in three
days, nineteen hours, and fourteen minutes in July, 1938.

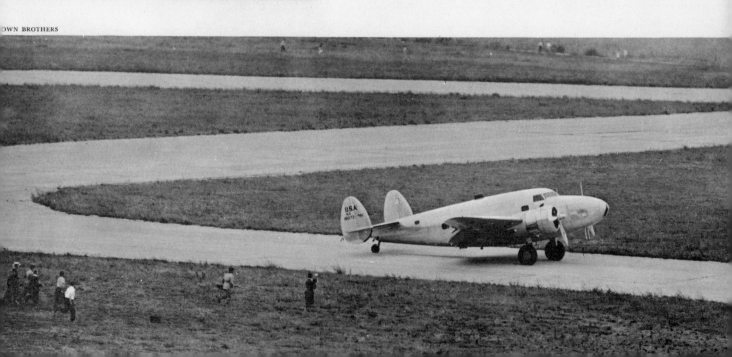

New Horizons

Flying at 70 miles an hour, the Question Mark *is shown above being refueled by a hose dropped from a plane captained by Ross G. Hoyt. The fuel line was caught by Major Carl Spaatz, who guided it into a tank in the fuselage. The fuel was then pumped by hand into wing tanks. The* Question Mark's *crew, seen left to right below after the wearying flight, comprised Sergeant Roy Hooe, Lieutenants Elwood Quesada and Harry Halverson, Captain Ira Eaker, and Major Spaatz.*

In January, 1929, an Army C appropriately named *Question Ma* during a period of searching f answers to new questions, broke world endurance records by remaing in the air over California for mc than 150 hours. Forty-three tim during the historic flight, a secor plane hovered less than twenty f above the Fokker and passed down it more than five thousand gallons fuel, as well as supplies and food f the five Army Air Corps fliers aboar Only when plugged grease outl stopped one of the Wright Whi wind engines did the plane return the ground.

The dramatic flight of the *Qu tion Mark* was just one of many e ploratory projects conducted by t Air Corps and Navy in the la 1920's and early 1930's. Congr had approved expansion of the t air branches, and both of them stro to develop new equipment and ne techniques.

Altitude records fell to men li Lieutenant Apollo Soucek of t Navy, who flew his Wright Apache 43,166 feet in 1930. Lieutena James Doolittle made the first tak off and landing on instruments September, 1929, and his work w carried on by the Air Corps's Capta Albert Hegenberger and by t Navy's Lieutenant Frank Akers, w made the first blind landing on aircraft carrier in July, 1935.

It was a period of tests and e ploration, as military fliers work steadily to find out just what they a their airplanes could do.

At right, six Marine F-4B's fly in echel Group flying occurred under officers l Captain H. M. Elmendorf, who led nir teen planes to a mass altitude record 1930, and Lieutenant Colonel Henry Arnold, who led a 1934 flight of ten Mar bombers from Washington, D.C., to Alas

Racing Thrills

America's best pilots convened each year at the National Air Races to display their skills and compete for cash awards. Huge crowds packed the grandstands and watched spellbound as the fliers cut pylons with incredible sharpness and flirted, sometimes too closely, with disaster.

The two most-coveted prizes were the Thompson Trophy, given for the fastest speed in a closed-course race, and the Bendix Trophy, awarded to the winner of a transcontinental derby. In these races, great pilots like Jimmy Doolittle, Roscoe Turner, Harold Neumann, Rudy Kling, James Haizlip, Jacqueline Cochran, and Frank Fuller, Jr., set new records and thrilled the crowds with their bravado. And it was the Air Races that gave impetus to the development of retractable landing gear, new fuels, and better engines—technological advances that were to be of great importance to the nation in the coming years of World War II.

BOTH: PRATT & WHITNEY

A highlight of the 1928 Air Races at L Angeles was the inverted flying of Na pilots D. W. Tomlinson, W. V. Dav and A. P. Storrs, known as the "S Hawks" (above). Military observers w saw them fly upside-down in Boeing F-2 with modified Wasp engines realiz the combat potential of such maneuve

The barrel-like Granville Gee Bee at l won the 1932 Thompson Trophy for Ji my Doolittle, who sped around the te lap, ten-mile course at a record-breaki 252 miles per hour. The Gee Bee, signed by Bob Hall, was dangerous as u as fast. Lowell Bayles and Russell Boa man were both killed flying Gee Be

Posters advertising the 1930 Air Races Chicago (right) promised thrills, but d not foresee the tragedy that was to m the meet. In the Thompson Trophy Ra a Curtiss Hawk flown by Captain Arth Page of the Marines crashed, fatally juring the pilot. The event was won Charles Holman, who flew 201 miles hour in a plane designed by Matty Lai

Speed Kings

Records of today," Frank Hawks said, "are the commonplaces of tomorrow." He and the other fast pilots of the 1930's made his statement come true.

When Hawks flew from California to New York in 1929, his time of eighteen hours and twenty-one minutes was considered astonishing. But by 1937, the transcontinental record was cut to seven and a half hours by Howard Hughes. Similarly, a speed of 194 miles per hour was good enough to win the 1929 Thompson Trophy for Douglas Davis, but a decade later, Roscoe Turner won the 1938 race by flying his Turner-Laird Special around the closed course at 283 miles per hour.

Thus records fell with amazing rapidity as daring pilots, who knew that their triumphs would be short-lived, vied for the right to claim the momentary title of fastest flier.

Lieutenant Alford Williams, shown above at the 1931 Air Races in Cleveland, was one of the Navy's greatest pilots. Winner of the 1923 Pulitzer Race with a record-breaking speed of 244 miles per hour, he was awarded the Distinguished Flying Cross in 1929 for his work as a test pilot. In a series of research flights, Williams studied the effects on aircraft of inverted flying maneuvers and correctly assessed their potential value in military combat.

Frank Hawks (right) earned the title "Meteor Man" with a series of record-smashing flights in America and Europe. Hawks, who was an Air Service pilot and then a barnstormer, was hired by the Texas Company in 1927 to promote its aviation products. He did so by flying from city to city and coast to coast, breaking speed records wherever he went. Hawks, who flew from Los Angeles to New York in twelve and a half hours in 1931, was killed in 1938 when his plane struck high-tension wires.

258

The small racer Pete *(above) was built in 1930 by Ben Howard, who won the 1935 Bendix Trophy with another of his own air-planes,* Mr. Mulligan. *Seated in the Wedell-Williams below is James Wedell, the winner of the 1933 Thompson Trophy.*

BELOW: *Roscoe Turner, the only three-time winner of the Thompson Trophy, leans against the Wedell-Williams that he flew in the 1932 competition. Turner, with his waxed mustache and powder-blue flying suit, was one of the most colorful racing pilots.*

One of many popular light planes was the Parks P-II, built in 1929 (above). Others were the Taylor Cub and the Stinson Reliant of 1937, which had a range of three hundred miles and carried a pilot and four passengers at 100 miles per hour.

The beloved humorist Will Rogers, shown below climbing out of a plane piloted by Billy Mitchell, was one of aviation's most influential boosters. Rogers and pilot Wiley Post were killed when their plane crashed near Point Barrow, Alaska, in 1935.

Flying for Fun

Private flying both for business and pleasure became a part of American life in the 1930's. The exploits of the record-breaking pilots had captured the imagination of the nation. Amelia Earhart and other women pilots like Jacqueline Cochran, Louise Thaden and Ruth Nichols had made flying glamorous, and popular personalities like Will Rogers had communicated their own love of aviation to their admiring public.

Many private persons, won to flying, bought light planes and joined aviation clubs, where they competed in aerial sports, including balloon bursting and parachuting, and participated in cross-country flights. Business and professional men bought small planes, too, to speed their travel on trips across the country. Aviation was no longer restricted to military and professional fliers. It was becoming a useful vehicle of transportation in everyday life—and it could also provide a great deal of fun.

Parachute jumping, demonstrated above by C.A.M. Scott of the Navy, was also a thrilling sport for civilians during the 1930's.

A Russian Flying Giant

The Soviet Union's emphasis on large air-craft culminated in the mammoth ANT-20 at left. Designed in 1934 by Andrei N. Tupolev, a pupil of the great aerodynami-cist N. E. Zhukovski, the eight-motor plane, called the Maxim Gorki, *weighed fifty-eight tons and had a wingspan of 210 feet. It was used chiefly for propaganda purposes until it was destroyed on May 19, 1935, in a collision with another airplane.*

FAMOUS AIRPLANES: U.S. 1928-1939

SIKORSKY S-38 1928

BOEING MONOMAIL 1929

NORTHROP GAMMA 1933

MARTIN B-10 1933

BOEING 247 1933

DOUGLAS DC-2 1934

MARTIN TRANSPORT 130 1935

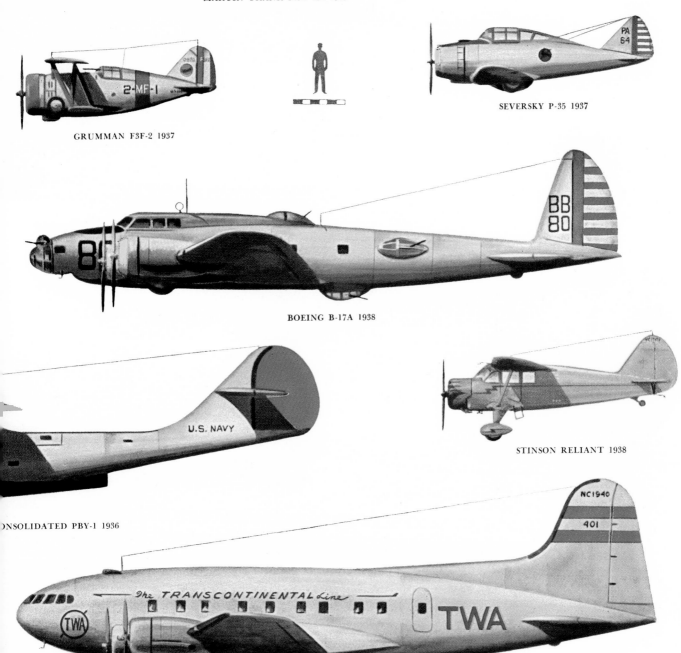

GRUMMAN F3F-2 1937

SEVERSKY P-35 1937

BOEING B-17A 1938

STINSON RELIANT 1938

ONSOLIDATED PBY-1 1936

BOEING 307 STRATOLINER 1939

RIGHT: *Transcontinental Air Transport's City of Los Angeles prepares to take off on its inaugural flight, July 8, 1929. At the controls is Charles Lindbergh, who had been hired by Transcontinental to survey its cross-country route, and who allowed the service to publicize itself as "the Lindbergh line." Transcontinental's service across America combined airplane and train travel by transferring the passengers to Pullman cars instead of flying them over mountainous areas. But although this hybrid service saved time, most travelers preferred the cheaper train service.*

BELOW: *Freight shipments are transferred from Railway to Air Express in 1932. The first scheduled Air Express service began on September 1, 1927, linking twenty-six cities. In 1928, the first full year of operation, four airlines—Boeing, National, Colonial, and Western—carried more than 17,000 Air Express shipments over routes that totaled 4,508 miles. The waiting Air Express plane in the photograph is a Hamilton all-metal monoplane, with a 400-horsepower Pratt & Whitney Wasp engine.*

Infant Industry

At first, fitful boom in American commercial aviation arrived at last in the late 1920's. Government support of the airmail, the sudden interest of big business in aviation, and the public's response to the long-distance record flights all combined to encourage commercial expansion. There were forty-four scheduled airlines in the United States by 1929. And although airmail routes had totaled only 2,800 miles in 1926, the figure had jumped to 30,000 miles only four years later in 1930.

The trouble, however, was that it was mail and not passengers that was providing the revenue. The vast majority of the public hung back, still unwilling to fly. New, safe, and economical planes were badly needed to induce enough air travel for profitable operations.

The negligee'd lady in the publicity picture above displayed the comforts of home in the lounge of a Fokker F-32 in 1929. One of the first four-engine airliners, the plane carried thirty-two passengers, but was too expensive to operate profitably.

The famous China Clipper *flies over the uncompleted Golden Gate Bridge at San Francisco (above) on November 22, 1935, the first day of Pan American's service to the Orient. The* Clipper, *commanded by Edwin Musick, was bound for the Philippines*

Queens of the Sky

At right is the reliable "workhorse of the air," Douglas's DC-3, which was equipped with an automatic pilot and soundproofing.

The modern airliner was born in 1933, when the Boeing 247 and the Douglas DC-1 made their initial flights. Both airplanes were the forerunners of rapidly-developed series of all-metal aircraft that featured cowled, air-cooled radial engines, retractable landing gear and variable-pitch propellers. They could carry passengers with safety and with speed, and—most important for their operators—they made commercial aviation a profitable business.

Most successful was the DC line produced by Donald Douglas and his dynamic chief engineers, James H. ("Dutch") Kindelberger and Arthur Raymond, who succeeded Kindelberger in 1934. The DC-1, a two-motor plane that could fly safely even if one engine failed, cost $307,000 to develop and produce. Only one was built, but the next version, the DC-2 of 1934, was reproduced more than two hundred times. Its multi-spar wing construction and split flaps allowed it to outperform all competition, and when a larger model, the DC-3, was built in 1935, it became the most popular airplane in the world. By 1946, when the last DC-3 was produced, 10,926 had been built, and by 1960 DC-3's had carried 600,000,000 passengers.

As domestic air travel boomed with the new planes, Pan American Airways began to push an air track across the Pacific, using Hawaii, Midway, Wake Island, and Guam as steppingstones to the Philippines. By 1936 graceful Martin M-130 Clippers were carrying mail and passengers to Manila, and by 1937 the route was extended by Sikorsky S-42's to Hong Kong, linking the United States to the Asiatic mainland more than 8,500 miles away.

Boeing's 307-B Stratoliner, a civilian version of the B-17 bomber, began carrying passengers for TWA in April, 1940. The first pressurized airliner, the four-engine transport could carry thirty-three passengers at 246 miles per hour. Aviation was growing at a fantastic pace, and domestic airlines in the United States, which had carried only about 6,000 persons in 1926, fifteen years later in 1941 were transporting almost three million people annually.

Professor Auguste Piccard (above) looks out from the gondola of the stratosphere balloon that carried him to 51,775 feet in 1931, and to 53,153 feet the next year.

The rocket-propelled glider at left was flown for ten minutes in 1929 by Fritz von Opel. A previous flight, in another glider, had been made by F. Stamer in 1928.

Below is the first practical helicopter, the Focke-Achgelis FW-61. First flown in 1936, it could reach 76 miles per hour and remain aloft for eighty minutes.

Pioneering

As the growth of commercial aviation spurred the development of conventional aircraft, men of new ideas and visions continued to explore and experiment.

The first rocket-propelled glider flight was made in Germany in 1928, while in America Dr. Robert Goddard steadily improved his equipment and fuel until he was able to launch a rocket to 7,500 feet in 1935. The first practical delta-wing aircraft was designed in 1931 by Dr. Alexander Lippisch of Germany, and the same nation saw the first flight of a practical helicopter in 1936. Frank Whittle of England and Hans von Ohain of Germany worked doggedly during the 1930's to design a workable jet engine.

Other pioneering efforts of the period included high-altitude balloon flights made by Auguste Piccard of Switzerland and by Captains Orvil Anderson and Albert Stevens of the U.S. Army Air Corps, who soared to 72,394 feet in the gondola of the *Explorer II* in 1935.

The Explorer II *rises to a record altitude over South Dakota in November, 1935.*

The Fate
of the Hindenburg

Zeppelin flights to South America were advertised by the German poster above. The service was operated by the Nazi government's Deutsche Zeppelin-Reederei, which usurped control of the flights from Dr. Hugo Eckener's Luftschiffbau-Zeppelin company in 1935. Most of the voyages to South America were made by the Graf Zeppelin, although the Hindenburg also flew to Rio de Janeiro occasionally. A third ship, the LZ-130, was scheduled to carry passengers in late 1937, but the Hindenburg crash ended the service.

Ten times during 1936, the gian Zeppelin *Hindenburg* made the round trip between Germany and th United States. Cruising quietly at 7 miles per hour, it gave its passenger who paid $720 apiece for the roun trip, a voyage of the utmost smooth ness and luxury.

The demand for reservation aboard the hydrogen-inflated airshi was so great that eighteen flights ha been scheduled for the 1937 seasor and extra cabins had been built to ac commodate more passengers. Ther were ninety-seven persons aboard o May 3, 1937, when the *Hindenbur* left Germany for its first voyage of th year to North America.

Head winds prolonged the fligh and thunderstorms delayed the land ing. But shortly after seven o'clock o the evening of May 6, the 804-foo Zeppelin prepared to moor at Lake hurst, New Jersey. Cables were low ered and the *Hindenburg* came dow to less than two hundred feet. Ther suddenly, disaster struck.

Flames burst from between tw cells of the upper stern, and withi seconds, sheets of crackling fire er veloped the tail section. As spectato watched in dumb horror, and scream ing passengers leaped from the shi the Zeppelin fell to the ground i twisted, flaming wreckage. Thirty-si lives were lost in the holocaust, an many of those who survived wer horribly burned.

The cause of the disaster was nev definitely established. There wer many theories, but all that seeme certain was that free hydrogen ha somehow escaped and had been ig nited. The *Hindenburg* tragedy which brought to an abrupt end th era of the great Zeppelins, remair an unsolved mystery.

Flames explode high in the air over Lakehurst, New Jersey, at the moment of catastrophe to the giant Hindenburg. Among the fatally injured was Ernst Lehmann, who had commanded the Hindenburg in 1936 and who was aboard as an observer during the last, tragic flight.

Rehearsal for World War

As aggressor nations plunged into limited wars in China, Ethiopia, and Spain in the 1930's, people slowly came to recognize that air power would undoubtedly be the decisive factor in any future world conflict. The stunning successes of new planes and techniques tested by the Germans, Italians, and Japanese served to convince the Axis powers of their own superiority. Only in time did these tragic examples strike home to shatter the complacency of unprepared, peaceful countries.

The small wars of the 1930's made it painfully clear that civilian populations would no longer be exempt from the horrors of conflict. In Ethiopia, Mussolini's son Vittorio observed with pleasure the bombs from his Caproni plane bursting "like flowers" among the thatched huts of primitive tribesmen. In Spain, Nationalist bombs killed 1,654 inhabi-tants of Guernica, whose anguish was later immortalized in a painting by Pablo Picasso. And in China, Japanese planes made flights of more than 1,200 miles over land and water to their targets, and demonstrated that distance no longer afforded security from long-range bombers.

These ruthless displays of air power frightened and shocked the observing world. The Germans had announced in 1935 that their air force was already equal to Great Britain's—and was approaching that of France, which still had the greatest number of planes, though many of them were obsolete. The British and French, aware at last of the crucial role of air power, began at a late hour to try to regain aerial supremacy, but their potential enemies moved at an even faster pace, continuing a military build-up that, for the first time, included powerful fleets of airplanes.

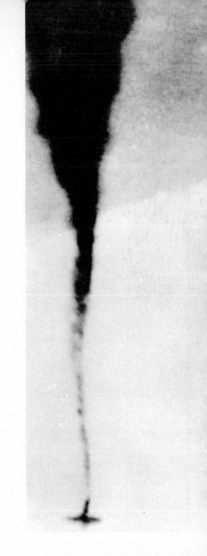

ABOVE: *A rare pre-World War II photograph shows Japanese pilots flying Nakajima Ki-27's in combat over China. First flown in 1936, these single-seat, low-wing monoplane fighters—later called "Nates" by Allied pilots—were famed for their maneuverability and had a top speed of 287 m.p.h.*

BELOW: *A squadron of Italian Fiat fighters takes off on a combat mission during the Spanish Civil War. More than 6,000 members of Mussolini's Aviación Legionaria aided Franco, flying more than 86,000 missions during the war.*

ABOVE: *Moroccan soldiers board a Junkers Ju-52 in North Africa. German transports ferried over 10,000 Moroccan troops to Spain in the revolt against the Spanish Republican government.*

At left, Italian bombers, commanded by Count Galeazzo Ciano, Mussolini's son-in-law, fly over the front lines in remote Ethiopia in 1935. The cruel, unequal conflict lasted just seven months.

A Giant Stirs

With war clouds darkening Europe and the Far East, Generals Henry H. Arnold, Frank Andrews, and others fought hard for a stronger American air force. But not until September, 1938, when President Franklin D. Roosevelt called for an enlarged Air Corps of 10,000 planes, did expansion really begin. The Air Corps, Arnold said, had finally "achieved its Magna Charta."

Although still hampered by isolationist sentiment and shortsightedness in Congress and elsewhere, the Air Corps was able to speed the production of new designs. America was not ready when war finally broke out in 1939, but the great Army Air Forces of the future were being forged.

UPI

At right, a group of Boeing P-26 pursuit planes roars above the clouds. The P-26, first flown in 1932, had a top speed of 234 miles per hour and set several speed and altitude records. It was both the U.S. Army Air Corps's first all-metal pursuit plane and its first monoplane fighter.

At left, three Boeing B-17's intercept the Italian liner Rex 725 miles at sea in May, 1938. The flight demonstrated the bomber's ability to attack an invader far offshore, but Navy protests resulted in the limiting of Air Corps operations to within a hundred miles of the American coastline.

Below is an aerial view of Randolph Field at San Antonio, Texas. The planes at bottom of the photograph spell out the word "wings." Randolph, Kelly, and Brooks fields trained hundreds of men as the Air Corps increased its quota of new pilots from 300 a year to 1,200 a year in 1939.

CULVER PICTURES, INC.

UPI

YEARS OF
ENDEAVOR

The Lindbergh Boom

Richard Mock, an aviation designer and executive, was studying aeronautical engineering at New York University when Lindbergh flew to Paris. He recalls the effect of that flight on his own career.

In the early days of 1927 we were aware that in the graduating class of the year before in aeronautical engineering, only one student had got a job in aviation, two or three in engineering of any sort, and the rest went into the bond business or worked for retail stores. So there was great apprehension about how we were going to get our bread and butter.

I wrote letters to some thirteen companies and organizations around March of '27—all the ones that I thought counted.

Then Lindbergh's flight was completed successfully. The result was that everybody who was in the aviation business expected a boom. Here was a group of people crying in the wilderness, and suddenly they were on the front pages. The net result was that *all* the companies that I had written to wrote offering me a job.

The Way to Berlin

The June, 1927, flight of Clarence Chamberlin and Charles Levine from New York to Germany came only seventeen days after Lindbergh's epic crossing to Paris. In this excerpt from one of his speeches, Chamberlin tells of the last part of his flight.

When we hit Lands End, England, the ceiling was down to about three or four hundred feet. I'm an over-or-under pilot; since the Hartz Mountains ahead in Germany were three or four thousand feet high, I was afraid to go under. So we went up top. The last place we saw in England through a hole in the clouds was Plymouth. Then we began to climb until, along about midnight, we were at 21,000 feet, with no oxygen, and I was getting a little tired.

Now Charlie [Levine] had never made a landing or a take-off, but he'd flown a plane a little in the air. So I said, "Charlie, you see that group of stars up there? Well, you keep your eye on that, and I don't care where you go in the next ten or fifteen minutes. I'm going to stretch out and get a little rest."

Well, he came to an extra high bank of clouds, and he kept pulling the stick back a little more and a little more, trying to stay up over the top until finally he pulled it up into a stall and off into a tail spin. I was back on top of the gas tank, and by the time I could get back into my seat to figure out which way we were turning and get the thing straightened out, we had fallen a little over 17,000 feet. Fortunately, we had another three or four thousand to go. I knew how low on gas we were, so it was no use going back up.

We put her in a slow glide and came on down through. We came out over water just as dawn was breaking. Charlie thought it was the North Sea; I hadn't the slightest idea what it was. As we got a little lower, we saw it was a river. On both sides of us the mountains were sticking up into the clouds. If we had come down a quarter of a mile on either side we'd have hit these mountains.

Well, I followed this river until we saw some rockets being fired off in the distance. The airport police at Dortmund, Germany, heard the engines and were firing up these rockets. So we flew down low over the field— we had a window that you pulled back—and I called out in my best high-school German and asked the way to Berlin.

Well, there was a little difference of opinion: some of them pointed this way and others pointed that way, with the result that while Charlie was flying he went the way he thought it was and while I was flying I went the way I thought it was.

Before we had left, somebody told us that all the railroads in Germany were laid out like spokes in a wheel, working out of Berlin. Well, I followed the only railroad, I think, that didn't go into Berlin. And we finally ran out of gas. We landed in one wheat field, bounced over a road, stopped rolling in another.

A lady and two boys came down the road on bicycles. When she found out I was in her wheat field, she was very angry and came over to chase us away; but when she heard our German, she got her children out of there.

The Lion Had a Parachute

The colorful Roscoe Turner, an imaginative businessman as well as a successful racing pilot, recalls some of the enterprising ways in which he made his living as a flier.

My Sikorsky was the largest airplane in the United States at that time [1927-28], and I used it for passenger carrying. I tried to start an airline with it from New York to Atlanta, but I couldn't get the necessary financial interest; so I used it as an advertising medium. I did more public relations work and advertising than probably any other aviator.

I went out with it one trip as a flying cigar store. It was an actual store on wings. It was tremendous advertising for the United Cigar Stores. Then, later on, I went out for the Curlee Clothing Company, flying their top salesmen and dropping them off in their territory.

Then I took the Sikorsky to Hollywood to help Howard Hughes finish his picture, *Hell's Angels*. I did all the flying. We made the plane look like a German Gotha bomber.

I also ran an airline for a group of businessmen out in Los Angeles and Nevada. It was the first high-speed airline in the world. We ran from Los Angeles to Reno and from Reno to Las Vegas and back to Los Angeles. At that time all the rest of the airlines were averaging about 85 miles an hour. Our average speed was 141 miles an hour. Some called it the

Roscoe Turner and his flying friend

"Alimony Special," because most of our trade was movie stars.

Of course, I enjoyed a very close friendship with William Randolph Hearst, and I had a standing invitation to his San Simeon ranch. He had a little airstrip there. Just a one-way field. When his big wheels from New York and Chicago came out there, why, he'd always call me up and ask me to fly them up to San Simeon. It didn't make any difference whether they wanted to fly or not. If Mr. Hearst told them to fly, they flew.

After we had discontinued the Nevada airline, I thought up the idea of buying a lion. The Gilmore Oil Company has a very beautiful lion-head trademark, so I persuaded them to animate it. I told them I'd take an African lion and fly around with it.

The lion liked to fly. The Humane Society made me build him a parachute, but he never used it. All the hotels gave us complimentary hotel suites because of the advertising they got out of it. It had never been done before, and it's never been done since. Oh, I think some guys have fooled around maybe with a mountain lion or something, maybe flown him a short distance, but I flew this lion all over the United States and Canada and Mexico. I kept him till he died. Now he's mounted in my front room.

"Good Girl . . ."

Mrs. Muriel Morrissey, sister of the dauntless Amelia Earhart, reminisces about the famous aviatrix.

If Amelia wanted to do something, she was going to do it, and there really wasn't much point in saying, "You can't do this."

She felt very strongly that women should win their own way and not be given any special consideration, economically or physically. She trained very definitely to stay awake, if need be, for eighteen hours at a stretch, and she trained herself to be able to undergo the same type of rigorous exercise that a man would.

That was when she was first considering the transatlantic flight in the *Friendship*. Of course, we didn't know what the reason for it was, but she used to eat very lightly, which worried Mother, because she couldn't see why Amelia wasn't eating things she'd always enjoyed. And sometimes we'd find out that she'd been up till three or four o'clock. Later on, of course, we found out that it was part of her self-discipline.

I have an interesting book which Amelia had at school. She cut from the newspapers and magazines clippings telling of things that women had done that men had always done before. One of the clippings is about the first Indian woman who was admitted to the Bar in Bombay, and one about a woman who was a member of the Bricklayers' Union in Toronto. There was one woman who came out with an article saying that she found it a little bit hard to do her job as she should and also run a home, but she said it could be done. Beside that Amelia had written in pencil, "Good girl, Helen."

We never thought too much about her making aviation a career, and I don't believe she did, even when she returned from the first *Friendship* flight. She planned to continue her work in the social welfare field. But the public wouldn't let her.

An Affair in Nicaragua

From 1927 to 1933 the United States Marine Corps and its small aviation section supported the Nicaraguan Guardia Nacional against rebels and bandits. Among the Marine pilots was Lieutenant Christian F. Schilt, who described in the following newspaper account the evacuation of wounded troops from Quilali, an operation which won him the Medal of Honor in 1928.

Quilali is in a deep hole, surrounded by high, rugged mountains. The only fairly level spot for miles around is the road running through the town. This is only 15 feet wide, with a 3-foot ditch running through it. Our forces had bandits all around them.

Our planes dropped picks and shovels to our ground troops. They demolished the houses on one side of the road, making a runway 70 feet wide and 300 feet long, and very rough. A high bluff is at one end of this quickly built emergency landing field and trees and a ditch at the other end, with a 5,000-foot mountain directly across the river.

On approval by Maj. Rowell, commanding Marine aviation in Nicaragua, wheels with tires eight inches wide were placed on a Corsair airplane, "Wasp" engine equipped. These large tires were necessary to insure greater safety and prepare the plane better to withstand the punishment it was to get upon landing at Quilali. Upon the completion of the runway I proceeded to Quilali and attempted a landing.

The first attempt was a failure. I approached for a landing in the normal way, but owing to the roughness, shortness and narrowness of the "field" a normal landing could not be made. On my next attempt, I decided to drop the plane into the "field." The first drop was about 10 feet. I rolled a short distance and bounced 30 feet. Then the plane hit the ground again, bounced 10 feet, and rolled up to the deep ditch at the end

Marine aviator Christian F. Schilt

of the "field." I got out of the plane, expecting to find half of it spread out on the ground. But I was surprised to find it intact. The first to greet me upon landing was Lieut. Gould. His first words were, "My God, Schilt, an angel from heaven would be no more welcome than you!"

My next worry was to get out of the "field" and back to semicivilization through the heavy machine gun fire the plane was under. After taking aboard Lieut. Richal, who had been wounded in the head, I was ready to attempt a take-off; two sturdy Marines held each wing tip while I started the engine. As it was speeded up, the Marines turned loose the wings simultaneously. I was catapulted forward into a ridge, which bounced me 10 feet. But the plane was fast gathering speed, and on the next bounce we remained afloat, and the plane was intact. . . .

On the ninth landing, an interplane strut was bent. This was straightened with an ax, wrapping the strut with wooden splints and safety wire. I made the last [the tenth] trip into Quilali without accident. All the wounded were evacuated to Octotal and after the last man was landed, we proceeded on a regular patrol flight over the bandit areas.

Fuel for Alan Cobham

Oil companies frequently played important roles in helping airlines establish new routes across undeveloped parts of the world. Henry Shaw, who was a British commercial pilot before he became manager of Shell-Mex Oil Company's aviation department, directed the "laying down" of fuel at remote points for many path-blazing flights, including the African survey flights of the great long-distance flier Sir Alan Cobham.

One African incident I remember very well. We had laid down supplies for one of Alan Cobham's flights up the Nile, down through Nyasaland, and down to South Africa. We had a tremendous job laying down those supplies. They had to go from the coast by road. Then where there were no roads they had to be carried by natives, each of the natives carrying two cases. Each case held two 4-gallon tins.

We had the signal that these supplies were in position, but it happened that one of the Shell inspectors was traveling near there on one of his annual visits and thought that he would inspect the stock. He opened one of the tins, and he was horrified to find

Cobham, relaxing during a long flight

it was full of water and not
trol. He opened several more and
y were all full of water.

We found out that one of the na-
es who did the last hundred miles
rrying these packages had dropped
tin, and out of it flowed what he
nsidered was water. He must have
ought, Why carry all this stuff to
ke Kivu, where there's lots of
ter? So they all made a pinprick
the bottom of the cans and a pin-
ck in the top and let all the fuel
w out. When they got near home,
y put these tins in the river, let
m fill up with water, and then
led the pinholes with clay.
Very smart, indeed. We found out
t in time to get a new supply there
o days before Cobham arrived.
at's the sort of thing we did en-
unter and had to overcome.

he First Stewardess

*nerica's first airline stewardess was
en Church of Cresskill, Iowa. She
ought that it was a good way to
mbine her training as a nurse with
r love for flying; in 1930 she sug-
sted the idea to Boeing Air Trans-
rt and got the job.*

first some of the pilots took the
ole idea of stewardesses as kind of
oke. Then they realized that they
ln't have to hand out box lunches
d take care of sick passengers any
ore.
I don't think I made many flights
en we went straight through. I
d an awfully hard time getting
ross Wendover on the Nevada line.
e always seemed to run into bad
ather there, and we had to sit it
t on the ground with no accommo-
tions. There was a little weather
tion there, where the passengers
t some space, but they usually slept
horse blankets on the floor.
The nearest place to the landing
ip where the passengers could eat
s the railroad station, but you had
walk through the mud to get
re and then walk back again.

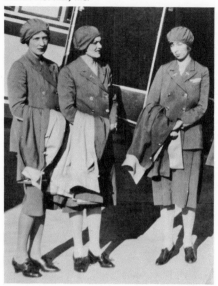

Ellen Church (right) and early hostesses

Sometimes it was necessary to make
arrangements for passengers to go by
train to their destination. That was
our responsibility too.

We spent more time with the passengers than the girls do today. It
was not like today, for we went slower
and had more time to show people
points of interest.

There was much more airsickness
than there is now, and ventilation was
pretty crude. There were heated
planes, but there must have been
leakage in some of them, leakage of
the exhaust fumes. In order to rid
ourselves of the fumes, we turned the
heat off and then wrapped up in
blankets. In looking back, I wonder
why anybody rode at all.

Refueling was sometimes interesting. Sometimes we had to land at an
emergency landing field and then we
had the gas in two-and-a-half- or
five-gallon cans. They would form a
sort of fire brigade, handing the cans
from one to the other, including the
stewardess and some of the passengers. Then, if we were some place
where there was no crew on the field,
somebody had to go out on the left
wing to the engine to do something
there. The pilot and the copilot were
busy inside, so the third member of
the crew had to go out on the wing—

and that was the stewardess. We did
it without a murmur because of the
argument that when a third person
was needed for something like that
the third person should be a man.

Dakar to Natal

*The opening of a new international
commercial route was often a supreme adventure. Didier Daurat, who
directed France's establishment of
the first transatlantic service between
Africa and South America, tells of
the strain and exhilaration common
to pioneers who were tying the world
together with air routes.*

The two services, Toulouse [France]
to Dakar [Senegal], and Natal [Bra-
zil] to Buenos Aires [Argentina] were
assured. But what remained was to
tie these two services together. It took
us several years to do it.

We did it first with *avisos*, small
boats. But they were very slow, and
it used to take us four nights and four
days from Dakar to Natal. In order
to honor our South American contracts, we had to make the ocean-
crossing by plane.

We had built another landplane,
the Laté 28, with a 650-horsepower
Hispano motor. This plane allowed
ten passengers to travel in relative
comfort. We made it into a seaplane,
and after proving that it could cross
the South Atlantic, we decided to fly
to South America.

We got to Senegal, where we had
a base on the river. And there, on
May 12, 1930, we received a message
informing us that the director of our
service in South America, Julien
Pranville, had been killed. On May
11, the plane carrying him had
crashed into the waters of the Rio
del Plata because of a bad fog. The
plane was flown by Elysee Negrin,
our chief pilot, and on board were
the radio operator, Pruneta, and two
Brazilian passengers. They were heading towards Natal to greet [Jean]
Mermoz and his crew on their arrival after crossing the South Atlantic.

281

Pranville's aircraft was floating on the dark waters of the river. The night was black and the fog was thick. Before the waters swallowed the plane, Pranville had only two minutes available to decide the assignment of the two air cushions that he thought could save two lives. What a terrible situation! Only two air cushions for five persons on board.

Then, Pruneta dived into the water saying: "Good-by forever, to all of you." Pranville and Negrin agreed to give the air cushions to the two Brazilian passengers. One of them drowned because his cushion didn't inflate well; Pranville, Negrin, and Pruneta died also. But the other passenger was saved; it was he who informed us of the tragedy. It was, I think, the first sacrifice by a commercial crew in order to save passengers.

I tell this because it happened at the brink of our attempt to fly across the South Atlantic. We had received proof of the fragility of human ambitions, and maybe this was what caused all of us in Senegal, who were putting the finishing touches on the plane which carried our hopes, to develop special techniques which allowed Mermoz to fly between Saint-Louis in Senegal and Natal in less than twenty-two hours.

It was both the first commercial flight for seaplanes on this route and a world record in straight flying. During the flight I was aboard an *aviso* at sea. The radio room was filled by the Senegalese crew, covered with perspiration from the boiler room. They refused to retire, as did the officers and sailors. Everybody was around the radio in a sort of communion with Mermoz.

It was a veritable festival of the airwaves. We received aboard the *aviso* all the messages to the plane. The messages were testimonials of the profound union which existed between men who didn't even know each other, from the banks of the Garonne to the borders of the Pacific. In French, in Spanish, in Moorish dialect, in Senegalese, in Portuguese —these messages gave the impression that all these men were striving for the same ideal. All of these men, united by a common will, were carrying, by their courage and experience, the seaplane which was flying from Senegal to Natal. This was one of the most moving experiences in my career. This spirit, which allowed us, in spite of the predictions, to realize a great piece of work, left indelible traces. We connected at last with South America, and we were the first ones to do it.

Setting a Record

During her many years of flying, Ruth Nichols established more than thirty-five speed, distance, and altitude records. Here she tells how she reached a height of 28,743 feet in March, 1931, to set a new world altitude record for women.

We had a propeller that had a certain pitch to it which would give you a very much better rate of climb—if you have a high pitch, you can climb faster, but you don't get anyplace. Here I was, flying an airplane that had a ground speed usually of 175 to 200 miles an hour, and I was headed westerly. I never made a single turn,

Ruth Nichols, after a record flight

and I landed in the same airpo after about an hour and a half flying time.

Of course, the reason for that w that I was climbing steadily at wh we call a high angle of attack. doing that, my ground speed w very, very slow. It came to a poin about fifty miles west of New Jers from where I took off, where n ground speed was zero. Then fina as I went up higher, I started losin ground and was going backward. was a great source of concern, to p it mildly, when I finally had reach my altitude peak and discovered th I was down to my last five gallons gasoline. I came down through t clouds and found myself out over t Atlantic Ocean. I could barely s the shore line, and I knew that th particular engine used gasoline ve rapidly. Coming in over the canyo of Manhattan I was pretty apprehe sive about whether that old engi was going to keep on going until I g to the airport at Jersey City. I did bother circling for wind direction just came in and landed, period.

That was in a Lockheed Vega, a the final barometric reading was a l tle higher than 28,000 feet. It w exceedingly cold, of course. As a ma

South Atlantic conqueror Jean Mermoz

of fact, I had thermometers in the [...]ng that broke at minus 40. It was [...]obably minus 60 degrees, from [...]at we gathered. I had on layers [...]n layers of warm clothing. Some[...]e had very kindly donated a rein[...]er suit, which was much more dra[...]tic- and attractive-looking than it [...]s warm, but I wore it on top of all [...]e layers, anyway.

The oxygen sets in those days were [...]tirely different from the equipment [...]d now. We didn't have enough [...]ney to buy the right kind, anyway; [...]vas pretty expensive, running up to [...]couple of thousand dollars. So I [...]t took a regular oxygen tank that [...]'d find anywhere, and we at[...]hed a rubber hose on the end of it. [...]put the hose in my mouth and [...]ked oxygen through directly from [...] tank. This little oxygen tank was [...]t on the wing, so if the wing was [...]nus 60 degrees, you can imagine [...]at the oxygen temperature was. [...]e first thing I knew, my tongue [...]ze into a solid ice ball, and it [...]sed a great deal of pain as well [...]a great deal of concern.

Young Man's Game"

[...]aska will always be indebted to its [...]sh pilots—men who for years [...]intained the only links between [...]ny of its settlements, and who [...]ped to open much of its wilder[...]s. One of them was Raymond [...]ersen, who operated his own flying [...]vice and later became president of [...]rthern Consolidated Airlines.

[...]ecided to come to Alaska during [...] Depression, inasmuch as there [...]n't appear to be much opportun[...]in the United States for anything [...]ept stunt flying and a little stu[...]t instruction, which was hardly [...] exciting way to fly, as far as I was [...]cerned. Alaska appeared to be [...] place where an airplane wasn't [...]oy or a carnival vehicle, but was [...]ually necessary and useful as [...]sportation. Being in Alaska didn't [...]nge my opinion one bit.

Flying in those days was strictly bush flying. We would serve various mining operations in the area, and out of Bethel we did a lot of emergency work, since the only hospital was at Mountain Village up near the mouth of the Yukon. If someone was hurt or sick, why, we would fly them over to the hospital. We'd gather them from all over the country.

It was an interesting type of work, inasmuch as you took care of practically all the needs of these people. As I'd drop my passengers off, I'd pick up some more for some other point along the Yukon. Nothing scheduled, but all just falling into place. As we would go to each of these places, folks would say, "I'd like to catch the boat leaving Seward on the sixteenth." So I'd say, "O.K., I'll take you to Anchorage on that trip." And the first thing I knew I had a pretty good load lined up.

In the meantime I'd take orders for everything from toothpaste to patent medicine and overshoes. Then I'd take my load to Anchorage, go around to all the stores, and shop for all these various people. We had a regular rate per pound that we charged our customers.

Occasionally a tractor would break down in one of the mining camps, and we would have to pick up parts for them and fly them back. We attempted never to charge people a charter rate if we could handle them at regular fares, and it worked out quite well. From that evolved our scheduled operation.

I also flew the first doctor around the lower Kuskokwim Yukon area, which was a very primitive Eskimo settlement. I took this doctor and helped him with the first vaccination for smallpox of all these natives. We went into the individual igloos and we had to talk these mothers into letting their babies get vaccinated.

There were harrowing experiences, but they were wonderful. I miss them. I miss those days. But it was a young man's game.

"I Had All These Goats"

Another Alaskan pioneer flier, Merle K. Smith, who later became president of Cordova Airlines, recalls one of his own experiences as a bush pilot.

In the old days we used to have what is now called unusual cargo. We called it good paying freight then.

There was a homesteader who decided that he needed fresh milk. So he sent to Seattle and ordered some goats. I loaded these goats into one of the old planes and started up there. Well, I had forgotten that goats like rope, and I had tied these goats to various places in the airplane with ropes so that they wouldn't get loose and annoy me or endanger the flight.

In about twenty minutes they had all the ropes chewed through. So then I had all these goats. They'd all frolic together. There must have been eight hundred pounds of goats; and they'd all get in the back of the airplane and I couldn't hold the nose down. They would all come up and chew on me a little bit, and chew my shirt, and I'd slap them away. But I decided not to do that any more, because the first time I did that, they all went to the back of the airplane. It got to be kind of a serious situation. By the time we got to where I could land these goats they had most of the fabric eaten off the inside of the airplane, and my shirt; and the seat that I was sitting on was pretty well stripped of upholstery. But these little things happened. If you came out all right, as in this instance—well, it was funny.

Katie's First Solo

Sports flying in the 1930's was sometimes dangerous, but almost always fun. Admiral Luis De Florez, the inventor of many aircraft devices for the United States Navy, recalls a bygone era of aviation country clubs.

The air was pretty much free of restrictions. People had little airplanes, and they had contests, contests in racing, in bomb dropping with sacks of sand, in bursting balloons, cutting toilet paper, spot landings, and, of course, acrobatics. A number of clubs sprang up and there were many team contests. These were very much in the same vein as a country-club polo team. We had air meets, with tin cups suitably plated so that people would risk their necks for them.

One particular organization was the Aviation Country Club on Long Island. In those days people wore helmets and goggles and nice white linen suits. They talked aviation, drank beer and tea, and whatnot. There were a great many women pilots; it was just fun.

The balloon-bursting was very interesting, a dangerous sport, finally banned by the Department of Commerce. A man would stand in the middle of the field with a balloon approximately two feet in diameter, and the airplane competing would be in position perhaps a mile down the field from there. Then the man would let the balloon go, and the plane would take off and try to burst it with its propeller. One of the interesting things was that if the pilot rushed the balloon too fast, it would very often go through the propeller without breaking; you had to calculate your speed. The danger came from the fact that fliers who were not skilled would follow the balloon directly up; they'd get so excited that they would stall and spin down to the ground. So in order to have a competition, we resorted to toilet-paper strafing, as we called it. You took a roll of toilet paper and threw it overboard, and that roll dropped in a straight line. Then you would turn and cut it. You had to cut it three times; your score was the number of seconds it took to cut it. After one of these meets, the whole countryside would be strewn with toilet paper.

Another group took to seaplaning. They had seaplane cruises, the same as the New York Yacht Club cruise, by invitation. There was a fleet captain who would arrange for moor-ings at the various stops. Usually the participants in the cruise would spend the night and have parties. The next day the cruise would go on, stopping somewhere for lunch at a beach. Sometimes they'd go to Canada, sometimes to Maine, sometimes to the Chesapeake. It was all done very informally with uniform jackets and cruise hats.

I was chairman of the flying committee for almost ten years, and during that period of time we didn't have a single fatality. The flying committee was pretty strict. We didn't want to give the sport a bad name.

There were a lot of amusing incidents. I remember one time we had an air meet at the country club and tried a comedy stunt. We had this German couple that ran the club, and we announced over the loud-speaker that Katie, the wife, had learned how to fly and that she was going to do her first solo. So we had Katie all dressed up in a helmet and goggles. In the meantime I'd gone in back and got her skirt and whatnot. I dressed up in the same clothes Katie wore, put a helmet on, walked out on the field after Katie had walked back through the clubhouse, and got into this airplane. I took off and flapped around all over the place and nearly stalled—I actually almost did break my neck. I finally came in and made about three attempts at landing. I landed the ship and then taxied up to the hangar and went in the back door. Then Katie came out with the same rig on. The people were indignant. They said, "You're the chairman of the flying committee—how dare you let that woman nearly kill herself in front of this crowd!"

We had considerable coverage by newspapers, and everybody thought the whole idea of aviation clubs would continue, the same way as golf and polo. But the war restrictions, maturity, and real-estate developments killed this gay and colorful phase of flying which probably will never return.

Father of Rocketry

On March 16, 1926, Dr. Robert *Goddard, after more than fifte* *years of research, made the first s* *cessful launching of a liquid-power* *rocket. Fire Department officials* *Worcester, Massachusetts, object* *to Goddard's experiments, and* *1930 he moved to Roswell, N* *Mexico, where he continued his p* *neering efforts. He outlined his pr* *ress in a report in 1935 to the Dan* *and Florence Guggenheim Found* *tion, which supported his research.*

In the first flight of the present ser of tests with gyroscopic control, March 28, 1935, the rocket as view from the 1,000-foot shelter travel first to the left and then to the rig thereafter describing a smooth a rather flat trajectory. This result v encouraging, as it indicated the pr ence of an actual stabilizing force sufficient magnitude to turn rocket back to a vertical course. T greatest height in this flight v 4,800 feet, the horizontal distar 13,000 feet, and the maximum spe 550 miles per hour.

In subsequent flights, with adju ments and improvements in the sta lizing arrangements, the rockets ha

Robert H. Goddard with an early rock

een stabilized up to the time propulsion ceased, the trajectory being a smooth curve beyond this point. In the rockets so far used, the vanes have moved only during the period of propulsion, but with a continuation of the supply of compressed gas the vanes could evidently act against the slip stream of air as long as the rocket was in motion in air of appreciable density. The oscillations each side of the vertical varied from 10° to 30° and occupied from 1 to 2 seconds. Inasmuch as the rockets started slowly, the first few hundred feet of the flight reminded one of a fish swimming in a vertical direction. . . . The continually increasing speed of the rockets, with the accompanying steady roar, make the flights very impressive. In the two flights for which the moving pictures are shown, the rocket left a smoke trail and had a small, intensely white flame issuing from the nozzle, which at times nearly disappeared with no decrease in roar or propelling force. This smoke may be avoided by varying the proportion of the fluids used in the rocket, but is of advantage in following the path of the rocket. The occasional white flashes below the rocket . . . are explosions of gasoline vapor in the air. . . .

The next step in the development of the liquid-propellant rocket is the reduction of weight to a minimum. Some progress along this line has already been made. This work, when completed, will be made the subject of a later report.

The Death of the Hindenburg

The last flight of the German airship Hindenburg was commanded by Captain Max Pruss. Following is his description of the flight's disastrous end at Lakehurst, New Jersey, on May 6, 1937.

The *Hindenburg* was the best and finest ship for passengers. It is very regrettable that we have no airships now. On an airship you had a won-

Captain Max Pruss

derful trip, not like an airplane where you can't see anything. It was very, very comfortable, and there was never any seasickness.

The *Hindenburg* could travel at 136 kilometers [84 miles] per hour. It held seventy-two passengers. We had not only passengers, but freight and mail and everything. We even had a car and airplanes on board.

We had a cabin for every passenger, hot and cold water, heating, and air conditioning. And a dining room and promenades you could walk on, as well as a lounge. There were four cooks on board. One was a pastry chef; the passengers had cake and bread every day. All the food was fresh. And we had a bar also; the passengers could have wine and all kinds of drinks.

We were able to make telephone calls to stations in Europe and America. And we had a grand piano on board, so we held a very good concert for radio stations in America.

The ship had four diesel engines with 1,200 horsepower each. Diesels and helium—that is the safest combination for the air because the helium cannot explode. But we had no helium. We had Hitler in Germany,

and the Congress of the United States refused to give us any helium.

I crossed the ocean 161 times in airships. In the *Hindenburg* I made ten round trips to the States and eight to South America. Then there was the disaster.

We had bad weather. About two o'clock we were over New York, made a few circles, and then went on to Lakehurst. Then we saw a big thunderstorm over New Jersey and knew we couldn't land and thought it better to go back to the sea. We went along the coast to Atlantic City and back, and we waited for the storm to blow over to the ocean.

Then we were under the storm, going to Lakehurst, and at seven o'clock we received a telegram that we could land. We went into a landing. During the landing, as the ropes were down, the explosion occurred.

I was in the control car. The explosion was under the cells of gasbags three and four in the aft. I heard a big noise and then I saw the flames. The flames were going through the whole ship and then forward to the bow. We were about 150 feet above the ground. My first idea when the explosion came was that the ropes had broken, but then I saw the flames and saw what it was. The stern fell and the bow shot up, because the gas was burning aft. I could do nothing but turn off the engines. As the control car came down to earth—we had under the control car a buffer, an air cushion—it bounced, and the ship was therefore at about a height of two meters [6½ feet]. The others in the crew jumped out. When the ship came down another time, I jumped out. Then the framework and all things came down, and I was under the burning cells and framework. I was in the hospital in the United States about four months.

It is very difficult to say what happened. The joint American-German Commission said: It might have been sabotage; it might have been lightning. Nobody knows.

CHAPTER 8

A Heinkel He-111 bomber flies over London's Thames River on September 7, 1940, the opening day of the German blitz on Englan

At first light on September 1, 1939, the Luftwaffe struck a hail of blows against the airfields of Poland. In forty-eight hours, German He-111 bombers, Me-110 "destroyers," and Ju-87 Stukas decimated the Polish air force, most of it on the ground; in ten days, the Polish army had all but ceased organized resistance. Hitler's uneasy ally Soviet Russia sent its hordes across the eastern border, and at the end of a month all Poland lay prostrate.

Britain and France, honoring their treaty obligations to the Poles, had meanwhile declared war on Germany. In time-tried opening moves, the French army took up positions in and behind the Maginot Line. Britain dispatched to the Continent a small expeditionary force, with an air component of one fighter wing, one bomber-reconnaissance wing, and a token independent air striking force. For seven months on the western front nothing happened. Americans called it a "phony war." Hitler, in his "Directive Number 1 for the Conduct of the War," had stipulated that "the responsibility of opening hostilities should rest unequivocally with England and France."

The later months of this "phony war" were overshadowed by a Russo-Finnish conflict. This "winter war" began on November 30, when the Soviets decided to take by force the Finnish bases they had been refused. Expecting little opposition, the Russians at first used obsolescent warplanes, holding back their newer designs. But the Finns put up a stiff resistance, and the 900-plane force originally committed by the Russians had to be expanded to nearly 2,000 before the little nation was finally overwhelmed in February, 1940.

A British blockade, meanwhile, was threatening to cut Germany off from her Scandinavian supplies. In reaction, Hitler struck savagely on April 9, 1940, to seize both Denmark and Norway. The Danes declined to fight. Norway's bravery cost her much. The German attack force, composed of warships, seven army divisions, eight hundred combat aircraft, and nearly three hundred troop-carrier planes, moved with surprise and precision. By the second day, all of Norway's major ports—Oslo, Bergen, Trondheim, and Narvik—were occupied and all her airfields in the south were taken over with nearly as great speed. As the RAF was unable to operate effectively in daylight at the distances involved, the Luftwaffe had control of the air, and soon sealed the doom of the Norwegians.

The Finnish crisis, with Allied inability to bring military assistance to an harassed friend, had brought down the French government of Daladier. The Norwegian fiasco now had a similar effect in England, and on May 10 the old war dog, Winston Churchill, succeeded Neville Chamberlain as Prime Minister.

Perhaps no single day of the whole six-year war was so fateful as that May 10. Even as Churchill took up the burdens of office, Nazi tanks, motorized columns, screaming Stukas, and parachutists had begun a brutal invasion of Holland, Luxembourg, and Belgium.

Despite resistance by the northern French armies and the British Expeditionary Force, the Germans were able on the first day to attack not only Rotterdam and capture its airfield but to pierce the whole Dutch countryside in the direction of the Moerdijk bridges, the vital link in the waist between northern and southern Holland. When these were lost after four and a half days, the Netherlands, on May 15, capitulated. The *coup de grâce* was delivered in barbaric measure by the Luftwaffe in a mass bombing of Rotterdam. For four days debate divided Churchill's newly-formed War Cabinet, but with this murderous low-level daylight attack on the famous Dutch seaport, hesitation ended, and the RAF Bomber Command was ordered to operate against the Nazi homeland. That night, for the first time, Allied aircraft—ninety-nine in all—dropped their charges on oil and communications centers in the Ruhr. Symbolically at least, the strategic air offensive against Germany had begun.

Meanwhile, Franco-British land strategy, which called for a wait-and-see attitude while the Belgians attempted to hold on along the Meuse and the Albert Canal, was going badly. The enemy's first assault, which included air-borne troops, had already leaped ahead of the intended Belgian line. Knowing well that the Maginot fortifications extended only along the frontier between Germany and France and not into Belgium, the panzers executed the main feature of German strategy and split the Allied front in two by a massive thrust between Belgium and France.

After the Nazi breakthrough, the Battle of France unfolded swiftly. The exhausted Belgians surrendered on May 27. The Germans, having turned toward the coast, methodically closed around the northern Allied forces a tight semicircle centered on Dunkirk. From that deadly noose, under an air umbrella provided by home-based RAF fighters whose mission was only sporadically interrupted by the Luftwaffe, the Royal Navy, aided by every seaworthy hulk in Britain, eventually saved the lives of more than a third of a million British, French, and other Allied troops.

With its now legendary lightning speed, the German war machine sliced deeper into France. On June 7 it reached the Somme; on June 9 Rouen fell; on June 10 it crossed the Seine. The "jackal, Mussolini," as Churchill dubbed him, chose that day to declare war and attack France in the south. Everywhere on the crowded, sunny French roads, the unresisted Luftwaffe bombed and strafed fleeing refugees and soldiers quite without partiality.

The inevitable fall of France came on June 20. Next day, at Compiègne, scene of Germany's World War I surrender, Hitler, in satanic elation, personally exacted the armistice. Britain, clutching her own and others' escapees, stood at last alone.

All thoughts now turned to a German invasion of Britain that everyone supposed Hitler, as with his other plans of conquest, had long prepared. There were, in fact, neither plans nor preparations. Operation Sea Lion was still mostly talk. Almost as though the war had succeeded beyond his expectation, Hitler hung back, uncertain what the next best move might be. "I can see no reason why this war need go on," he told the Reichstag on July 19, hinting that England would find him ready to make terms. When Churchill brushed aside all suggestion of parley, Hitler's last remaining hope of avoiding a long war was to attack.

While the German generals and admirals were wrangling over how and where to get ashore, how to nullify the British navy, and how to keep reinforcements and supplies moving across the Channel, the battle for mastery of the air began.

The opposing air forces entered the contest realizing that they were "poised on the top of a huge wave of fate"—whichever way it fell, much beside the personal fortunes of the combatants would be decided. As of mid-July, Goering, on his side, disposed of three air forces: Luftflotte II in Belgium and the Low Countries with Albert Kesselring in command, Luftflotte III in northern France under Hugo Sperrle, and Luftflotte V in Denmark and Norway under Hans-Juergen Stumpff. The first two together possessed roughly 900 fighters (Me-109's and Me-110's), 875 bombers (He-111's, Ju-88's, and Do-17's), and 300 dive bombers (Ju-87's). Luftflotte V had only 157 aircraft, 34 of them fighters. On the British side, the RAF fighter force consisted of forty-six squadrons of Hurricanes and Spitfires and two of Defiants. The total number of British single-engine fighters was between six and seven hundred.

Since early June the Luftwaffe had been skirmishing in night raids over England, testing the nerve of the people and the mettle of RAF Fighter Command. Pressure against the defenders had so increased that by July 10 the British felt the main offensive to be imminent. The first phase of the battle actually started on July 2, with heavy pounding of the Channel ports and convoys and nightly bombing of towns and cities all over England, Scotland, and Wales. German tactics aimed at luring RAF fighters into combat prematurely, but Sir Keith Park, the great commander of No. 11 Group, responsible for London and the South of England, wisely held his strength for heavier onslaughts to come.

From August 8 the attacks intensified, and the main targets now became airfields and radar stations on the south and east coasts. On the 13th, which the Germans called Eagle Day, and which marked the real beginning of the main offensive, the Luftwaffe flew 1,485 sorties, lost forty-seven aircraft, but failed to inflict serious damage. RAF Fighter Command defended with 700 sorties, losing thirteen machines. On the 14th, a quiet day, the Germans lost nineteen planes, the British eight. The high tide of the battle thus far was reached on August 15, with the Germans making 1,786 sorties, the greatest number flown by either side at any time. During a day of widespread, incessant conflict, plotters in the RAF control center at Stanmore observed apprehensively that the attackers consistently outnumbered the defenders; but the Luftwaffe did not achieve a breakthrough. The British claimed 182 of the enemy shot down, while the Germans reported 134 kills for a loss of thirty-four. After the war it was learned that the actual totals were seventy-five German and thirty-four British aircraft lost.

To the Germans it seemed that the British would have required three times the number of fighters they actually possessed to put up the defense that everywhere greeted them. The first secret was radar, primitive as it was, and the supporting communications that permitted effective, flexible control of the fighters from the ground. The Luftwaffe had no radar and no radio control of its aircraft. Each German mission was a set piece, planned in detail beforehand; there could be no improvisation during the battle. The second British secret was tactics. Sir Hugh Dowding, the Fighter Commander, and Park, his lieutenant in the south, decided to meet the enemy as close to the coast as possible, thereby exploiting the short range and superior eight-gun firepower of the Spitfire. Despite the opposition and later bitter criticism of formidable opponents, Park also insisted on using flexible squadron tactics rather than wing tactics, in committing his forces to battle.

After a brief lull due to bad weather, the Luftwaffe, on August 24, returned to full-scale attack. It did so with apparent determination to smash the hard core of Fighter Command that had hitherto eluded it. Realizing that failure to concentrate geographically and numerically had proved costly as well as ineffectual, the Germans now attempted to breach the defense with hammer blows by close formations. Through the rest of August and the first days of September, Spitfire and Hurricane squadrons were confronted by masses of up to forty bombers escorted by more than one hundred fighters, as fighter airfields and the command posts of London's defenses were hit in more than two thirds of thirty-three attacks.

The German mass tactics now began to swamp the squadron tactics of Fighter Command, eating into replacements of pilots and machines. In two weeks the RAF lost 277 aircraft as against 378 lost by the Germans. Worse still, the British lost 231 pilots, killed and wounded—a quarter of the available force. Just as the attrition was becoming intolerable, Goering again switched his plan of attack. This effect had a deeply ironical cause.

On the night of August 24, owing to a navigational error, Nazi bombs fell on central London for the first time. Believing the attack deliberate, Churchill made a suggestion to Sir Charles Portal, the chief of Bomber Command. Hitler and Goering were astounded when, the following night, RAF bombers made a reprisal raid on Berlin. Eighty-one British planes did what Goering had boasted could never be done. After Berlin

was attacked a second time on August 26, Hitler vowed to wipe Britain's cities off the map.

Goering conferred with Kesselring and Sperrle at The Hague on September 3. As usual, opinions differed. Believing the RAF still had plenty of fighters, Sperrle favored continuing current tactics. Kesselring thought the RAF was finished. Goering stated that the British fighters were withdrawing beyond London, out of range of the German fighters, and that only if London, the heart of the Empire, were in mortal danger would England risk her last fighter reserves. Two against one: the switch to London was ordered.

The Reichsmarschall took command in person, his headquarters an armored train hidden in a tunnel at Cap Gris-Nez. Hitler had been told that the next phase of the battle would decide the air issue and make invasion possible or, as Goering thought, unnecessary. In Britain, the morning of September 7 began with a seemingly routine attack on airfields, but, at 4 P.M., radar plotters noticed several large enemy formations over Calais. Instead of splitting up as they usually did when the coast was reached, the German aircraft appeared to be stacking up in layers, much above their customary altitude. They hit London in two waves—three hundred bombers with six hundred fighter escorts employing new flexible tactics. The attacks went on throughout the night, with the populous East End and London Docks the principal targets. The fires burned into the dawn. Goering, elated, telephoned his wife: "London is in flames." The blitz was on.

Many Londoners thought the invasion had started. Church bells were rung, road blocks thrown into place, the Home Guards alerted. Actually what had begun was an ordeal of death and destruction which for length and intensity no city on earth had yet suffered. There were few more mass daylight raids, though for eighty-five nights London was pummeled and pounded. But the RAF and the ack-ack took a heavy toll of the intruders, and the "hearts of oak" of the people of London never faltered in courage nor wavered in defiance.

The blitz on London continued until spring, but long before that it was clear that the Luftwaffe had failed miserably. Before September ended, Hitler had postponed Operation Sea Lion to October, and when October came he put it off until the next year. In reality it was put off forever. With the threat of invasion past, the British took stock of what had happened to them and what they must do in the future. By a very narrow margin, a hair's breadth, they had escaped. The Germans had failed to achieve the first prerequisite to success against England—control of the air—for on control of the air the second prerequisite, control of the narrow seas, depended. Though it went on to other victories in other theaters, the German air force never really recovered from the experience of the Battle of Britain. For a while, Hitler still paid rhetorical tribute to his Eagles, but he never quite trusted Goering again: the Luftwaffe was not invincible and the Reich was not invulnerable to enemy air action.

For a would-be world conqueror, Hitler's strategy was curious. He was a land animal and scorned both sea and air power because he could not understand them. He did not see that air power was an all-embracing, strategic power, truly analogous to the sea blockade of the days before the airplane, but more potent because more direct. So, despite its seemingly independent position within the German armed forces, he subordinated the Luftwaffe to his land-minded strategy, which depended for success upon interior lines of communication, and upon commitment to but a single main tactical front.

The top leadership of the Luftwaffe—Goering, Milch, Udet, Kesselring, Jeschonnek, Sperrle, Stumpff, Schmitt, and the others—did little to educate the Fuehrer in air doctrine because they were nearly as ignorant of the true nature of air power as he was. At no stage in the build-up of the Luftwaffe was there co-ordination of strategy and technology. The basic weakness of the Luftwaffe was lack of comprehensive thinking and planning, and of effective command and control machinery for implementing decisions.

The German weakness in air technology was not merely a question of the selection and production of types of aircraft, of armor and armament, of radar and other navigational aids. From the beginning to the end of the war, the Germans had on the drawing boards and in various stages of test and production some of the world's finest airplanes, including both a rocket-propelled fighter (the chunky Me-163 with a speed of 590 miles per hour but a rapid consumption rate of fuel that limited its time in the air) and the first jet-propelled plane, the He-178. Nor was it a question of prejudice for or against bombers. Hitler and Goering both wanted bombers. But whatever the types, Hitler was obsessed with what he called "offensive war"—by which he meant unceasing attack—and by incessant attacking, without due regard to when, where, and how, he threw away the Luftwaffe and bled Germany to death.

The Battle of Britain may have been lost by Germany before it began. First, if it had come two months sooner, the RAF would have been far less well prepared. Second, if after Dunkirk, Hitler had turned at once and invaded England instead of pursuing the French army, Britain as well as France might have fallen, for at one moment the British had only one equipped division available for the island's defense.

Fatal flaws in the Luftwaffe's performance were detailed in a series of reports to Washington by an American observer, Colonel Carl Spaatz. Spaatz noted that German night bombers failed to close British ports on the Channel and on the east and west coasts, and thereby force shipping into the Clyde where U-boats could easily have sent it to the bottom. Many lucrative targets far from the main concentration of RAF fighter airfields could have been bombed with low losses, even if with some strain on the bombers' range. Escorting day fighters were erroneously tied to the bombers for close support instead of being allowed to pursue RAF fighters in running combats. Consequently, bombers and fighters flying together in close packs became ready marks for the Spitfires and Hurricanes. Bombers employed singly or in threes were wasted in weak attacks on scattered, militarily unprofitable targets all over the country. The practice of having one experienced pilot lead a bomber formation otherwise manned by inexperienced crews was self-defeating, because the RAF fighters soon learned that by shooting down the leader in head-on attack they could often disperse a whole formation.

These lessons were lost least of all on the RAF, which, in the high tradition of its first chief, Lord Trenchard, was devoted to the development of true offensive air power. Vital though it was to the whole war, the Battle of Britain was defensive and, as such, an interruption of the RAF's determined plan for a strategic bombing offensive. From the moment Churchill had taken over from Chamberlain, bombing had been settled policy. The limiting factor was the unhappily small number, restricted range, and low payload capacity of Bomber Command's aircraft. It was also evident that, for the present, the Germans could prevent large-scale attack by unescorted bombers, and that at night, with existing navigation aids, darkness alone was enough to preclude the identification of precision targets.

There was some consolation, however. The Battle of Britain had made clear that Germany was not going to win the war in a matter of weeks. There would be time to improve the planes and accessory equipment and to apply a plan of systematic bombing.

The sweep of war, meanwhile, had been widening. Always anxious to extend his empire on the cheap, Mussolini had invaded Egypt and Kenya on September 13, which forced Britain hastily to reshuffle her thinly-spread land forces in India, Australia, and New Zealand to meet the threat to the vital link in her lifeline through the Mediterranean and Suez. On land, the Italians were checked by Wavell at Sidi Barrâni, while the British navy, on November 11, won a resounding victory at Taranto and restored to itself supremacy in the Mediterranean Sea. Three of the six capital ships of the Italian fleet were put out of action by aircraft from H. M. S. *Illustrious*. On December 11 Wavell moved against the Italian army and in sixty-two days cleared Egypt and Cyrenaica. His little, poorly-equipped army, spearheaded by the Desert Air Force, crushed Mussolini's legions and captured 130,000 prisoners.

The new year, 1941, began well; but before it was very old, Germany, with the acquiescence of Bulgaria and Rumania, put the torch of war to Yugoslavia and Greece. Yugoslavia was quickly subdued. The Greeks, aided by a small British expeditionary force, resisted for a fierce moment but, virtually without air strength, were soon quelled. The British retired to Crete, the strategic key to the eastern Mediterranean, but their attempt to hold the island and its three airfields was hopeless without fighter defense. Under the bludgeonings of the Luftwaffe, followed by paratroop assaults and landings of troop-carrying gliders and aircraft, the doom of the Cretan garrisons was sealed.

Wavell in Libya meanwhile found himself between the mass of the Italian army in his rear in East Africa and a possible hop by the Germans across the Mediterranean into North Africa. Choosing to meet the nearer danger first, he attacked Eritrea from Khartoum and Italian Somaliland from Nairobi. By April 6 the capitals of both countries were in British hands. Though the mopping up took some hard fighting and lasted till the end of November, Mussolini's dream of empire in Africa was demolished.

While Wavell was thus occupied, the Germans had planted a large contingent of the Luftwaffe on Sicily, and of tanks in Libya. Faced with the latter, the British army had no choice but to fall back on Egypt, leaving a garrison on the coast at Tobruk. Under the constant blows of the Luftwaffe, the navy was hard put to keep open the Narrows between Sicily and Malta on which the life of Malta depended. The Mediterranean picture was darkening.

The war at sea took a dramatic turn when, at the end of May, the Germans sent out the fast new battleship *Bismarck* to prey on shipping in the Atlantic. A large force of British capital ships set forth in pursuit. In the first engagement the *Hood* was hit by the *Bismarck* and blew up, but the *Bismarck* was also hit. Early next morning, May 25, the *Bismarck* was lost to her pursuers. Some thirty-one hours later, she was found again by an RAF Catalina flying boat. On the evening of May 26, Swordfish planes from the carrier *Ark Royal* landed two, possibly three, hits on the *Bismarck,* whereupon her steering went out of control. Destroyers continued to lob torpedoes at the wounded

ship throughout the night. **On the morning of May 27,** British capital ships moved in for the kill.

The fate of the *Bismarck,* pride of the German navy, re-emphasized that land war offered Germany her only hope of victory. The successes in Greece and Crete, on the trail of her fading Axis partner, Italy, had proved extremely costly, with little glory and no booty. The path to India through the Middle East was still blocked by Britain and the little countries friendly to her, and seas and an ocean lay between. But there was an alternative theater and a more glittering prize, and Hitler decided to make a supreme effort to obtain it.

At dawn on June 22, 1941, the Wehrmacht, with the assistance of Finns, Hungarians, Rumanians, and later, Italians and Spaniards, smashed with 170 divisions across the 1,000-mile Russian frontier. As usual, the operation was spearheaded by the Luftwaffe with 2,770 planes.

Nazi successes came rapidly. Massed near the border on unprotected airfields, Russian planes were surprised and destroyed on the ground in hundreds during the opening attacks. In the air, battle-hardened German pilots swept the skies. Fantastic victory scores were reported. Even the slow Stukas once more came into their own. By the end of the war, Hans Rudel, the renowned dive-bomber pilot, was credited with destroying more than five hundred Russian tanks, enough to equip a whole tank corps.

While the good summer weather lasted, the dazzling successes of the Luftwaffe continued. Russian fighters could not match the Messerschmitts, and their bomber forces were virtually wiped out. Their most effective air weapon was the Il-2, a new, heavily-armored ground-attack plane which they used with great courage and determination.

Although by the end of 1941, more than 8,000 Soviet planes had been destroyed in the air and on the ground, the Nazis badly miscalculated the technical capacity and productive power of the Russian aircraft industry. While many of the western factories were overrun, new plants at Irkutsk and Semenovka, at Kazan and Novosibirsk, were beyond the reach of German two-engine bombers. Now Germany's lack of a long-range strategic air force began to hurt, for at the end of 1941 the battered Russian air force was beginning to recover its strength.

Hitler was sarcastically bitter in denouncing the Luftwaffe's technical capabilities and production. Goering, stung by his taunts, passed the buck to Ernst Udet, his old friend and a World War I ace, who was unfortunately miscast in the role of inspector-general and chief of the technical department of the Luftwaffe. When the early Russian winter showed up the poor preparation of German aircraft for such conditions, Goering heaped blame on Udet. Patriotic, popular, and conscientious, Udet cracked under the strain. Late in November, 1941, he put a pistol to his head and killed himself. Though Goering reported the suicide as a test-flight accident, many knew where the real fault lay and saw in Udet's death the nemesis that awaited the Luftwaffe and all Germany.

All the assumptions on which German air power was built were proving wrong. The war was no longer limited to Europe only. The Fuehrer was no longer satisfied when the Luftwaffe beat up the enemy air force at the start of each campaign. The German air force of just before the war had not, as it then so confidently believed, attained all the capabilities it would ever need, and the cancellation order of August, 1940 —which had stopped research and test on all aircraft that could not be put into production within one year —was now seen to have been a hideous mistake.

Aside from doctrine, the main reason for not developing long-range strategic bombers had been that such a program would have overtaxed the country's resources when reserves of oil and bombs and combat crews were already very short. Now the Russian war, though it pointed up the need for such aircraft, actually deferred, rather than spurred, their development. The thinking in the Luftwaffe at this point was that a strategic bomber fleet could only be created if the Russian campaign ended quickly and the terrible drain on the economy that it caused was halted. Still further changes in German air concepts were soon to be brought about by the growing threat posed by the bombing offensive from the British Isles against the Reich itself.

In line with Churchill's conviction in the fall of 1940 that "only the Air Force could win the war," the RAF, under its new chief, Sir Charles Portal, had set resolutely to work. Between October, 1940, and March, 1941, the main concern, apart from the Battle of the Atlantic, had been with precision bombing against oil and rail targets in the Ruhr and elsewhere.

The retired but still redoubtable Lord Trenchard and others protested that Britain was too nice in her bombing. Trenchard called for a massive bomber build-up and an offensive against every corner of the Nazi homeland. While his fiery views were not wholly endorsed by the RAF leadership, two basic policies were emerging. The principal bombing effort would be made at night, and the principal objective, though the targets themselves would be military, would be German morale.

Hardly had the night-bombing offensive gotten under way when a crisis developed that called the whole program into serious question. In June the

Prime Minister took alarm when night photographs disclosed that only one in four aircraft reporting attack on a German target actually got within five miles of it and, in heavily-defended areas like the Ruhr, only one in ten. Then, on November 7, 1941, four hundred bombers took off to strike at Berlin, the Ruhr, and other targets; thirty-seven did not come back. Annoyed and dismayed, Churchill "advised" that Bomber Command be "conserved" in order to "regather their strength for the spring."

The war had now been in progress for two grim years. Though the people of the United States were not yet directly and formally engaged, they had already given many hostages to fortune.

On September 28, 1938, on the eve of Munich, President Roosevelt had directed that, in view of the deteriorating international situation, the national defense required an actual rate of production of 10,000 long-range airplanes a year, backed up by a production potential of 20,000 a year—a decision that was called the "Magna Charta" of American air power.

Munich-time also brought to the top command of the U. S. Army air arm one of the country's pioneer military aviators—a newswriter somewhat ludicrously called him a "white-haired old gentleman"—Henry H. ("Hap") Arnold, just turned fifty-two and now a brigadier general. Vigorous, bold, and far-seeing, he was one of America's most dynamic war leaders and the man chiefly responsible for organizing and directing the greatest aggregation of air power the world had ever seen—an air force of nearly 2,500,000 men and over 75,000 aircraft.

As Arnold took over, the Air Corps was emerging from a doctrinal dispute that had been going on since 1917. The dominant view now was that bombing was the basis of air power, that daylight bombing was fundamental to precision as opposed to area attack, that bombers—because of the limited range of existing fighters—would have to fly without escort, and that bombers could achieve enough defensive firepower to enable them to operate without prohibitive losses. Fighter development had lagged behind bomber development, due to the soon-discredited theory of "bomber invincibility," overemphasis of the interception function as opposed to escort, and such technical misconceptions as the multiseat fighter. Whatever the cause, when war broke out no serious effort had been made in the United States to convert single-seat interceptors into escort fighters by extending their range.

Arnold was anxious to apply or adapt to the American air situation the lessons to be learned from either friend or foe. In the spring of 1939 Charles A. Lindbergh, who had been living in England and France, returned to America. The day after he landed he and Arnold had an important conference at West Point where, after lunch, they sat unnoticed in the bleachers while a baseball game was in progress. Arnold later wrote: "Lindbergh gave me the most accurate picture of the Luftwaffe, its equipment, leaders, apparent plans, training methods, and present defects that I had so far received." What Lindbergh told him galvanized Arnold into redoubled activity. With President Roosevelt's knowledge and approval, he asked the flier to get into uniform and serve on a board to revise the military characteristics of all aircraft under consideration in the Air Corps expansion program. In assuring that America's air capabilities surpassed anything the Germans had or were planning on, the findings of this "Lindbergh board" were of inestimable value. Though Lindbergh later got into dispute with Roosevelt by opposing what he considered a dangerous drift toward intervention in the European war when the United States was still unprepared and had not been attacked, Arnold's opinion of him was not changed by the uproar. When war came, Lindbergh, no longer in uniform, continued to act as technical adviser to the Air Force, testing airplanes in combat in the Pacific and even shooting down a couple of Zeros.

The French debacle of May-June, 1940, led the President to issue his famous call for 50,000 airplanes. By this he meant that annual production should go to 50,000 and that the combined air strength of the Army and Navy should total 50,000 airplanes— 37,000 for the Air Corps, 13,000 for Naval aviation.

Arnold knew that, however high the goals, a large proportion of U. S.-produced aircraft would go to friendly countries already fighting. Still, he was determined to keep a balance between the procurement of airplanes and the training of combat and maintenance crews. By this means, whatever its size, the Air Corps would have the trainers, bases, buildings, transport, and gasoline that were as necessary for building air power as were combat planes.

At the same time, Naval aviation was being rapidly expanded. In 1938 aircraft carrier tonnage limit had been 40,000 tons; in June, 1941, this was increased by 79,000 tons, and in July by another 200,000 tons. The ceiling on useful airplanes was simultaneously raised to 15,000. Attempts were even made to equip destroyers with catapults and planes, but the experiment was later abandoned.

Throughout 1940 and 1941 the defense picture in the United States was one of growing preparedness. Before one expansion program could be completed, a larger program would be called for. All these demands, foreign and domestic, rapidly converted the haphazard peacetime economy into a vast industrial machine—an "arsenal of democracy." The Battle of Britain brought the destroyer-bases deal. The blitz on London produced the Lend-Lease program, inaugurated in March, 1941. The disaster in Crete, the campaign in the North African desert, and the U-boat war led to the President's declaration of an "unlimited national emergency."

The military services had by now laid their plans for action in any eventuality. In July, 1941, President Roosevelt asked for an estimate of the forces "required to defeat our potential enemies." The Air War Plans Division responded with a document known as AWPD/1, which turned out to be an accurate forecast of the peak air strength of the Air Force in World War II. The air mission, it stated, would be to destroy Germany's industrial war-making capacity, to restrict Axis air operations, and to prepare and support a final invasion of Germany. An accompanying map showed that of forty-two groups of heavy and medium bombers based on the British Isles, twelve bomb groups were to be B-29's, with another twelve B-29 groups based in the Middle East. Actually, the very heavy bombers did not become available soon enough and were never used against Germany.

Although the German attack on Russia drew the United States closer to the anti-Axis countries, it also stimulated the appetite of Japan for conquest. In July, 1941, with the connivance of Vichy France, the Japanese took over Indochina. The United States, Britain, and Holland retaliated with economic sanctions against Japan. Throughout the fall diplomatic talks were kept up between Washington and Tokyo, but the Japanese fleet, cut off from its oil sources, was burning up reserves. Cordell Hull demanded that Japan disgorge not only Indochina but also her gains on the Chinese mainland. This was asking the tiger to give up its kill. To the new, militaristic premier, Hideki Tojo, it seemed that his country must accept unbearable demands or resort to force to break the strangling blockade. On December 1 an imperial conference decided that Japanese honor demanded war.

Early on December 7 a powerful Japanese carrier force that had secretly left Japan on November 28 under Vice-Admiral Chuichi Nagumo reached a point some two hundred miles north of the Hawaiian Islands. At dawn a first wave of 183 planes roared off for Pearl Harbor, their mission to neutralize American air defenses. The American commanders in the Pacific, convinced that aggression, if it came, would start in the Far East, had taken no defensive measures, though they had been warned to expect "an aggressive movement in any direction." The Japanese surprise was complete. At 7:55 A.M., the raiders struck, strafing and dive-bombing American planes on the ground and leaving the air almost free for following waves of bombers and torpedo planes.

Protecting the first wave of bombers from the carriers *Akagi* and *Kaga* were forty-three Zeros, the best carrier-borne fighters in the world. They shot down four of twenty-five Air Corps planes that got into the air. Then 170 planes from Nagumo's other carriers roared in. Bombing and torpedoing almost without interference, they either sank or damaged all eight of the American battleships in the harbor. Twelve B-17's flying in from California found themselves in the middle of the battle with guns stowed away and no ammunition. By 9 A.M., the raiders were gone. At a cost of twenty-nine planes and fifty-five men, they had killed more than 2,000 Americans and virtually destroyed American power in the Pacific.

In the Philippines, the story was much the same. Despite advance warning, both Clark and Iba Fields were devastated, and rows of American planes were shot up on the ground. By nightfall on December 9, only twelve out of thirty-five operational bombers and thirty fighters were left. American offensive air power on Luzon had ceased to exist.

On the 10th, in the Gulf of Siam, where they were steaming without fighter escort, the British battleship *Prince of Wales* and the battle cruiser *Repulse* were sent to the bottom by Japanese land-based torpedo bombers. Of this loss Churchill wrote: "In all the war I never received a more direct shock."

The ancient concept of the capital ship as mistress of the seas was shattered forever. In a classic test of air power against conventional sea power, the airplane had won. Billy Mitchell's old contention, that no surface ship, however powerful, could survive determined air attack unless protected by friendly aircraft, had been spectacularly vindicated.

Dominant in the air, Japan now had naval supremacy in the Pacific and in East Asian waters, and she used it to the hilt. With no effective air defense, the bastions of the Far East fell one after another. Hong Kong, Singapore, Malaya, were all lost. The Dutch East Indies, Borneo, the Andamans, and Burma—all were conquered. The Burma Road was cut and China left in isolation.

Their humiliation at Pearl Harbor left the American people stunned and infuriated. They got their first taste of revenge on April 18, 1942, when James Doolittle, now a Lieutenant Colonel, led a flight of sixteen B-25's off the aircraft carrier *Hornet* and, in the first attack on the Japanese homeland, bombed Tokyo.

Early in May a far-ranging B-17 spotted a Japanese convoy moving south to occupy Port Moresby, the Allied base in New Guinea. The ensuing Battle of the Coral Sea was the first naval engagement in history fought without the opposing ships making contact. In two days of confused but vicious fighting, American Naval planes sank the light carrier *Shoho* and damaged the *Shokaku*. The Japanese sank the carrier *Lexington* and damaged the *Yorktown*. Strategically, the Coral Sea was an important American victory, since the Japanese invasion fleet was turned back, and the threat to Port Moresby was averted.

Still Japan pushed on. The next move was a two-pronged offensive designed to capture Midway and establish bases in the Aleutians. Admiral Isoroku Yamamoto assembled a tremendous striking force of battleships, carriers, cruisers, destroyers, submarines, and supporting vessels — more than 150 ships and 1,000 carrier-based planes. The purpose was to push Japan's defense perimeter farther from the home islands and to force the remnants of the U. S. fleet to fight a final, decisive battle.

Yamamoto's first error was in dividing his air strength by consigning two of his carriers to the Aleutian task force. His second was in failing to detect soon enough the two American carrier task forces, under Rear Admirals Raymond A. Spruance and Frank J. Fletcher, that were converging on threatened Midway from Pearl Harbor. After severe losses of American Brewster Buffaloes and Douglas TBD Devastators which were no match for Zeros, Dauntless dive bombers in less than five minutes smashed into flaming wrecks three Japanese carriers—the *Akagi, Kaga,* and *Soryu.* The fourth enemy carrier in action, the *Hiryu,* hit the *Yorktown.* Later, the *Hiryu* was set afire by planes and sunk by an American submarine. The crippled *Yorktown* was also finally lost to a submarine's torpedo.

Robbed of his air power, Yamamoto was obliged to retire without achieving any of his objectives. His only gain was the occupation of Attu and Kiska, two chilly islands in the Aleutian chain. Though far from finished as a fighting power, Japan never recovered from the loss of the cream of her combat fliers and so many irreplaceable technicians and maintenance crews. When Yamamoto signaled his withdrawal message, "Occupation of Midway is canceled," he signaled in effect that, though the war in the Pacific was far from over, the decision was no longer in doubt.

Blitzkrieg

Born of the spirit of the German airmen of the First World War, inspired by faith in our Fuehrer ... thus stands the German Air Force today, ready to carry out every command of the Fuehrer with lightning speed and undreamed-of might."

Thus trumpeted Hermann Goering on September 1, 1939, as Germany invaded Poland. With overwhelming technical and numerical superiority, German planes wiped out 90 per cent of Poland's air force. And on September 25, the first large-scale bombing of a major city began as Ju-87 Stukas (left), flying at 210 miles per hour, screeched down on Warsaw and bombed the Polish capital into submission in two days. It was a fast and heady first victory for Hitler's Luftwaffe—and a chilling preview of a terrifying new power.

A German pilot (above) flies over the front lines in Poland while his observer mans the machine gun. The Germans, with a combat force of over 1,500 planes, rapidly eliminated air opposition and used their unchallenged fighters for ground-strafing.

The grim German painting below depicts Stuka dive bombers over the Vistula River in Poland in September, 1939. The original, painted by Otto Bloss in February, 1940, was among Nazi combat art captured by the Allies at the end of the war.

Times of Trial

In Denmark, Norway, Luxembourg, Holland, Belgium, and France, the story was the same: unprepared men, too late and with too little, were overwhelmed. As Hitler's armies rolled forward, fighters and bombers of the Luftwaffe paced the Nazi conquests.

For one triumphant moment only, in May, 1940, the indomitability of man's spirit frustrated the juggernaut. Hemmed in at Dunkirk, shattered remnants of British and French units waited to be captured. For the moment, Hitler sent his armor elsewhere—and the miracle occurred. Every type of British ship raced across the Channel protected by every British combat plane available. The RAF "capped" the beaches, held off the Luftwaffe, and allowed more than 350,000 men to be saved from what had seemed certain surrender.

ABOVE: *A defiant British soldier, trapped on the beach at Dunkirk, fires at a German plane. Many of the bombs dropped on the troops by Luftwaffe aircraft that got past the RAF were smothered in the sand and caused relatively few casualties.*

298

ABOVE: *Allied troops huddle on the sand at Dunkirk under strafing and bombing attacks by German planes. Thirty-two RAF squadrons, comprising every kind of British fighting aircraft from Spitfires just off the assembly lines to antiquated Hawker Hector biplanes, fought desperately to maintain control of the air over the beaches. Their efforts were successful long enough to save most of the 1,200 ships and small boats that received the lines of waiting men and transported them across the English Channel.*

LEFT: *While the evacuation was in progress, British planes helped hold off Germans who were pressing against the perimeter. The photograph looks back from a British Battle bomber that has just attacked a column of German troops on a French road near Dunkirk. Bombs can be seen bursting alongside the horse-drawn convoy, while soldiers flee across the field at right. German air attempts to drive off the RAF cost the Luftwaffe more than seven hundred aviators during the Dunkirk evacuation; but the Nazi backlog of planes and fliers was far greater than Britain's.*

299

Battle of Britain

In the summer of 1940 the power of the Luftwaffe was turned loose on Great Britain. Certain that they could wipe out the RAF, the Germans bombed British airfields and installations and battled the outnumbered RAF pilots in the air. As the British people watched with pride and courage, English fliers in Spitfires and Hurricanes fought above the home island, giving the invaders more than they received. "Never . . . was so much owed by so many to so few," said Winston Churchill.

Still, British losses were great, and by September the situation was ominous. Then Hitler changed tactics. Daylight raids dwindled, and the nighttime bombing of cities began. It was now the turn of British civilians, and they rose to their "finest hour." Night after night the wail of sirens sent defiant populations into subways and shelters, while firemen and volunteers steadfastly battled seas of fire set by Goering's planes. Overhead, the RAF continued to fight ferociously, downing German bombers and their fighter escorts.

Destruction was great; large parts of many cities were reduced to rubble. In London alone, more than 20,000 persons were killed and 25,000 seriously injured. But when failure led Hitler to end the blitz in May, 1941, the English people knew they had beaten the Luftwaffe.

LEFT: *A smiling and confident Hermann Goering interrogates a pilot who has just returned from a mission over England. Admiring airmen look on, while one of them snaps a photograph of the Reichsmarschall.*

OVERLEAF: *The dome of St. Paul's Cathedral rising above the flames and smoke of burning London during the night of December 29, 1940, seemed to symbolize the courage and determination of the British.*

UPI

ABOVE: *A German Dornier 215 bomber, on its way to England, flies past the island of Guernsey in the English Channel on September 13, 1940. The Do-215, which carried a crew of four and a bomb load of 2,200 pounds, had a range of nine hundred miles.*

BELOW: *RAF pilots race toward their Spitfires. The shortage of pilots was acute, and the men had to fly several times each day. At the beginning of September, 1940, the average squadron had only sixteen pilots instead of the usual twenty-six.*

PICTURE PRESS AGENCY, LTD.

The Nazi Tide

In Africa and the Balkans, in the Atlantic and the Mediterranean, Axis aggressions steadily broadened the arena of war.

In April, 1941, to secure his southern flank before attacking Russia, Hitler hurled his armies, supported by almost 1,000 planes of Luftflotte 4, against Yugoslavia and Greece. Nine RAF squadrons, supporting the Greek forces, fought until they had only twenty-four airplanes left. These had to be evacuated to Crete when the Greeks were overwhelmed.

With Greece in their hands, the Germans decided to capture Crete with a massive air-borne assault. The assignment was given to the Eleventh Air Corps, whose parachute and glider-borne troops were an elite force. With almost complete air superiority, the Germans struck on May 20. More than five hundred Ju-52's and one hundred gliders ferried troops to the island where—according to the Daedalus legend—man first flew with wings. The defenders, mostly New Zealanders, resisted furiously. German casualties were heavy—more than 4,500 men killed or missing and nearly two hundred Ju-52's damaged or destroyed. But in the end the Royal Navy was forced to evacuate the remnants of the garrison, suffering heavily from dive bombers as it did so.

It was a brilliant air victory for the Nazis, but an expensive one, for the island was of little use to them.

LEFT: *A German airplane, on fire, plummets to earth during the air-borne invasion of Crete. Bombing and strafing of British defenses prepared the way for the paratroops and glider and transport landings.*

RIGHT: *A war painting by Charles Cundall, capturing an episode of the conflict in the Atlantic, shows a British Hudson bomber and a flying boat, circling over a trapped German U-boat on September 8, 1941.*

The Arsenal of Democracy

Stunned by the fall of France and the seemingly invincible might of the German Luftwaffe, the American people looked suddenly to the state of their own air power. Army and Navy aviation, for so long the stepchildren of the armed forces, were given what amounted almost to blank checks and directed to expand as fast as possible.

The needs seemed overwhelming. American aviation had to be built up, but overseas democracies, fighting with their backs to the wall, were desperate for American planes and equipment. Under Lend-Lease, commitments were made to Britain that had high priority. Existing American plants began operating round the

clock, and new factories were built across the nation. Manufacturers of nonmilitary products retooled to aviation needs, and the output of planes soared from 6,000 in 1940 to 19,000 in 1941.

Both the Army and Navy, meanwhile, rushed the completion of new training facilities. The draft brought in recruits, some of whom were soon on their way to new bases in Alaska, Iceland, and the Caribbean. The mere spending of funds could not fully compensate for oversights of the past, but by mid-1941 the United States was well embarked on an air program designed to meet the ominously-mounting crisis.

At left, Douglas A-20 bombers fly over a portable landing mat at Marston, North Carolina, during warlike maneuvers held in November, 1941. The "Battle of the Carolinas," and a similar exercise in Louisiana two months earlier, gave Army, Navy, and Marine pilots an opportunity to test new equipment. Almost 850 planes participated in North Carolina, including Lockheed P-38, Bell P-39, and Republic P-43 fighters. The Douglas A-24 dive bomber was tested, and precision bombing was conducted by B-17's, as 500,000 men first gained experience in air-ground techniques.

Thousands of new pilots, like those marching toward their training planes at Randolph Field, Texas (below), were graduated between July, 1939, and December, 1941. Most Air Corps cadets received their primary training at civilian schools, and then went on to basic and advanced training at Randolph or at nearby Brooks and Kelly Fields. In July, 1940, new schools were opened at Maxwell Field in Alabama and at Moffett Field in California. In addition, training programs at existing fields were greatly accelerated as the annual quota for new pilots rose to 33,000 in 1941.

Attack in the East

"Russians," wrote Werner Baumbach, the Luftwaffe's General of the Bombers, "were simply regarded as subhuman." When the German military machine struck suddenly at Russia in June, 1941, Hitler's ground and air forces treated the Russian people in that light, blitzing soldiers and civilians alike and alienating whatever anti-Communist elements might have existed within the country. The devastation wrought by the Germans during their first few months of hard-smashing advance is symbolized in this painting by German artist Wilfried Nagel of an air attack on a Russian horse-drawn convoy, retreating toward Moscow.

308

The Rising Sun

Since 1931, when they had first intervened in China, the Japanese had been marked as aggressors. But the rest of the world had done little to halt them, and by 1941 their shadow extended over much of southeast Asia. Though there were many who still believed that an appeal to reason would pull them up short, it was far too late. Military leaders were firmly in power, and a well-oiled armed machine was on the march.

Among the keys to their power, underrated by western nations, were strong air arms of the army and navy that included many advanced types of planes, including the superb Mitsubishi carrier-based Zero fighter. The Zero had weaknesses—principally lack of armor—but in the days after Pearl Harbor, its firepower, range, and maneuverability made it more than a match for every fighter that the surprised and hard-pressed American Air Corps and Navy could bring into the struggle against it.

The Japanese pilots above were members of the Cochin China Air Force, establishe[d] in March, 1940, by the Japanese-controlled National Government of China. Two yea[rs] earlier, the Japanese had set up another puppet air force in conquered Manchuri[a]

The Curtiss P-40B's on the muddy Burmese field at right were flown by the "Flyin[g] Tigers," an American volunteer unit that fought the Japanese from December, 194[1] until July, 1942, when it became the 23rd Pursuit Group of the U. S. Army Air Force[.]

Japanese instructors and trainees (below) climb into two-seater versions of th[e] Zero fighter. Zeros with Nakajima Sakae engines first saw action in China [in] 1940, when they escorted bombers on raids against Chungking and other inland citie[s.]

The leader of the "Flying Tigers" was Brigadier General Claire Chennault (below). In eight months his group of some 250 men shot down 286 Japanese planes.

Day of Infamy

At dawn on December 7, as the crews of a secret task force cheered them off (left), airplanes of Japan rose from carrier decks and roared toward Pearl Harbor, about two hundred miles away. The first waves knocked out Ford Island (right) and other ground installations. As flames rose from the wreckage of hangars and planes that never got into the air, Japanese bombers attacked, at will, undefended ships (below).

Japanese Victories

The days following Pearl Harbor produced shock after shock for the Allies. With little air opposition, Japanese planes paved the way for conquests in southeast Asia and the Pacific. Americans cheered a gallant defense of tiny Wake Island, during which a handful of Marine Wildcats helped fight off the Japanese invasion fleet. Ten days later, a larger force with two carriers appeared and finally overwhelmed the island.

Elsewhere, Japanese planes and ships swept the Allies from one defensive position after another. American sea defenses were crippled at Pearl Harbor, and British sea power in the East all but disappeared as Japanese planes, in short order, sank the *Prince of Wales, Repulse, Cornwall, Dorsetshire, Hermes,* and *Vampire.* Only at the Coral Sea, in May, were the Japanese temporarily halted.

314

LEFT: *A war painting by Japanese artist
Kenichi Nakamura shows torpedo bombers of the Japanese 22nd Air Flotilla sinking the British battleship* Prince of Wales
and the battle cruiser Repulse *in the Gulf
of Siam on December 10, 1941. The Japanese lost three planes to antiaircraft fire.*

RIGHT: *Tokushiro Kobayakawa, another
Japanese artist, painted the sinking of the
British cruisers* Cornwall *and* Dorsetshire
*on April 9, 1942. Eighty Val dive bombers
from a task force under Vice-Admiral
Nagumo, victor of Pearl Harbor, caught
the ships three hundred miles off Ceylon.*

BELOW: *Smashed by bombs and torpedoes
during the Battle of the Coral Sea, May
8, the* Lexington *begins to sink as her
crew goes over the side. American Naval
fliers from the* Lexington *and* Yorktown
*sank one Japanese carrier, damaged an-
other one, and turned back a New Guinea
invasion force during the pivotal action.*

USAF

As Naval crew members watch anxiously, one of the big B-25 bombers starts its take-off r
down the pitching deck of the Hornet. In the foul weather, the take-offs were precario
Though all of the airplanes managed to get away safely, several almost fell into the se

The Doolittle Raiders

Not until the aircraft carrier *Hornet* had taken them far out to sea did the fliers who had volunteered for Lieutenant Colonel James Doolittle's "dangerous and highly important mission" learn where they were going. On April 18 the *Hornet* would be five hundred miles from Japan, and on that day they would take off from the carrier in their sixteen B-25's and bomb Tokyo.

Unforeseen problems beset the daring raid. Early on the 18th, Japanese vessels spotted the *Hornet* and its companion carrier, the *Enterprise*. Doolittle and Vice-Admiral William F. Halsey, who commanded the carriers, decided on an immediate take-off, though the ships were still some 670 miles from the target. From a deck that rose and fell with the rough sea, and off a runway only a third as long as the B-25's usually required, the raiders soared into the air and headed toward Japan.

Flying extremely low to avoid inter-ception, thirteen of the B-25's swept in over Tokyo, while three others headed for targets south of the capital. Led by Doolittle and by Major John Hilger, Captains David M. Jones and C. R. Greening, and Lieutenants Edward York and Travis Hoover, the Army fliers dropped their bombs and sped on unharmed, planning to land in China.

As darkness approached, the weather was bad, and their fuel ran low. One by one, they bailed out or made crash landings. Most of the fliers were found by friendly Chinese. One crew landed near Vladivostok, and the Russians interned them. And two planes came down in Japanese territory; three of the eight crewmen were shot, and five imprisoned.

The bold raid did little actual damage to Japan. But American planes over Tokyo, even for "thirty seconds," rattled Japanese confidence and gave a boost to the morale of the U.S., smarting from a string of reverses.

Friendly Chinese escort some of the fliers through a village after the raid, one of them holding the arm of Major John Hilger, who was hurt when he crashed. The casualties and plane losses made Doolittle think at first that the mission had been a failure.

If enemy bombers, intent on knocking out American plants, had reached Seattle during the war, they might well have ignored the suburban area above. Actually, the "earth" was burlap, the "grass" spun glass, and the "leaves" chicken wire. Beneath the camouflage was Boeing's main assembly plant, where workers produced 6,981 B-17's. Below, two girls inspect a "back-yard garden" on the roof of the Boeing factory.

Production Line

Rosie the Riveter" and "graveyar shift" entered the American vocabulary as men and women worked side by side on the home front, pouring out planes for the fighting front. Shifts came and went round the clock producing in 1942 almost 48,000 planes. Two years later the figure was more than 96,000.

The vastly expanded aircraft industry, much of it on the West Coast, was aided by automobile plants that converted to making planes. The Government altogether spent an estimated $45,000,000,000 for aircraft in World War II, and a total of 300,000 military planes were produced. The United States, said Lieutenant General William S. Knudsen, who headed the Air Technical Service Command, "smothered the enemy in an avalanche of production the like of which he had never seen or dreamed of."

Douglas Aircraft's assembly lines produced over 30,000 airplanes during the war, including 5,000 SBD Dauntless dive bombers (above).

The Battle
of Midway

From Japan, an armada of two hundred ships and seven hundred planes bore in for the kill. Its mission: to seize Midway, destroy the remnants of the U.S. fleet, and win the war. Though heavily outnumbered, America had broken the Japanese naval code and knew the enemy was coming. As an ambush, Admiral Chester Nimitz flanked the invaders with the carriers *Enterprise, Hornet,* and *Yorktown*—and waited.

On June 4, 108 Japanese planes hit Midway's defenses, chewing up a Marine fighter squadron in anti-quated Buffaloes. When island-base bombers and Devastators from th lurking carriers tried with desperat courage to attack the Japanese flee they were slaughtered. Thirty-five ou of forty-one Devastators were los Then, while the battle raged at lo level, the ambush suddenly worked Out of the clouds screamed Daunt less dive bombers, destroying thre Japanese carriers in five minutes.

Later, the Japanese lost anothe carrier and a cruiser, and the Amer icans lost the *Yorktown*. But pilots heroism had won a decisive battle.

т: *Douglas SBD Dauntless dive bombers were the eventual victors at Midway. Their* *den attack at a slanting 70-degree angle from 17,000 to 2,500 feet caught Vice-Admiral* *uichi Nagumo by surprise and scored nine mortal hits on his carriers. The Japanese* *the big carriers* Akagi, Kaga, Soryu, *and* Hiryu *in the battle as well as 332 planes* *some 2,500 men, and were forced to call off their Midway invasion plans.*

ow: *A spectacular aerial shot during the battle shows the Japanese carrier* Kaga *cir-* *g desperately to try to avoid American dive bombers. Earlier, the 26,900-ton ship,* *ose name meant "Increased Joy," had been the target of low-flying American torpedo* *nes and bombers, which suffered terrible losses from Zeros and antiaircraft fire.* *til the arrival of the SBD's, Midway had appeared to be a great Japanese triumph.*

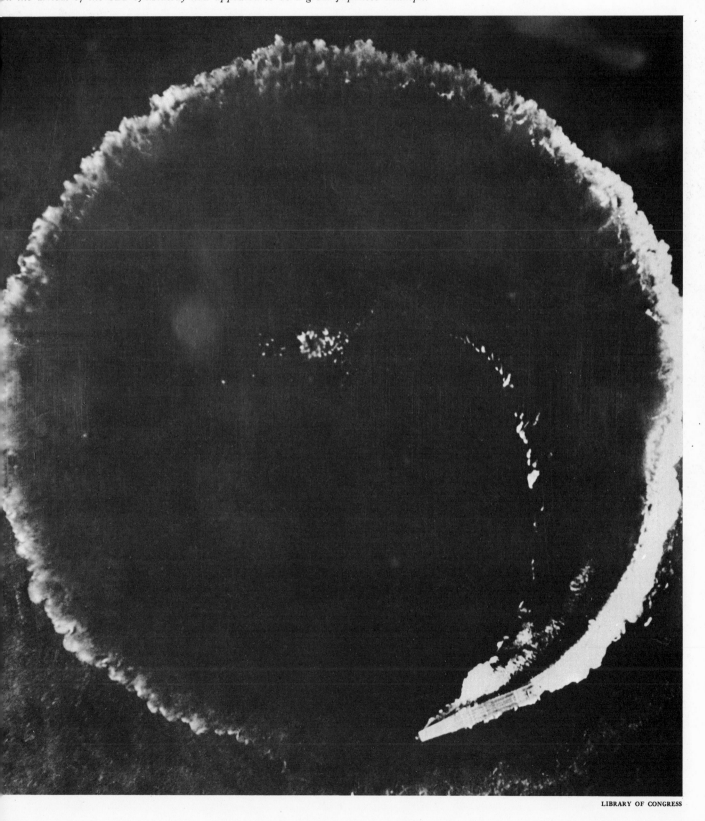

ENGINES
OF DEATH

Udet and the Me-109

Willy Messerschmitt, who built his first airplane in 1923, has designed many famous aircraft, including the jet-propelled Me-262, which saw action late in World War II. He recalls here a skeptical reaction to his most successful plane, the Messerschmitt Bf-109, popularly called the Me-109.

When we were building the 109, General Ernst Udet, head of the Luftwaffe's technical division, came to me and said, "I heard about your development of a new fighter airplane. How about letting me see it?" That was in 1935, a few days before the first flight of the airplane. So I took Udet into my shop and he looked at the airplane, shaking his head, and climbed up the ladder to the cockpit, which was opened. Udet, of course, was one of the most famous World War I pilots, flying biplanes and these open planes. He climbed in and the mechanic closed the canopy, and Udet didn't look enthusiastic at all. We were quite downhearted. When he got out, he patted me on the back and said, "Messerschmitt, this will never be a fighting airplane. The pilot needs an open cockpit. He has to feel the air to know the speed of the

Messerschmitt (right) with Goering

airplane. And then you'd better [put] on another wing on top and put a f[ew] wires and struts on, and then you[']ll have a real fighting airplane."

"Clouds of Warplanes"

In May, 1940, President Franklin [D.] Roosevelt electrified the free wo[rld] with an appeal for the production [of] 50,000 airplanes in the United Stat[es.] American industry met the challen[ge,] but H. Mansfield Horner, gene[ral] manager of Pratt & Whitney Aircr[aft] at the time, tells of one initial reacti[on] to the President's request.

When the President called for his [fa-]mous 50,000 airplanes, we did[n't] know whether he meant an ann[ual] rate or a total force of 50,000. La[ter] on he said he meant 50,000 per ye[ar.] I think that would really have shak[en] us up if we'd believed that at the tim[e.]

We brought in licensees—we we[re] the ones that first originated th[at] thought. We couldn't take the p[ro-]duction expansion without spreadi[ng] ourselves too thin. The first one [we] brought in was Ford. That was a ve[ry] interesting period. The whole feeli[ng] of the people at Ford was that th[ey] could do this with their left hand. [In] fact, Mr. [Henry] Ford himself sa[id] that if somebody'd tell him to, [he] could build a thousand fighters a da[y,] including the engines, and do it [all] in his tool room. That was the gene[ral] atmosphere which we were ve[ry] much concerned about, because [we] wanted to make the thing go. We f[elt] that if they did take this approac[h] they were going to mess things [up] something awful. So we finally p[er-]suaded them to send a group of to[ol] and production engineers to take [a] good look at our place. They did, a[nd] then they had the difficult job of te[ll-]ing Mr. Ford that this was a re[al] undertaking. Not only couldn't th[ey] do it in their tool room, they couldn[']t do it in the whole Ford complex [of] facilities! They would have to bui[ld] themselves a brand-new plant. Th[ey] did, and they did a great job.

"We Won't Let It Fly"

When it finally appeared, the P-47 Thunderbolt, built by the Republic Aviation Corporation, was one of the best fighter planes of the war. Alexander Kartveli, its designer, recounts some of the difficulties encountered during its development.

We built the airplane and it was very successful. We exceeded our promised speed by 20 miles—it would go 420 miles per hour. Then they tested the wing for tortional frequency. Although most airplanes had a frequency of about 2,700 cycles per second, the P-47 showed only about 2,400. So they told me, "You'll have to jack up the frequency; otherwise we won't let it fly."

To jack up the frequency is very difficult. It's like changing the beat of your heart. So we were all disgusted. Then our forces captured a Messerschmitt, and we measured its frequency. It happened to be something like 900. It was lower than ours. So I said, "You'd better send a wire to Hitler to ground his airplane—it's no good." As a result, they passed the Thunderbolt, low frequency and all.

But then we had another problem. After a certain maneuver, the tail of the airplane would come off, and it would crash. At first we didn't know what to do or where to turn. It was designed according to all the rules; it had passed all the tests; and yet too often she would dive and pull out, and the tail would come off.

So we junked the old tail, stopped everything for a few weeks, and worked night and day designing and testing a new tail. Part of the tail was fabric-covered and that part was blowing loose. So we made it all-metal and finally overcame the trouble.

We also had problems with aileron control and longitudinal control. When you exceeded a certain speed you couldn't move the stick, and the pilots didn't know what to do. They would dive until they would gradu-

CULVER PICTURES, INC.

Alexander Kartveli

ally decrease their speed and then the stick would come back. That was a new phenomenon for us and it was very exciting. We finally worked out a way of flying to avoid this particular danger. We established the limit of diving angle and diving speed. Finally we put on so-called dive breaks which would prevent that condition and make flying easier.

This type of engineering is a very nerve-racking business because so many things can go wrong, and you are dealing with human life. You get stomach ulcers, you don't sleep nights, you don't eat. But the final satisfaction of seeing your plane fly is a tremendous reward which makes up for all the suffering.

"Hap" Arnold

Robert Gross, who was president of the Lockheed Aircraft Corporation, reminisced in 1959 about General Henry H. Arnold, chief of the Army Air Forces—and the principal military driving force behind the build-up of American air power.

General Arnold was a very stern and hard taskmaster; he was never satisfied with any performance. He made you do better than you could, because

he demanded more than you had in you and wasn't satisfied with anything less.

"Hap" was not an engineer, of course, though he was scientifically oriented. You could discuss engineering problems with him. We didn't often, because when he visited us his time was always very, very limited. I've seen him come in and spend less than half an hour, just exhort us to do more, and then leave. He'd just tell us the costs of failures, urge us on to higher levels, and then go along. This was his real contribution, I'd say. He was the driving force that got his suppliers to promise more and do more than they thought they were able to do.

Why did we respond to his exhortations as we did? In the first place, he was personally a very likable, forceful person; you couldn't sit and look at Arnold and talk to him for a few minutes without reaching a very intense level of rapport. He sort of picked you up and carried you along. Secondly, we were afraid of him. He'd berate up one side and down the next, and we were afraid he'd order us out of business or something, and take the place over. Finally, there was our own conscientious need to do our best. There's no question about it, he was 100 per cent in his work, with no competitive diversions of any kind. He pressured us with his own absolute dedication.

"Put on the Girls"

Jacqueline Cochran, a racing pilot and holder of numerous air records, served with the British Air Transport Auxiliary before becoming head of the U. S. Women Airforce Service Pilots (WASP). Here she tells of some of the many contributions made by women fliers during the war.

Late in 1940 General Arnold said they needed pilots desperately for ferrying airplanes from Canada to England, and he asked me if I could be of any help. I said I would be

323

WASP leader Jacqueline Cochran

happy to volunteer, and my services were immediately accepted.

It was a difficult task with a high mortality rate. I got shot at over the North Atlantic, and others did too. We usually got to England with only about two and a half hours of fuel to spare, and that is hazardous.

When I was there in England, they asked me if I would recruit a group of American women. I came back and recruited, and finally I took twenty-five women to England. They all fulfilled their contracts, and some stayed until the war was over. We were used in ferrying work; I ferried for eleven months. We landed planes like the Hurricane and the Spitfire in fields where I wouldn't land my Lodestar today if I could avoid it. When planes were damaged in flight, the boys often put them down in the first field and we girls would then take the damaged planes to a depot. When a mission was being organized, ferry pilots would assemble the planes —we would fly perhaps five different types in a day—and after the planes were returned, we would disperse them and put them on satellite fields.

Then General Arnold came in June, 1942, and said, "You'd better come home." I recommended strong-

ly that we take on a group of women and train them. The girls proved to be simply remarkable.

For instance, one day I got a call to come into General Arnold's office. He said, "What do you know about the B-26?" I said, "I don't know a thing except the scuttlebutt that it's a so-called hot airplane." The men were saying that they were willing to be killed in war, but they wouldn't fly the B-26. But we were tooled up for them, and we needed them desperately, so we had to build them. They proved to be all right afterward.

I flew the plane and didn't see anything so difficult about it. I came back and said to General Arnold, "I can cure your men of walking off the program. Let's put on the girls." So we had 150 girls flying B-26's. They towed targets while live bullets were being shot at the targets from B-24's. They did 70,000 hours of tow work, and with that all-girl crew there was only one minor accident and not a single fatality. They also did radio control work—a girl would fly the airplane and another girl would sit beside her and fly another plane without anybody in it. She would control the other airplane over the target lines, where men would shoot the plane down. It was an exceedingly difficult operation and a hazardous one, but we never had a fatality on that, although we did have seven pilots, of whom two were girls, killed by sabotage.

The girls also tested new engines, and did some instructing, too. They were marvelous instructors. Men preferred them because they were more patient.

One time I saw a girl get out of a P-51. That was one of the most difficult planes to fly. Obviously, she was going to have a child. "What are you doing flying a P-51?" She started boohooing and saying her husband was in combat and she wanted to do her part. I said, "A pregnant woman has no business flying," but I couldn't help but admire her.

Spitfire Pilot

Through 1940 and 1941 British fighter pilots held the Luftwaffe at bay in the West. In this excerpt from his memoirs, Wing Leader, *Group Captain J. E. Johnson of the RAF, who became the top British ace of the war with thirty-eight victories, describes his first kill over France during the summer of 1941.*

Ahead of me, not more than three hundred yards away, three Messerschmitts climbed steeply as if they were being hauled up three sides of a pyramid. Their prey at the apex of the pyramid was a solitary Spitfire flying straight and level, and although I didn't know his call sign I shouted to him: "For Christ's sake, break." But it was too late, for the combined fire of the 109's smashed into his belly, and exploding cannon shells ripped through his port wing like a cross-cut saw slicing through a wooden plank. The wing drifted down lazy as an autumn leaf, but the crippled Spitfire fell into a vicious spin.

The Messerschmitts stayed to fight and the sky was full of aircraft. It was a dangerous place for a lone pilot, and I looked around, always turning, for the nearest section of

Captain J. E. Johnson

pitfires so that I could join forces. uddenly a 109 arced up in front of ne at two o'clock and the enemy lot put his aircraft into a gentle ive. I was very close to him and ould see the square wing tips and ne tail struts of a 109-E. . . . I swung ly Spitfire to get behind him and nought: This is it. Nail him, and get ut. Clear your tail first.

I was dead line astern of the Messerschmitt and hit him behind ne cockpit with the eight machine uns. As the range closed, I contrived o spray the 109 with bullets and the lot half-rolled on to his back and ettisoned his hood. I remembered ill Burton's precise instructions conerning enemy pilots who bailed out —"I'll court-martial any member of nis squadron who fires at a parahute"—but this chap was still inde the cockpit and I hammered him nce more. A shapeless bundle broke way from the Messerschmitt, and vhen I circled to watch it, I saw the arachute break open. Feeling a deep xultation at this sight, I drove the pitfire round in a steep, tail-clearing urn, since the combat had peraps lasted several seconds and much ould happen in this time. But the sky eemed empty of all aircraft and I ped across the Channel and landed t Hawkinge to refuel.

A Little Fillip"

n the dark days after Pearl Harbor lmerican morale was first lifted by he bold B-25 bombing attack on ^okyo. General James Doolittle deribes the raid he led from the carier Hornet *on April 18, 1942.*

'he weather when we took off was ery rough. That, however, was good, ecause there was a strong wind lowing and the only worry we had vas that we might have to take off in dead calm. If so, then it would ave been very difficult to get airorne with the very heavy load that ve had. So we were delighted to ave a rough sea and plenty of wind.

Doolittle (right) with General Arnold

The target maps were distributed as soon as we put to sea in the *Hornet*. Each crew made a very complete study of the target area and all of the terrain in that vicinity so that we could find each target readily, bomb it promptly, and get out rapidly. Mine was a target in the military plant, more or less in Tokyo. We went in low, dropped our bombs, and got out as quickly as we could.

There was moderate, inaccurate flak. None of the planes was shot down, though many of them had hits. In my own case, I saw five fighters converging on me. I swung very quickly round two little hills, did an S turn, and the fighters turned also, but they didn't make the second half of my S. And the last I saw was the fighters going off in the opposite direction, apparently trying to pick me up. So I did not get shot at by fighters; it was only this one group of fighters that actually formed and was preparing to attack.

After getting out to sea, we turned half right and went to China.

When we were ready to land at Chuchow, we found that the weather was bad, and the homing device that was supposed to direct us to the field didn't answer. We found out later that the plane bringing in the device had crashed, killing all aboard. This was the most critical point, I guess. We realized that it was impossible to land at our destination, that we would have to either crash-land or jump.

I was very distressed. I realized that we had accomplished the first part of our mission, which was to bomb Japan, but I felt very distressed because the second part of our mission was to collect all our aircraft and make them available to the people in the CBI [China-Burma-India] theater. There was dense fog when we got to the coast, and we had to climb right into the fog. We had two airplanes that crash-landed right near the coast, in the water. So the likelihood of saving the aircraft was remote or nil. I felt very badly about having lost my entire force of aircraft and having scattered my entire force of men all over a considerable area of China.

Two men were killed in one crew, but the other eight were picked up by the Japanese, tried, and three of them were executed. One was starved to death. The other four we got back, after the war was over. They were in very bad shape.

The raid had three advantages, really. The first advantage was to give the people at home a little fillip. The news had been all bad until then. The second advantage of the raid was to cause the Japanese to worry and feel that they were vulnerable. The third and most useful part of the raid was that it caused a diversion of enemy aircraft and equipment to the defense of the home islands which the Japanese badly needed in the theaters where war was actually going on.

The actual damage done was minimal. We had sixteen airplanes with one ton of bombs each, only sixteen tons of bombs; in the later raids they were dropping five thousand tons of bombs in one raid! Sixteen tons compared with five thousand is pretty puny.

CHAPTER 9

Paratroopers drop from C-47's of the U.S. Twelfth Air Force to spearhead the invasion of southern France on August 15, 1944.

ALLIED TRIUMPH

American war strategy included two major premises: "Europe first" and the build-up of forces in Britain for an air offensive and for the early recrossing of the Channel by Allied armies. Whatever hopes Allied air leaders may have had that Germany could be defeated by strategic bombing, it was clear that the air offensive would have to take place within a land-sea-air strategy. But with fires burning everywhere, the build-up of American bomber forces in the British Isles had to be slower than the pre-Pearl Harbor plans had envisioned. On January 27, 1942, it was agreed that the first two heavy bomb groups available should form the nucleus of an American air command in Britain, which would "operate independently in cooperation with the British Bomber Command." On February 4 Brigadier General Ira C. Eaker left the United States to prepare for the reception of American air units in England, and early in June Major General Carl Spaatz arrived with the first contingent and formally took command of the Eighth Air Force.

At the same time, Churchill journeyed to Washington. Since Christmas, the Coral Sea and Midway had been the only bright spots in a gloomy world. The German summer offensive was under way in Russia. The Crimea had already fallen, and the Nazis were bearing down on the Caucasian oil fields and possibly the Middle East. In North Africa Rommel had begun to move in May, and on June 13 had defeated the British at Knightsbridge. Now, on June 21, while Churchill was conferring with Roosevelt, a telegram arrived which the President silently handed to the Prime Minister: "Tobruk has surrendered, with twenty-five thousand men taken prisoners."

Churchill suggested that the Americans, who were anxious to be in some major action in 1942, might create a strategic diversion in northwest Africa. The American chiefs of staff resisted, arguing that even a small bridgehead in France would be preferable to anything that might be done in North Africa. Haunted by the memory of Dunkirk, the British refused to join in a cross-Channel operation in 1942. By the end of July, the Americans found themselves committed to invade North Africa, and on August 7 Lieutenant General Dwight D. Eisenhower, American commander of the newly-formed European theater, was named to lead the new expedition.

In England, meanwhile, the first B-17E arrived on July 4, 1942. American faith in daylight bombing was still strong, despite early German and British failures. It had not really been tried—not with the high-level precision techniques that Americans believed essential. Confidence was based on two things: first, the Norden bombsight, held to be capable of "pickle-barrel" accuracy from great height; and second, two great bombers, the B-17 Flying Fortress and the B-24 Liberator. Their speed, range, and durability had already been proved in the Pacific; and in formation, armed with ten or more heavy machine guns each, they could bring tremendous firepower against attackers.

Some of the British were skeptical about daylight bombing. Others, like Trenchard, believed that, whatever the problems, it was infinitely more desirable— even necessary—to bomb by day and by night, right around the clock, than to do either alone.

Unquestionably, area bombing at night by RAF Bomber Command had made great progress in 1942. The new bomber commander, Sir Arthur Harris, intended to wipe out Germany's cities systematically, acre by acre. He believed that with existing equipment true precision bombing was impossible and, in any case, probably a meaningless refinement. The American idea of going for the jugular vein did not appeal to him; he felt the result was more certain—if less tidy—when the whole organism was smashed.

The striking power of Bomber Command was vastly increased in 1942. Older, slower, less capacious aircraft were replaced by more Halifaxes and the redesigned Manchester, now called the Lancaster. The weight of single bombs rose from two to eight thousand pounds. Average strength available per mission went up from forty-two bombers in January to 261 in December. Pathfinder navigation aids in the form of air-borne radar now made it more nearly certain that targets could be found in overcast and at night.

The Ruhr was at last heavily bludgeoned in a series of mounting blows, culminating, on May 30, in a mass attack on Cologne, the first of three 1,000-bomber raids. The munitions towns of northern Italy were also hit, Turin being the first city to feel a full-scale attack with 8,000-pound bombs. On some operations, losses amounted to 10 per cent and in a few instances rose even higher, but Harris believed the results justified the risks.

On July 4 the U.S. Eighth Air Force went into action with borrowed RAF airplanes. And on August 17, flying with strong Spitfire escort—and with Eaker, the bomber commander, in the lead ship of the second flight—twelve Fortresses bombed the railroad yards at Rouen, while six others carried out a diversionary sweep. All returned safely, and the mission seemed a good omen for daylight precision bombing.

Through the first week of September, ten more attacks were made on targets within the operating radius of the fighters. Accuracy was so good that it looked as if the day bombers would be able to land 40 per cent of their bombs in a 1,000-yard circle around the aiming point. Luck changed abruptly on September 7 when the weather turned bad and the bombing went wild. Still, losses were low—only two bombers in eleven missions.

A new phase of the American effort began on September 8, when Spaatz was ordered to strip the Eighth Air Force of a good part of its still meager strength to provide units and planes for a new air force—the Twelfth, under Brigadier General James H. Doolittle—which would assist the forthcoming invasion of North Africa. The pared-down Eighth, somewhat disheartened by the postponement of its own mission, flew three more operations in October. On the 9th, over Lille, German fighters shot down four out of 108 bombers. Worse still, only nine bombs were plotted within five hundred yards of the aiming point. For the rest of the year and into the spring, the Eighth Air Force and RAF Bomber Command were directed to give protection to Allied convoys bound for North Africa and were obliged to waste their effort in bouncing bombs off the twelve-foot-thick roofs of submarine pens in the Brest peninsula.

November, 1942, marked three great climaxes of World War II. The first was the Battle of Alamein, in which the British Eighth Army, under its new commander, Lieutenant General Bernard L. Montgomery, broke the back of Rommel's Afrika Korps and sent it into retreat. In a series of stupendous actions from October 24 to November 5, Montgomery was mightily assisted by the RAF's Desert Air Force, under Sir Arthur ("Maori") Coningham, and the U.S. Ninth Air Force, under Lieutenant General Lewis H. Brereton, who earlier had been in India.

The second November climax was the Battle of Stalingrad, a German disaster of the first magnitude. Furious fighting had been going on there since August. As the Russian winter closed in, a massive Soviet counterattack struck the Germans on November 19, hurled them back, and ultimately closed around the Sixth German Army. During December, 1942, and January, 1943, nearly five hundred aircraft were lost in a frantic attempt to deliver the 550 tons of supplies needed daily by the encircled troops. The Germans even tried using their new four-engine bomber as a transport. This was the Heinkel He-177, just coming into limited production after many design difficulties. Losses were unbearable: within a few weeks a thousand highly-trained airmen were sacrificed. And their efforts were wasted. In February, 1943, the Sixth Army surrendered.

The third climax occurred on November 8, 1942, with the Allied invasion of northwest Africa. Three well-timed task forces—two from England moving on Algiers and Oran and a third headed from the United States to Casablanca—caught the enemy off guard. Brief opposition was met from Vichy French forces, but by November 10, Algiers and Oran had been taken and all French units in Morocco had surrendered.

The Allied problem was to secure Tunisia before the Germans could build up enough strength to hold it. Supported by paratroops dropped at Bône and other key points, Allied troops got to within twenty miles of Tunis on November 28 only to be driven back two days later by superior German forces. The high tide of Allied advance passed, and supplies, reinforcements, and aircraft bogged down in mud.

Perhaps the unhappiest part of the operation was the air situation, in which responsibility for support was unwisely divided between the American Twelfth Air Force, under Doolittle, and the British Eastern Air Command, under Sir William Welsh. Units were strung out throughout the invasion areas, and local ground commanders assumed operational control of tactical aircraft, dissipating the meager air strength. Coordination was virtually impossible and could only be effected by the Allied Commander in Chief personally. Early in December, Eisenhower sent for Spaatz to come down from England and take charge. Tactical air commanders were restored to control of their own units, and a system of coordination between ground and air commanders was established. Spaatz emerged as Eisenhower's acting deputy for air.

In January, 1943, Roosevelt and Churchill met at Casablanca and adopted the policy of "unconditional surrender." They also decided that when Tunisia had been won, Eisenhower should proceed to the capture of Sicily in order to re-establish Allied control of the Mediterranean. At the same time, Churchill also proposed to Roosevelt that the American air forces based in Britain abandon daylight bombing and join the RAF in night operations. Called to the conference, Eisenhower and Spaatz resisted, knowing that the United States was already developing long-range fighters that would become available by the time the Eighth Air Force had reached sufficient bomber strength to make deep penetrations of Germany. Long argument failed to convince the Prime Minister that daylight bombing was feasible. Eaker came down from England and in a private interview with Churchill made a point-by-point case for daylight bombing. Not without lingering doubts, Churchill at last withdrew his opposition. Before the conference ended, the Combined Chiefs of Staff issued a directive for a combined bomber offensive by the Eighth Air Force and RAF Bomber Command, operating by day and night against a common schedule of priority targets.

North Africa was now made a separate theater under Eisenhower. Spaatz was to command all the air forces in northwest Africa, while Sir Arthur Tedder coordinated air activities throughout the Mediterranean, especially those eastward of Tunisia and thus beyond Eisenhower's jurisdiction.

On February 14 Rommel, retreating before Montgomery's British Eighth Army, joined up with the Axis forces already in Tunisia and settled in the Mareth Line. The Germans struck the weak Allied center, breached the line in the bloody battle of Kasserine Pass, and were stopped only as they pressed into Algeria. This was the last great adventure of the Afrika Korps. In March, operating from newly-built forward airfields, Spaatz achieved control of the air in Tunisia. The Eighth Army, moving in from Libya behind massive air and artillery preparation, took the Mareth Line, and Rommel went home to Germany pleading ill health. The Northwest African Air Forces now pounded the Sicilian ports and shipping to pre-

vent the Germans from reinforcing or escaping. B-17's pulverized thirty acres of dock area in Palermo; and on April 18 four squadrons of American P-40's caught nearly one hundred Ju-52's and their fighter escort over the Gulf of Tunis, shooting down more than fifty in ten minutes with the loss of only six Warhawks. The final ground push began on April 22, supported by as many as 2,000 air sorties a day. Tunis and Bizerte fell on May 7. Huddled against the sea, cut off from escape by sea and air, the entire Axis force in Africa—270,000 men—surrendered on May 13.

Before the invasion of Sicily could be supported by air, it was necessary to subdue the neighboring island of Pantelleria and gain its bases for fighters too short-legged to operate from Tunisia. Bombed incessantly for a month, the island surrendered on June 11, the first instance of the conquest of territory by air power.

Sicily itself was given a similar pounding. A thousand planes and almost all thirty-one of its airfields were put out of action before D-Day, July 10. With the air over land and sea under Allied control, only a dozen of the armada of 3,000 ships were lost, mostly at night, and the American, British, and Canadian forces went ashore virtually unmolested by enemy air attacks. From July 14, Allied air supremacy was almost complete, and North African Air Force planes were free to bomb airfields in France and Italy and make strategic attacks against Italian rail centers.

After Casablanca, the commitments of American air power to other theaters had kept the strength of the Eighth Air Force in England, now under Eaker, too low to damage the Reich. Until spring, its nominal force was from two to six groups, and only half of these were operational. A hundred-plane mission was a rarity. The idle commitment to invulnerable submarine pens continued to exact its toll. U-boats, nevertheless, gave the Eighth Air Force its first opportunity to attack Germany when, on January 27, 1943, the construction yards at Wilhelmshaven were hit.

Even yet, there were no long-range fighters and no nose turrets to give protection against head-on attack. The development of the combat box, a tight stack of bombers with mutual defensive fire, helped somewhat. Still, losses above 10 per cent were common, and in an attack on Bremen on April 17 sixteen of 106 bombers were lost.

By the summer of 1943, the Eighth Air Force received six new heavy groups. Aircraft, ball bearings, and oil were the high-priority enemy targets, and the oil refineries at Ploesti, Rumania, were singled out to be hit. The Eighth lent three of its B-24 groups, and the Ninth, still based in North Africa, two of its groups, for a minimum-altitude, radio-silence, surprise attack, on August 1, 1943, on this supposed oil arsenal of the Reich. In the execution, the lead groups turned too soon and alerted the defenses. Fifty-four of 177 Liberators dispatched were lost, in return for about 40 per cent of the capacity of Ploesti which, in a few months, was nearly back to its usual efficiency. The courage and devotion of the crews was by far the most important aspect of the mission.

The Eighth Air Force realized that in 1943, owing to RAF Bomber Command's 1942 successes and the mere appearance of the new Flying Fortress weapon against Germany, the Luftwaffe would be waiting for revenge. In target planning, Ploesti oil had been a tossup with the Messerschmitt single-engine fighter works at Regensburg and Wiener Neustadt. The two attacks were finally made concomitant, though the Ploesti task force was to bomb Wiener Neustadt and the Eighth, Regensburg. Ball bearings being high on the target list, an attack on Schweinfurt was thrown in for good measure. Regensburg was to be hit first, and the force was to fly on to bases in Algeria—an early shuttle-bombing attempt. By striking after the Regensburg contingent, the Schweinfurt effort was expected to escape enemy opposition. Both operations could be given fighter support only part of the way.

The Regensburg wave of 146 bombers took off from England on the morning of August 17. As expected, the German fighters savagely attacked the top and bottom elements of the combat wing. Twenty-four bombers went down, but every building of the Messerschmitt plant was damaged and the planes flew on to Africa unopposed. Bad weather held up the Schweinfurt wave for three and a half hours. Instead of the feeble resistance of spent German fighters, it encountered the Luftwaffe rested and refueled. In and out, the task force lost thirty-six bombers, and more were crippled, in exchange for eighty direct hits on the ball-bearing works.

A second raid on Schweinfurt on October 14 cost sixty of the 291 attacking Fortresses. Though no formation of American bombers was ever turned back, the worst that the opponents of daylight bombing had prophesied had come true. Heavily-armed bombers, it was now seen, could not protect themselves against massive fighter attack. The German tactics of loosening up combat formations by firing long-range rockets from twin-engine "destroyers" and then having their single-engine fighters go after cripples or stragglers was effective and deadly. "Feathering a prop over Germany," said one American pilot, "is like writing to the boys at the mortuary for space on their slab!" It was the last deep daylight penetration attempted by the Allies until long-range fighter escort appeared four months later in February, 1944.

After the second Schweinfurt raid, the Germans dispersed their ball-bearing plants. German industry, though severely battered, was showing remarkable recuperative powers; and German fighter production in December, 1943, was higher than it had been in June. Yet, the Nazis fully realized the potential disaster that awaited them. Invading Russia in 1941, the German army had been supported by 50 per cent of the Luftwaffe. Now, at the end of 1943, only 20 per cent stood behind the army; the bulk of the German fighter squadrons had wheeled around to meet mounting day and night bombing in the west.

The Allied invasion of Italy, meanwhile, had begun on September 3 with Montgomery's landing in Calabria. The American Fifth Army, in an attempt to cut off the supposedly retreating Germans, landed higher up the boot at Salerno, below Naples, on the 9th. With Allied fighters operating at the limit of their radius, the going in the beachhead was rough. When the Germans counterattacked, American paratroops were dropped and stopped their advance. With the full weight of Allied air, naval, and ground fire assisting, General Mark Clark was able to make contact with Montgomery on September 16. Spaatz then turned his bombers against the remaining enemy airfields in the south and quickly rebased his own fighters on them as they became available. From then on, the Allies had control of the air over Italy.

Naples fell on October 1, and the Eighth Army reached an equivalent point on the east coast, thus freeing the complex of airfields in the Foggia Plain. In a few weeks the Allied advance found itself stopped by the rugged Italian terrain, bad weather, and a fortified barrier that the Germans called the Gustav Line. Here the Allies sat through the winter. The capture of the Foggia airfields, however, had provided bases from which strategic bombers could at last reach targets in central and southeastern Europe. To exploit the advantage, the U. S. formed a new strategic air force—the Fifteenth, under Major General Nathan F. Twining—to be based in Italy.

In November and December, Roosevelt and Churchill again met, at Cairo and at Tehran. Closer cooperation with the Russians was attempted, and Stalin agreed to let the American heavy bombers have shuttle bases in the Ukraine. The war in Italy was to be curtailed and all possible effort concentrated on the build-up for a cross-Channel invasion of the Continent in the summer of 1944. The command team developed in the Mediterranean was moved to London. Eisenhower was designated Supreme Commander, with Sir Arthur Tedder as his deputy. Spaatz became commander of the U.S. Strategic Air Forces in Europe, controlling the operations of the Eighth and the Fifteenth. Eaker was sent from England to head the Mediterranean Allied Air Forces, and Doolittle replaced him as commander of the Eighth. The war in Europe was about to enter its final phase.

On the eastern front, the summer of 1943 had spelled continued disaster for the Germans. Starting at Kursk, near the center of the long line, Soviet forces began a gradual but steady rollback of the invaders. Enormous battles of tanks and aircraft were fought at Orel, Smolensk, and finally Zhitomir. Day after day, cities and towns were liberated. By the end of the year, the whole front, from Leningrad to the Crimea, was rolling westward.

On the other side of the world, during all this period, a different kind of war had been raging fiercely. Daunted at Midway, the Japanese had pushed aggressively forward elsewhere. In July, 1942, they had started a drive across the mountainous spine of New Guinea toward Australia, and on September 17 were only twenty miles from Port Moresby. Major General George C. Kenney at this point organized the U.S. Fifth Air Force and, largely by knocking out enemy airfields, began systematically to gain control of the air over New Guinea. Allied troops, many of them airlifted from Australia, turned back the Japanese, who held on stubbornly at Buna until January, 1943.

Admiral Chester W. Nimitz, Navy commander in the Pacific, had meanwhile begun a campaign to take Guadalcanal, where the Japanese were building an advanced airfield. The First Marine Division landed at Guadalcanal and Tulagi on August 7 and occupied the airfield, which soon came under heavy Japanese air and naval counterattacks. The small unit of Marines hung on gallantly, and from the airstrip day after day Marine Wildcats rose to battle Japanese bombers and fighters that swarmed down the Solomon Islands "slot" from Rabaul.

For weeks the issue at Guadalcanal was in doubt. Four major naval battles were fought for possession of the island. Japanese reinforcements swarmed ashore, and on the night of October 13 shells from the battleships *Haruna* and *Kongo* reduced the airfield to a shambles. The Americans fought back with every type of combat plane available. On November 11 they smashed a desperate attempt by the Japanese to land new troops, sinking seven out of eleven transports and damaging the rest. Six thousand Japanese soldiers and all their supplies were lost.

After long, bitter fighting, the Japanese finally abandoned Guadalcanal in February, 1943; and Marine and Army troops, under the direction of Admiral William F. "Bull" Halsey, moved on to capture other strongholds in the Solomons. The Japanese were dogged defenders and made island-hopping extremely

costly to the attackers. It took two months to conquer New Georgia and longer to subdue the nearby islands. But once the tide of war turned, it began to ebb rapidly for the Japanese. In March planes of the Royal Australian and United States Fifth Air Forces smashed an entire Japanese convoy of eight transports and eight destroyers into flaming wrecks in the Bismarck Sea. The cost to the Allies was only six planes.

The Japanese suffered a dramatic blow of another sort in April. On the morning of the 18th, Admiral Isoroku Yamamoto, said to possess the best military mind in Japan, took off from Rabaul in a Betty bomber to inspect Japanese airstrips on Bougainville in the northern Solomons. American monitors, able to read and decipher enemy coded messages, knew where he was going, and when; fifteen minutes before Yamamoto reached his destination, he was jumped by waiting Lockheed P-38's, shot down, and killed.

Salamaua and Lae, the main objectives of the Allied advance in New Guinea, held out against American and Australian troops under General Douglas MacArthur until mid-September. Gradually it was realized that the most effective way to deal with the far-flung Japanese strong points was to strangle their long supply lines with air power. In the fall of 1943 and early in 1944, the Thirteenth Air Force, Navy planes from the Solomons, and eventually the Fifth Air Force did just that to Rabaul, neutralizing the anchor of the Japanese position in the southwest Pacific. Farther north, progress was also made. In November, 1943, in the Gilbert Islands, the atoll of Tarawa was captured after a heroic and exceedingly bloody fight. Moving westward in February, 1944, a landing was made in the Marshalls, and Kwajalein was taken with its harbor and airfield. Here, for the first time, the Japanese were deprived of territory they had held before the war. Its capture was a symbol that the power of the Rising Sun was soon to set.

Another threat to Japanese power was now building up in the United States and on airfields in central China. The threat was the Superfortress, the B-29, plans for which had been laid down in 1939-40. To operate the big planes from China required the building of huge air bases in India and China and airlifting supplies over enormous distances. The first B-29 attack of the war was made on May 27, 1944, from India against Bangkok. Full-scale use against the Japanese homeland from the advanced bases would come later. Meanwhile, C-46's—and, later, four-engine C-54's—of the Tenth Air Force carried supplies to China over the "Hump" of the Himalayas. The pilots fought 100-mile-per-hour winds and blinding snowstorms, flew at night to avoid Japanese fighters, wrestled their heavily-laden transports over mountain ranges 16,000 feet high, and faced the constant hazard of forced landings in remote and terrible terrain. "Five hundred and sixty miles of aerial dynamite," one flier called the run over the Hump.

In Europe, the long-awaited invasion of France was about to take place. By early 1944, long-range P-51 fighters were beginning to arrive in England in significant numbers, and the range of the P-38's and P-47's had been extended by the use of droppable wing tanks. To gain control of the air over the invasion areas before D-Day, Spaatz's bombers struck a major blow at the German aircraft industry in a "Big Week" of concentrated operations in February, 1944. The RAF cooperated with five heavy night attacks. A large dent was put in German aircraft production when it was needed most. On March 4, 6, and 8 the daylight bombers, escorted by Mustangs, attacked Berlin in force. The whole of the Reich now lay open to the American heavies. Though losses were often severe, Spaatz relentlessly struck at important targets on every possible occasion. To cut down the Luftwaffe still faster, he ordered the fighters to skirmish ahead of the bombers to seek out and kill the enemy fighters. In February and March the Luftwaffe lost eight hundred day fighters in the west. Though the planes might be replaced, the pilots could not, and the German air force began to decline rapidly.

In an effort to increase the firepower of their interceptors, the Germans weighed their warplanes down with rocket-firing devices, extra cannon carried in gondolas, even air-to-air bombs. As a result, when the sleek, long-range Mustangs suddenly appeared over Berlin and other cities deep inside the Reich, the aging German fighters were completely outclassed.

Even if they had been able to match the Allies in quality, the Germans could no longer hope to stop the tidal wave of air power rolling over them. In 1944 alone the United States produced 96,318 planes —more than twice the total American production in all the years prior to World War II. British factories were pouring out a stream of Lancasters, Halifaxes, Mosquitoes, Spitfires, Tempests, Typhoons, Beaufighters, and other combat types. When it came to hauling devastating bomb loads, the Lancaster was the war's most successful heavy bomber, but the British de Havilland Mosquito was also highly annoying to the Germans. Its great speed made it almost immune to fighter attack—until German jets became operational—and its wooden construction made it difficult to detect by radar. It was used for just about everything: bombing, photo-reconnaissance, night fighting, antisubmarine patrol, and "intruding"—following enemy aircraft back to their own fields and shooting them down as they tried to land.

In the planning phase before D-Day a sharp difference of opinion arose among the Allied air commanders over target priorities. One group, led by Tedder, favored a concentrated campaign against communications. The other, for which Spaatz was spokesman, favored a smashing attack on oil. Eisenhower decided on the communications plan. In the end, the U.S. Strategic Air Forces, aided by the RAF Bomber Command's unremitting attacks on German cities, knocked out both target systems. The strategic bombing offensive may have been long in coming, but it was now beating the German homeland to pulp.

When the invasion was launched in the dark and windy hours before dawn on June 6, the Luftwaffe was able to fly only a few sorties in opposition. Over the invasion forces in 4,000 ships, 11,000 Allied planes formed an iron canopy. Three divisions of airborne troops were dropped into Normandy before daylight. During the first day, the U.S. Eighth and Ninth Air Forces, between them, flew 8,722 sorties, while the RAF, in daylight, flew 5,676.

In the following weeks the Allies retained complete mastery of the air in Normandy. The interdiction campaign prevented rapid movement by German reinforcements into the combat area. Still, the German defense was stubborn, and the development of the battle was slowed. On July 25, for five miles along the Saint-Lô-Périers road, the Eighth and Ninth Air Forces blasted an enormous hole through which the American army was able to break out. Lieutenant General George S. Patton now began the first of his famous dashes across the French countryside. On August 7, when the Germans attempted to cut the American spearheads, they were caught in a British-American pincers movement at Falaise and the panzers were bombed and strafed into ruins. The remnants now headed for the Siegfried Line.

On August 15 France was invaded from the south by American and French troops after elaborate preparations by the Fifteenth and Twelfth Air Forces. Pushing up the Rhône Valley, the invasion forces met up with the main body of Eisenhower's command on September 11. In this operation—as throughout the Battle of France—the American tactical air forces were writing a new page in the history of warfare through the intimate, powerful, almost omnipresent air support given the armies. Between these air forces and the ground forces they worked with, it was, as Patton said, a case of "love at first sight."

In a desperate attempt to split the Allied armies, Hitler in December launched a short but sharp offensive in the Ardennes. Known as the Battle of the Bulge, this maneuver carried the German armor fifty miles before it was stopped. For a week, bad weather prevented the Allied air forces from attacking, but when the skies cleared on December 23 the twenty-five German divisions in the Bulge were pounded unmercifully. The Luftwaffe tried to operate with its former sting, but it suffered heavy losses due to inexperience of the crews. By New Year's, the Bulge was over.

The last twelve months of the war saw the introduction of Hitler's vengeance weapons, the V-1 and V-2, and the use of the first jet aircraft by both the British and the Germans. One week after D-Day, the V-1 flying bombs—in effect small pilotless jets with a speed of 390 to 410 miles per hour and a range of 150 miles—began to drone across the Channel, inflicting punishing damage on a horrified but unwavering London. By August the RAF had fifteen day squadrons and six night fighter squadrons assigned to V-1 interception. Seven of the new Gloster Meteor jet fighters went into action and destroyed thirteen buzz bombs. Revolutionary German fighters—the Messerschmitt Me-262 jet and the world's first rocket airplane, the Me-163—came too late and in too few numbers to put a serious crimp in the Allied bombing offensive. Also too late to be of serious help to the Germans was the Junkers Ju-287, the first heavy jet bomber. Potentially more deadly was the V-2 missile which stemmed from earlier research with liquid-propellant rockets by the American scientist Robert H. Goddard. Carrying a 2,000-pound warhead, the V-2 had a range of 220 miles reached at speeds up to 3,600 miles per hour over an arched flight path sixty miles high at its peak.

Despite these spectacular developments, the whole German war machine by early 1945 was slowly and inexorably grinding to a halt. In January and February the Western Allies knifed into the Rhineland. The Russians pressed westward from Warsaw to the Oder. In March the Rhine was crossed. In April the Ruhr was taken and the last German defenses in the west collapsed. On April 16 Spaatz announced the end of the strategic air war—the bombers had run out of targets to destroy. On the 25th American and Russian ground forces met at the river Elbe. At last, on May 7, Germany surrendered unconditionally. The captured Nazi leaders unanimously asserted that the war in Europe had been decided by air power.

The Pacific war was also slowly moving toward the climax. The final phase began in midsummer of 1944 with the Marianas operation against Saipan, Guam, and Tinian, only 1,500 miles from Japan. The invasion, preceded by neutralizing air attacks on Truk in the Carolines, was executed by a task force whose size dwarfed that of the whole Japanese navy. The amphibious assaults were provided heavy air support by U.S. Navy, Marine, and Seventh Air Force planes. Japanese commanders knew that if the Marianas

were lost, massive bombing attacks on the home islands would begin. Still, they did not consider their position hopeless. In the Marianas they had at least five hundred land-based planes. In the Philippines, Vice-Admiral Jisaburo Ozawa had assembled a fleet of seventy-three vessels, including five battleships and nine aircraft carriers. Task Force 58 under Admiral Marc Mitscher was larger, and this time the volume of antiaircraft fire that American ships could deliver was almost unbelievable. Nevertheless, Ozawa hoped to exploit the superior range of his lighter aircraft, stay beyond the reach of the American carriers, and if necessary run shuttle missions to Japanese land bases where his planes could refuel and rearm to strike the American fleet on their way back. After destroying the U.S. fleet, he could then whip the isolated invasion troops in the Marianas.

"The fate of the Empire," said Premier Hideki Tojo, "rests on this battle." Even as Army troops and Second and Fourth Division Marines fought for a foothold on grimly-defended Saipan, and Third Division Marines stood by for a landing on Guam, a titanic sea and air battle commenced. For the Japanese, nothing went right. Before Ozawa's fleet could reach the combat zone, Grumman Hellcats had shattered the Japanese land-based air force. When Ozawa hurled his planes at the American carriers in four separate waves, Hellcats clawed them to pieces. "If this plane could cook," one ecstatic American pilot cried, "I'd marry it!" Japanese losses were fantastic: 366 planes. In the "Marianas Turkey Shoot," as it was called, some American fliers were credited with six victories on a single mission. American combat losses were twenty-six planes.

Submarines and air attacks from Mitscher's carriers destroyed a large part of Ozawa's fleet and sent the remnants reeling back, damaged and demoralized. From that victory, the American Navy turned toward the Philippines. In heavy strikes against Japanese bases on Okinawa and Formosa, Hellcats crippled the enemy's land-based air power, then turned south to help protect landings on the east coast of Leyte.

Again while the beachhead battle was in progress, the Japanese fleet attempted a major disruption. The result was the Battle of Leyte Gulf, fought and won by the ships and fliers of the Seventh and Third Fleets, commanded respectively by Admirals Thomas C. Kinkaid and William F. Halsey. Once more, the Japanese were overwhelmed. The giant battleship *Musashi*, hit by at least thirty bombs and twenty-four torpedoes, rolled over and sank. Two other battleships and four carriers went down. In the air, Zeros were slaughtered. In one engagement Commander David S. McCampbell shot down nine enemy aircraft; he went on to become the Navy's top ace, with thirty-four confirmed victories. In the savage fighting that followed, Army Major Richard I. Bong brought his score up to forty confirmed kills and was withdrawn from combat, the number-one American ace of all time.

From Leyte, the action moved to Mindoro, and from there to Luzon, the invasion of which occupied much of January, 1945. Corregidor was taken with a paratroop drop on February 16. By the beginning of March, Manila was in American hands.

A principal reason for the seizing of the Marianas had been to gain islands that could be used as bases for the long-planned B-29 very-heavy-bomber operations against Japan itself. The Twentieth Air Force, intended as a global air force and commanded personally by Arnold, controlled all B-29's. The Superforts began to arrive on Saipan in October, 1944, and flew their first mission—to bomb Truk—on the 28th. On November 24 Brigadier General Emmett "Rosie" O'Donnell, of the 73rd Wing, led 111 B-29's against Tokyo. The new strategic bombing force did not escape the usual operational problems—slow build-up, lack of fighter escort, bad weather, poor accuracy, and a low rate of operations. In the end, two answers were provided: LeMay and Iwo Jima. Major General Curtis E. LeMay, a division commander with the Eighth Air Force, was sent out from England to take charge of the B-29's and put them in fighting shape.

Iwo Jima is a rocky island in the Bonins about halfway between Japan and the Marianas. Its value as a base for fighters and as an emergency landing field for B-29's limping back from Japan to the Marianas was inestimable. Before the operation, it was supposed that its capture would take four days. It took four weeks and one of the bloodiest battles of the entire war. For seventy-two days before the Marines went ashore on February 19, 1945, planes and ships bombarded the rock—five and a half miles long and two and a half wide—almost round the clock, trying to soften it up. When the landing was made, the Japanese, hidden in underground defenses, fought like demons. But in terms of American fliers' lives eventually saved, the island was worth what it cost.

In the over-all Pacific war, the next stage was to wrest the Ryukyus from the enemy, as these islands formed a natural springboard for an assault on Japan. The last and most violent amphibious campaign of the Pacific struggle began on March 18, with preparatory air strikes by Admiral Mitscher's Task Force 58. Okinawa, the main island, was invaded on April 1 by Army and Marine troops. As always, the Japanese garrison resisted fiercely, and the operation was not concluded until June 21.

No longer able to match American planes and fliers, the Japanese air force now turned to suicide tactics in which the *kamikaze* pilot crashed his explosive-packed plane onto a target, most frequently a ship. During the Okinawa operation these kamikazes made about 1,900 attacks and caused the U.S. Navy some of the heaviest damage of the war.

In March, LeMay decided to break from standard Air Force practice and use his B-29's to bomb the cities of Japan at night in low-level attacks with incendiaries. The resulting devastation was spectacular. The first fire raid on Tokyo killed 80,000 people, destroyed a quarter of the city's buildings, and laid waste an area of fifteen square miles. Almost from the beginning of these attacks, the B-29's had mastery of the skies over Japan. Fighter escort was unnecessary, armament became a nuisance. Many of the bombers had their guns removed and the space filled up with more incendiaries.

With their home islands a nightmare, further Japanese resistance was senseless. Nevertheless, they had seventy divisions of ground troops, and perhaps 5,000 combat planes, of which at least 3,000 would be used as kamikazes. It was the knowledge on the American side that these forces could inflict untold additional casualties that led to the decision to use the atom bomb. On August 6, in a searing flash of flame, the city of Hiroshima disappeared. On August 9 Nagasaki was hit.

In the face of such appalling weapons, it was impossible for even the die-hards in the Japanese government to justify further resistance. On August 15 the Emperor accepted the surrender terms. Over the blackened ruins of Japan, the calm summer skies held terror no longer.

General Henry H. Arnold, photographed above just after a tour of combat theaters in early 1943, had to cope with the logistical needs of eleven American air forces, each of which pleaded desperately for more planes and men. "A letter from [General William O.] Butler in Alaska," Arnold wrote later, "summed up the mail from all of them: 'I need everything!' " To add to the strength of any one commander "probably meant taking it away from some other theater, from some of your own people."

U.S. Bombers

American air power made its European debut during the summer of 1942. On June 12, Colonel Harry Halverson led thirteen B-24's on a first daring, long-distance raid against the oil refineries at Ploesti, Rumania. Taking off from Egypt, 1,000 miles from the target, the bombers surprised the enemy. All the planes got safely away, though one B-24 crashlanded later.

The first American mission from England took place, appropriately, on the Fourth of July. Six aircrews, flying A-20 Boston bombers borrowed from the RAF, joined six British crews on a low-level raid against air bases in Holland. The Germans were warned by radio from a picket ship off the Dutch coast, and two of the bombers flown by Americans were shot down. The bombardiers of two of the other planes were so confused by the camouflaged targets that they failed to drop their bombs at all.

More auspicious was a raid on August 17 against the railroad yards at Rouen. A dozen B-17 Flying Fortresses, like the one shown being loaded at an English base with three-hundred-pound bombs (right), completed their mission without losses. In the fall the North African invasion diverted planes and men and temporarily stalled the build-up of U.S. air strength in England. But as the Eighth continued to stab at the enemy, American crews matched the courage and ability of veterans.

On one occasion, for instance, nine B-17's, turning back from a canceled mission against Rotterdam, were jumped by more than twenty German fighters. The Americans fought their way back to England, but in one bomber the pilot was injured and the copilot killed. The bombardier, who had been washed out of flying school, took over the controls and flew the plane back home on two engines.

336

On a Wing
and a Prayer

During 1943 the Allies increased their air attacks on key points in Hitler's Fortress Europe. In July British bombers turned Hamburg into an inferno. Dropping strips of tin foil to confuse the German radar system, the RAF dumped tons of incendiary and high-explosive bombs on the city. When the ten days of sustained raids were over, 70,000 people were dead, and Hamburg as a city had almost ceased to exist.

The Luftwaffe, however, was still able to inflict punishing losses bombers that attacked strategic ta gets farther inland, beyond the ran of escorting fighters. Almost o third of the B-24's that made a lo level raid on Ploesti in August we shot down. Sixty planes and th crews were lost on August 17 in rai against Schweinfurt and Rege burg, and, in October, 148 bombe were lost in six days. The Combin Bomber Offensive was damagi Germany, but the cost was high.

An intimate look at the price paid by the men who carried out the strategic bombing of Europe is provided by these photographs. At left, a B-24 Liberator, its aft section in flames, continues to roar ahead after it was hit by antiaircraft fire over Quakenbrück, Germany. A moment later, the whole plane exploded. Below, a torn bomber of the Fifteenth Air Force drops away from its companion B-24. Despite injured wings, crippled engines, and other serious conditions, some bombers made it home, their crews often flying with little more than perseverance and a prayer.

At left, a B-24 of the Ninth Air Force flies over the burning Astra Romana refinery at Ploesti, Rumania, during the raid of August, 1943.

Global Bases

Mechanics change an engine at Munda, New Georgia, in the painting above by Robert Laessig. After fierce fighting, the Solomon Islands strip fell to the Americans in August, 1943. The Japanese lost 350 planes in their futile attempt to hold the base.

ARMY TIME-LIFE COLLECTION, DEFENSE DEPT.

At an American base in the Aleutians, depicted above by Ogden Pleissner, ground crews watch planes returning from a mission. On the opposite page is the American airfield at Kweilin, China, where the buttes helped to provide concealment.

In the Pacific and the Far East, Japanese confidence was still high in the late summer of 1942. In their conquered territories were ample supplies of oil, rubber, minerals, and food. Only with submarines and a few remotely-based aircraft could the Allies interfere with Japanese access to these supplies.

Moreover, aggression and expansion were still proceeding. China's life line, the Burma Road, was cut. The Zero was still the best fighter plane in the Pacific, and under its air-cover the campaign to isolate Australia was moving ahead.

Serious reversals began to occur in August. In New Guinea the Allies commenced to push back the Japanese, and on Guadalcanal in the Solomons an invasion by Marines turned into the start of an American counterthrust. Once the tide turned, Japanese difficulties mounted, particularly in the air. New U.S. fighters held their own against the Zero and gradually won control of the skies. And on the ground, in a growing number of locations that began to form links in a chain around Japan, bases were built for the increasing units of Allied planes that were arriving in the Pacific.

With an industrial technology and know-how that paled Japanese efforts, American engineers and Seabees constructed the bases in record time. Men and equipment poured from ships just behind invading forces, or were flown in by air to clear, grade, and level strips. Where the Japanese had used steam roller and manual labor, American engineers and Seabees utilized heavy trucks, bulldozers, graders, and drag lines to knock down jungles.

Even before fields were finished, fighters would fly in, heralds of big air forces that would soon turn them into important offensive bases.

340

South Pacific

On a captured Japanese airfield at Guadalcanal, American forces established the first Allied air base in the Solomons. Henderson Field was, depending on the weather, either a gummy mudhole or a dust bowl, and the pilots who served there experienced all the hardships and tensions of jungle combat that characterized the torturous climb up the Solomons.

Living amid insects and tropical downpours, they suffered from dysentery, malaria, and fungus. Adequate equipment was often lacking. And as the pilots took to the air, they did so with the knowledge that the enemy's fighters were faster and more numerous than their own.

But under the command of Marine Brigadier General Roy Geiger, they shot down scores of enemy planes. "[They] fought on day after day, while their friends were killed around them," Australian Commander Eric Feldt said later, and "it was their unabated aggressiveness, taking to the air at every alarm, that began the decline of the Japanese Air Force."

BELOW: *A dramatic sequence of action photographs shows the death of an Allied plane. Two Douglas A-20 Havocs are first seen attacking Japanese installations at Karas in Dutch New Guinea. In the second picture, one of the planes is hit by antiaircraft fire and its pilot loses control. As the crippled craft plunges into the water and then explodes, its companion flies past.*

ABOVE AND BELOW: USAF

LEFT: *White phosphorus incendiary bombs, dropped by American airplanes, burst over Lakunai, one of the four airfields at Rabaul, New Britain. Three Japanese gun emplacements may be seen in the lower third of the photograph. Rabaul, a heavily-defended naval and air station, was a prime target for the Allies. By the end of October, 1943, the number of planes there had been cut by two thirds.*

BELOW: *The second-ranking Marine ace, with twenty-six Japanese planes to his credit, was Captain Joseph Foss of South Dakota, who was awarded the Medal of Honor for his achievements at Guadalcanal. His squadron, VMF-121, shot down 208 enemy aircraft, more than any other Marine unit. The top Marine fighter pilot was the colorful leader of the "Black Sheep" squadron, Major Gregory "Pappy" Boyington, who had twenty-eight kills.*

US NAVY

FAMOUS AIRPLANES: 1939-1945

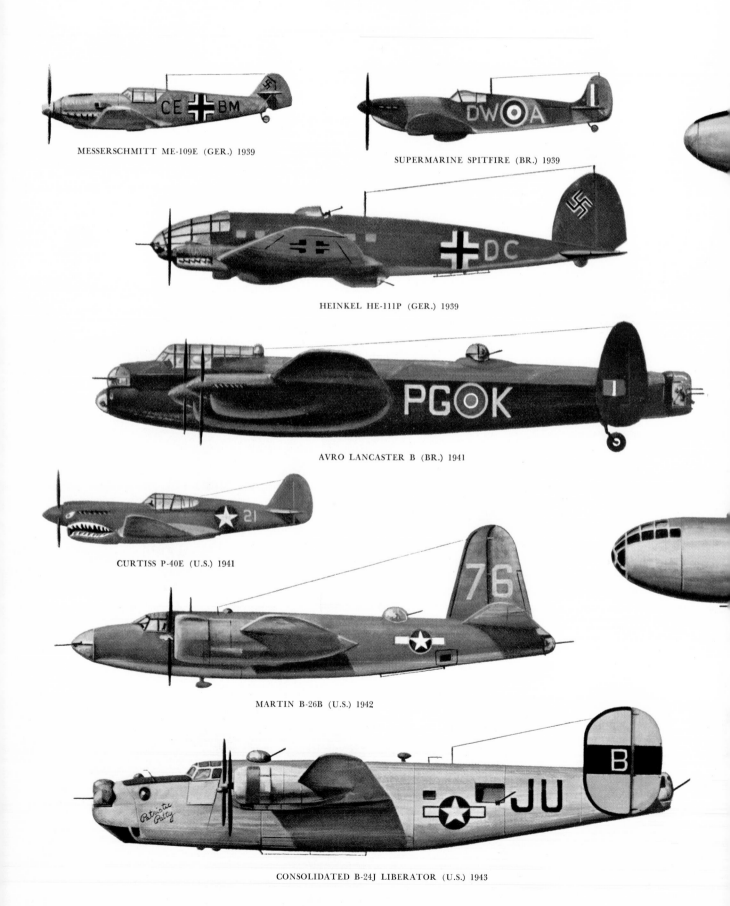

MESSERSCHMITT ME-109E (GER.) 1939

SUPERMARINE SPITFIRE (BR.) 1939

HEINKEL HE-111P (GER.) 1939

AVRO LANCASTER B (BR.) 1941

CURTISS P-40E (U.S.) 1941

MARTIN B-26B (U.S.) 1942

CONSOLIDATED B-24J LIBERATOR (U.S.) 1943

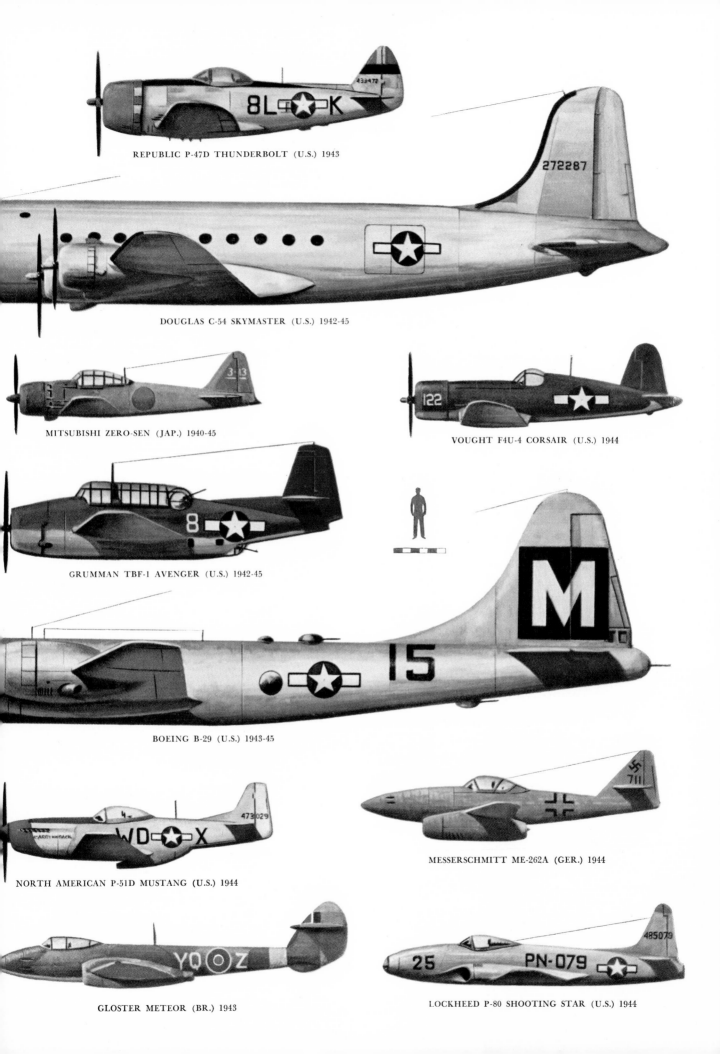

REPUBLIC P-47D THUNDERBOLT (U.S.) 1943

DOUGLAS C-54 SKYMASTER (U.S.) 1942-45

MITSUBISHI ZERO-SEN (JAP.) 1940-45

VOUGHT F4U-4 CORSAIR (U.S.) 1944

GRUMMAN TBF-1 AVENGER (U.S.) 1942-45

BOEING B-29 (U.S.) 1943-45

NORTH AMERICAN P-51D MUSTANG (U.S.) 1944

MESSERSCHMITT ME-262A (GER.) 1944

GLOSTER METEOR (BR.) 1943

LOCKHEED P-80 SHOOTING STAR (U.S.) 1944

Attacking Europe

When long-range fighters finally became available, the American Air Forces set out in earnest to accomplish General "Hap" Arnold's directive: "This is a MUST . . . *Destroy the enemy Air Force wherever you find them, in the air, on the ground, and in the factories."* The slogan, "Victory Through Air Power," which Major Alexander de Seversky had used in marshaling U.S. public opinion behind a strategic air offensive in Europe, began to come true.

On January 11, 1944, eight hundred American bombers, escorted by Mustangs, struck three major German aircraft factories. On the same day the Mustangs claimed over 155 German planes in the air. On March 6 the Allies dropped over a thousand tons of bombs on Berlin and shot down 176 Luftwaffe fighters.

American losses were sometimes also high, but the savage poundings disrupted German transportation and communication, shattered military and industrial targets, and seriously set back Nazi production.

After D-Day, the attacks mounted in intensity, and in time the offensive, hitting Germany from all sides, destroyed Hitler's war might.

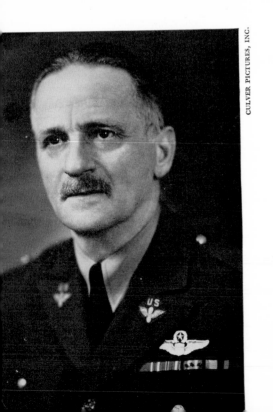

The commander of the U.S. Strategic Air Forces in Europe was Lieutenant General Carl Spaatz (left). After D-Day, his bombers concentrated on destroying the Nazis' fuel supplies. By September, 1944, gasoline production in Germany had fallen to 25 per cent of the normal output. And by January, 1945, enemy airfields were crowded with planes without fuel to fly.

Flying Fortresses unloose a torrent of bombs on a German communications center (above). In June, 1944, the Americans rained 120,000 tons of bombs on Germany.

The wreckage of railroad yards at Limburg, Germany (right), is seen after a raid by bombers of Major General Samuel E. Anderson's 9th Bomber Command.

The top American ace in Europe was Major Francis S. Gabreski (below). A member of the Eighth Air Force's 56th Fighter Group, the P-47 pilot was credited with thirty-one victories in the air, plus two and a half planes destroyed on the ground.

Death in the Sky

While bombers blasted German aircraft plants and fuel supplies, Allied pilots overwhelmed the Luftwaffe in the air. In February and March, 1944, the Germans lost eight hundred day fighters in battle, and by D-Day the Allies had full control of the air over Normandy. After that the Luftwaffe died fast.

Those who fought the German pilots never questioned their courage or competence. By the end of the war, twenty-nine German aces were credited with over one hundred victories each. Major Erich Hartmann claimed 352 kills, although many were no doubt "probables."

Each of the Allies had its own heroes and aces. Russia's top flier, I. Kozhedub, claimed sixty-two victories. Britain honored many men, including Douglas Bader, who led a fighter squadron brilliantly although he had two artificial legs. American aces included Robert S. Johnson, George Preddy, John C. Myer, David Schilling, John T. Godfrey, and Francis S. Gabreski.

OVERLEAF: *The end of Nazi Germany is symbolized in this stark view of the ruins and mud-filled shell holes of Wesel, pulverized by Allied air power. The northern Rhine city was bombed for a month prior to the offensive of March 24, 1945, when some 3,000 planes and gliders ferried the First Allied Airborne Army into the area.*

USAF

The gun-camera sequence of photographs at left, taken by an American fighter, shows a Messerschmitt Me-109 during the instant of its destruction. First the attacker comes in behind the Me-109. Then bullets set the German plane's belly tanks on fire. Finally, in the last photo, the blazing Messerschmitt blows up.

A Luftwaffe pilot, legs spread grotesquely, falls from his Focke-Wulf FW-190 (below). The dramatic photograph was taken over Belgium by Major James Dalglish of the Ninth Air Force's 354th Fighter Group. Flying a P-47, Dalglish riddled the German plane with .50-caliber bullets, forcing his adversary to leap.

352

The photograph above, by Edward Steichen, shows a pilot aboard the carrier Lexington awaiting the drop of the checkered flag before taking off in his TBF Avenger. The Navy torpedo plane could fly at 271 miles per hour. Grumman built 2,290 Avengers within a two-year period.

The take-off from a Japanese carrier is depicted at right in the war painting by Shori Arai. After 1942 there were no great carrier-versus-carrier duels, since the Allies had land bases from which to cover offensives. By that time, also, new American flattops outclassed the Japanese carriers.

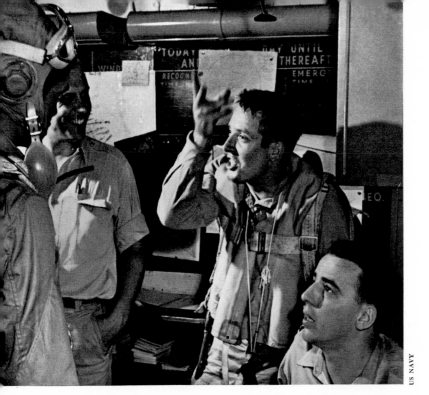

*he exhilarated Navy pilot above is telling his companions in the ready room of
e Yorktown about the bombing of Wake Island. Planes from the largest fast carrier
rce yet assembled—the Essex, Lexington, Independence, Belleau Wood, and Cow-
ns, as well as the Yorktown—made six strikes against Wake on October 5 and 6,
943. Twelve U.S. planes were lost, but twenty-two enemy aircraft were destroyed.*

Carrier War

In the sparkling waters of the South and Central Pacific, carrier task forces and their men and planes fought a continuing series of sea-air battles that steadily destroyed Japanese power.

On November 11, 1943, as U.S. Navy planes from the carriers *Essex, Bunker Hill,* and *Independence* prepared to launch the day's second strike against Rabaul, more than 120 Japanese aircraft swooped down on the American fleet. A wild, forty-six minute melee followed, during which more than forty enemy planes were destroyed, and not one of the American ships was damaged.

The successful defensive action typified the direction the Pacific war was taking. Confidently, Admiral Nimitz announced: "Henceforth, we propose to give the Jap no rest."

AF

Up the Ladder

As the Americans captured island after island from the Japanese, they perfected the strategic coordination of air, naval, and land forces that became the familiar pattern of the war in the Pacific.

An example was the campaign that seized the Marshall Islands. For weeks before the amphibious landings, Army and Navy pilots, based on the recently-captured Gilberts, pounded the enemy airfields with bombing and strafing attacks. Then, late in January, 1944, Task Force 58 moved up, and planes from its twelve carriers gained control of the air over the Marshalls.

On January 31, troops landed on Kwajalein Atoll, and took it with the support of tactical air power and gunfire from the ships offshore. On February 17, landings began on Eniwetok, which had been pounded by American planes for three weeks. And from the 14th to the 22nd, planes of Task Force 58 and the Seventh Air Force struck at Japanese bases in the Marianas and the Carolines, preventing them from sending aid to the Marshalls. By the end of the month, secure possession of the most important points in the Marshalls had been attained.

US NAVY

The F4U Corsair at left fires five-inch rockets at enemy hill positions on Okinawa. The F4U, first flown in combat in February, 1943, could reach 400 miles per hour. Many Japanese felt it was the best Allied fighter plane.

B-25's of the Fifth Air Force drop parachute-bombs on the Japanese airfield
at Dagua, New Guinea (above), in February, 1944. Dagua and other airdromes
around Wewak were neutralized prior to the Allied attack on Hollandia.

355

Kamikazes

During the last ten months of the war in the Pacific, at least 5,000 Japanese airmen sacrificed their lives in attempts to save their homeland by diving their planes into Allied warships. They accounted for 50 per cent of American vessels damaged throughout the entire war.

One officer, J. Bryan, III, of the *Yorktown*, described how he felt during an attack: " . . . you try to keep your terror under cover. . . . You jump aboard the first train of thought that runs through your mind, to escape your imagination's conjury—the blast, the crumpled bulkheads, the pinioned leg, and the flames . . . " Kamikazes, however, were the last gasp of a dying air force.

US NAVY

LEFT: *A suicide plane spins past the flight deck of the U.S.S.* Sangamon *before crashing into the sea. The organizer of the kamikaze forces, Vice-Admiral Takijiro Ohnishi, commander of the First Air Fleet, originally called for volunteers as the American invasion fleet neared the Philippines.*

RIGHT: *A breathless instant in another kamikaze attack was photographed from the battleship* Missouri, *as a plane bore down through smoke and spray on the gun crews. The name* kamikaze *(divine wind), commemorates a storm that saved Japan from invasion in the thirteenth century.*

BELOW: *A painting by Iwata Sentaro depicts a group of kamikaze pilots waiting to take off on their final mission. Another special Japanese air unit dedicated to mass suicide attacks was known as Jinrai Butai* (Corps of Divine Thunder). *Its pilots flew glide bombs called* ohkas.

The Franklin

On March 19, 1945, as planes from Vice-Admiral Marc Mitscher's Task Force 58 pounded targets on the Japanese home island of Kyushu, a single-engine enemy airplane swept out of the clouds and dropped two 500-pound bombs on the carrier Franklin. *The fires and explosions that followed (left) killed 772 men, but the survivors, many of whom had been on the carrier when a kamikaze gouged a forty-foot hole in her deck in October, 1944, fought to save the listing ship. An unsuccessful follow-up attack did no additional damage, and the* Franklin *limped back to America under her own steam.*

359

The Defeat of Japan

Congested cities, their buildings made mostly of wood, became tinderboxes on the home islands of Japan during the last months of the war. From March, 1945, B-29's of the 21st Bomber Command rained tons of jelly-gasoline incendiary bombs on sixty-nine major Japanese cities, razing almost 180 square miles and bringing death to more than 250,000 of the Emperor's subjects.

Then on August 6, as Allied forces prepared to invade Japan, a single bomb, equivalent in force to 20,000 tons of TNT, was dropped on Hiroshima. This first atomic bomb, which destroyed 60 per cent of the city, brought a fiery death to 80,000 persons and injured an equal number. Three days later, a second and more powerful A-bomb fell on Nagasaki. Terrible as they were, these weapons ended the war, and spared both sides the casualties of a bloody invasion.

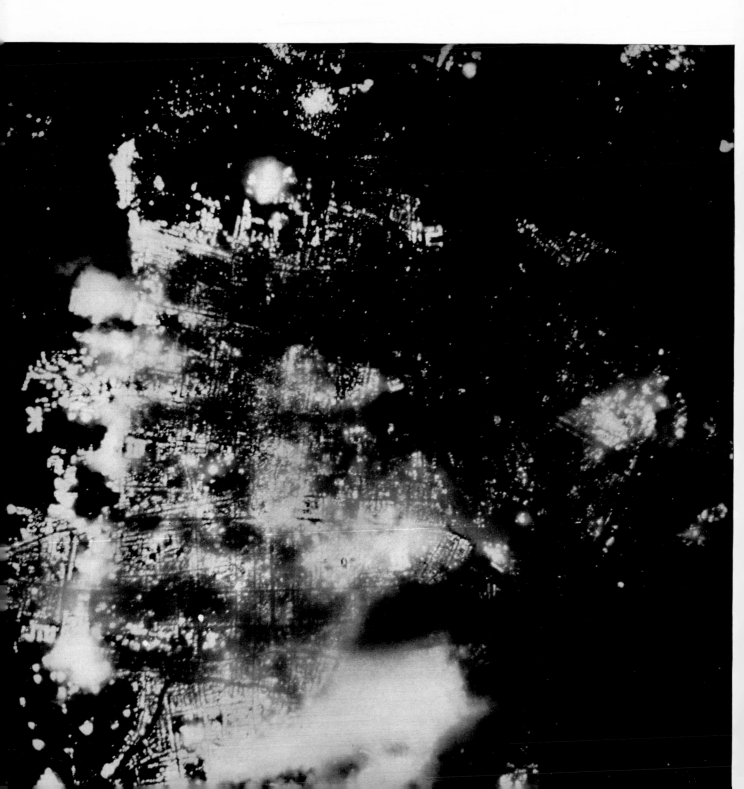

USAF

ABOVE: *Between July 10 and August 15, pilots of American Task Force 38 and British Task Force 37 literally blasted the remains of the once-powerful Japanese navy out of existence. This photo shows the destruction of the battleship* Haruna, *one of eighty-six large vessels sunk close to Japan.*

LEFT: *An incendiary attack on August 1, 1945, leaves night fires raging across most of Toyama, a Japanese aluminum production center. During the summer of 1945, B-29's often hit four cities in a single night, sometimes dropping leaflets first to warn the population to take shelter.*

RIGHT: *The August 9 atomic bomb, dropped from Major Charles W. Sweeney's B-29,* Bock's Car, *sends a mushroom cloud over Nagasaki. The explosion shook the plane, 29,000 feet in the air, "as if the B-29 were being beaten by a telephone pole." More than 35,000 people died in the city.*

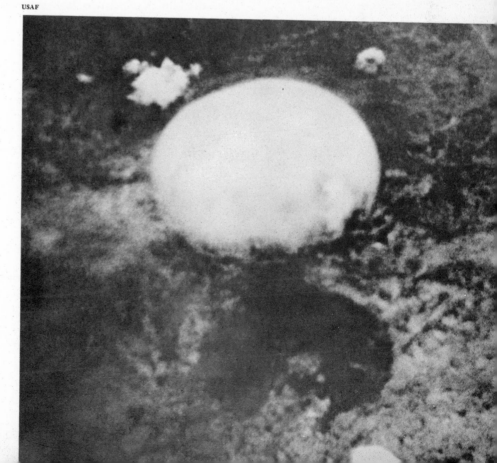

THE RULE OF AIR POWER

First Mission

In the summer of 1942 American air attacks began in earnest against Hitler's European fortress. Though it might not have been their toughest, the first mission to most men was usually an unforgettable experience. General Ramsay Potts, at the time a captain with the U.S. Army Air Forces' 93rd Bombardment Group, had flown across the Atlantic to England with his B-24 unit. Soon afterward he took off on his first mission—to bomb Nazi-held Lille, France.

It seemed to me that we had no sooner formed up and turned toward France than we were over there. This was because we had a tail wind of about 110 miles an hour. So we were going pretty fast, flying at about 23,000 feet.

We were supposed to have some fighter escort, but we didn't see them. Very shortly after we'd penetrated the coast, we ran into some FW-190's, and these 190's made attacks from different directions. I had a tail gunner who was a pretty good man, but shortly after the first attack I couldn't contact him on the radio and I thought that perhaps he'd been hit. So I sent the engineer back to find out. He came back and reported that the man was in a state of shock—not from being hit, just from fright—and he had frozen up. He wasn't firing his guns; he wasn't talking to anyone on the intercom.

Then my left-wing man got hit, and his airplane caught on fire, and I got a report that nine chutes were seen. This, coming on the heels of this problem with the tail gunner, was another sort of psychological shock, because the man flying the plane on my left was my closest friend in the squadron.

Anyway, we overshot the initial point to turn on the bomb run because of the very high wind; as a consequence, we actually made a very poor bomb run. We were being subjected to severe fighter attacks during that time. We dropped our bombs, but later we determined that we didn't hit the target. We turned toward home, and here we were going against the wind. Up until this point it had seemed that we were flying for a very short time, with everything happening; now I kept looking down at the French landscape and it seemed to me that we were hardly moving at all. Minute after minute rolled by, and it was an interminable time, throughout which we were getting these sporadic fighter attacks. There had been flak over the target too, which, since it was the first time we'd run into anything like that, was a little bit nerve-racking.

Finally we got home. We had two airplanes make crash landings on the field, and they tore off their landing gears and one of their wings. Then we got news that another plane had crash-landed on the beach.

I remember going back to my quarters after the interrogation and trying to light the small potbellied stove we had with some sort of cinders that passed for charcoal. I was so cold—I think not only because it was damp and chilly, but also I suppose I was experiencing a kind of shock reaction from this mission, plus evidence of fear, I suppose. I don't remember throughout the rest of the war ever again feeling as fearful about going on these missions as I did right after this first one. I couldn't get warm. I put on all kinds of sweaters and heavy jackets and even wrapped a big tartan blanket around myself, and kept trying to get the fire going so I could get warm.

North African Base

In the global war fliers and their planes coped with every sort of airfield. General Joseph Atkinson recalls one in Algeria which he used in late 1942 when he commanded the U.S. 97th Bombardment Group.

Our flying field was called Tafaraoui near Oran. Anyone who's ever been here will never forget it. It's the world's biggest mudhole. I've never seen soil composition like it. It looked like a light-colored sand when it's dry. Then, when it rained, it was impossible to walk any distance and nearly impossible to make any progress at all.

All we had in the way of transportation were a few jeeps, and so we had no way of getting the bombs over to the airplanes. We got hold of a few bomb dollies, but the mud was of such a consistency that the dollies would just become sleds. So we put a rope around the bombs and dragged them through the mud to the airplane, and hepped them up by hand onto the bomb shackles— and it was one hell of a job.

Decision for Victory

General Ira C. Eaker, participant in many historic moments of aviation before the war, was commander of the U.S. Eighth Air Force in Europe when he attended the Casablanca Conference in January, 1943. He tells of a critical decision made at the Conference—and of the coining of a memorable phrase.

When I got to Casablanca, General "Hap" Arnold told me that President Roosevelt had acceded to Mr. Churchill's request, and that we would give up daylight bombing and join the RAF in night bombing. I told General Arnold that that made no sense at all. I said, "Our planes aren't equipped for that, and our crews aren't trained for night bombing. The great tragedy of it is, too, that it will give the Germans just the respite they need. They will not have to man their west wall in the daytime, so that will cut their needed troops in two, and give them more men to put on the eastern front and more fighters to use."

General Arnold said, "If you feel that strongly about it, I'll arrange for you to see the Prime Minister tomorrow morning."

General Eaker and mascot in England

I spent the evening setting down all the reasons why we should continue daylight bombing. The next morning, I went over to the old P.M.'s villa. He came down the stairway in his RAF commodore's uniform. He took the paper and he said, "Now, you understand there's no lack of confidence in you. I greatly admire the operation of these gallant young men you are leading. But my mother was an American, and it just breaks my heart to see these wonderful young Americans sacrificed. Air Marshal [Arthur T.] Harris tells me that your losses are sometimes 10 per cent on a mission." Then he sat down on a couch and read the paper. He was sort of half reading aloud, muttering at this paragraph and that, and he came to the paragraph that said, "If the RAF bombs by night, and we bomb by day, bombing around the clock, the German defenses will get no rest." He repeated the "bombing around the clock" phrase. And when he finished, he said, "You have not convinced me that you are right, but you have convinced me that you should have your opportunity to prove your case. When I see your President, I will tell him that I withdraw my objection, and

that I advise that we continue the daylight bombing for a certain length of time."

A week or so after my return to London, I got a call from an aide that the P.M. was going to talk about the Casablanca Conference in the House of Commons, "and he wonders if you'd like to come." He made his speech, and he came to one point in the speech and he said, "The RAF will continue to bomb by night. The American bomber force will bomb by day. Bombing around the clock"—and he looked up at the gallery where I was sitting—"bombing them this way, around the clock, will give the Germans no rest." He took that phrase, but he had to be sure that I knew that he knew it was not deliberate plagiarism. So it was Churchill who saved our daylight bombing offensive.

Command of the Air

Through the early months of 1944 Allied air forces, struggling for control of the skies above Europe, incurred heavy losses. Much of the responsibility for grave decisions rested on the shoulders of the commander of the U.S. Strategic Air Forces in Europe, General Carl Spaatz, one of America's leading air officers from 1916 until his retirement as Chief of Staff of the Air Force in 1948. General Spaatz recalls an episode of the critical months prior to the Normandy landings.

I remember having a conversation with General Eisenhower. We had had some pretty heavy losses. On one raid we had lost thirty or forty planes, and he asked me whether we could take the losses.

I said, "What's that got to do with it? Are we getting control of the German air force? If we have to take the losses to control them, then we have to take it, that's all." You can't have a war and worry about that. What you have to worry about is whether you're winning or not. If you have a loss purposelessly, then that's stupid. But if you're winning, then it's not.

At the end of 1943 the German air force was still pretty strong, and there was no hope of making an invasion of Europe if we were going to be met by a strong German air force. They had to be subdued or forced back, and we had to do both —and we did it. The net result was that there were only about three or four German airplanes that appeared at the Normandy invasion. If they'd had two or three hundred airplanes there, that thing would have become a shambles.

"One Big Rat Race"

Lieutenant Colonel Robert S. Johnson, one of the numerous fighter pilots who helped escort U.S. bombers on raids against the Continent, became America's second-ranking ace in the European theater (after Francis S. Gabreski), downing twenty-eight enemy planes in less than eleven months. Here he tells of a mission to Germany on March 15, 1944, when he scored three of his victories.

There were twenty-four fighters escorting our 180 bombers, but sixteen boys had gone off in search of enemy aircraft. So I was there with eight fighters, trying to protect the bombers. Then I saw forty or fifty condensation trails way to the north, and I headed north to meet them.

I took very special pains to be clear on the radio, and I reported our exact position until I actually made contact with the enemy. I was real happy I did, because as I neared the big mass of condensation trails above me, I looked directly ahead and below, and there were another fifty enemy planes, perhaps more. And over to my right, there was another big group.

We dived straight into the ones below us and flew right through them, with guns firing. Then we turned and came in behind them. They

started rolling over, diving toward the earth. The group above us came down to help them, and the other group on the right came down too. There was one mad swirl of airplanes spinning around there within an area of five miles.

Well, we stopped them about three miles north of our bombers. My continuous calling brought eighty or ninety of our P-47's and P-38's, and there was one big rat race. There was absolutely no room in that sky for anyone. You can imagine the noise and the screaming of the airplanes— probably 150 or so enemy and roughly one hundred of us, all wide-open engines, all guns firing—and then about two or three miles south of us a whole row of bombers, sixty wide, heading for Berlin. You can imagine the noise that was heard on the ground below. Any tiny little spot that you could see of open sky, you would try to head that way, because otherwise you'd have had mid-air collisions.

Well, that particular day there were so many enemy planes available, all you had to do was fire your guns and you were going to hit someone. That was the day I got three. I don't know how many others my

Robert Johnson (left) before a mission

shots brought down—there were just masses of airplanes—and we had no idea how many we hit.

I only lost one of my guys, and I don't know yet how he was lost. I had to do some real heavy twisting to keep away from mid-air collisions, but I didn't get a scratch. In fact, none of our boys had a bullet in him, except the one that was lost.

Fighter Pilots In Tanks

Close support by tactical Air Force planes of fast-racing ground armor units helped hasten final victory in Europe after the D-Day landings. General Elwood Quesada, who headed the 9th Tactical Air Command, recalls what was probably the ultimate in such cooperation.

The Saint-Lô breakthrough was, in my opinion, the most pertinent battle of the campaign. Before it occurred, I did everything I could to urge General [Omar] Bradley to concentrate his armor, and have the armor go through on a narrow front, and move fast thereafter. As an inducement to get him to adopt my approach to the problem, which was admittedly the approach of an airman, I promised him that each column would have a fighter cover from dawn until dusk, and that they would work as a team.

This was the start of our tank-airplane teams. We put fighter pilots in the tanks with an aircraft radio. They could talk to the crew of the aircraft in terms that were meaningful to fighter pilots. We had found that the average tank commander, when he tried to talk to the airplane, would say things like, "You see that tree over there—the green one?" To a pilot all trees are green and he can't distinguish one single tree. A pilot in a tank would say, "The target is twelve o'clock, two miles," or something like that—meaningful terms.

The problem was, what aviators would go in the tanks? Much to my surprise, they competed for the so-called privilege. They liked it.

General Elwood Quesada

So this was a very, very successful operation and proved to be a real bonanza. In our chase across Europe it couldn't have worked better because sometimes the tanks would be many miles ahead of their supporting units. The tanks could tell the airplanes where the targets were when the airplanes couldn't find them, and the airplanes would tell our tanks where the German tanks were to avoid surprise. So it made both forces effective. It was so successful that it was somewhat pathetic. The Germans would have a small contingent of tanks lying in ambush, and before they knew it, they themselves were ambushed. It was a slaughter, an outright slaughter.

Gliders In The Jungle

On March 5, 1944, glider-borne troops in the CBI theater opened an Allied offensive in Burma by establishing a base behind Japanese lines. Colonel John R. Alison, an American fighter ace with seven victories, describes the dramatic episode.

I think it was perhaps the most difficult mission I ever flew. I had never flown a glider, but I assumed I could. The afternoon before the flight I got in one and had them pull me up in the air—we were towed by C-47's, two gliders behind a C-47—and drop me so I could get the feel of it.

Then that night we took off to land behind the enemy lines. We flew without light, across rough terrain. We landed in a clearing in the jungle. The clearing was not smooth and the gliders were overloaded. They were coming in at too high a speed. We were hitting logs, we were falling into holes, and then gliders were crashing into each other. Twenty-three men were killed in the landing, and we had about sixty injured the next morning. But we had over five hundred men in and ready to fight.

Fortunately, the landing area wasn't fortified. We were afraid it would be, because the Japanese apparently got our plan. We had two places on which we were going to land that first night, but on last minute reconnaissance we found that the Japanese had blocked one of the areas with logs. If we had tried to go in there, it would have been terrible. The other landing area hadn't been blocked, and that's where we went.

Oh, we had all kinds of fantastic incidents with these gliders, landing and piling up, and going into trees. It all seemed much worse in the darkness, particularly when men were hurt and you didn't know how many. It looked like a tremendous problem.

That first night we lost one of our radio gliders en route. The other one got in, but it was damaged. Because of the accidents, I tried to send word out to stop all airplanes still towing gliders. The radio operator could only get out one word, and he got the wrong code word. He sent out the word for "disaster." That's the only message that they received in India. They thought we were all lost.

In the morning we had the situation well under control; we had our airport started. When we got our radio station established, I picked up the phone and called [Colonel] Phil Cochran in India. General [Orde] Wingate was at the radio with him. Phil asked, "How are you doing?" "We're doing all right," I said, which was incredible to them. Phil and Wingate—Wingate had wept when the word came back, "disaster"—had thought the whole thing was off. Phil said, "Can you make an airstrip there?" I said, "We're going to be ready this afternoon."

We had bulldozers, horses, and engineers on the gliders, as well as fighting troops, so by that night we had a rough landing strip. I think we took in over one hundred airplanes that night all loaded with troops. From then on we were in business.

Kamikazes

Admiral James S. Russell, who served with U.S. carriers in the Pacific, describes a destructive kamikaze attack by Japanese fliers off the Philippine Islands in 1944.

We in the carrier force [Task Force 38] had been cleaning out every field in the northern Philippines. Our fighters would go in every day or two and knock down everything in sight and burn up everything on the

Admiral James S. Russell

365

ground. We were enjoying a wonderful free hand, flying across Luzon and sinking ships coming down the western shore of the Philippines to Leyte to reinforce the Japanese fighting against us on that island.

Then the U.S. forces ashore thought their flying fields were in good-enough shape, and they announced that they would take over control of the air over the islands. But when we no longer struck the island airfields, the Japanese started building up their air strength, and it wasn't long till we had some strong raids coming out after us.

One day our fighters knocked down all but six of a group of about fifty Japanese aircraft. The first thing we knew, the survivors were coming down on us in slanting suicide dives.

The *Enterprise* sawed the wing off the one that was coming at her, and he dropped into the sea and blew up when he hit. The *San Jacinto* knocked down the one that was diving on her. I think the *Belleau Wood* also knocked one down, but the one that came down on the *Franklin* went smack through the flight deck. He actually hit with such impact that he went through just forward of the after-elevator and burst in the elevator pit. That set the *Franklin* on fire.

Well, another one came down and dropped a bomb on us, but missed. We said, "He's the fellow that's supposed to go home and tell the story." We were mistaken. He made an attack on the *Belleau Wood* across formation from us. It became evident that he was going to crash on the deck and sweep along and burn the airplanes. Apparently he was killed before he arrived at the deck, because he fell below the deck and crashed into the stern where, unfortunately, he hit the pilot's ready room and killed several men. So in our task group we had two carriers on fire out of four, all because we did not clean out the fields on the beach opposite us.

"It Was . . . Horrifying."

Saburo Sakai, the top-scoring Japanese ace to survive the war, was credited with sixty-four air victories. The following excerpt, from his book Samurai, *recounts a deadly battle over Iwo Jima in June, 1944.*

. . . then I saw what was to me the most hideous of all the hundreds of air battles in which I had fought. I glanced down to my right and gaped.

A Hellcat rolled frantically, trying to escape a Zero which clung grimly to its tail, snapping out bursts from its cannon, no more than fifty yards behind. Just beyond the Zero, another Hellcat pursued the Japanese fighter. Even as I watched, a Zero plunged from above and hauled around in a tight diving turn after the Grumman. One after the other they came in, in a long snaking file! The second Zero, intent upon the pursuing Hellcat fighter, seemed entirely unaware of a third Hellcat following in its dive. And a third Zero, watching the whole proceedings, snapped around in a tight turn and caught the trailing Hellcat without warning.

It was an astonishing—and to me, a horrifying—death column which snaked along, each plane following the other before it with determination, firing at the target before its guns. Hellcat, Zero, Hellcat, Zero, Hellcat, Zero. Were they all so stupid that not one pilot, either Japanese or American, guarded his weak spot from the rear?

The lead fighter, the Grumman, skidded wildly as it hurled back smoke, then plunged toward the sea. Almost at the same moment the pursuing Zero exploded in a fireball. The Hellcat which had delivered the death blow remained in one piece less than two seconds; cannon shells from the second Zero tore its wing off, and it fell, spinning wildly. The wing had just ripped clear of the fighter when a blinding flash of light marked the explosion of the Zero.

Saburo Sakai in 1952

And as the third Hellcat pulled up from the explosion, the cannon shells of the third Zero tore its cockpit into a shambles.

The five planes plunged toward the sea. I watched the five splashes. The last Zero rolled, turned, and flew away, the only survivor of the melee.

Tokyo in Flames

On the night of March 9, 1945, American B-29 bombers, flying from the Mariana Islands and coming in over Tokyo at 5,000-feet altitude, devastated the Japanese capital with fire bombs. General Thomas Power, who led the raid under the direction of General Curtis LeMay, commander of the U.S. Twentieth Air Force, describes the mission.

That fire raid was the most destructive single military action in the history of the world. In fact, that raid caused more casualties than the atom-bomb attacks on Hiroshima and Nagasaki. If you had sat up there as I did and watched the fire develop, you would understand that.

I don't remember the exact number of bombs we dropped, but it must have been tens of thousands because these fire bombs break up and a B-29 can carry close to 20,000 pounds of bombs.

The best way to describe what it looks like when these fire bombs come out of the bomb bay of an airplane is to compare it to a giant pouring a big shovelful of white-hot coals all over the ground, covering an area about 2,500 feet in length and some 500 feet wide—that's what each single B-29 was doing! There must have been well over three hundred airplanes, all of them spewing these white-hot incendiaries. They started fires everywhere. Of course, Tokyo was a highly inflammable city, and as the fire swathes widened and came together, they built up into one vast fire.

From a military point of view it was a tremendously successful raid. Over fifteen square miles were burned out. We took a pretty good licking in our outfit. As a matter of fact, we lost seven airplanes on that one mission. But, surprisingly enough, we did not lose a man on the next four missions. Of course, when the target is heavily defended, the first unit to come in is exposed to most of the defensive firepower. But once the fire gets going and everything starts going to hell, the defenses just fall apart completely.

General Thomas Power

The Hiroshima Bomb

Colonel Paul W. Tibbets, Jr., commander of the Enola Gay *(named for his mother), the B-29 that dropped the world's first atomic bomb, tells of the destruction of Hiroshima on August 6, 1945.*

As far as I was concerned it was a perfect operation. We got out of there without any trouble. We heard the blast and felt it; it rocked us exactly as they said it would. In other words, we made our turn, and as we leveled out of our turn the flash occurred. The man in the tail gunner's position said, "I can see it coming," meaning the shock wave. He had been told to watch for this. Well, by the time he said that, the first one hit us. It was a real wallop—a real bang. It made a lot of noise and it really shook the airplane. The second hit us with less force, and the third one was very negligible.

When we got hit by the shock wave, I rolled right into another bank, a little bit easier this time and came right on around, because with all this going on, I wanted to get a look at it. There was the mushroom growing up, and we watched it blossom. And down below it the thing reminded me more of a boiling pot of tar than any other description I can give it. It was black and boiling underneath with a steam haze on top of it. And, of course, we had seen the city when we went in, and there was nothing to see when we came back. It was covered by this boiling, black-looking mess. We made some photographs real quickly and as we did that we approached this big cloud. Well, of course, I knew I didn't want to fly into that cloud; I knew it was hot with radiation. So we turned off. We were at 33,000 feet. I told the boys, "O.K. now, let's get all the air speed we can and get offshore." I knew that if they shot us down over the water there would be Navy vessels or submarines to pick us up. We did see one fighter, but he didn't

USAF

Paul Tibbets after the Hiroshima raid

come anywhere near us, and it was an easy flight home.

The mood was very quiet. Everybody was tired. It was all over. Here we were out over the water and everybody knew that it was just a ride home now, so we took turns sleeping. I had lain down and slept for about an hour, I guess. The reaction didn't set in for another day. The guys who were working on the airplanes weren't impressed until the information was public; then they came in with their eyes wide open and asked, "Gee, is it true?" Then, of course, everybody got to feeling real proud of the part he got to play in it. I imagine some pretty wild tales flew around; the stories got pretty big.

I felt nothing about it. I was told —as a military person—to do something. I recognized, as somebody said a long time ago, war is hell. I don't know how many people were killed; I didn't want anybody to get killed. But let's face it, if you're going to fight a war, you fight it to win and use any method you can. It wasn't my decision to make morally, one way or the other. I did what I was told. I can assure you that I can sleep just as peacefully at night as anybody.

367

An X-15, carried aloft under the wing of a B-52, tests its fuel jettison system before being dropped for a high-altitude flight.

POSTWAR

The months following V-J Day saw a drastic and dangerous decline in the air power of the free world. Taught by centuries of experience that global responsibilities outlast wars, the British were carefully slow in releasing their military aircrews. But the Americans, convinced that their monopoly of the atomic bomb gave them all the security they needed, joyfully began beating their swords into new automobiles and their spears into television sets.

As a result, American air strength simply melted away. So rapid was the demobilization that equipment worth millions of dollars rusted into junk overseas for lack of trained personnel to care for it. On V-J Day the U.S. Army Air Forces had two and a quarter million men. By the end of the year, fewer than 900,000 remained, and by the spring of 1947 the air force of the most powerful nation on earth had shrunk to a fraction over 300,000 men, of whom only 25,000 were flying personnel.

Since V-J Day, meanwhile, sentiment in the United States had been building for the creation of a unified national military establishment, with Army, Navy, and Air Force departments under a Secretary of Defense. Within this framework, the older services could at last agree to make absolute the independence of the Air Force, which, under the stress of conflict, had achieved actual if not statutory autonomy. These changes went into effect in September, 1947, after passage of the National Security Act. In the new setup, James Forrestal became the first Secretary of Defense; Stuart Symington, Secretary of the Air Force; and General Carl Spaatz, the first Chief of Staff, United States Air Force.

"Unification," as the reorganization was somewhat euphemistically called, was not a victory for Billy Mitchell's concept of a single, unified national air force. As a matter of fact, each service—Army, Navy, Marine Corps, and Air Force—was now to a greater or lesser degree organized around air power and had its own air component. But, for all the compromises, there was little doubt that the Air Force had emerged as the dominant military service, and that air power had been confirmed as the nation's first line of defense.

Starved for consumer goods, the American people at the same time had been clamoring happily for more of everything—including air travel. The public no longer feared or distrusted flying. Some 13,000 DC-3's had been built; they seemed as reliable as rocking chairs. More than 1,100 DC-4's had come off the assembly lines. By the end of the war the big four-engine Douglas transports, aided by a military version of the graceful Lockheed Constellation, were carrying 44 per cent of all military air cargoes, daily spanning the Atlantic as casually as if it were a lake. At the end of hostilities, many of these airplanes became available for civilian use at a fraction of cost. With them, and with huge and newer cargo-carrying Curtiss C-46 Commandos, independent airlines like Slick, Riddle, Resort, and the Flying Tigers sprang up to help meet the demand for freight and passenger service. "Non-skeds" they were called, since often they adhered to no fixed schedules.

Fierce competition among American airplane builders, plus years of experience, made the postwar piston-engine American transport the most successful passenger-carrying aircraft in the world. While the major airlines raced to see which could be the first with non-stop transcontinental service, excellent short-haul aircraft like the Martin 404 and the Convair CV-240 appeared. In 1948, in an effort to attract still more customers, the major airlines offered reduced "aircoach" fares. By 1957 these "tourist" flights were accounting for almost 40 per cent of all domestic passenger traffic and 65 per cent of international traffic.

Meanwhile, the British were not idle. English engineers had become increasingly interested in the turboprop airplane, a compromise between the piston engine and the pure jet, which seemed to offer the best combination of speed and economy for the short-haul type of air traffic that prevailed in Europe. As a result, Britain was the first to build such an engine, the Rolls-Royce Trent, which was first tested in a Gloster Meteor in September, 1945. Three years later, the British flew the first turboprop airplane in history, the Vickers V-630 Viscount.

The year after the war, the United States armed services staged some dramatic flights that helped remind the public that military aircraft were still around —and still capable of great things. In October, 1946, the *Truculent Turtle,* a twin-engine landplane, designed by Lockheed and the Navy, flew nonstop and without refueling from Perth, Australia, to Columbus, Ohio—a distance record of 11,236 miles that remained unbroken for fifteen years (until January, 1962, when an Air Force B-52H flew 12,519 miles, from Okinawa to Spain). Soon afterward, the Air Force sent a B-29 on a 9,500-mile flight from Hawaii to Cairo, Egypt, by way of the North Pole.

By this time the spectacular B-36 was in the air. Ordered in 1941 as an intercontinental bomber that could strike Berlin from American bases in case of Hitler's conquering England, the huge plane weighed more than six times as much as a B-17 and was powered initially by six pusher propellers driven by conventional reciprocating engines. It could carry a 10,000-pound bomb load 10,000 miles.

Already it was obvious that such piston-driven monsters were headed for extinction; compared to the onrushing jets they were cumbersome and slow. But in the growing tensions between the East and West, the B-36 was a necessary interim aircraft and a deterrent to potential warmakers.

In fighter planes the change-over from piston engines to jets was already well advanced. German and British pioneering in this direction had led to substantial progress during the war, but America was not far behind. The first jet airplane to fly in the United States was the experimental Bell XP-59A Airacomet. Powered by two General Electric turbojets based on a British model designed in the 1930's by Frank J. Whittle, it was rushed to completion in 1942. It was never put into production; its speed was too slow for a jet, and its range was too limited. But it was an important test vehicle, and was followed by the faster Lockheed P-80, the Air Force's first operational jet fighter,

which was in the air by January, 1944—though it saw no combat until the Korean conflict.

In 1944 the Bell Aircraft Corporation had also been working on an experimental rocket plane to be known as the X-1. Douglas, too, had been developing a jet single-seater, the D-558, which was later to be powered with rocket engines and called the Skyrocket. Both these planes were designed to break through what had been considered a serious technological obstacle to aviation progress: the sound barrier. Early attempts to achieve supersonic flight were extremely hazardous. In Great Britain Geoffrey de Havilland, son of the designer, carried out assaults on the invisible barrier with great courage and determination. But on September 27, 1946, his swept-wing DH-108 disintegrated at or near the speed of sound, and he was instantly killed.

Just over a year later, on October 14, 1947, a twenty-five-year-old American combat veteran named Charles Yeager climbed into the tiny, needle-nosed Bell X-1 whose four rocket motors could gulp their entire fuel supply in two and a half minutes. Carried aloft by a B-29 and air-launched over Muroc Dry Lake in California, the X-1 zoomed above 37,000 feet and flashed through the critical transonic area to a speed of a little over Mach 1, the speed of sound. In September, 1948, using a later version of the plane in which young de Havilland had met his death, the British also broke the sound barrier.

Unfortunately, however, in this postwar period peaceful scientific research was not the prevailing urge throughout the world. In the summer of 1948 the Soviets moved to test the morale and unity of the Western Allies. With Berlin isolated deep in the Russian zone of occupied Germany, they imposed increasingly severe restrictions on the land routes used by the Western powers to supply their sectors of the city. By June 22 all surface traffic had been halted.

But the Allies had been guaranteed the use of three air corridors, each twenty miles wide, leading from West Germany to Berlin. Faced with the choice of abandoning the two million Berliners in their sectors of the city or attempting the task of supplying them by air, the British and Americans did not hesitate.

The Berlin airlift was a brilliant demonstration of technical competence and international and interservice cooperation. American Navy tankers brought huge supplies of aviation fuel to Bremerhaven. Navy cargo planes joined the Air Force C-54's in round-the-clock flights to Berlin. The Army's Transportation Corps trucked cargo to the planes. British air tankers took over responsibility for hauling all petroleum products to the beleaguered city. German civilians worked furiously to extend and maintain runways.

By January, 1949, the airlift was providing enough food to permit the individual Berliner's food ration to be raised from 1,600 to 1,880 calories daily. As spring came, and the weather improved, so did efficiency. On a single day in mid-April, in an effort that became known as the "Easter Parade," a total of 1,398 flights brought a record-breaking 12,940 tons into the city. Watching glumly, the Russians evidently decided that the airlift had become a Cold War victory for the Allies. The next month they ended the blockade.

Balked at Berlin, international communism looked for a more promising pressure area, and found one in Korea. That country had been divided ever since the Soviet Union had occupied the northern portion to receive the surrender of Japanese troops in 1945. Beyond the strategic defense perimeter of the United States, South Korea was a tempting target for aggression. On June 25, 1950, backed by a small Soviet-equipped and Soviet-trained air force, Communist North Korean troops crossed the 38th Parallel.

American air power was almost immediately engaged. On June 27, flying from bases in Japan with orders to protect the evacuation of American citizens, long-range Twin-Mustang F-82 fighters intercepted a flight of five YAK's and shot down three of them. That same day, half a world away in New York, the Security Council of the United Nations approved a resolution urging members to "furnish such assistance to the Republic of Korea as may be necessary to repel the armed attack and to restore international peace and security in the area."

This made the defense of South Korea an international responsibility, and some of the members of the United Nations did "furnish assistance." But essentially the struggle that followed was a clash between the forces of international communism and the United States. By June 29, American B-26's and B-29's were in action, plus a handful of F-80 jet fighters. By July American carrier planes—Grumman F9F Panther jets and Douglas AD Skyraiders—were hammering enemy supply lines, and the U.S.S. *Boxer* was setting a transpacific speed record carrying a load of 145 Mustang fighters and other planes.

At first, such antiquated warplanes seemed adequate. The North Korean air force was virtually destroyed, and their ground forces driven back toward the Yalu River, which marked the Manchurian border. But on November 1 six Russian-built MIG-15 jet fighters attacked a flight of Mustangs just below the Yalu. One week later, the first all-jet air battle in history took place between the MIG's and F-80's. The Shooting Stars had difficulties against the newer swept-wing Russian fighters, but they destroyed one of the MIG's. The United Nations ground force advance

and the unification of a free Korea were more than the Chinese Reds could tolerate. On November 26 they crossed the Yalu in force and confronted the United Nations with an entirely new war.

It was imperative that the American Far East Air Forces hold the initiative in the skies if the U.N. ground troops were not to be overwhelmed. Fighter-bombers gave close support, and airdrops of vital supplies helped the encircled Marines fight their way back from the Changjin Reservoir. In mid-December the first F-86A Sabres arrived in Korea. Though they were a great improvement over the F-80's, they were still inferior in performance to the MIG's. But American pilots flying them proved to be more skilled and aggressive than their adversaries, and the Sabres made an effective record.

Both sides were hampered by political considerations that limited military operations. The United Nations forces could not bomb enemy supply bases in Manchuria without the risk of touching off another world war. The Reds could not fly combat missions from Manchuria without inviting reprisal; they had to stage their aircraft into North Korean airfields which were pounded constantly by U.N. bombers. Their efforts to keep these airfields operational were so unsuccessful that their ground offensive bogged down for lack of air support. In June, 1951, the Soviet delegate to the United Nations suggested that cease-fire discussions begin.

They did begin, but the fighting went on for another two years. In the summer of 1952 American air commanders tried to break the stalemate by bombing North Korean power stations, including the great generating plant at Suiho on the Yalu River, which was supplying electricity to war plants in Manchuria. Intelligence reports indicated that the Suiho strikes cost northeast China 23 per cent of its power requirements.

Limited though it was geographically, the Korean struggle was a full-scale war. Red China's twenty-two air divisions included some 1,800 aircraft and at least 1,000 jets. These were held at bay by improved F-86F Sabres, which in the later months of the war established an overwhelming superiority in combat with the MIG's. In May, 1953, Sabre pilots claimed fifty-six MIG's destroyed. Only one Sabre was lost, and the pilot was rescued. In June seventy-five MIG's were claimed, and the Sabres had no losses at all.

In the spring of 1953 fighter-bombers of the Fifth Air Force carried out a pair of attacks that may well have been decisive in bringing an end to the sullen war. The rice economy of North Korea depended on controlled irrigation from reservoirs that stored water for the rice-growing seasons. On May 13, fifty-nine Thunderjets attacked and damaged the massive irrigation dam at Toksan. That night the waters broke through in a devastating flood, wiping out rail lines and highways. Three days later, ninety F-84's broke the dam at Chasan, dropping bombs into the reservoir and using the water itself to transmit the blast effect. Again there was a disastrous flood. Under such pressure, the Red negotiators at Panmunjom modified some of their hitherto unyielding attitudes, notably their demand that all prisoners of war be repatriated regardless of their wishes. At last, on July 27, an armistice was signed.

Neither side could claim total victory, but the United Nations' two main objectives were achieved: naked aggression was halted, and South Korea's independence secured. For such limited success, air power could claim a large share of the credit. The Communists claimed repeatedly that if they had had the kind of air support on which the U.N. forces had relied, they would have driven their foe into the sea.

While the air battles had raged over "MIG Alley" in Korea, commercial aviation had put the first jet transport into operation. This was Britain's de Havilland Comet, which appeared in 1952 on BOAC routes to South Africa, Ceylon, and the Far East. Some felt the plane had been rushed into service, but for the next two years the graceful Comets were queens of the skies. Then, in 1954, disaster struck.

On January 10, taking off from Rome in good weather and climbing to its flight-plan altitude of 36,500 feet, a Comet suddenly and inexplicably disintegrated, carrying thirty-five people to their deaths in the sea near Elba. No distress signal was heard. The pilot of the Comet was making a normal radio report; his voice ceased abruptly in mid-sentence. All Comets were grounded and subjected to rigorous inspection. Then, on April 8, the same thing happened to another Comet over the Mediterranean. Again there was no warning—just instantaneous failure of a magnificent and proven airplane.

The Comet crashes shook the aviation world. But the whole history of aviation is the story of man's ability to recover—and learn—from disaster. The Comet accidents spurred the British to one of the most remarkable pieces of aerial detective work ever accomplished.

Groping in four hundred to six hundred feet of water with giant grabs and underwater television, salvage vessels recovered fragments of the airliner that had fallen near Elba. Meanwhile, back in England, three Comets were turned over to government engineers to serve as guinea pigs for exhaustive tests.

Two of the planes were flight-tested in every conceivable way. The fuselage of the third was encased in a huge tank containing 200,000 gallons of water. Every five minutes, by flexing the wings with hydraulic jacks and by raising and lowering water pressures inside the submerged cabin, engineers were able to reproduce stresses equivalent to a normal three-hour flight. Finally, after "flying" the equivalent of 9,000 hours in its watery tomb, the metal skin of the pressure cabin split open. Microscopic examination indicated that the cause of failure was metal fatigue, which occurred much earlier than any computation had indicated. Later, the critical piece of wreckage was recovered from the sea, revealing the same type of failure. The results of the investigation were made public in a candid and forthright report. Steps were taken to eliminate the weakness. Aviation moved on.

By now it was moving at dizzying speed. Throughout the 1950's, experimental aircraft driven by increasingly powerful rocket engines leaped to one record after another. At the same time, supersonic military aircraft were becoming standard equipment, with designers in Britain, France, the U.S.S.R., and other countries advancing along parallel lines. With the lessons of the Korean War still fresh in mind, Americans scored the most firsts. In 1953 the Air Force put into production the Pratt & Whitney J-57 turbojet engine, whose thrust of some 10,000 pounds made Frank J. Whittle's original jet design seem almost like a toy. The first operational fighter to achieve supersonic speeds in level flight was the North American F-100 Super Sabre, which set a world's speed record of 822 miles per hour in August, 1955. The "Century" series of supersonic fighters continued with the twin-jet McDonnell F-101 Voodoo; the Convair F-102 Delta Dagger; the Lockheed F-104 Starfighter, capable of flying supersonic straight up; the Republic F-105 Thunderchief, a radar-equipped fighter-bomber designed to carry nuclear as well as high-explosive bombs; and the Convair F-106 Delta Dart. For the Navy, a Vought F8U-1 Crusader carrying full combat equipment won the Thompson Trophy in August, 1956, with a speed of 1,015 miles per hour—an extraordinary performance for a plane capable of landing on an aircraft carrier.

One of the most significant aerodynamic discoveries of this period came from the laboratories of the National Advisory Committee for Aeronautics. Experimenting with transonic wind tunnels, NACA engineers found that air resistance could be significantly reduced by lengthening the nose of a supersonic aircraft and indenting the fuselage so as to give it a "wasp-waist," or "Coke-bottle" shape. Discovered and verified in 1952 by Richard T. Whitcomb, the "area-rule" concept was followed in the design of such fighter planes as the Navy's Grumman F11F-1 Tiger and the Air Force's F-102. It was also incorporated into the world's first supersonic bomber, the Convair B-58 Hustler, which first flew in November, 1956.

While piloted aircraft were driving toward the outer limits of mechanical tolerance and human endurance, the descendants of the old German vengeance weapons were following an inexorable evolution of their own. In the United States the Air Force developed the Martin Matador, and the Navy experimented with the Vought Regulus. These were subsonic, pilotless aircraft, carrying a warhead and driven by a turbojet engine after a rocket-assisted take-off. The Air Force also worked on two long-range pilotless bombers, Northrop's SM-62 Snark and North American's SM-64 Navajo. Compared to the buzz bombs of World War II, the Snark had tremendous range: its J-57 jet engine could keep it in the air for four or five thousand miles. But its subsonic speed made it vulnerable to enemy countermeasures. Even the Navajo, which was designed to be faster, finally had to be canceled after more than three quarters of a billion dollars had been spent on it—though it contributed considerable knowledge to future developments in guidance, rocketry, and aerodynamic configuration.

Another air-breathing, air-supported weapon was Boeing's IM-99 Bomarc, a pilotless winged missile designed to rise from the ground, seek out, and destroy incoming enemy aircraft. Launched by rocket power, the Bomarc was equipped with two ram-jet engines that enabled it to climb to high altitudes at speeds up to Mach 2.5, and made it a threat to any conventional bomber.

But now the winged, manned aircraft itself was facing competition in the development of fearsome descendants of the V-2. At new and expanded research centers, manufacturing plants, and test sites in New Mexico, California, Alabama, Florida, and elsewhere, work progressed on both intermediate range and intercontinental ballistic missiles. In September, 1956, a U.S. Army rocket team headed by former German V-2 experts, including Wernher von Braun, fired a Redstone rocket with solid-fuel upper stages 3,000 miles down the Caribbean range from the missile test site at Cape Canaveral, Florida. This rocket carried a dummy fourth stage. If propellant instead of sand had been loaded aboard, the fourth stage could have been sent into orbit around the earth. Thirteen months later, achieving the necessary escape velocity of some 18,000 miles per hour, the Russians hurled the first man-made satellite into space. The Russian *Sputnik,* a highlight of world-wide scientific activity in connection with the International Geophysical Year, aroused the American public's support for an accelerated program in the United States that would ensure an adequate supply of intercontinental ballistic missiles, as

well as boosters that would put America ahead of Russia in the exploration of space.

Research and development were quickened in both fields, and in the fall of 1959 the Air Force added the first Convair Atlas ICBM's to its operational defenses. At the same time, work progressed on newer missiles and on the more powerful Saturn booster. The latter would be particularly important to the space program, which was also taking large strides forward. Despite Soviet firsts in orbiting the world, both with unmanned and manned vehicles (Yuri Gagarin circled the earth three times on April 12, 1961, and four months later Gherman Titov achieved seventeen orbits), the U. S. National Aeronautics and Space Administration's civilian-run Mercury Project, using Atlas carriers, thrilled the American people in February and May, 1962; with full publicity so that no one could doubt their achievements, Lieutenant Colonel John H. Glenn, Jr., and Lieutenant Commander Scott Carpenter each orbited the earth three times.

The successes in outer space marked the dawn of a brand-new era in the story of man's conquest of flight. Space medicine, metallurgy, physics, and a host of scientific fields faced a future of expanding horizons. Programs designed to orbit and probe the moon, establish space stations, and reach distant planets demanded more powerful boosters, complex satellite systems, and space vehicles capable of carrying crews that could navigate at will through space and in and out of the earth's atmosphere.

The spectacular rise of the long-range rocket and the first successes in space provided a new assessment, also, of the piloted aircraft as a military weapon. Ever since the formation of the U.S. Strategic Air Command in March, 1946, the chief defense of the free world had been the retaliatory threat of its manned long-range bombers. Over the years it had been built up into a magnificent force-in-being, disciplined, dedicated, polished to split-second combat readiness.

In 1951 SAC began receiving its first B-47's, six-engine, jet-propelled medium bombers with swept-back wings and tail surfaces. Carrying a crew of only three men, the B-47 became for a time the work horse of SAC; more than 1,300 were built by Boeing before production was discontinued. By August, 1954, the production model of the B-52 was ready. These huge eight-engine jets cost eight million dollars apiece, as compared to an average cost of $315,000 for the old B-29; but they could fly at speeds of over 600 miles per hour and carry a formidable variety of weapons, including air-launched missiles. In 1956 the supersonic, delta-winged B-58 medium bomber took to the air, and on March 6, 1962, dramatized its astounding capability when one of them flew round-trip from Los

Angeles to New York in four hours and forty-two minutes, beating the sun, as it were, by covering the New York-Los Angeles leg in two hours, fifteen minutes, and twelve seconds.

To some fliers, the work with rockets and missiles had originally seemed to foretell a military "push-button" future, when manned aircraft—both the SAC bomber and the fighter plane—would be obsolete. Early-warning radar lines, like the Air Force's Ballistic Missile Early Warning System (BMEWS), combined with retaliatory ICBM's carrying nuclear warheads and ground-launched antimissile defense missiles, seemed to preclude the usefulness of the military aviator. But it soon became apparent that strategic bombers would be needed for some time to complement ICBM's, and that an antimissile missile was still far in the future. Moreover, if manned military craft were approaching an end of usefulness within the atmosphere, they were just beginning a new chapter in the rarefied higher altitudes and in space.

The transition was vividly dramatized by the X-15, North American's experimental high-altitude plane. In 1959 the X-15 made its first free flight, released from under the wing of a B-52. By June, 1962, this man-made needle with a volcano in its tail had reached an altitude of 250,000 feet. In November, 1961, with air friction heating its skin to 1,100 degrees, it had exceeded its design speed of Mach 6, reaching Mach 6.04, or 4,093 miles per hour. And there was still plenty of "stretch" in it; engineers predicted that it would ultimately fly faster than Mach 7 and reach a height of 500,000 feet, almost one hundred miles above the earth—or the area of satellites and orbiting space vehicles.

At the same time, other aircraft—still in preparation—showed the outlines of a future in which fighting men would continue to fly. The Air Force's RS-70 (originally the B-70) was planned to be a Mach 3 reconnaissance-strike bomber, able to cruise at over 30 miles per minute—faster than the muzzle velocity of a rifle bullet. Weighing half a million pounds, this stainless steel and titanium monster would fly at almost 80,000 feet. It would be driven by six General Electric J-93 engines delivering 180,000 pounds of thrust—or one third as much power as that generated by Hoover Dam. At Mach 3 the aerodynamic heating level would be around 550 degrees, yet inside the bomber the four-man crew would work in a shirt-sleeve environment without having to wear pressure suits. Three prototypes were being built. The cost: something over a billion dollars.

In the early 1960's the United States Air Force moved also toward a total vault into space with another craft. Under the project name of the X-20, it planned an outer-space manned vehicle; here a giant multistage Titan III rocket would be used to boost a space glider that would reach speeds of Mach 25, or 17,500 to 18,000 miles per hour. The X-20 would represent a marriage of the ballistic missile and the winged aircraft, and would be America's first truly maneuverable space craft.

Despite such attention to defense matters, progress in flight during the late 1950's was not limited to military and space activity. The first jet transport to fly in the United States was the Boeing 707, which made its initial test flight on July 15, 1954. In 1958 it was carrying passengers in almost vibrationless comfort at speeds of close to 600 miles per hour and at altitudes above 30,000 feet. The next year it was joined by the Douglas DC-8, with similar performance. In Europe, by this time, the Russians had an all-jet transport in service, the Tu-104; the British had introduced their improved Comet 4; and the French had designed a twin-engine jet, the Caravelle, with the engine pods attached to the fuselage just in front of the tail surfaces—an innovation that reduced cabin noise and made possible an efficient, unencumbered wing. Such aircraft were a delight for the air traveler, but their high initial cost and sharply-increased carrying capacity brought problems that still await solution.

As aviation approached the sixtieth anniversary of powered flight, the scope and variety of air activities seemed almost limitless. No prophet, however gifted, can accurately forecast the developments still to come. Commercial transports undoubtedly will soon be pushing through the sound barrier. Helicopters, which came of age during the Korean War and later found a hundred uses, will become increasingly varied in function and design. Nuclear-powered aircraft may appear, and airplanes may be boosted to great heights by jets or rockets, and then—seventy miles up—proceed to any destination on earth in a hypersonic glide.

One thing is certain: we live in an age of fantastic challenge and achievement. Time is being telescoped. Man lived on the earth a thousand thousand years before he flew, yet less than the span of one man's lifetime separates the epochal Glenn orbiting of the earth and that day on the North Carolina shore when the Wrights, braving a freezing head wind, lifted the first airplane into the air for the first immortal flight. That realization makes almost anything seem possible —if man is wise enough to wear his wings well.

ABOVE: *The first jet plane, the Heinkel He-178, powered by Hans von Ohain's centrifugal-flow turbojet engine, flew on August 27, 1939, at Rostock, Germany.*

BELOW: *Frank Whittle tested a jet engine on the ground in 1937. On May 15, 1941, he had his initial success in the air with England's first jet, the Gloster E-28/39.*

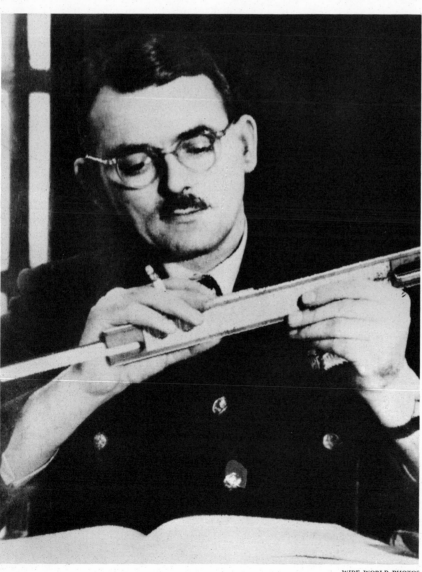

The Jet Age

For generations men had been interested in the possibility of designing aircraft based on the principle of Sir Isaac Newton's Third Law of Motion (to every action there is opposed an equal reaction). In 1930 a first important step in this direction was achieved when a British patent was granted to Frank Whittle, a twenty-three-year-old RAF officer. His design called for a jet engine in which air, drawn in at the front, was mixed with fuel, ignited, and ejected from the rear in a violent reaction that propelled the airplane forward.

While Whittle worked to perfect his design, a German, Dr. Hans von Ohain, labored along parallel lines and developed an engine that powered the world's first jet plane (upper left). By 1942 the first jet combat plane, the Messerschmitt Me-262, appeared in Germany and was rushed into production. Though it was designed as a fighter, had no bombsight, and possessed too short a combat range to be effective, it went into service late in 1944 as a bomber.

Meanwhile, Britain's second jet, the Gloster Meteor, also appeared in combat; and a Whittle engine sent to the United States in 1941 served as the prototype for the power plant that boosted America's first jet, the XP-59A, into the air in 1942.

Jet craft appeared too late to affect the outcome of World War II. But in the postwar years, the new planes soon proved their superiority over conventional aircraft in speed, power, economy of fuel utilization, and simplicity of design.

RIGHT: *A Lockheed P-80 executes a roll over irrigated fields in Arizona. This early American jet fighter, first tested in 1944 with a power plant derived from a British de Havilland jet, later became the F-80 Shooting Star used in the Korean War.*

Berlin Airlift

To the aggressive Communist world, the Berlin airlift of 1948-49 was a stunning setback. It was also a testament to heroic airmen and to the energies and initiative of the free nations of the West.

American and British cargo-carrying planes reached Berlin at intervals of three minutes, day and night. Pilots had one chance to land; if they missed, they left the area to avoid stacking. Unloading time was cut to forty-nine minutes per plane—enough pause for a cup of coffee before crews took off again. In the first six weeks some pilots averaged as little as four hours sleep per day.

Despite the huge traffic, expert planning by the Military Air Transport Service and other units kept accidents low. In fifteen months there was only one mid-air collision.

Cigar-chomping Curtis LeMay (left), vigorous Commanding General of the U.S. Air Forces in Europe, hastily organized the Berlin Airlift in June, 1948. By the time the Russians lifted the blockade in May, 1949, LeMay and his colleagues had surmounted staggering operation and maintenance problems and had delivered 1,588,293 tons of supplies in 196,031 flights to the isolated city.

Berliners (below) watch a C-54 transport taking off from Tempelhof airfield to return to one of the four West German dispatching bases: Fassberg, Celle, Wiesbaden, and Rhein-Main. Pilots like American Lieutenant Gail Halvorsen, who dropped bags of candy to children at the end of a runway each time he made a landing, symbolized the human link that bound Berlin to the fliers.

The Korean War

In the first phase of the conflict in Korea, American air power quickly proved the lesson learned in World War II. A month after hostilities began, Lieutenant General George Stratemeyer, commander of the U.S. Far East Air Forces, commenced a systematic disruption of North Korean supply lines and the destruction of the Communists' sources of supply. Within two months, he announced that his bombers had knocked out "practically all of the major military industrial targets strategically important to the enemy."

But the war was not ended. With one foe disposed of, a new one appeared. In November, 1950, Chinese Communists entered action from a sanctuary that could not be attacked. Air Force, Navy, and Marine planes battled Russian-built MIG jets over the Korean peninsula; and with F-84 Thunderjets and F-86 Sabres as escorts, B-29 Superfortresses pounded strategic targets in North Korea and in the area of the Yalu River border. But the principal fountainheads of the Communists' strength were protected, and the war dragged on, illustrating again—though this time by an inability to carry it out—the lesson of World War II.

Nevertheless, Americans controlled the air over the battlefields. "Without the support . . . of your air and naval forces," said North Korean General Nam Il at the truce negotiations, "your ground forces would have long ago been driven out of the Korean peninsula."

LEFT: *A dramatic combat photograph, taken from an Air Force RF-80 photoreconnaissance plane, shows an F-80 in action over North Korean rice paddies. The American Shooting Star has swept past a Communist T-3C tank (bottom), set fire to a car, and strafed a village sheltering enemy troops and vehicles.*

ABOVE: *A fifth victory on May 20, 1951, made Major James Jabara the first jet ace. His final score of fifteen was topped by Captain Joseph McConnell's sixteen.*

BELOW: *A Sikorsky HRS-1 evacuates Marine casualties after bringing up replacements. By war's end, helicopters had rescued more than 10,000 persons.*

MARINE CORPS PHOTO

An unusual experimental plane was the Bell X-5, shown being tested over the South west desert for the National Advisory Committee for Aeronautics in 1951. The plane wings could change the angle of their sweep in flight and provide data on swept wing

Supersonic Flight

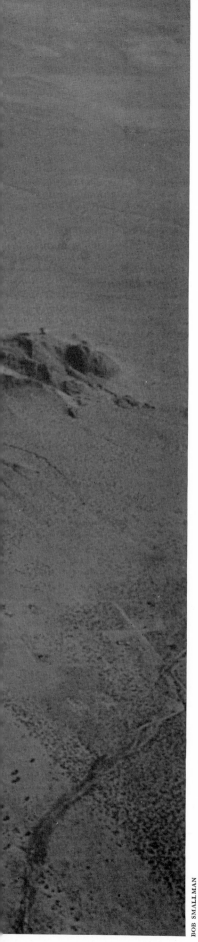

In World War II, combat pilots making power dives approaching the speed of sound had found their controls freezing up and their planes being shaken by severe buffeting. The problem arose, basically, from the compressibility of air. When a plane flies through the air at the speed of sound (approximately 760 miles per hour at sea level and about 650 miles per hour above 35,000 feet), the air particles ahead do not have time to change their position and follow the shape of the oncoming wings or fuselage. Instead, they are compressed into a shock wave, or wall of "thick" air. Jet engines at first did not have enough power to push through this wall, and the problem of penetrating the sound barrier gave postwar aviation a dramatic challenge.

When planes began probing the sound barrier, engineers began measuring their speed in Mach numbers (named for Dr. Ernst Mach, an Austrian physicist who had experimented with supersonics). Under this system, Mach 1 equals the speed of sound at a given altitude, and Mach 2 is twice as fast. Speeds between Mach 1 and Mach 5 are known as supersonic, and above Mach 5, hypersonic.

Charles Yeager's first supersonic flight (slightly above Mach 1) on October 14, 1947, in the Bell X-1 was followed by a string of further test flights in a variety of experimental craft. In August, 1951, William Bridgeman flew a Navy Douglas D-558-II Skyrocket at Mach 1.89, and in December, 1953, Yeager took a Bell X-1A to Mach 2.5—1,650 miles per hour. Almost three years later, after tests by Major Frank Everest and Captain Iven Kincheloe, a new plane, the X-2, also made by Bell, was flown at Mach 3.2 by Captain Milburn G. Apt, who was killed when the craft went out of control.

Other planes, flown by service and civilian pilots, pushed both speed and altitude records steadily higher; and by June, 1962, test flights of the North American X-15 rocket plane had taken the heat-resistant craft to an altitude of 250,000 feet—about 47 miles—and a speed of Mach 6.04 —4,093 miles per hour.

Test pilots Charles E. Yeager and Arthur Murray (right) pose in partial-pressure suits in front of the X-1A.

LEFT: *A Boeing B-52F Stratofortress shows its eight jet engines in pods beneath the wings. Later models carry four GAM-87 Skybolt missiles with a 1,000-mile range.*

RIGHT: *A Russian fighter-interceptor of the Cold War flies above Moscow in 1961. A Mikoyan design, it has two turbojets and a rocket engine and carries two missiles.*

BELOW: *A B-47 Stratojet, with crew of three, soars skyward with a JATO (jet assist take-off) boost. Lockheed and Douglas helped produce the Boeing-designed plane.*

Years of
Cold War

The peril to the free world, continuing after Korea, was clear for all to see: in a surprise attack long-range bombers, carrying thermonuclear weapons, could rapidly destroy a nation's ability to resist. Determined that there would never again be a Pearl Harbor, the American people looked to the Strategic Air Command to create an aerial force in readiness whose rapid and massive retaliatory striking power would deter the plans of a potential aggressor.

Under General Curtis LeMay, SAC flung a network of airfields in friendly countries around the world, berthing them with Convair B-36's.

The giant six-engine bomber, the biggest ever built, carried nuclear bombs and could reach any target on earth. Jet speed was added to SAC's deterrent force by the B-47 medium bomber, and in time the B-36 was replaced by the faster and more versatile B-52 jet global bomber.

OVERLEAF: *Aerial refueling helped SAC keep part of its force always air-borne. A KC-135 tanker operator (called "Clancy") lowers a pipeline boom (left) to a B-52.*

THE BOEING COMPANY

Fighters and Airlifts

On May 13, 1957, a unit of F-100 Super Sabres flew nonstop from London to Los Angeles, more than 6,700 miles, dramatizing the world-wide mobility of the U.S. Air Force's Tactical Air Command.

Rounding out an air power "second to none," urged by General Hoyt S. Vandenberg in 1953, TAC's family of supersonic fighters, reconnaissance aircraft, and mobile troop carriers and cargo planes is both a combat command and a supporting force. Air strike and airlift forces can move quickly to any "brushfire" war or trouble spot from Lebanon to Thailand. In support of NATO and tactical air units in Europe and the Pacific, TAC also provides fighter and troop-carrier squadrons.

Pioneer long-distance flights by jet fighters, troop-carrier maneuvers, intercontinental airlifts, and in-flight refueling all helped TAC develop its capabilities during the 1950's. By 1962, in a demonstration of their ability to cope with localized "hot spots," TAC personnel were training South Vietnamese in counter-guerilla air operations.

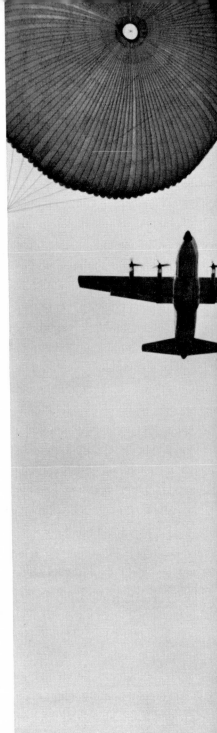

ABOVE: *TAC C-130 Hercules turboprop transports spot-drop cargo for the 82nd Airborne Division during 1962 exercises.*

LEFT: *A supersonic F-100, backbone of TAC in the 1950's, is zero-launched for a quick take-off within a short distance.*

RIGHT: *The McDonnell F-110 is a TAC version of the Navy's F4H, which set a speed mark of over 1,606 miles per hour.*

The New
Navy

In an age when control of the sea meant control of the air above it, a progressive U.S. Navy experimented rapidly with new craft and new concepts. To deliver attack wherever necessary, carriers with angled decks and nuclear power were planned to provide far-ranging bases for fast, versatile planes.

In the Korean War and thereafter as guardians of peace in the Cold War, catapult-equipped carrie[r] berthed planes like A3D Skywarrio[r] (with a 3,000-mile range); A[3] Vigilantes (with a Mach 2 speed)[;] F3H-2 missile-launching Demon[s] and F8U supersonic Crusaders.

At the same time, the Navy adde[d] Polaris-firing, nuclear-powered su[b] marines and furthered research in [a] variety of fields, including rocket[s] and high-altitude flights.

vy research has been typified by experiments with vertical take-off planes like the onvair XFY-1 (right). The delta-wing hter, tested in 1954, also settled back to vertical four-point landing on its tail.

e U.S.S. Enterprise (below), the world's st nuclear-powered carrier (with eight essurized water reactors), took to sea in 52 with an air group and crew of 4,600. s flight deck covers four and a half acres.

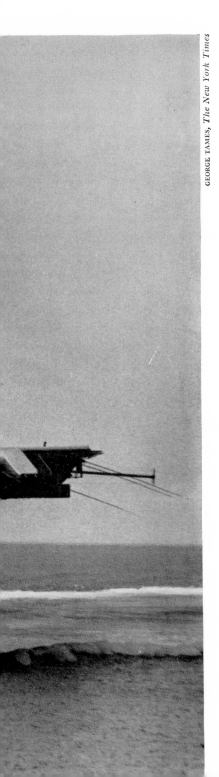

UNITED STATES AIR FORCE
032

CONVAIR B-36D 194

U.S. AIR FORCE

BOEING B-47 STRATOJET 1947

N4479P

PIPER AZTEC 1960

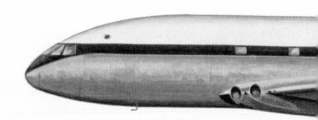

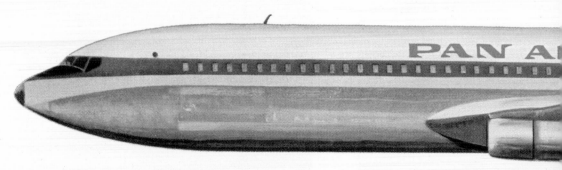

PAN AM

BOEING 707-320B 1962

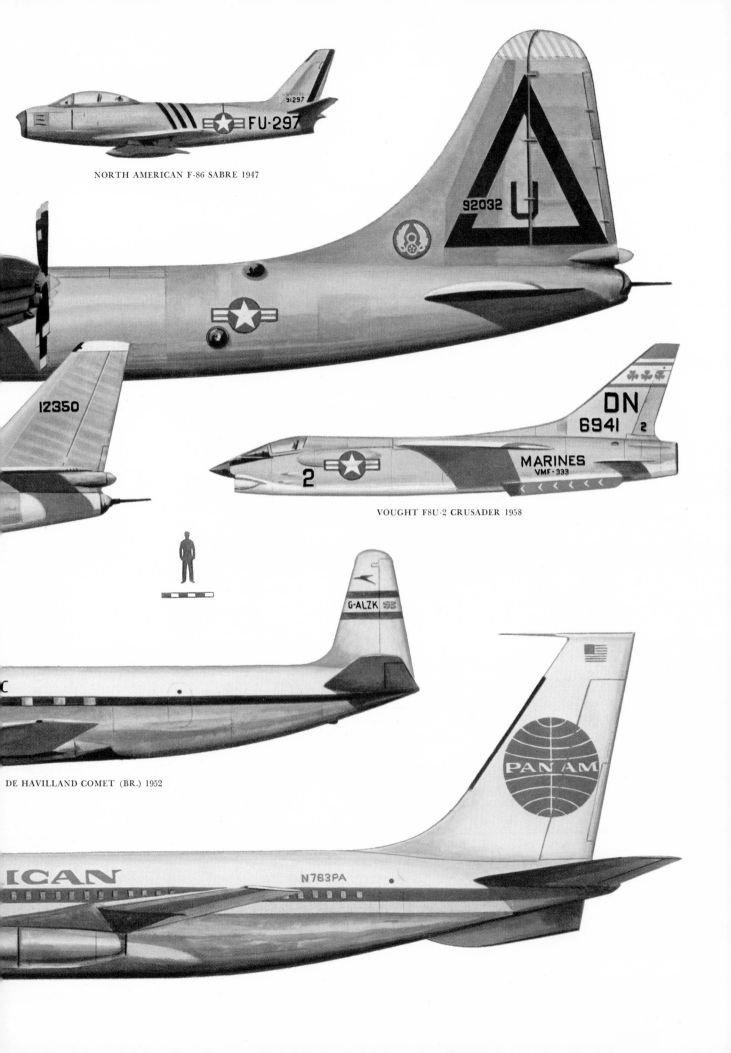

NORTH AMERICAN F-86 SABRE 1947

VOUGHT F8U-2 CRUSADER 1958

DE HAVILLAND COMET (BR.) 1952

At its July, 1961, Aviation Day celebration in Moscow, the Soviet Union unveiled the world's largest helicopter, capable of lifting a prefabricated house (as shown above), or carrying 180 soldiers.

Flying in formation at right are four Sikorsky HSS-2's, a 1958-59 amphibious antisubmarine model, adaptable as a 28-passenger commercial vehicle or as a troop carrier with a rear loading ramp.

Merely by shifting his weight in the desired direction, the soldier-pilot of the U.S. Army "Flying Platform" above achieves the ultimate in one-man military mobility. Rotors beneath the platform sustain the unique helicopter, designed in 1955 by Hiller.

Hovering Craft

The meteoric development in the design and use of helicopters during the years since the start of World War II has been due principally to the drive and vision of a single man, Igor Sikorsky.

In 1939, the Russian-born American, already famous for his giant flying boats, designed and built the VS-300, the prototype of the modern helicopter. Fully operational by 1941, Sikorsky's machine had a single main lifting rotor, as well as a small vertical one at the tail to offset twisting effect and supply directional control—a combination used in 90 per cent of current models. Three subsequent Sikorsky types were hurried into production, and more than four hundred of them saw service in World War II. In postwar years other builders, including Bell, Piasecki, Hiller, and Kaman, entered the field to compete with Sikorsky. In 1946 the two-seater Bell 47 became the first helicopter certified for commercial use. By 1956 large U.S. and European companies were operating big passenger-carrying helicopters between cities and outlying airports.

After the dramatic demonstration of the helicopter's military potential in Korea, Sikorsky developed the S-56, able to carry thirty-six fully-armed Marines, and the S-58, an effective craft for antisubmarine patrol.

Today, "flying bananas," "bubbletops," and all shapes and sizes of what are familiarly called "whirlybirds" and "choppers" seem to fill the air. Whether transferring a V.I.P. from an airport to the White House lawn, rescuing flood victims in Japan, exploring inaccessible canyons, opening up jungle wilds, or retrieving missile cones at sea, the helicopter gives evidence of living up to its boosters' claims that in time there will be almost no limit to the services it can perform in the air.

Travel by Air

Military transport aviation had familiarized air travel to thousands of servicemen and civilian officials during World War II, and in the postwar years international and domestic air transport boomed. Airports in America and overseas expanded and expanded again to handle passenger, freight, and mail business.

By 1961 the U.S. industry alone, with 49.6 per cent of international traffic, had an annual payroll of over a billion dollars. There were fifty-six certified American lines, carrying more than fifty-eight million passengers and some 885,000,000 ton-miles of freight per year.

Jets, which made air travel even more attractive, heightened the problem of airspace. And still, in 1962, two thirds of the American people had yet to make their first flight.

TONY LINCK

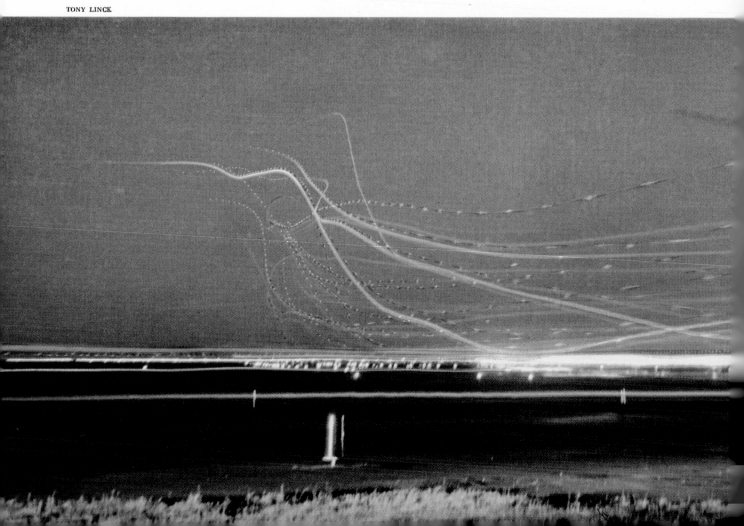

ABOVE: *Lockheed's 300-mile-an-hour Constellation was as fast as the Japanese Zero when it first flew in 1943. The Air Transport Command used it during the war as the C-69. Later, it blazed commercial routes for TWA to Europe and the Near East and provided luxury coast-to-coast service in the United States.*

LEFT: *Though it proved uneconomical for U.S. commercial service, Boeing's Stratocruiser of 1949 was one of the most popular planes ever built. Used on transoceanic and long-distance routes by Pan American, Northwest, and others, it seated seventy-five people and had a lower deck lounge and bar.*

BELOW: *Like the shadow of a passing era, the shape of a Super-G Constellation is caught in this night photograph of New York's $371,000,000 jet-age International Airport at Idlewild. One of the world's busiest, handling air traffic from all parts of the world, it averages some 726 take-offs and landings each day.*

TONY LINCK

Private Planes

The view at left of a 1960 "fly-in" to a gathering of private plane owners at Lock-haven, Pennsylvania, typifies the phenomenal growth in the use of small planes in the postwar years. Where once private planes were generally used for pleasure flying, they are now mainly employed as work vehicles. The pattern was set in the 1920's by Alaskan and Canadian bush pilots who opened the Far North with small, rugged craft like Junkers, Norsemen, and de Havilland Beavers and Otters. Today, in the United States, corporations shuttle company personnel from city to city in Lockheeds, DC-3's, and Aero Commanders. Professional men visit their clients in Pipers and Beechcraft; Western ranchers inspect their stock from low-flying Cessnas; and surveyors fly over watery reaches in Grumman amphibians. Private planes tie-down in long lines at almost all American airports, and the total fleet, approaching 70,000, is bigger than the air forces of both the United States and Russia combined.

399

Officers at Headquarters, North American Air Defense Command, Colorado Springs, Colorado (above), direct a twenty-four-hour watch on the continent. The screens plot aircraft and shipping activity, as well as space detection and tracking by the Arctic BMEWS line and other sensors

Convair's B-58 Hustler (left) was the Air Force's first supersonic bomber. Initially flown in November, 1956, the three-place craft is a medium bomber with four turbojets in pods. An analogue computer is tied to the plane's radar, inertial and star-tracking navigational systems

The Ramparts
We Watch

On May 1, 1960, a high-flying Lockheed U-2 was downed in Russia while flying a reconnaissance mission for the U.S. Central Intelligence Agency. The episode again dramatized the use of the air as an arena for major moves in the Cold War.

But an aerial camera that could photograph large parts of Soviet territory with piercing sharpness from a plane flying in the neighborhood of supersonic speed at 60,000-feet altitude also symbolized the state that aviation had reached. Almost every branch of science has contributed today to open new vistas for flight that the Montgolfiers and Wrights could not have imagined.

Defense necessities still give a military coloration to most of aviation's more startling advances. The triumph of a John Glenn, orbiting the earth, was part of the civilian Mercury project, undertaken by the National Aeronautics and Space Administration. But as it launched America toward a new frontier of flight, it served also to remind the free world that all theaters of the heavens are still ramparts to guard.

The defenses of those ramparts are an increasingly complicated skein of supersonic bombers, missiles with nuclear warheads, radar warning lines, and sophisticated computer systems.

In time, military use of the air may become unnecessary. But until then, men on peaceful missions must fly in the shadow of air forces and in regions dominated by missiles.

A smoke ring, caused by the firing of the rocket in the below-ground, silo-shaped launch site, circles skyward ahead of a 6,300-mile-range Minuteman missile. Some eight hundred Minutemen, one of the Air Force's family of ICBM's (others: Atlases and Titans), will be berthed at U.S. bases.

TOWARD
NEW
HORIZONS

Farewell to Propellers

The jet age reached maturity after World War II, but the first U. S. jet, the Bell XP-59A, was tested in secrecy over California's Mojave Desert in 1942. Lieutenant General Laurence C. Craigie was the first military test pilot to fly the jet fighter.

The testing took place up on the north end of Muroc Dry Lake, which was an excellent place to carry on these tests. In these early days, we needed a long run to get off; it actually took two miles. Also, Muroc was very remote from civilization, and this was a highly-classified project.

As I think back on that first flight, I always remember two very distinct impressions. One, I was tremendously impressed, just in the process of taking off, with the smoothness and the quietness, because all my flying life I'd been used to propellers—and the take-off with a propeller airplane, of course, is the noisiest period. When you suddenly find yourself flying with this absence of vibration and noise, it's tremendously impressive.

The other was just an accident of that particular airplane. We had a system built into that first airplane which was going to take some of the heat from the engine itself and bring it up between the two layers of glass which formed the windshield so that it wouldn't fog up. Through a failure in this early system, I was getting hot air piped directly into the cockpit. This was in October, on a very hot day out in the desert. So my other impression was one of extreme discomfort. On that first flight, I went up to about 10,000 feet and went at about 350 to 375 miles per hour.

As I said, it was a highly-classified project. So when we got out to Muroc for the tests, we were concerned over the fact that with that nice, clear air, people driving by on the highway three quarters of a mile away would see this airplane, and finally someone would realize, "I've never seen a propeller on that airplane."

I got to thinking about this, and came up with an idea. I had them build a big balsa-wood propeller around a ring. You could just stick the ring of this propeller over the rather pointed nose of the airplane whenever the airplane was outside the hangar for maintenance work, and it completely disarmed anyone who might have been suspicious.

On the very first flight, October 2, when Bob Stanley was flying, we got frantic telephone calls from the training base five miles south, asking us if we wanted any help. "You've got a plane flying around now that's on fire," they said. They didn't realize what they had seen. They'd seen this jet flying, and the combustion was not good on this early engine. If you looked at it from the side, you could see a black streak behind the airplane, but if you were behind the airplane looking up, that column of black smoke made it really look as if the airplane was on fire.

"A Good Way to Travel"

The effect of World War II on the airlines is described by Cyrus R. Smith, president of American Airlines and a pioneer in commercial aviation since 1928.

After the war we were, in a sense, starting all over again. Many of the planes that formerly belonged to the airlines had gone into military service during the war, and few if any of those ever came back. The DC-4, or C-54 as the military people called it, was one project that the airlines had under way when the war broke out. The entire production went to the Army, however, and the airlines got none. But we bought quite a few when the war was over.

Then, with the cooperation of Douglas Aircraft, we got the DC-6, which was pressurized and a somewhat faster airplane. Our problem was that we had no money to pay for the airplanes. It was difficult to finance aviation enterprises in those days—they had no record of historical earnings. But we did raise the money, and we did buy the airplanes.

I think one great effect of the war was that people became accustomed to traveling in airplanes. We had carried, on our own service, some seven million soldiers, and we'd taken the newness out of traveling by air. The people were pretty well used to flying, and they acquainted their families with the fact that it was a good way to travel. We thought, when the war was over, that there would be a very rapid expansion of business—and there was.

"Boy, It Sure Went!"

On October 14, 1947, Muroc Dry Lake was the scene of another historic flight: after being dropped from a speeding B-29, Captain Charles Yeager flew the Bell X-1 past Mach 1 to become the first man to break the sound barrier. Yeager, a World War II fighter pilot, recalls the event.

Prior to a drop you always had a feeling of anticipation. You wondered whether or not everything would work all right. But it's like flying a combat mission; it's the waiting that hurts you.

Once you were dropped, at about 25,000 feet, you were on your own and you felt perfectly at home. Actually, you just sort of floated a little bit when the mechanism released you from the B-29. You were subject to a falling sensation for a minute until you could level the airplane out and fire your rockets, and then it flew like a conventional airplane, except that you had rocket power and no noise and no moving parts. Boy, it sure went when you fired off your rockets!

I've tried to think back to that first flight past Mach 1, but it doesn't seem any more important than any of the others. I was at about 37,000 straight level, and it was just a matter of flying the airplane. It flew very nicely and got up to .97 on the Mach

indicator, and then the meter jumped to about 1.05 as I accelerated past the shock wave that was on the nose of the airplane. I was kind of disappointed that it wasn't more of a big charge than it was.

I had a couple of cracked ribs that day, by the way. I had been fooling around at a dude ranch the night before, and a horse flipped me. I ran my elbows through a couple of ribs. I didn't tell any of the guys. As I recall, it hurt quite a bit, but there's not a lot of strain in flying an airplane like the X-1, except when closing the door—you have to pull up real hard on the lever, and that was the worst part. But you're sitting in there and nobody can see you and you can grimace all you want to.

Total Snafu

The test pilot's lot, never an easy one, is summed up dramatically in this reminiscence of a single flight by Major General Albert Boyd, who headed many flight test programs for the U.S. Air Force.

I was flying the XB-45 bomber at Wright Field on a hot August morning in 1949. Immediately after takeoff, the gear failed to retract; it retracted only about a quarter of its travel, and it jammed in this position. We flew at an altitude of about 13,000 feet for quite a while, attempting to extend the gear. In the meantime the pressurization cooling system had failed, my communication system had also failed, and so had the electrical system and the number-four engine. We were suffering from heat; we couldn't communicate with anyone. The only choice we had was either bailing out or crash-landing. We didn't have ejection seats then, and bailing out wasn't a simple thing because we had to go out through an exit in the nose. So I elected to come down and bounce the airplane on the runway, striking the gear, attempting to lock it in place. But this didn't change the

General Albert Boyd during jet tests

position of it, so we elected to make a crash landing on the runway.

As I came around and turned on final for the landing, the right inboard landing flap failed at the inboard hinge, at an indicated air speed of about 150 miles and an elevation of about four hundred feet. When this big flap failed and rotated around on top of the wing, it caused the airplane to roll violently, practically on its back. At this low altitude, and with the other conditions being what they were, I knew this was the end. I didn't think there was a possible way of recovery, but I did all, as anyone will, to survive: I applied full power on the three good engines, and took advantage of what altitude I had to recover. I rolled out over the trees, just missing them, and then we staggered all the way around the field, carrying full control. It required all the aileron and all the rudder to maintain level flight. I asked the copilot and the flight engineer if they didn't want to bail out once we were back up to about 1,500 feet, and they said no, they'd stay.

So we made it around the field without having even enough control to align the airplane with the runway. We were about thirty degrees

403

off. Just as soon as we got over the fence we touched down on the sod. Any flat piece of ground looked wonderful—just to get it on a piece of flat ground. As I closed the throttles, and we touched down, the gear folded right away, and the airplane started skidding across the field, taking runway lights with it. We were going over that runway just as if we were going through a wheat field. We skidded a mile, and toward the end of the skid we saw a big ditch out ahead, and it looked as though the airplane would skid into it. Again, we thought we'd had it. But we skidded up practically to the edge of the ditch—and stopped. That was about as close as one can come.

War With the Communists

The crucial role of air power in the Korean War is made plain by General Otto P. Weyland, who served from 1950 to 1954 as Vice-Commander and Commander of the U.S. Far East Air Forces and of the United Nations Air Forces.

We were far outnumbered on the ground; there was no question about it. But when the Chinese ground forces intervened, they were not accompanied by concomitant air power. Now a big army takes a lot of supplies, but we were cutting them off. The Communists came to the conclusion that they would never achieve any goal unless they could overcome the disparity in the air.

They had been operating out of Manchuria, but the MIG was a short-range airplane compared to ours, and they couldn't get down as far as our main ports and establishments, operate effectively, and still get back home. The obvious solution for them was to establish forward airfields. So they started construction of four jet airfields about sixty or seventy miles inside North Korea, in from the Yalu River. The first thing they did was to put in a large concentration of antiaircraft. They had more

General Otto P. Weyland

flak around those positions than even the best German airfields had in World War II. It was rough. And they were under the umbrella of the fighter effort from across the Yalu where they had radar control. What they hoped to do was to establish a clutch of airfields, and then move in fighters and have local air superiority. Then, I suspect, they were going to establish another clutch of airfields further forward and then move their fighters forward. Then they could move in their offensive aircraft.

Well, I watched the airfield construction carefully, and I just let them go on with the building of them until they got about 75 to 90 per cent complete. We'd photograph them every day we could. When they were nearing completion, then I laid very, very heavy air strikes on the airfields. We put on a very heavy fighter escort. This was one occasion on which the Communist fighters really fought. They were pretty vicious about it. And we learned that you can't protect bombers with fighters against high-speed jet airplanes. We lost quite a few B-29's, but then I shifted to night operations, and we knocked out the airfields—all of them. But the Communists just went right back

to work and doubled the labor force on them. We kept after it, and after about three months it became obvious to them that they would never succeed in making the airfields operational. They finally gave it up as a bad job. That was a decisive element in the Korean War. That proved that they were not going to get their aircraft where they could really use them. In other words, we maintained unquestioned air superiority right up to the last day.

Jet Ace

Colonel James Jabara, who had been a fighter pilot in World War II, shot down fifteen Communist planes during the Korean War. He describes his fifth victory—which made him the first jet ace.

When we first got to Korea, we had seventy-five F-86's, and the Chinese had at least five hundred MIG's. Now, that's a lot of MIG's. I always felt that the MIG was a better airplane than our F-86 above 30,000 feet, which was where most of our fighting was. The MIG could outperform us; it was lighter and had as much thrust as we did. But we had better gun sights, and our airplanes were sturdier-built. And we had better training, more discipline, aggressiveness, and the desire to get the job done. That's why we shot down some 850 airplanes, and lost only fifty-six of our own.

On the last mission of my first tour I got my fifth and sixth MIG. We got up to the Yalu River, about sixteen of us, and about sixty-five MIG's came across the river. We dropped our fuel tanks as soon as we saw them, but I could only get one of mine to drop, unfortunately. Normally, you'd get out of there and go home, but I picked out one MIG out of a flight of four. I hit him at about 30,000 feet, to slow him down a bit—I had a radar gun sight, the first time I ever used it. Then I was able to get up another five hundred feet, and he just blew up. The pilot did get out, and I took some good pictures of him.

As I was taking these pictures, I was bounced by six MIG's. This was at 25,000 feet, and we were all going in a big circle. I could hear their cannon shells exploding; it sounded like a popcorn machine. I was able to get around and shoot down the number-six MIG. Then a couple of our boys came down to help me out. On the way back, I was so low on fuel that I had to shut my engine off and glide. But before I got back to our base, I started the engine back up and landed. It was quite a scrap.

"Something Very Unusual"

The air defense of the United States is a serious business, but it has had its lighter moments. William P. Lear, inventor of many air navigation aids, including the F-5 automatic pilot for jets, recounts one amusing experience.

We were flying from Las Vegas to Los Angeles, and I had my three children with me. They had these air-defense identification zones out there, and when you went through, you had to identify yourself or they'd come up and take a look.

William P. Lear

Well, I had forgotten to file that I was coming into the Los Angeles area. All of a sudden, a jet came up underneath my nose and went off into the sky. That was a warning to me that he was going to come up and take a look. One jet stands off back here, and another one looks at you—I guess the one standing back is to shoot you down if you don't handle yourself properly.

Anyway, I realized that there was going to be somebody flying right alongside of me, so I had my little son sit in the pilot's seat. He was four years old, and he thought he could fly. I put the plane on autopilot, and he grabbed hold of the wheel and twisted it, but he couldn't do anything because he couldn't overpower the autopilot.

Then I went in back, and I had all of us press our noses against the windows in back, because I was afraid that if they saw this green hornet of an airplane with this little man flying it, they'd get desperate and shoot it down. I wanted them to see that we were back there.

This fellow came up finally in a P-89, and he looked in each window. Then I could see him looking at this little boy flying this airplane, with nobody in the other seat, and he just went zoom back to his base.

When I got home, I called the base and said, "Did you have a report of an unidentified airplane today?"

He said, "Yes. But the pilot would not talk. He wouldn't say what he saw, but he said it was something very unusual."

It must have really scared him.

Crossfield and an F-100

In supersonic planes like the D-558-II Skyrocket and the X-15, test pilot Scott Crossfield has broken innumerable records. None were like a particular barrier he smashed in 1954.

It was my first flight in the F-100 in the NACA stability-control program. I got a fire warning during the flight,

Scott Crossfield in the X-15

so I stopped the engine. At that time there was still considerable controversy over the ability of that airplane to make a dead-stick landing. But dead-stick landings in rocket airplanes were my business, so I made one, and it was not particularly difficult. It came off very nicely.

Now, I had been flying the Skyrocket, and after landing it I had the habit of letting it coast up the ramp and stop near the hangar doors. Well, I don't know what possessed me, but I tried to do that with the F-100 that day with the engine off, and of course with no hydraulic power either. The handbook said that without the utility hydraulic system you were on exactly three cycles of the brake, and it was right. I pumped the brake three times, but the airplane kept rolling and I went into the hangar and came out through the aluminum hangar wall.

That was probably the worst experience I ever had in an airplane, even though it was pretty humorous. The damage was really not very great, except to the wall and to my pride. But Chuck Yeager and the others gave me credit for breaking one barrier that they weren't interested in breaking—the hangar wall!

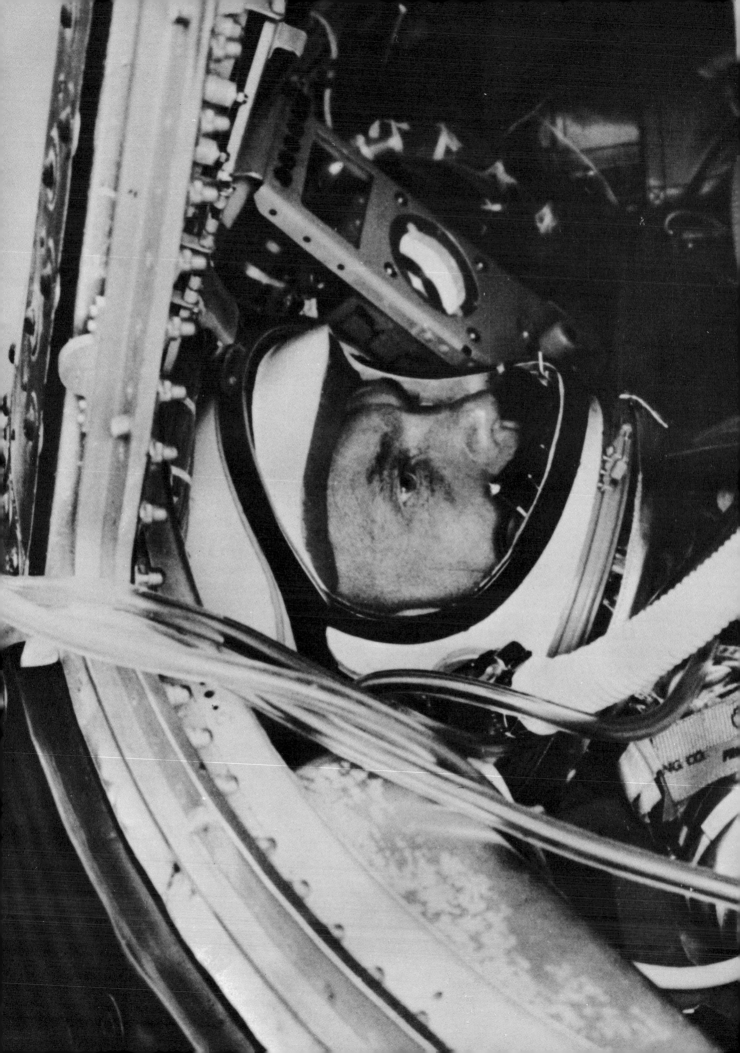

The Future

On February 20, 1962, Lieutenant Colonel John H. Glenn, Jr., orbited the earth three times in a Mercury space capsule, the Friendship 7. *In four hours and fifty-six minutes, he traveled 80,428 miles and saw the sun set four times. Following are excerpts from his speech delivered before a joint session of Congress six days later.*

Data from the *Friendship 7* flight are still being analyzed. . . . But these things we know. The Mercury space craft and system's design concepts are sound and have now been verified during manned flight in space.

We also proved that man can operate intelligently in space and can adapt rapidly to this new environment. Zero G, or weightlessness, at least for this period of time that we're talking about, appears to be no problem. As a matter of fact, lack of gravity is a rather fascinating thing. Objects in the cockpit can be parked in mid-air. For example, at one time during the flight I was using a small hand-held camera. Another system needed attention at that particular moment as I started to take a picture. So it seemed quite natural . . . to park the camera in the air, go ahead and do what I wanted and then take up the camera again. . . .

There seemed to be little sensation of speed although the craft was traveling at about 5 miles per second—a speed that I, too, find difficult to comprehend. . . . I feel we are on the brink of an area of expansion of knowledge about ourselves and our surroundings that is beyond description or comprehension at this time.

Our efforts today and what we've done so far are but small building blocks on a very huge pyramid to come. . . . Knowledge begets knowledge. The more I see, the more impressed I am not with how much we know but with how tremendous the areas are that are as yet unexplored.

407

ACKNOWLEDGMENTS

The Editors are grateful to Charles H. Gibbs-Smith, Marvin W. McFarland, and the following individuals and institutions for their assistance and counsel in the preparation of this book, and for their cooperation in making available documentary and pictorial material in their collections:

Air France, Paris: Jean Dabry
Air Transport Association of America, Washington, D. C.: Phyllis Goldenberg
American Airlines: James B. Devine, Gayle Williams
American Antiquarian Society, Worcester, Massachusetts: Marcus A. McCorison
American Aviation Historical Society, Los Angeles: James J. Sloan
Mrs. Leslie P. Arnold, Leonia, New Jersey
Edmond Audemars, Paris
Bibliothèque Nationale, Paris: Jean Vallery-Radot
Warren Bodie, San Jose, California
The Boeing Company: Mark E. Nevils, Donald E. Rees, Elmer C. Vogel
Peter M. Bowers, Seattle
British Overseas Airways Corporation: David H. Lobb
Harry Bruno, New York
Richard M. Bueschel, Mt. Prospect, Illinois
Vincent J. Burnelli, Washington, D. C.
Chicago Historical Society: Mrs. Mary Frances Rhymer
Mrs. Alfred A. Cunningham, Alexandria, Virginia
Charles Dollfus, Paris
Douglas Aircraft Company: J. B. Messick, H. K. Gagos
Eastman House, Rochester, New York: Beaumont Newhall, Robert M. Doty
Etablissement Cinématographique des Armées, Paris: Commandant Darret
Mrs. Robert E. Gross, Los Angeles
Peter M. Grosz, Princeton, New Jersey
Beckwith Havens, New York
Imperial War Museum, London: Alfred J. Charge
Institut du Transport Aérien, Paris: Henri Bouché, Henry Beaubois
Institute of Aerospace Sciences, New York: S. Paul Johnston, Elizabeth Brown
International Business Machine Corporation, New York: Ernest Shipman
Kansas State Historical Society, Topeka: Robert W. Richmond
Egon Krueger, Oberpfalz, Germany
The Library of Congress, Washington, D. C.: Virginia Daiker, Mrs. Suzanne Cooper
Lockheed Aircraft Corporation: Bert W. Halloway, Erik Miller
University of Michigan, Transportation Library, Ann Arbor: Leo Natanson
Mrs. Thomas DeWitt Milling, Washington, D. C.
Musée de l'Air, Paris: Colonel Rougevin-Baville, Comte Arnauld de Castillon de Saint Victor
Musée Carnavalet, Paris: Jacques Wilhelm
National Air Museum, Smithsonian Institution, Washington, D. C.: Philip S. Hopkins, Paul E. Garber, John Albertson, Louis Casey
National Archives, Still Pictures Branch, Washington, D. C.: Forest L. Williams, Walter V. Barbash, Joe D. Thomas
National Maritime Museum, Greenwich, England: M. S. Robinson, E. H. H. Archibald
The New York Times: Shirley Baig, Michael O'Keefe
North American Aviation: A. J. Montgomery
Pan American World Airways: Jerry Lister, Julie Smith
Pratt & Whitney Aircraft, East Hartford, Connecticut: George J. Flynn
Klaus F. Pruss, Frankfurt, Germany
Republic Aviation Corporation, Farmingdale, New York: Leon Shloss
Dr. Douglas R. Robinson, Pennington, New Jersey
Colonel Paul A. Rockwell, Asheville, North Carolina
Royal Aeronautical Society, London: F. Smith
Ryan Aeronautical Company, San Diego, California: William Wagner, Betty Churchill
Brigadier General Robert L. Scott, Jr., Phoenix, Arizona
Thompson Ramo Wooldridge, Cleveland and Los Angeles: M. S. Griffin, James R. Lewis
Trans World Airlines, New York: Donald B. Moyer
U.S. Air Force, Magazine & Book Branch, Washington, D. C.: Major James Sunderman, Major Gene Guerny, Captain Joseph A. Skiera; Air Force Museum, Wright-Patterson Air Force Base, Ohio: Mrs. Frances R. Biese, William J. Ratsch, Jr.; North American Air Defense Command, Colorado Springs: Colonel Barney Oldfield; Air Force Pictorial Art, Washington: Lieutenant Colonel George C. Bales, William H. Winder; Public Information, New York: Captain James C. Sparks, Sergeant George Zimmerman
U.S. Army, Department of Historical Properties, Washington, D. C.: Mrs. Marian McNaughton
U.S. Marine Corps, Washington, D. C.: Historical Branch, Colonel W. M. Miller, Richard M. Long; Public Information, Colonel D. R. Nugent, Lieutenant Colonel P. N. Pierce, Gladys M. McPartland
U.S. Navy, Magazine & Book Branch, Washington, D. C.: Commander Russell L. Bufkins, Lieutenant Commander F. A. Prehn, Lieutenant (j.g.), A. E. Holt; Exhibit Center, Arlington, Virginia: Lieutenant Commander B. H. Pester; Combat Art, Charles D. Lawrence
Wisconsin State Historical Society, Madison: Paul Vanderbilt
Jerry Witkin, New York

The majority of the interviews from which excerpts were taken for the special sections, "In Their Words," were conducted for American Heritage under the direction of the Columbia University Oral History Office by Kenneth W. Leish. Acknowledgment is also made to Dr. Donald F. Shaughnessy and Mrs. Sandy Jensen for other interviews and to Dr. Louis M. Starr for overall direction of the project, and Mrs. Elizabeth Mason for her assistance.

Grateful acknowledgment is made for permission to quote from the following works:

Myths and Legends of China by E. T. Chalmer Werner, George G. Harrap & Co., Ltd., London
The Ramayana of Valmiki, translated by Hari Prasad Shastri, Shanti Sadan, London
Social Life in Britain from the Conquest to the Reformation by G. G. Coulton, Cambridge University Press, New York
The Notebooks of Leonardo da Vinci, edited by Edward MacCurdy. Reprinted by permission of Harcourt, Brace & World, Inc., New York
The Papers of Wilbur and Orville Wright, edited by Marvin W. McFarland. Reprinted by permission of McGraw-Hill Book Company, Inc., New York, and Oberlin College, Oberlin, Ohio
Letters from France of Victor Chapman. Reprinted by permission of Chanler Chapman, Barrytown, New York
Wing Leader by Group Captain J. E. Johnson. © 1956 by Chatto & Windus, Ltd. ©1957 by Ballantine Books, Inc. Reprinted by permission of Ballantine Books, Inc.
Samurai! by Saburo Sakai as told to Fred Saito and Martin Caidin. Reprinted by permission of E. P. Dutton & Co., Inc., New York
"Fight and Flight in Nicaragua" by Frank Schilt, USMC. Reprinted by permission of North American Newspaper Alliance

The Editors are also indebted to the following basic works on aviation:

The Aeroplane by Charles H. Gibbs-Smith, Her Majesty's Stationery Office, London, 1960
The Air Forces of the World by William Green and John Fricker, Hanover House, New York, 1958
Ceiling Unlimited by Lloyd Morris and Kendall Smith, The Macmillan Company, New York, 1958
Histoire de l'Aéronautique by Charles Dollfus and Henri Bouché, L'Illustration, Paris, 1938
A History of the United States Air Force, 1907-1957, edited by Alfred Goldberg, D. Van Nostrand Company, Inc., Princeton, New Jersey, 1957
Sky High by Eric Hodgins and F. Alexander Magoun, Little, Brown and Company, Boston, 1935

U.S. Copyright is not claimed for color plates on pages: 25, 50-51, 54, 57, 63, 92-93, 97-101, 132-37, 140-41, 174-77, 180-83, 209-13, 257-72, 297, 308-15, 337-48, 353-57, 377-400

Photography: Michelaides-Paris; Zoltan Wegner-London

INDEX

B-52 Stratofortress, 368-69, 371, 374, 375, 384-85
Boeing 40, 202
Boeing 247, 244-45, 264, 269
Boeing 307 Stratoliner, 265
Boeing 707, 375
Boeing 707 320B, 392-93
F2B, 256
IM-99 Bomarc, 374
Minuteman, 401
Monomail, 264
P-26, 277
Stratocruiser, 397
XB-15, 249
XB-17, 249
X-20 Dyna-Soar, 375
BOEING COMPANY: 318
BOELCKE, OSWALD: 161-62, 173, 190
BOHME, ERWIN: 162
BOMARC. See Boeing
BOMBARDMENT, aerial: in Ethiopian War, 247; first by airplane, 151; first by balloon, 44; in Korean War, 372-73, 381, 404; Mitchell's demonstrations of, 200-201, 218-19; in Sino-Japanese War, 248; in Spanish Civil War, 247-48; in World War I, 161, 163, 165, 166-67, 171, 175, 181, 185, 189, 191-92; in World War II, 288-95, 297-99, 301, 304, 312, 314-17, 320-21, 325, 328-35, 336, 338-39, 343, 346-48, 353-55, 357, 359, 360-61, 362-67
BOMBER, development of: in World War I, 163, 185, 211; in World War II, 248-49, 274, 277, 328-29, 332, 334, 335, 376; post-World War II, 371, 373-75, 384-85, 400-401, 403-4
BOMBSIGHT: 192, 223, 328, 404
BONG, RICHARD I.: 335
BOOTLEGGING: 199, 234
BORELLI, G. A.: 14, 97
BOSTON: 221
BOSTON. See Douglas
BOSTON AIR MEET (1910): 124
BOYD, ALBERT: 403-4
BOYINGTON, GREGORY: 343
BRADLEY, OMAR N.: 364
BRAUN, WERNHER VON: 374
BREESE AIRPLANE: 243
BRÉGUET, LOUIS: 122
BRÉGUET 14: 183
BREMEN, Germany: 330
BRERETON, LEWIS H.: 329
BREWSTER BUFFALO: 295, 320
BRIDGEMAN, WILLIAM: 383
"BRISFIT." See Bristol
BRISSON, M.-J.: 60
BRISTOL AIRCRAFT: 124
  Bristol 142, 244
  Bristol Scout, 160, 161
  F2B "Brisfit," 183, 188
BRITAIN, Battle of: 286, 289-91, 301
BRITISH AIR TRANSPORT AUXILIARY: 323-24
BRITISH ARMY AEROPLANE NO. 1: 120
BRITISH OVERSEAS AIRWAYS CORPORATION: 373
BROCK, WILLIAM: 253
BROOKINS, WALTER: 143, 154
BROOKS FIELD, Texas: 277, 307
BRONTE, EMORY: 242
BROWN, ARTHUR WHITTEN: 200, 208
BROWN, WALTER F.: 244
BROWNE, ROSS: 152-53
BROWNING, JOHN: 99
BRYAN, J., III: 356

BRYAN, WILLIAM JENNINGS: 157
BUFFALO. See Brewster
BULGE, Battle of the: 333-34
BUNKER HILL, U.S.S.: 353
BUREAU OF AERONAUTICS, U.S.
  Department of Commerce: 203
BURMA: 310, 365
BURNELLI, VINCENT J.: 203
BURNELLI RB-2: 212
BUSH FLYING. See Alaska
BUTLER, WILLIAM O.: 336
BYRD, RICHARD E.: 204-5, 228, 238, 242, 250

C

C-1. See Douglas
C-2. See Fokker
C-46. See Curtiss
C-47. See Douglas
C-54. See Douglas
C-130. See Lockheed
CR-3. See Curtiss
CAIRO CONFERENCE: 331
CALABRIA, Italy: 331
CALDWELL, CYRIL C.: 191-92
CALIFORNIA ARROW: 71
CAMEL. See Sopwith
CAMP D'AUVOURS, France: 129
CAMPBELL, DOUGLAS: 181, 193-94
CAPRONI, GIANNI: 215
CAPRONI AIRCRAFT: 164, 215, 274
CARAVELLE: 375
CARLSTROM, VICTOR: 157
"CAROLINAS, Battle of" (U.S. Army maneuvers): 307
CAROLINE ISLANDS: 334, 354
CARPENTER, M. SCOTT: 374
CASABLANCA CONFERENCE: 330, 363
CASUALTIES: first in an airplane, 121, 129; first in a balloon, 43-44, 53
CAUDRON AIRCRAFT: 174, 182
CAVALLO, TIBERIUS: 15, 37
CAVENDISH, HENRY: 15, 32, 41
CAYLEY, GEORGE: 80-81, 88-89, 110
CENTRAL INTELLIGENCE AGENCY: 401
CESSNA AIRCRAFT: 399
CHAMBERLAIN, NEVILLE: 249, 288
CHAMBERLIN, CLARENCE D.: 205, 239, 242, 250, 278-79
CHAMBERS, REED: 194
CHAMBERS, WASHINGTON IRVING: 155, 179
CHANUTE, OCTAVE: 83-84, 85-86, 102, 113-15, 119
CHAPMAN, VICTOR: 162, 178, 191
CHARLES, J. A. C.: 41-43, 48-49, 72
CHATEAU-THIERRY: 165
CHENNAULT, CLAIRE L.: 248-49, 311
CHICAGO: 221
CHINA: folklore of, 11, 23-24; invention of kite, 11, 24; Korean War, 372-73, 381, 404; war with Japan, 247-48, 274-75, 310-11, 332-33, 340
CHINA CLIPPER. See Martin
CHURCH, ELLEN: 281
CHURCHILL, WINSTON: 288-91, 293, 295, 301, 328, 330-31, 363
CIANO, GALEAZZO: 275
CIERVA, JUAN DE LA: 215
CIGOGNES (STORK) SQUADRON: 190-91
CIRCULAR FLIGHT, first: 119
CITY OF LOS ANGELES: 266

CIVIL WAR (American), balloons in: 45, 64-65, 75-76
CLARK, MARK W.: 331
CLARK FIELD, Philippine Islands: 295
CLIPPER. See Martin
CLOUDSTER. See Douglas
COBHAM, ALAN: 133, 204, 280-81
COCHIN CHINA AIR FORCE: 310
COCHRAN, JACQUELINE: 256, 260, 323-24
COCHRAN, PHILIP G.: 365
CODY, S. F.: 120, 135
COFFYN, FRANK: 154
COLD WAR: 373-75, 384-85, 388-91, 400-401
COLI, FRANÇOIS: 204-5
COLLISHAW, RAYMOND: 186
COLOGNE, Germany: 329
COLONIAL AIR TRANSPORT: 202, 266
COLUMBIA: 239
COLUMBIA AIRCRAFT CORPORATION: 204
COMET. See De Havilland
COMMANDO. See Curtiss
COMMERCE, U.S. DEPARTMENT OF: 203
COMMERCIAL AVIATION: British, 199, 206, 216, 232, 234, 371, 373, 375; Dutch, 199, 216; first jet service, 373; first passenger service, 151; first stewardess, 281; French, 199, 216-17, 281-82, 375; German, 199, 216; government-subsidized, 199, 216, 243-44; Russian, 375; U.S., 151, 199, 203, 243-44, 245, 246, 266-67, 268-69, 279, 281, 370-71, 375, 395, 396-97, 402-3. See also individual airlines, Dirigibles, Helicopters
CONDOR. See Curtiss
CONDOR LEGION: 248
CONINGHAM, ARTHUR: 329
CONSOLIDATED AIRCRAFT:
  B-24 Liberator, 324, 328, 335, 336, 338-39, 344, 362
  PBY-1, 264-65
CONSTELLATION. See Lockheed
CONVAIR AIRCRAFT AND MISSILES:
  Atlas ICBM, 374
  B-36, 371, 385, 392-93
  B-58 Hustler, 374, 400
  F-102 Delta Dagger, 373
  F-106 Delta Dart, 373
  XFY-1, 391
COOLIDGE, CALVIN: 201-2
COPPENS, WILLY: 166
CORAL SEA, Battle of: 295, 314-15
CORDOVA AIRLINES: 283
CORNU, PAUL: 135
CORNWALL, H.M.S.: 314-15
CORREGIDOR: 335
CORRIGAN, DOUGLAS: 250
CORSAIR. See Vought
COSTE, DIEUDONNÉ: 250
COUTELLE, JEAN-MARIE-JOSEPH: 54-55, 74
COWPENS, U.S.S.: 353
COWPER, WILLIAM: 73
CRAIGIE, LAURENCE C.: 402
CRETE: 292, 304
CROCKER, H. G.: 220
CROSSFIELD, SCOTT: 405
CRUSADER. See Vought
CUNNINGHAM, ALFRED A.: 155
CURTISS, GLENN: and Aerial Experiment Association, 120, 130-31; and Lincoln Beachey, 157; dirigible engines of, 71, 120; early airplanes

of, 120, 122, 130-31, 148, 157, 164, 179; exhibition team of, 124, 148-49, 154, 155; flying school of, 124, 130; and Langley "aerodrome," 105; record flights of, 122-23, 130, 138; seaplanes of, 124, 125, 130-31, 185; and U.S. Army, 157, 179; and U.S. Navy, 130-31; and Wright lawsuit, 120, 131
CURTISS AIRCRAFT:
  America, 125, 141
  C-46 Commando, 332
  CR-3, 226
  Condor, 245
  F-5-L, 183
  Hawk, 256
  JN-4D Jenny, 164, 181, 182, 196, 198, 206
  June Bug, 120, 130-31, 140
  Navy-Curtiss (NC) flying boats, 199-200, 208-9, 212
  Oriole, 212
  P-1, 213
  P-36, 249
  P-40, 249, 344
  R3C-2, 227
  Triad, 141
CURTISS FLYING SERVICE: 237-38
CYCLONE ENGINE. See Wright Cyclone engine

D

D-1. See Junkers
D-7. See Fokker
D-558. See Douglas
DC AIRPLANES. See Douglas
DH AIRPLANES. See De Havilland
DR-1. See Fokker
D-DAY: 333, 346, 348, 364
DAEDALUS: 11, 20, 34-35
DAGUA, New Guinea: 355
DAILY MAIL PRIZES: 121, 123, 125, 154, 199, 200
DALADIER, EDOUARD: 288
DALGLISH, JAMES: 349
DAMIAN, JOHN: 12
DANIELS, JOHN T.: 109, 115
DANTI, GIOVANNI: 13
DAUNTLESS. See Douglas
DAURAT, DIDIER: 281-82
DAVIS, DOUGLAS: 258
DAVIS, NOEL: 204-5
DAVIS, W. V.: 256
DAYTON-WRIGHT RACER: 212
DEFENSE, U.S. DEPARTMENT OF, established: 370
DEFIANT: 289
DE FLOREZ, LUIS: 283-84
DEGEN, JACOB: 97
DE HAVILLAND, GEOFFREY: 124, 134, 160
DE HAVILLAND, GEOFFREY (younger): 371
DE HAVILLAND AIRCRAFT:
  BE-2, 160, 162
  Comet (1934), 245
  Comet (jet), 373, 375, 392-93
  DH-2, 182
  DH-4, 163, 164, 167, 183, 189, 198, 200, 232
  DH-9, 163, 206, 232
  DH-9A, 163
  DH-108, 371
  Mosquito, 333
DELAGRANGE, LÉON: 120, 122, 126-27
DELTA DAGGER. See Convair
DELTA DART. See Convair
DEMOISELLE: 122, 140

L.V.G. C-II: 182
LZ ZEPPELINS. *See* Dirigibles
LAFAYETTE ESCADRILLE: 162, 175, 178, 191
LA GUARDIA, FIORELLO: 181
LAHM, FRANK P.: 124, 151, 181
LAIRD, MATTY: 256
LAKUNAI: 343
LAMBERT, ALBERT: 239
LANA, FRANCESCO DE: 14, 28, 44
LANCASTER. *See* Avro
LANCER. *See* Republic
LANDING GEAR, retractable: 88, 94-95, 203, 227
LANGLEY, SAMUEL PIERPONT: 84-85, 105
LANGLEY, U.S.S.: 201, 223, 249
LANGLEY MEMORIAL AERO-NAUTICAL LABORATORY: 203
LANSDOWNE, ZACHARY: 225
LATHAM, HUBERT: 121-22, 132, 139, 153
LAUNOY-BIENVENU HELICOP-TER: 97
LAW, RUTH. *See* Oliver, Ruth Law
LAWRANCE, CHARLES L.: 204
LEAR, WILLIAM P.: 405
LEBAUDY, PAUL and PIERRE: 45, 70-71, 124
LE BLANC, ALFRED: 143
LE BRIS, JEAN-MARIE: 94-95
LEFEBVRE, EUGÈNE: 122, 139
LEHMAN, ERNST: 273
LEI KUNG: 11
LEIBNITZ, GOTTFRIED WIL-HELM: 14
LeMAY, CURTIS E.: 335, 366, 379, 385
LENNOX, COMTE DE: 61
LEONARDO DA VINCI: 12-13, 26-27, 36
LESLEY, JOHN: 12
LEVAVASSEUR, LÉON: 119-21, 139; Antoinette aircraft and engines, 120, 121, 139, 140, 153
LEVINE, CHARLES A.: 242, 250, 278-79
LEWIS MACHINE GUNS: 160, 249, 295
LEXINGTON, U.S.S.: 315, 352, 353
LEYTE GULF, Battle of: 334-35
LIBERATOR. *See* Consolidated
LIBERTY ENGINE: 164
LIBRARY OF CONGRESS: 203
LIGHTER-THAN-AIR CRAFT. *See* Balloons and Dirigibles
LIGNES AÉRIENNES FARMAN: 217
LILIENTHAL, OTTO: 78, 83, 102-3, 112-13
LILLE, France: 329, 362
LIMBURG, Germany: 346
LINCOLN, ABRAHAM: 65
LINDBERGH, CHARLES A.: influ-ence on aviation of, 242-43, 250; "the Lindbergh line," 244, 266; as military adviser, 293-94; transat-lantic flight of, 204-5, 230, 239
LIPPISCH, ALEXANDER: 271
LIU AN: 11
LLOYD GEORGE, DAVID: 138
LOCKHEED AIRCRAFT: 243
  C-130 Hercules, 388
  Constellation, 370, 397
  F-80 Shooting Star, 372, 376, 381
  F-104 Starfighter, 373
  L-10 Electra, 245, 246-47
  Lockheed 14, 246
  P-38, 249, 307, 332, 333, 364
  P-80, 345, 376
  Truculent Turtle, 371

U-2, 401
  Vega, 213, 243, 246
LOCKLEAR, ORMER: 196
LOCKWOOD, RALPH: 220
LOENING, GROVER C.: 179, 210
LOENING M-8: 183
LONDON, air raids on: in World War I, 166; in World War II, 286, 290, 301, 334
LONDON-MANCHESTER RACE: 123
LOS ANGELES, U.S.S.: 247
LOUGHEAD, ALLAN H.: 243. *See also* Lockheed aircraft
LOUIS XVI: 41, 48
LOVETT, ROBERT A.: 185
LOWE, THADDEUS S. C.: 64-65, 75-76
LUCIAN: 35
LUFBERY, RAOUL: 178, 193
LUFTHANSA GERMAN AIR-LINES: 216
LUFTSCHIFFBAU-ZEPPELIN: 272
LUFTWAFFE: 247-49, 288-93, 297-99, 301, 304, 306, 308, 324-25, 336, 338-39, 346, 348-49, 362-64
LUKE, FRANK, JR.: 165, 187
LUNARDI, VINCENT: 42, 53
LUZON: 335, 366
LYONS, HARRY W.: 243

M-1. *See* Ryan
M-130. *See* Martin
MB-1. *See* Martin
MB-2. *See* Martin
MacARTHUR, DOUGLAS: 154-55, 332
MACCHI M-39: 227
MACH, ERNST: 383
MACHINE GUNS. *See* Armament
MACKINTOSH, THOMAS S.: 61
MACON, U.S.S.: 247
MACREADY, JOHN A.: 201, 220, 235-36
MAISONFORT, MARQUIS DE: 44
MAITLAND, LESTER G.: 242, 252
MALONEY, DANIEL: 103
MALTA: 292
MANCHESTER. *See* Avro
MANILA, Battle of: 335
MANLY, CHARLES M.: 84, 105
MANNOCK, EDWARD: 166, 186
MAREY, ETIENNE-JULES: 98-99
MARIANA ISLANDS: 334-35, 354, 366
MARIE ANTOINETTE: 41
MARSHALL ISLANDS: 332, 354
MARTIN, GLENN L.: 179, 210-11, 235, 244
MARTIN AIRCRAFT AND MIS-SILES:
  B-10, 249, 264
  B-26B, 324, 344, 372
  M-130 China Clipper, 268-69
  MB-1, 211
  MB-2, 212, 218
  Martin 404, 370
  Martin Matador, 374
  TT, 141, 179
  Transport 130, 264-65
MASON, MONCK: 44-45, 75
MATADOR. *See* Martin
MATHY, HEINRICH: 166
MAUGHAN, RUSSELL A.: 201, 220, 227
MAXIM, HIRAM: 82
MAXIM GORKI: 263
MAXWELL FIELD, Alabama: 307
MAYER, DAVID: 97

McCAMPBELL, DAVID S.: 335
McCONNELL, JAMES: 178
McCONNELL, JOSEPH: 381
McCURDY, J. A. D.: 155
McDONNELL AIRCRAFT:
  F3H-2 Demon, 390
  F4H, 388
  F-101 Voodoo, 373
  F-110, 388
McNARY-WATRES ACT: 244
MEERWEIN, C. F.: 32
MERCURY: 18
MERCURY PROJECT: 374, 401, 407
MERMOZ, JEAN: 281-82
MESSERSCHMITT, WILLY: 322
MESSERSCHMITT AIRCRAFT:
  Me-109 (Messerschmitt Bf-109), 248, 289, 322, 324, 325, 344, 349
  Me-110, 288, 289
  Me-163, 291, 334
  Me-262, 322, 334, 345, 376
METEOR. *See* Gloster
MEUSE-ARGONNE OFFENSIVE: 167
MEUSNIER, JEAN-BAPTISTE MARIE: 42-43, 60
MEXICAN BORDER EXPEDI-TION: 164, 179, 192
MEXICAN WAR: 44
MICHELIN CUP: 154
MIDWAY, Battle of: 295, 320-21
"MIG ALLEY": 373
MIG 15: 372, 381, 404-5
MIKOYAN AIRCRAFT: 384
MILCH, ERHARD: 291
MILITARY AIR TRANSPORT SERVICE: 378
MILLING, THOMAS DeWITT: 124, 181, 192
MINDORO, Philippine Islands: 335
MINUTEMAN. *See* Boeing
MISSILES: 334, 374, 375, 390, 401
MISSOURI, U.S.S.: 357
MR. MULLIGAN: 259
MITCHELL, R. J.: 227
MITCHELL, WILLIAM: 260; as Assistant Chief of Army Air Service, 200-201, 218-22; court martial of, 202; in World War I, 165, 167, 181, 195, 198
MITCHELL BOMBER. *See* North American
MITSCHER, MARC A.: 124, 334, 335, 354, 359
MITSUBISHI AIRCRAFT: 247, 248; Zero-Sen, 248, 295, 310, 321, 334-35, 340, 345, 366
MOCK, RICHARD: 278
MOFFETT, WILLIAM A.: 201-2, 222, 247
MOFFETT FIELD, California: 307
MOISANT, ALFRED: 148
MOISANT, JOHN B.: 143, 148
MOISANT, MATILDE: 148
MOLLISON, JAMES: 250
MONOMAIL. *See* Boeing
MONS, retreat from: 172
MONTGOLFIER, ETIENNE and JOSEPH: 40-42, 47-48, 63
MONTGOMERY, BERNARD L.: 329, 330, 331
MONTGOMERY, JOHN J.: 103
MOORE-BRABAZON, J. T. C.: 121, 123, 153-54
MORANE-SAULNIER AIRCRAFT: 141, 160, 161
MORGAN, J. P.: 202
MORRISSEY, MURIEL: 279
MORROW, DWIGHT: 202
MORROW BOARD: 202, 203

MORSE AIRCRAFT: 219, 226
MOSELEY, CORLISS: 226
MOSQUITO. *See* DeHavilland
MOUILLARD, LOUIS-PIERRE: 82-83, 112
MOZHAISKI, ALEXANDER F.: 81
MUNDA, New Georgia: 340
MURRAY, ARTHUR: 383
MUSASHI: 334
MUSICK, EDWIN: 268
MUSSOLINI, BENITO: 247, 289, 291
MUSSOLINI, VITTORIO: 274
MUSTANG. *See* North American
MYER, JOHN C.: 348
MYTHS. *See* Folklore

NC FLYING BOATS. *See* Curtiss
NADAR. *See* Tournachon, Félix
NAGASAKI: 335, 360, 366
NAGUMO, CHUICHI: 294, 315, 321
NAKAJIMA AIRCRAFT AND ENGINES: 247, 275, 310
NAM IL: 381
NAPLES: 331
NAPOLEON: 44, 54
NATIONAL ADVISORY COM-MITTEE FOR AERONAUTICS: 203, 243, 373, 382, 401
NATIONAL AERONAUTICS AND SPACE ADMINISTRATION: 203, 374, 401
NATIONAL AIR RACES: 256, 258
NATIONAL AIR TRANSPORT: 202, 244, 266
NATIONAL SECURITY ACT: 370
NAVAJO. *See* North American
NAVARRE, JEAN: 162
NAVY-CURTISS (NC) FLYING BOATS. *See* Curtiss
NELSON, ERIK: 237
NESTEROV, P. N.: 163
NETHERLANDS: 288, 336
NEUMANN, HAROLD: 256
NEW BRITAIN: 343
NEW GEORGIA: 332, 340
NEW GUINEA: 315, 332, 340, 342, 355
NEW ORLEANS: 221
NEW YORK INTERNATIONAL AIRPORT (Idlewild): 397
NEW YORK *SUN:* 75
NEW YORK UNIVERSITY, School of Aeronautics: 203
NEW YORK *WORLD* PRIZE: 124
NEWTON, ISAAC: 14, 376
NICARAGUA: 280
NICHOLS, RUTH: 260, 282-83
NIEUPORT AIRCRAFT: 140, 160, 162, 163, 175, 178, 182, 185, 191
NIGHT BOMBING: in World War I, 166, 191-92; in World War II, 289, 290, 293, 301, 328-29, 330, 333, 335, 360-61, 363, 366-67
NIMITZ, CHESTER W.: 320, 332, 353
94TH AERO SQUADRON, U.S.: 165, 193-94
97TH BOMBARDMENT GROUP, U.S.: 362
93RD BOMBARDMENT GROUP, U.S.: 362
NINTH AIR FORCE, U.S.: 329, 333, 339, 349
9TH BOMBER COMMAND, U.S.: 346
9TH TACTICAL AIR COMMAND, U.S.: 364
NOBEL, ALFRED: 68